It was nearly three o'clock before the horses were saddled and Madame Knight and Hester were ready to embark on their journey.

Philena and Hester said their final, tearful farewells. A small group of neighbors and friends followed the horseback riders to the place where Moon Street forked. "Good-bye! Good-bye!" they shouted.

As Philena's horse moved further and further away from Hester, Hester felt as if she were watching herself becoming smaller and smaller. A memory returned. Hester recalled when she was a little girl and glanced for the first time into Madame Knight's looking glass. She thought she was seeing her sister smile and reach out to her. She even tried to lift and look behind the looking glass, certain that Philena must be hiding there. When she discovered her sister had vanished, she burst into tears and cried inconsolably.

That was how she felt at this very moment: abandoned and alone.

Books by Laurie Lawlor

The Worm Club
How to Survive Third Grade
Addie Across the Prairie
Addie's Long Summer
Addie's Dakota Winter
George on His Own
Gold in the Hills
Little Women *(a movie novelization)*

Heartland series
Heartland: Come Away with Me
Heartland: Take to the Sky
Heartland: Luck Follows Me

American Sisters series
West Along the Wagon Road, 1852
A *Titanic* Journey Across the Sea, 1912
Voyage to a Free Land, 1630
Adventure on the Wilderness Road, 1775
Crossing the Colorado Rockies, 1864
Down the Río Grande, 1829
Horseback on the Boston Post Road, 1704
Exploring the Chicago World's Fair, 1893
Pacific Odyssey to California, 1904

American SISTERS
Horseback on the Boston Post Road
1704

Laurie Lawlor

Aladdin Paperbacks
New York   London   Toronto   Sydney   Singapore

First Aladdin Paperbacks edition February 2002

Text copyright © 2002 by Laurie Lawlor

ALADDIN PAPERBACKS
An imprint of Simon & Schuster
Children's Publishing Division
1230 Avenue of the Americas
New York, NY 10020

Also available in a Minstrel ® Books hardcover edition.
The text of this book was set in Cochin.

Printed in USA
10 9 8 7 6 5 4 3 2 1

Library of Congress Control Number 2001096795

0-7434-3626-1

For Rebecca Burton Mills,
who helped take care of
Sis and Sis

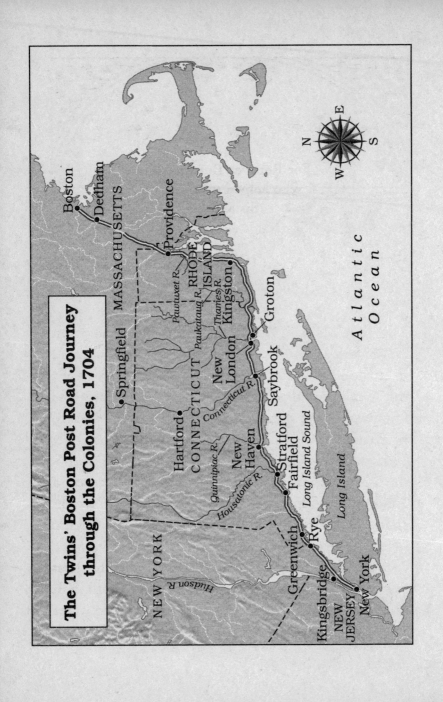

The Twins' Boston Post Road Journey through the Colonies, 1704

Boston
Dedham
Providence
MASSACHUSETTS
Springfield
Pawtuxet R.
Pawcatuag R.
RHODE ISLAND
Thames R.
Kingston
New London
Groton
CONNECTICUT
Hartford
Saybrook
Connecticut R.
Quinnipiac R.
New Haven
Stratford
Fairfield
Long Island Sound
Housatonic R.
Long Island
NEW YORK
Hudson R.
Greenwich
Rye
Kingsbridge
NEW JERSEY
New York
Atlantic Ocean

N E S W

Introduction

The first mail in North America was sent from New York City on January 22, 1673, and arrived in Boston on about February 5th. Nobody knows the name of the first postrider, but everyone knows the route he took through New Haven, Springfield, Brookfield, Worcester, and Cambridge. The route was later called the Boston Post Road—the first link in what would one day become a 3,000-mile chain of trails and roads that would span the continent from the Atlantic to the Pacific Oceans.

A little more than two decades after the first postrider made his trip, another important and unusual person followed the same route. Her name was Sarah Kemble Knight. She was a thirty-eight-year-old Boston shopkeeper who was keen-eyed and sharp-tongued, and, fortunately for posterity, she kept a diary about her 270-mile journey on horseback. It was an unusual trip at the time for a woman to make independently. She faced swollen rivers without bridges, plus bears, winter storms, uncertain accommodations, bad food, and, often, bad directions. On occasion she took advantage of the company and presence of postriders, who carried the mail for colonists.

This novel is based on her wonderful diary, which was published for the first time in 1825. Only a few facts are known for certain about Sarah Knight. She was born on April 19, 1666, had one daughter, and spent most of her life in Boston. She was widowed at an early age. A unique and independent woman for her time, she managed to develop keen business skills and knowledge of the law. She ran a shop and a farm, operated an inn, and purchased and sold several hundred acres of land. She died September 25, 1727, was buried in New London, Connecticut, and left behind for her daughter the sizable sum of 1,800 pounds.

Chapter 1

"We have no birthday."

"Doesn't matter."

"Who's older?"

"Not important."

Hester sighed. In eerie, matching movements she and her twelve-year-old twin sister, Philena, scrubbed the keeping-room floor of the house on Moon Street. *Dip-twist-slop-circle right-circle left.* Every week followed a familiar pattern. Monday — washing; Tuesday — ironing; Wednesday — mending; Thursday — churning; Friday — cleaning; Saturday — baking; Sunday — Sabbath. Days and weeks and months and years rolled in and out as predictably as the tides in Boston Harbor. Nothing ever seemed to change except the weather and the seasons.

Hester paused to watch Philena work. *I remember her dreams. She feels my pain. I used to find this reassuring. Now sometimes her face seems repulsive. May God forgive me.*

"What?" Philena said and frowned.

"Nothing," Hester replied quickly. She turned away so that her sister could not see her blush.

"Aren't you going to help? Can't do this all myself," Philena said. She sat back on her heels and dipped the rag in the bucket, then smacked the wet rag hard on the floor. *We are a pair of hands: she the right, and I the left. Exactly the same, except that she is always better.*

Hester smiled. Her sister should be more careful. It was so easy to read her thoughts—as easy as it was for Philena to read hers. On hands and knees, without looking at each other, the sisters danced their rags across nicks and knotholes that stared like eyes. Their rags *hush-hushed* across the broad pine boards and waltzed around the legs of the stools and the legs of the long plank table where the girls ate their meals with Madame Knight's boarders.

To keep her clothing clean as she worked, Hester had rolled up the waist of the black-and-white silk crepe petticoat and white shift, the cast-off clothes of Polly, Madame Knight's fifteen-year-old daughter. Philena did not care that her plain muslin apron was already soiled at the knees or that the hem of the front of her worn, dark-green shift was soggy.

Like her sister, Philena kept her long brown hair parted in the middle and tucked under a white cap that hid overlarge ears. Both girls had the same dark eyes and the same pale skin and the same thin lips. Except for their clothing, they were the same. Their voice, their laughter. The loping way they walked. The birdlike way they fluttered their hands when they were nervous. The careless way they chewed their food. Everything about them was identical. Even the secret name they had given each other was the same: Hester-Phina.

Since before they were born they had been together. As babies they slept curled in the same cradle, one sister sucking the other's thumb. They shared everything: trencher, spoon, mug, clothes, comb, blanket, bed. The only possessions they kept from each other were their thoughts. And even these sometimes escaped into communal use if they weren't careful.

Very, very careful.

Hester and Philena's lives had become so predictable, so alike, so inseparable that they could never have guessed how everything would suddenly change that bright October morning in 1704.

A little bell rang in the shop that adjoined the keeping-room. "Customer," Hester said. She tilted her head toward the open shop door. A gust of unseasonably warm wind from the busy Boston streets mingled with the shop's smells of ink powder, dried codfish, lead pencils, lamp black, chocolate, coffee, and linseed oil.

Footsteps. From where Hester and Philena crouched on the keeping-room floor, they had a fine view of customers' shoes and pant legs and skirt hems. Hester gave her sister the sign to begin the Game. They both knew the rules. One cough meant yes. Two meant no. The Game's only question never altered: *Is this one our mother?*

The customer's black shoes were scuffed and worn down so unevenly at the heels that she walked in a painful, lopsided manner. What they could see of her patched skirt was muddy and torn. Hester coughed twice loudly. This could not be the one. *Too poor, too pathetic.* In her mind, their mother was rich. She never walked anywhere. She rode in a carriage with two fine white horses. The fact that she had given Hester and Philena away as babies must have been a simple, youthful mistake. Perhaps she had never forgiven herself. Perhaps she longed to find them again.

Philena peered at the customer's battered shoes and coughed once. She felt hopeful. She always felt hopeful that they would be reunited. And yet she was realistic. A poor woman could not afford to keep twins who were hungry and bawling all the time. It made sense that their mother had been an unfortunate soul, a hapless victim of poverty.

Neither Hester nor Philena ever thought much about their father. They lived in a household ruled by women. Polly had a mother. Madame Knight had a mother. Goodwife Kemble had a mother long dead but still discussed with so much vehemence that she seemed alive and quarrelsome as ever. To have a proper mother was a measure of one's worth. To not know who their real mother was always made Hester and Philena feel disconnected and disembodied, like smoke or mist. They had no birth story, no early, warm mother-memory—nothing to hold on to but each other.

"Thou art Madame Sarah Knight?" the customer asked in a tired, thin voice. She addressed their mistress in the formal, respectful way that was the custom between strangers.

"I am," Madame Knight answered impatiently from behind the counter.

There was a short pause, and then as quickly as the scuffed shoes had appeared, they shuffled across the floor. The bell rang. The door shut. The customer vanished.

"Wrong again," Hester hissed. She wrung out the rag. "If she were the one, she'd have asked for us."

"Maybe she doesn't know we're here," Philena said softly and pushed up her damp sleeves. "It was eleven years ago. A long time."

Hester snorted. She liked her grand story better. The carriage and the fine white horses. If she were going to be rescued from the life of an indentured maidservant, she wanted a marvelous improvement. "What use is there in trading one life of hardship for another?"

Philena didn't answer. Instead she began scrubbing again, harder and fiercer than before. *She always has to have the last word.*

Hester decided to cheer her sister, who took the Game much too seriously. She sang:

"Oh, Cape Cod girls they have no combs,
Heave away, heave away!
They comb their hair with codfish bones.
Heave away, heave away!
Heave away, you bully, bully boys!
Heave away, and don't you make a noise,
For we're bound for Australia!"

Philena joined her sister in a crooning duet:

"Oh, Cape Cod boys they have no sleds.
They slide down hill on codfish heads.
Heave away, heave away!"

Philena giggled, glad not to feel angry anymore. She could never stay mad at Hester very long.

"Oh, Cape Cod cats they have no tails,
They blew away in heavy—"

"Enough of that disreputable song!" Madame Knight shouted from the shop doorway, one pudgy fist on her wide hip. In her other fist she held a crumpled piece of paper. Her face was flushed and her blue eyes blazed. She was a short, stout woman of middle age with a famous temper that once again seemed about to explode.

Hester and Philena exchanged looks of caution. *Now what's wrong?*

"Why my old mother taught that horrid song to you, I shall never understand," Madame Knight declared.

"But Mistress—" Philena protested.

"Goodwife Kemble told us it is a proper working song," Hester added. She considered it her duty to finish her sister's sentences for her, especially when she knew that what Philena intended to say was not going to sound particularly convincing.

"It's a working song for sailors," Madame Knight said with great vehemence. She jammed a lock of graying hair into her second-best lace cap. "Let me remind you that *you* are not sailors. You are maidservants. This is not a ship and my mother must one day realize that. Oh, woe is me to be a poor widow in such an impossible situation! Perfidious servants who can't be trusted, a mother who thinks she's still on her father's sloop, and a daughter with impossible, grand fancies."

Hester shot an amused glance at her sister. *Polly's impossible, that's true enough.* Philena bit her lip and tried not to grin.

"Perhaps," Madame Knight growled, "I should forbid you to spend so much time with my mother. She is not a proper influence."

"We love and respect Goodwife Kemble," Hester said and made a fawning little curtsy. Every word she said was true. No one was quite as dear to them as Goodwife Kemble. Although the elderly woman had a habit of wandering off course sometimes and forgetting where she was, she told the most exciting stories about pirates who cruised the coast. And she was the one person in the Moon Street household who ever showed them the least bit of affection.

Madame Knight took a deep breath and glanced about the keeping-room. "How much pewter have we left?"

"A few plates. A bowl," Hester said. She knew exactly what was in the wooden cupboard against the wall. It was her job to polish the pieces that had not already been traded for cash. "Why do you ask, Mistress?"

Madame Knight did not answer. When her gaze fell on the only chair in the room, the one with the faded embroidered pillow, she scowled. "God rest his soul," she mumbled bitterly. She seemed to be speaking directly to her late husband, whose untimely death had caused her sudden fall in fortune. Madame Knight turned to the girls again. "I have much to do and I do not know how I'll manage before this afternoon. What time is it?"

Hester and Philena shrugged. Mentioning the missing clock at this particular moment did not seem like a very safe idea. Had Madame Knight already forgotten she had traded the clock to pay for last year's firewood?

"It's late and this may be my last chance. My very last chance. I will speak with you when I return. A matter of great urgency has come up," Madame Knight said. She hurriedly stuffed the paper into her pocket, which hung from a string tied around her ample middle.

Hester cleared her throat. "I can go to market for you," she volunteered. She liked nothing better than to put a basket on her arm and wander aimlessly among the colorful stalls of fish and vegetable vendors near the noisy harbor.

Madame Knight shook her head in a distracted fashion as she picked out a few plates from the cupboard and wrapped them in her apron. "This will be a much longer journey than a mere trip to market," she said. "Watch the shop for me. I will be back in a trice." She hurried out on to Moon Street.

"What was that all about?" Philena asked.

"A longer journey," Hester said. She quickly finished the floor and stood up. "Nothing that concerns us, I'm sure. We never go anywhere."

"But she said it did. She said she wishes to speak with us. 'A matter of great urgency.' That must mean something bad."

"Why do you always worry so much? Certainly she has more chores for us. Nothing else."

Philena pouted. "I do not like the sound of it."

"Be still," Hester replied. "And help me dump this bucket."

Together they lifted the heavy bucket by the handle and staggered outside. For several moments they stood in the small grassy spot behind the house, out of the wind. The sun warmed the tops of their heads and their shoulders. And for several moments, they luxuriated in doing nothing.

"Pssst!" Cato called. He peeked around the corner of the house. "Madame gone?"

"Yes," Philena replied, glad to see him. But before Philena could ask him how he was and where he had been, Hester interrupted.

"She'll be back soon," Hester warned. "Hurry now. What news?"

Cato leaned against the weatherbeaten house with the exaggerated laziness of the old men who gathered on the village green. "Much news maybe," Cato said and smiled at Hester as if Philena were not there.

Philena sighed. Shyly, she studied Cato's broad tawny face and laughing black eyes. Her only friends already belonged to her sister. Cato was Hester's friend. He worked outdoors and did the heavy work. He unloaded the merchandise and took care of Madame Knight's four horses. Barely fourteen, he had been a slave since he was taken as a very young boy from his Indian family in the Carolinas. Unlike Hester and Philena, he would receive no Freedom Dues when his time was up. He would always be a slave. That was just the way things were, Hester always reminded Philena. Some people were free. Some people were indentured servants who had to work a certain amount of time for their masters without pay. And some people were slaves. The same way that some people had mothers and some people didn't.

"Speak, boy!" Hester urged. She looked to her left and right. Any moment Madame Knight might come bustling up the narrow street and end their conversation and free time.

"I hear Madame say she make money soon. Lots of money," Cato said slyly. "She say she be rich."

"Where did you hear that?" Hester demanded.

"She come out the shop. Right away she a-calling to Master Thatcher across the way. She a-smiling and a-waving. Very bright and happy. So happy, she not kick me when I pass." Then he added in a low, confidential voice, "Even so, I going fast out of here."

Hester rolled her eyes. Cato was always bragging about running away, even though they all knew the punishment if he were caught. A severe beating and maybe the loss of one ear. And yet he said he didn't care. He said he was determined to escape back to his tribe in the wilderness of the Carolinas. No one would dare follow him.

"Madame Knight won't get rich selling a few more pewter plates," Philena scoffed. "She must have some new scheme."

"Maybe she know where pirate treasure," Cato suggested. His dark eyes glimmered. "Captain Kidd bury Spanish gold on hidden beach before they hang him. Maybe she go dig and get rich."

Philena licked her lips. The famous English pirate, Captain Kidd, had been captured and hung three years earlier. His short, violent life was told to them with great eagerness by Goodwife Kemble, who read of his exploits in broadsheets and newspapers that came all the way from London. These well-worn pages circulated up and down Moon Street. "They say he hid jewels and doubloons and pieces of eight in a sea chest. Madame Knight might—"

"Might what? If you believe everything Cato says," Hester interrupted with a nasty laugh, "you are a bigger fool than I thought."

Cato frowned. Philena felt herself shrinking.

Once again she became the left hand. The one of lesser rank. The one bitterly rebuked for not being clever, for being awkward and wanting a graceful manner.

"How you know Captain Kidd not make her rich?" Cato declared angrily. "She find treasure and you be sorry."

"Ahoy!" a shrill voice called from the kitchen window.

"Goodwife Kemble," Hester and Philena murmured. Instantly, Cato vanished.

Chapter

2

"Drop anchor and come aboard, Girl," Goodwife Kemble demanded. She swung open the shutter for a better view. Long ago she had given up calling either twin anything but Girl.

Hester sighed. Philena fidgeted. "We're busy, Mistress," Hester called back to her. Hester knew if they went inside to talk to Goodwife Kemble, they'd be trapped in the kitchen for hours.

"Not too busy to make fast," Goodwife Kemble replied, her raspy voice rising. She had good strong pipes when she gave orders. "I haven't heard your catechism. Now splice your patience and cruise down along into the galley. Be quick."

Reluctantly, Hester left the bucket beside the

back-door step. She and her sister trudged into the house. The old woman kept the kitchen as neat and trim as the deck of a well-run ship. Although she was nearly fourscore years, Goodwife Kemble was spry enough to climb out on to the roof to repair shingles or scamper up a ladder to wash the second-floor windows. She said she liked to go aloft, and protested loudly when her daughter ordered her down.

"So, I hear you're going to sea," Goodwife Kemble said. She sat on a bench with a gray shawl wrapped around her thin shoulders. She held the worn head of her cane in her gnarled hands.

Hester shrugged. "Madame Knight said something about a journey. She didn't mention anything about taking us along."

"She's not taking both of you. Just one. You." Goodwife Kemble lifted the tip of her cane and gave Hester a nudge. "That's why I want to hear your catechism. You set sail today."

"Today?" Hester said in amazement.

"Where?" Philena bleated. "Why?"

"My daughter won't say," Goodwife Kemble confessed, then added in a hushed tone, "I warned her she's sailing too close to the wind. But there's no stopping her when she's in this reckless state of mind."

Hester winked at her sister. *Just another of her fancies. Pay her no mind.* "Now, now, Mistress . . ." she began, half-smiling.

"Don't 'mistress' me. I've sounded it out. She's going. And she's taking one of you and Polly with her. Now say your catechism, the both of you," Goodwife Kemble commanded.

Only one of us? Philena gulped. To humor the ancient woman, she and Hester did as they were told.

"Come now and stand still beside each other," Goodwife Kemble said when they were finished.

"Do we have to?" Miserably, Philena twisted her apron. "Madame Knight says—"

"We must watch the shop while she's away," Hester interrupted.

Goodwife Kemble frowned. She had lost most of her teeth. When she scowled, her pitifully tooth-shaken mouth seemed to collapse like bread dough. It was difficult for Hester or Philena to believe that she had once been the most beautiful woman to ever sail 'round the Horn.

"My Sarah's too fat and too old to be wandering

the countryside rigged on a horse," Goodwife Kemble said. "What if she meets with Indians or bears or wolves? She can't shoot a gun. And what if the weather turns owlish? What if there's a gale? What then? You remember last winter—a season of more than ordinary cold and wind and deep snow. Why must she go in October, with bad weather ahead? She says nothing, but acts sly and says I'll be taken care of handsomely when she returns. How can she think that delivering the personal belongings of Mr. Trowbridge to his family will afford her such a great reward?"

Hester and Philena exchanged secret glances. *Great reward?* They had always considered Mr. Trowbridge a miserly, lonely, crooked-backed man. He had been one of Madame Knight's many boarders. Before he died, he had worked as a scrivener — a job Goodwife Kemble explained to mean a person who worked in a lawyer's office writing on pieces of paper in beautiful penmanship. He passed away one evening two weeks before and had been quickly buried. All that he left behind were some clothing and a mysterious, small trunk that was locked tight. Perhaps Madame Knight was being promised something valuable in Mr. Trowbridge's will.

Philena winked at her sister. *Maybe gold coins hidden in the trunk. Just like Captain Kidd's sea chest.*

"Girl!" Goodwife Kemble leaned forward and examined closely each of the twelve-year-old maidservants. "You can't fool me. I raised you, don't forget. I know all your impudent tricks. Now hold still for once."

Reluctantly, Hester and Philena froze. With elbows intertwined they seemed like a set of pale, identical roots found beneath a rotting log or an apple split perfectly in half or the same line of a hymn sung over and over. It was dizzying to look upon them at the same time. The startled eye moved from one to the other and back again as if to ask, "Can this be? Which is which? Who is who?"

Once a week for as long as they could remember, Goodwife Kemble ordered them to say their catechism and then stand beside each other for her inspection. "Stand up straight," she barked. She reached out with her cane and pushed Hester closer to Philena. "Who is tallest?"

"She is," Philena said, not bothering to look up.

"Who is smartest?"

"She is," Philena said. She glanced at her grinning twin sister.

"Who is the prettiest?" Goodwife Kemble demanded.

"She is," Philena mumbled, even though they had been told all their lives that they looked exactly alike.

"Who is the most patient, prudent, and prayerful?"

"She is," Philena said.

"Who is the most dutiful, kind, and loving?"

For a long moment Philena paused. "She is," she said finally. She felt a choking inside her throat. *What if Hester really does leave me behind?*

"God go with you," Goodwife Kemble said and studied Philena closely. She bowed her head and made an extra silent prayer. "Amen."

"But you said I'm not the one who's leaving," Philena protested, her voice quavering.

Goodwife Kemble glared at Philena. "Do not be saucy and impudent with me, Girl! I know exactly *who* you are."

Philena whispered her apology and made a little curtsy. She felt glad when Hester grabbed her arm and pulled her outdoors. But just as they stumbled toward freedom, Madame Knight caught them both by the necks of their dresses and hauled them into the house again like two flounders dangling from a hook.

Before they could protest, they found themselves standing in the middle of the keeping-room.
Goodwife Kemble hobbled in from the kitchen
and took a seat in the corner. "Is it true?" Philena
asked Madame Knight.

"Goodwife Kemble said—"

"A journey today—"

"But I won't go."

"Can you ever speak without interrupting each
other?" Madame Knight demanded. She dabbed
her sweating forehead with a handkerchief. "Your
habits are most irritating."

"Sorry," Hester said.

"Sorry," Philena echoed.

"I wished to tell you myself," Madame Knight
said. She paced before them. "Once again my mother
has completely disregarded my instructions."

Goodwife Kemble beamed happily. She liked
nothing better than a bit of mutiny now and then.

"We leave this afternoon," Madame Knight continued.

This afternoon. Hester and Philena's faces filled
with shock. Their mouths hung open in disbelief.
Can it be possible? The idea of separation stunned
them. For several moments they could not think of

anything to say. Philena stared at a knothole. Hester studied her dirty feet.

And then Hester began to weep. Of course when she began to weep, so did Philena. Soon they were both wailing louder and louder until Madame Knight put her hands over her ears and had to shut the front door for fear that the neighbors would think she was abusing her servants.

"Enough!" Madame Knight cried. "It is only a journey. We leave today and we shall return as soon as we can. There is not a moment to lose. We are already late in our departure. I need one of you to stay here to watch the shop and help my mother. I need one of you to go to assist me and Polly. What is more simple to understand than that?"

Neither Hester nor Philena was willing to understand. All that they knew was that their lives would be wrenched apart. The thought was as painful as if they were both about to have an arm torn away.

"I cannot go," Hester choked between sobs. "I cannot."

"Do not make her," Philena protested. "She is all that I have in the world."

"You thankless wights!" Madame Knight declared. "I took you in out of the goodness of my heart. I raised you. When the Boston authorities brought you to me, scrawny as a pair of stray cats, I said I'd feed you and dress you and house you. Bring you up as proper Christians. For what? A few miserable shillings a year they give me. You *owe* me your time. You owe me far more than just that. You owe me your lives."

Hester and Philena shivered as if the room had suddenly become very cold.

"You will do as I say," Madame Knight said, "or you will find yourselves in worse circumstances. Your time can be disposed of easily enough. I could send one of you to Virginia. Do not cross me on this." Her gray eyes looked hard. Her mouth's expression was stony.

Philena rubbed her face with her dirty sleeve. Hester sniffed loudly. They had heard this story and this threat countless times. They knew they still had nine years left on their indentured contract. In nine years they would reach their majority—age twenty-one—and they would be free. Until then, Madame Knight could split them apart anytime she wished and sell their remaining time to anyone who wanted to buy a servant's services. And the very worst place for a servant was Virginia. Some rumors said it was the hard labor and the beatings. Others claimed it was the heat and the disease. Whatever the reason, servants sent to Virginia plantations were never heard from again.

"Come now, Girl," Goodwife Kemble said gently to sniffling Hester and Philena. "You'll simply keep your weather eye peeled and you'll be reunited when spring comes again. That's not so far off. Why don't you both go above deck for some fresh air? You're going to make yourself pretty nigh fin out if you keep up your blubbering."

Gratefully, Hester and Philena stumbled out the back door. They walked down the path to the rail fence that separated Madame Knight's property from the common pasture. "We could run away," Philena suggested.

"You sound as foolish as Cato."

"You could pretend you were ill and unable to travel."

"She'd simply take you instead." Hester cocked her head. Beyond the pasture they heard the *clank-*

clank-clank of the blacksmith shoeing horses. *For the journey.*

Hester blew her nose loudly. "And I suppose you know why Madame Knight chose me for the journey?"

"Because you are the tallest, prettiest, smartest, most kind, dutiful, and loving?"

Hester made a face and shook her head. She felt surprised by how wretchedly stupid her sister could be sometimes. "She picked me to go with her to keep me out of trouble — far from home and far away from the shop. She left the good twin behind. I've heard her tell Goodwife Kemble that you're the pliable one. The one who never vexes or contradicts. The one who always counts correctly the customers' pence for the pins and needles and thread. She trusts you."

"You confess your faults too easily, Hester-Phina," Philena replied.

Hester smiled at the sound of their special name. It seemed a kind of comfort. She watched Philena sit on a stump and pick a scraggly sprig of wayward mint. Philena twirled it between her callused fingers. The sharp green smell reminded her of biting salt spray along the ocean when they went to gather clams. By the time Hester returned, it might be spring again. *Clamming season.* That was what Goodwife Kemble had said. Spring seemed like a long way away.

"Don't look so sad. Now you're making me miserable, too," Hester said and frowned. "What choice do we have? None. You know that. I must go. And soon I'll return and everything will be just the way it was before I left. I promise."

Philena slumped forward. "We have never been apart. Never." She crushed the mint in her fist, then tossed it as far as she could. "I think I might die without you."

Hester gave her a playful shove. "You will be fine. I will be fine, too," she said in a bright voice.

But they both knew she wasn't telling the truth.

"Girls, that's enough lying about lag-last, shiftless, and useless," Madame Knight bellowed from the doorway. She gathered her long skirt to keep it from the mud and hurried out of the house. Over one plump arm she carried a basket filled with gifts from their neighbors. Jams and jellies and fresh bread wrapped in clean cloth. "There is work to be done. And Polly? Where is she? We will never be ready to leave at this rate."

"Haven't seen her, Mistress," Hester replied. Madame Knight's only daughter was the apple of her eye. Polly could do no wrong. Over the years Hester and her sister had learned that it was safest not to speak when Polly's name was mentioned. Saying anything almost always landed them in trouble.

"Come here and take this," Madame Knight said. When the girls came closer, Philena took the basket from her. "Which one are you? Doesn't matter. See what you can fit into the tuck-a-muck. And don't forget the box of food when it's time to leave. We shall be lucky to find decent provisions not outrageously priced at inns along the Post Road."

While Philena disappeared into the kitchen, Hester followed Madame Knight to the barn. "Mistress, can you tell me where we're going?" Hester asked.

"No, I cannot," Madame Knight replied. "I have been told not to reveal our destination."

Mr. Trowbridge's relatives are certainly a suspicious lot! Hester decided to rethink her strategy. "What route shall we travel?" she asked innocently while inspecting the three enormous, restless horses.

They looked down at her with big eyes and stomped their big hooves. They curled their lips to reveal long, sharp, yellow teeth. The sight nearly took her breath away.

"We will ride south along the Post Road," Madame Knight said, "toward New York."

"We are going to New York?" Hester asked. She felt sick to her stomach. She had only ridden half a dozen times in her life. "Is that not very far?"

"I did not say we are going to New York, Girl. I said we are riding in that direction."

Suddenly, Hester felt confused and disheartened. *Doesn't she know exactly where she's going?* She looked into the eyes of her mistress's horse and did not feel the least bit of confidence. The villainously ugly creature of faded, sunburned sorrel color had a crazy, wild glare. The other two horses, called pacers, were so abnormally broad-backed and broad-bodied that riding them would be like sitting on a table with her feet hanging over the side, resting on the sidesaddle's double stirrups. She and Polly would practically need ladders to climb atop their backs. Even so, there was always the possibility of falling off or being knocked to the ground. *This journey is headed toward disaster.* "Mistress, why can you not—"

"You know the old saying," Madame Knight warned, " 'Curiosity killed the cat.' I suggest you ask no more questions—"

"Mama?" Polly cried. She scurried around the barn. The whites of her large gray eyes were red. Her pale face was streaked with tears. "I cannot go with so few dresses. It isn't fair. What will people think when they see me wearing the same dress over and over again? I will be humiliated."

Madame Knight took a deep breath. She put her dimpled fists on her broad hips and looked at her pretty, wailing daughter. "We have no choice, my dear. There is not space."

"I won't go then," Polly announced.

Hester breathed a great sigh of relief. She would be glad to make this ill-fated trip without the bothersome, spoiled creature.

"We have already discussed this," Madame Knight replied mysteriously. "This is your opportunity to meet quality people. You have never been outside of Boston. Now, my dear, please dry your eyes and finish packing your clothing. I am sure that we will find plenty of fine dressmakers in New Haven."

New Haven! Hester scowled. They were going all the way to New Haven for a new wardrobe for Polly?

Madame Knight's comment seemed to make perfect sense to her daughter. With revived spirits, Polly shoved her way past Hester. "Out of my way, Girl," she snarled and marched back to the house.

Hester could not retaliate. Not with Madame Knight watching. *Just wait*, she thought.

It was nearly three o'clock before the horses were saddled and Mr. Trowbridge's belongings were fastened with ropes behind Madame Knight's saddle. She and Polly and Hester said their final, tearful farewells before setting off behind fat Captain Luist, who promised to accompany them as far as the first town on the Post Road. A small group of neighbors and friends followed the horseback riders to the place where Moon Street forked. "Good-bye! Good-bye!" they shouted.

Philena stood outside the shop and waved a handkerchief and sobbed as if her heart would break. She could not believe that Hester was really leaving. All afternoon she had denied that such a thing would happen. As she watched her sister ride away, she felt a terrible wrenching emptiness that throbbed like a toothache. *What will I do without Hester?*

Hester took one look back at her sister standing in the muddy street. Hester blinked hard and tried to appear brave as the sidesaddle rocked dangerously from side to side. *Indians. Cold wind. Deep snow. Bears and wolves.*

As she moved farther and farther away from Philena, she felt as if she were watching herself becoming smaller and smaller. A memory returned. Hester recalled when she was a little girl and glanced for the first time into Madame Knight's looking glass. She thought she was seeing her sister smile and reach out to her. She even tried to lift and look behind the looking glass, certain that Hester-Phina must be hiding there. When she discovered her sister had vanished, Hester burst into tears and cried inconsolably.

That was how she felt at this very moment: abandoned and alone.

Chapter

3

On Friday afternoon I, Polly Knight, leave home in Company with my Deer Mother and our madeservant who is most disagreeable & tedious & complains mightily about her horse who is abnormally broadbacked & slow. I wish she did not join us. Weather clear. I keep this record of our Travel to remynd me that disappointments & Enjoyments are often so blended together, by the good Providence of God, that comfort may be drawn by the Prudent Man, even amidst tryals and difficulties. This being my first true Journey away from home I am eager to gaze upon Marvels in taverns such as a Fine Large White bear brought from Greenland or a Sapient Dog who can light lamps, Spell, read and Tell tyme. I Have heard *of such things from my Dear friend Mehitable Parkman who is better than any Sister. This Afternoon jolly Captain Luist travels with us as far as Dedham, where we plan to meet the Postrider heading West. Captain tells us Frightfull tales of Indians & Skalpings but Mother is determined to Procede even tho no postrider comes. We rest ourselves then go on Alone. 12 Miles to the place where we will spend the Night. What they call the Post Road is little more than a trampled Cow path between trees some places. God keep us Safe.*

—Polly Knight

Weary and sore, Madame Knight, Polly, and Hester arrived at an inn called the Good Woman Tavern that evening. A great painted sign hung over the door showing a figure of a woman with no head. "What is the meaning of that?" Polly demanded. "She has no face. We cannot see her eyes or her mouth. How do we know she is good?"

"Perhaps she is good because she is headless and therefore silent," Hester muttered. She had had nearly enough of Polly's incessant chatter about the color of the maples and were they nearly as bright as the ones back in Boston and how she would like to see the militia drill in New Haven and could they possibly be better dressed and more dignified than the ones back in Boston? Hester was glad when she could climb down from her horse, stretch her weary limbs, and escape from Polly's grating voice.

"I shall do the talking to the innkeeper," Madame Knight announced. It took Hester and Polly and a groomsman with a crooked leg to help lower her from her horse. She was wearing a sad-colored woolen round gown of camlet made with puffed sleeves that came to her pudgy elbows and were finished with knots of ribbons and ruffles. On her head she wore a close round cap that did not cover her ears. She adjusted her heavy woolen short cloak on her shoulders and carefully counted the three saddlebags and tuck-a-muck containing their food. She instructed the lame groomsman to carry these inside where they'd be safe, and woe to him if he dropped or damaged or lost anything. The horses were led to the barn to be unsaddled and fed.

With great dignity Madame Knight pulled open the heavy wooden door. The sight of her mistress's purple gloves of soft kid startled Hester. *Where did these come from?* The bright gloves extended to Madame Knight's elbows. Surely the minister at the meeting house back in Boston would never have approved of such a new and immodest fashion. Hester studied the gloves. Now that they were far away from any prying Moon Street eyes, were they allowed to wear whatever they wished? Could they do what they felt like? These new possibilities both exhilarated and befuddled Hester.

She stood nervously outside the inn door. *What shall I do when I go inside?* Without her sister, she was uncertain how to act. Hester had grown so accustomed to organizing and directing Philena, she didn't know what to do when she was on her own and had no one to boss around or prompt.

"Come now!" Madame Knight hissed from the open doorway at Hester and her daughter. "Do as I say and do not, I repeat, do not speak to anyone until I signal that this is appropriate. Remember, we are among strangers now."

Polly nodded with the great seriousness. Hester gulped and followed her mistresses through the door. The smoky tavern was loud and dark. The place smelled of tobacco and stale ale and sweat. A great fire blazed in the stone fireplace. Men in greasy leather pants leaned against the wall with their large muddy boots outstretched. They smoked long clay pipes and talked and joked and laughed with a heartiness that seemed oddly disconcerting. Other men huddled forward, their whiskered faces hidden in the enormous tankards they cradled with both arms on a long trestle table. No one looked up when Madame Knight and the girls entered.

Fearlessly, Madame Knight sailed around the strangers and the haphazard benches and stools and found the only empty table near a grimy window. She pointed to indicate that the girls should take a seat. Then she slowly lowered herself on to a bench. Polly flicked a greasy rind of pumpkin and a grizzled piece of bone from a stool before she sat down. Madame Knight leaned forward, careful not to soil her precious gloves. She folded her sausage-like fingers together and waited as if she were sitting in a pew at church.

The tavern became completely quiet. The men's heads swiveled. They gazed at the newcomers in astonishment and horror. Madame Knight coughed a nervous cough. She looked at the gawking strangers and said politely, "I understand from the sign that accommodations are six pence for a single meal. A quart of beer is one penny. But why is it that fire and bed, diet and wine and beer between meals is just three shillings a day? Does this not seem unreasonable?"

No one spoke. They only stared.

Hester squirmed and wondered if they should leave. She had never in her life been in a tavern except the one on Moon Street where everyone knew everyone. Here she did not recognize one familiar face. She felt uneasy and anxious. *They are looking at us, judging us.* "How far to the next inn?" she whispered to Madame Knight. "I do not think, Mistress, that we are wanted here."

Madame Knight refused to retreat. She leveled an imperious gaze about the place. "Where is the proprietor so that we might be served? We are hungry and have traveled a long way today." A few of the men sitting close by picked up their tankards, belched, and then edged farther away from Madame Knight and the girls. This behavior only seemed to unnerve the sociable woman more. Her eyes darted here and there.

"Captain Blood," someone murmured.

Madame Knight gave a halfhearted, friendly grin

to no one in particular. Perhaps she thought her charm would somehow convince these strangers to accept her.

"Mother?" Polly whined softly. "Do you not think we should leave?"

Hester drummed her fingers on the greasy table edge. She heard the words again. "Captain Blood," a low voice muttered. The hairs on the back of her neck stood up.

Madame Knight unfolded her gloved hands. She rose to her feet in one surprisingly graceful movement. It was clear that she had decided they would never have dinner unless she took matters into her own hands. "This captain. Where is he? I wish to speak to him and demand service."

Someone chuckled in the shadows. "Can't."

"Why not?" Madame Knight demanded, her voice indignant. "Speak, man. Don't hide thyself like a worm."

Another fellow laughed, though not loudly. "Thou canst not speak to Captain Blood for he cannot speak to thou." A tall, thin man with a leaping Adam's apple jumping about the collar of his shirt stepped into the firelight. He had a spattered apron tied around his waist and carried a mildewed rag.

"Dost thou own this establishment?" Madame Knight asked icily. "Dost thou always treat strangers so badly?"

"Pardon me, madame, but no one ever sits there," the aproned man explained.

Without thinking, Hester took her hands from the table and put them in her lap.

"No meal has been served at that place in years," he continued.

"Why?" Madame Knight demanded.

"Captain Blood's wife, long dead now many years."

Hester gripped her hands together very tightly in her lap. She watched the other strangers pause and lean forward or cock their heads to one side. Everyone in the room was listening.

"When Captain Blood's wife finds someone sitting at that place," the aproned man continued, "she smashes all plates, all dinners set upon that table, small or great, cloth or no." He picked up a dirty tankard and wiped his free hand on his apron.

Madame Knight clucked her tongue. "Nothing more than a preposterous story to terrify travelers. Well, sir, I am not afraid. We came to eat. So serve us and quit your far-fetched tales."

The man in the apron appeared immovable. He scratched his long greasy hair, tied back with a leather string. "Hear me out. This story is true," he said in a serious tone. "Time and again watchers were set near this very place. They were told not to take their eyes from the spot nor take themselves from the room. Yet something always happened."

"What?" Madame Knight demanded. This time her voice did not sound so bold.

"An alarm of fire. A call for help. A summons from the landlord. This but for a single moment, but in that moment eyes were taken away from that table and then *smash! crash!* The dinner was thrown upon the floor, trenchers and spoons and cups scattered and strewn everywhere."

The indignant flush was gone from Madame Knight's cheeks now. She looked pale and flustered. "And so how dost thou know it is a ghost that does this work?"

"What else could it be?" The man shook his head. "Captain Blood many years ago left port with a wife and came home with an angry spirit. That is all we know. She haunted him to an early death, never once giving the poor man the satisfaction of enjoying his ale in peace nor his mutton in quiet."

Hester edged farther away from the table. An icy chill seemed to hover nearby and she had the sudden urge to leap to her feet and run out the door. Somehow her feet were as heavy as iron. She could not move.

"Mama?" Polly whimpered. "I am not hungry. Can we go now?"

"So thou wilt not serve us here?" Madame Knight demanded. "Then we shall move. Girls, let us sit at another table to appease this apparition."

Hester and Polly gladly made their way to new stools, sharing a table with a greasy, bearded man who smelled strongly of ale and tobacco. His nose was bulbous and dark with veins and when he smiled at them his teeth were missing or black in places. Hester gulped. After hearing about Captain Blood and his evil wife, she did not trust anyone in this strange place. As soon as they moved, the hubbub and conversation resumed.

"We shall have the dinner, whatever it may be," Madame Knight told the aproned man, who came to the table and made a quick wipe across the surface. "I am looking for a guide. Dost thou know of anyone from this quaking tribe who might take us to the next station in the morning?"

The man in the apron glanced about the tavern. "Anyone here going toward New Haven who might take this lady along past the swamp?"

"I will pay for services," Madame Knight added.

No one volunteered.

"I will pay double for services," Madame Knight announced. She winced even as she said these words. She did not part easily with her money.

A tankard thumped on their table. "I'll take thou where the Post Road goes," the man with the bulbous nose and bloodshot eyes said. "For a dram of cider and a half a piece of eight."

"John, does your wife know where you're a-going?" the man in the apron demanded. "You aren't supposed to be wandering."

"Don't plague me! I know the way," John replied in a slurred voice. He tipped his tankard back and drained every last drop.

"I'll seal the bargain with a dram," Madame Knight declared. From her belt she untied her pocket containing a small leather bag of coins. She smacked these on the table and indicated to the aproned man that she'd have a dram herself.

In horror Hester and Polly inspected the wobbly new guide. Madame Knight downed the tankard and then carefully wiped her mouth with a dainty handkerchief. When their dinner arrived, it was a cold and bony mass of overcooked fish. Hester nibbled on a piece of hard pumpkin and Indian mixed bread with no butter. Every so often she glanced over at the haunted table and felt relieved that they were as far away as they were from the ghost of Captain Blood's wife.

That evening the innkeeper showed them to their room, one of only a few private chambers in the building. They had to climb up a ladder to a loft while carrying a flickering candle. There was but one tall bed in the small room. It had a feather comforter on it and a thin, worn quilt ragged around the edges. The room was so cold, they could see their breath.

"Now, Mother, how can we sleep in just one bed the three of us?" Polly complained.

" 'Tis better than sharing with a stranger," Madame Knight declared. "We bought a whole bed, not a half. And the inn's full tonight."

"But what of her?" Polly insisted, pointing a haughty finger at Hester. "It will be too crowded in the bed."

Hester stubbornly moved her foot back and forth on the gritty surface of rough, wide pine planks. "There's no spare blanket," she said. "I'll catch a chill sleeping on the floor on such a night as this."

"She's right," Madame Knight said wearily. She climbed with some effort into the bed and removed her shoes. She dropped each one on the floor with a thud. Then she pulled back the coverlet and climbed in wearing all her clothing. "Girl, you can sleep at the edge. But mind that you do not take all the covers from us."

After some effort, they made ready to go to sleep. Polly said her prayers and Madame Knight blew out the candle. Hester lay her head upon the sour-smelling pillow. She lay on her side at the very edge of the sagging bed and stared into the darkness. She thought of Captain Blood's wraith-like wife haunting the floor below them. She sniffed and pulled the ragged edge of the quilt up to her neck and shoulder.

In moments the room rocked with the sound of

Madame Knight's loud snores. Polly, obviously warm and snug in the valleylike middle of the bed, was soon asleep, too. Hester felt cold and wide awake and very alone. This was the first time she had ever slept without her sister. She wondered what Philena was doing at that very moment. *Does she miss me?*

Chapter

4

Saturday—We do not remain long at the Good Woman to rest ourselves even though my Great weakness requires every Indulgence my dear mother can afford. I believe I bear my ride beyond anyone's Expectation but horrid Girl berates me this morning beyond endurance. My mother says hush Not to pay her any mind for she is far from her familiar other Half, namely one twin, and I keep calling her Girl and this makes her most Upset. "After all these years do you Know not my Tru name?" she cries. What a foul-tempered lazy Girl she is not even willing to help me comb out my hair. Such rebellious carriage! And she nothing more than an indentured Maid. She's proms'd faithful Service for the years till her majority *and in the mean time gets housing and keep and Freedom Dues, which she speaks of with such rapture that she makes it sound Like a goodly Fortune. Does she know not she is but a chattel to us? If she were mine servant I would Beet her I tell My mother for her pure insolence. Now she can have no contrivance with her sister and so does vent her spleen on me. Such unnatural Creatures twins are. I am glad I am an only chyld.*

The early morning was dark and misty and smelled of wood smoke and coming snow. A small sliver of moon hung low in the sky when Madame Knight, Polly, and Hester awoke. They tried to rouse John, wrapped in a moth-eaten buffalo robe downstairs on the tavern floor before the fire.

"Wake up, sleeping dog!" Madame Knight hissed and poked him with her foot.

"Go away, woman!" John growled. "Let me sleep."

"Thou promised to take us on the road and if thou dost not, thou shall receive no payment."

John swore some oaths and stumbled to his feet. He looked old by firelight. Hester wondered if such an antique man would bear up under a

long day's ride. He staggered to the privy where
he was gone a very long time before he finally
reappeared. By then Madame Knight had instructed the groom to resaddle their horses and
make ready their packs for the day ahead. As soon
as John swung his leg over his horse's sway back,
he headed north.

"Mistress!" Hester called. "He goes back to
Boston."

Disgusted, Madame Knight called back John,
who was almost asleep in the saddle. Hester gave
her drowsy horse a good nudge and they began to
follow the muddy path between the trees. An owl
hooted somewhere close by, a sign that gave
Hester pause. She wondered if it might mean bad
luck but said nothing to Madame Knight or to
Polly. She had already had an argument with
Polly that morning and did not wish to make the
peevish girl more disagreeable than she was
already.

Hester's stomach growled. She hoped there'd be
something for them to eat in the tuck-a-muck
when they stopped to rest. But neither John nor
Madame Knight seemed interested in lingering
along the path. Dew-heavy branches bent low.

Cold water sprinkled Hester's shoulders and head and slid down her neck. *Was there ever such a miserable morning?*

Slowly, the sun began to creep up from the horizon and the sky began to lighten. In silence they ambled single-file. Without warning, John turned precariously in his old saddle tied together with dirty pieces of rope and called to Madame Knight, "What brings you along the Post Road in the autumn of the year with snow soon upon us?"

Madame Knight leaned forward slightly as if to keep herself in readiness in case her horse decided to caper. "I am going to New Haven to settle a family and business matter which may have much bearing on my future prosperity," Madame Knight replied.

Business matter. Future prosperity. When Hester heard these words, her ears pricked up immediately.

"A long, dangerous way for a woman to go alone," John said. He turned and spit into the woods. "You must have a considerable sum waiting for you in New Haven to take such a risk."

Madame Knight did not reply for several moments. "I have my reasons. They are private reasons."

John guffawed. "Don't worry. Shan't tell nobody."

Still, Madame Knight refused to reveal her secret. Instead, she gave her horse a little kick. The horse lumbered forward. The little trunk belonging to Mr. Trowbridge wobbled and jangled as she passed John, who did not seem to realize he'd been snubbed. In a loud voice, he entertained them with tales of adventures and eminent dangers he had escaped. "Once I came upon a catamount and had to wrestle it to the ground and strangle it with my bare hands," John boasted. "Another time I tamed a poisonous snake, then chopped off its head with my knife, all while I was running through the wood so's to escape a wild she-bear about to rip me limb from limb."

"I didn't know but we had met with a hero disguised," Madame Knight said over her shoulder. "Surely the bravest man in all of Massachusetts Bay Colony."

Hester could tell from the tone of her voice that Madame Knight did not believe a word of John's story. Hester liked to tell her sister equally wild tales, but she always made it clear to Philena that they were only make-believe—not true incidents.

Even so, it always amazed Hester how gullible Philena was and how willing she was to pass along tales of Hester's bravery. *Was anyone ever so believing as my sister?* Hester worried that in her absence her sister might be tricked unfairly. It was too easy to impress her.

As they rode on they came to a very thick forest filled with fog. "Beyond this," John warned, "lies a terrible swamp."

"Is there another way around it?" Polly demanded fearfully.

John shook his head.

Hester felt more and more anxious. There were Indians in the woods of western Massachusetts. In the *Boston News Letter* Polly had read aloud stories of people being taken captive. She'd read of massacres. How could Madame Knight have been so foolish? They had no gun and only this silly, weak old man for protection.

Finally, they stopped and dismounted and ate some of the food from the tuck-a-muck. "Do not feel fearful," John announced. He spouted crumbs as he spoke. "I have Universal Knowledge of the woods."

"And what, pray tell, is Universal Knowledge?" Madame Knight demanded as she nibbled daintily.

"It is the great comprehension of all things wild. My grandfather was a woodsman. My father was a woodsman. My brothers were woodsmen. And I am—"

"A great tippler and a great liar," Madame Knight said and remounted her horse. "If you have such a wonderful awareness of the woods, why did we find you in the tavern?"

John put one wobbly foot in his stirrup and swung his other leg over the saddle with great effort. He stared down his bulbous nose at Madame Knight. "One cannot stay in the woods *all* the time."

Polly slapped her reins across her horse's neck and moved closer to Hester's horse. The dark, misty shadows between the stunted pines and thorny bushes seemed to waver like something alive. For the next several hours they wandered along a path filled with briars. The path narrowed, then suddenly ended.

"Where are we?" Madame Knight demanded.

"Lost!" Polly wailed.

John swore loudly. "This way. I know it." He

turned his horse around and they retraced their steps. And for several more hours they zigzagged among cedars and pines. Hester had a sinking feeling that she had already seen these trees before. Her stomach growled and she felt certain they would never find their way out of this forest.

Soon the sun began to set. Ahead a clearing appeared. "Just as I suspected!" John declared. "We're almost there."

They left the forest and came upon a swamp filled with fearsome sounds and strange, disagreeable odors. "Oh, save me!" Hester cried. Her horse struggled up to its knees in thick black mud. She perched ready to jump from the horse into the brambles, certain that at any moment her horse would sink over its head in quicksand. But amazingly, the horse's broad hooves lifted with a terrible sucking sound and she was carried over the sloughy spot.

Ducks and geese flew overhead. Ragged soft cattails shredded and bent as they passed by. The seeds scattered, white and windblown. Hollow stems of dried grasses whispered and bent as a breeze pushed past them. In the brambles Hester spied a pair of red eyes watching her. The musty smell of the swamp rose up all around her and spread a kind of coolness along the ground. The sudden drop in the temperature made her tremble. She wrapped her woolen cloak around her shoulders and longed to sit beside a blazing fire.

"How far?" Polly asked in a hopeless voice. She tried to brush dirt from her cloak. "This mud is terrible. I scorn to be drabbled."

"Not too much farther," John promised. And sure enough, in the distance they saw a lone house with a light burning in the window. The horses began to move more quickly, as if they knew the trail's end was near. John was first to lower himself to the ground. He held his horse's reins as he knocked on the door.

A young, curious woman peeked through a crack. "Law for me," she cried, "what in the world brings you here at this time of night, John?" She opened the door wider and saw Madame Knight and the girls. The woman's neck was long and her eyes bugged out like that of a frog. "I never seen women on the road so dreadful late in all the days of my life. Who are you and where are you going? I'm scared out of my wits. Lawful heart, John! Can't believe it's you. How-de-do! Where in the world are you going with this woman and these girls? Who are they?"

John, stoop-shouldered with weariness, motioned for Madame Knight, Polly, and Hester to dismount. Then he promptly disappeared inside the house without offering to help them unharness or feed their horses.

"Well, there's an ungrateful scoundrel!" Madame Knight grumbled. She carefully lowered herself off the horse and led the tired animal to a falling-down shed. Polly and Hester were too tired to quarrel and followed her.

When they finally came inside the house, they found John sitting by the fireplace making himself very comfortable. From his pocket he dug out a pouch of tobacco for a smoke. Instead of offering Madame Knight a place to sit down or some food, the frog-eyed woman kept talking, asking more silly questions about where they were going and why they were going and when they'd be returning and what did they think they were doing scaring a body so badly in the middle of the night like this?

"Good woman!" Madame Knight said angrily. "I do not think it my duty to answer such unmannerly questions. We have not eaten properly yet today and are nearly famished." She paused and added a bit more kindly, "I have come here to have the post's company with us tomorrow on our journey." She flung off her cloak and carefully removed her gloves. She sat beside the fire. Polly and Hester, not knowing where to leave their muddy cloaks, simply sat upon them on a bench in an exhausted daze.

The young woman seemed impressed by Madame Knight's appearance and air of importance. She ran upstairs and when she returned it was obvious that she had put on jewelry—at least three or four rings and a glittering silver thimble, which she wiggled in the air to make sure everyone noticed. "Would you like to take a seat on the best chair?" she asked and waved her hands before her face. "We have a cold bite of bacon and some biscuit. I can fry the meat for you if you like," she said. Before she prepared the meal, she took off her rings and thimble. "These are nothing. Mere trifles," she announced to no one in particular. "I never pay them much heed." She did not appear to notice when she accidentally knocked the little thimble from the corner of the table. It rolled under Hester's foot.

When she was sure no one was looking, Hester picked up the thimble and, without thinking, tucked it inside her pocket, which hung from a string around her waist. For once, the preacher's threats about sin and Everlasting Punishment never crossed her mind. It was as if their journey along the Post Road had carried them to a place where all familiar rules and consequences no longer applied. She ate her dinner quickly and forgot about the thimble.

"Here is your payment as we agreed," Madame Knight said to John when they were finished with their greasy meal. She gave him his money, which he accepted eagerly. Hester wondered if he had worked for so much in as many months.

"You'll be needing lodging, too, I suppose?" the young woman asked, clearly impressed by the little bag of coins that Madame Knight seemed to distribute so freely.

Madame Knight nodded wearily. The talkative young woman showed them a little room in a back lean-to, which was so small, even the narrow bed nearly filled up the whole room. The bed stood so high that Hester and Polly had to help Madame Knight climb on a chair to reach it. Madame

Knight handed Hester a blanket and she pulled out a pallet that had been tucked under the bed for what must have been many years.

Hester felt as if she were sleeping in a long narrow cave. When she looked up she saw the wall on one side and the side of the tall bed on the other. She shut her eyes and had the terrible sensation that she was falling into deep, black mud. Exhausted, she turned her head on a sad-colored pillow, which she soon discovered was plagued by fleas. The bugs bit her face and neck all night. After many sleepless hours, she remembered the thimble tucked in her pocket and felt strangely pleased to have taken it.

Chapter

5

Since the moment Madame Knight, Polly, and
Hester left on their journey, the house on Moon
Street had become a regular hurrah's nest. Right
away Goodwife Kemble began ordering Philena
about as if she were the only crewmember on a
full-rigged ship.

"Look lively!" Goodwife Kemble shouted and
thumped her cane against the ceiling of the kitchen.
The floor beneath Philena's bed gave a loud knock.

Philena sat bolt upright in the cramped, dark
loft. Her sister's bed was empty. Her terrible
dream was true. *She's gone.* Reluctantly, she dressed
and scrambled down the ladder to set the fire and
make breakfast.

"I'm captain now," Goodwife Kemble declared. And although it was Saturday, which was the usual day to bake a dozen or more loaves of bread for the week, Goodwife Kemble announced that because the sun was shining and the wind was stark calm, it was a perfect day to do the laundry.

Philena sighed. She hated doing the laundry. It would be an even longer, more hateful job working alone. But she had no choice. Goodwife Kemble was in charge.

At breakfast it seemed very strange not to share a trencher of gruel with Hester. How odd to have her own spoon, her own leathern cup of cider to drink. "There's no use looking so forlorn, Girl," Goodwife Kemble announced. "We've plenty of work to do."

Philena looked up from her breakfast. In all the years of living at Madame Knight's, she could not remember one time that anyone called her Philena. *Why is that?* She stirred the gruel slowly. She quietly said her name aloud just to remind herself. "Phi-len-a," she whispered. It still sounded unfamiliar. *Who's she?*

"What?" Goodwife Kemble asked.

"Nothing," Philena answered. *I'm always Us or*

We. Never Me. But now here she was, all by herself. She looked about the room self-consciously. *She's gone.* Philena felt strange, as if she'd forgotten something important. Her other self. She felt as naked as if she were walking down Moon Street without a proper cap.

The kitchen seemed far too quiet with chatty Polly and Madame Knight gone. *Hester always does the talking for me.* Philena tried to think of something to comment upon. The weather? The work? Philena racked her brain.

Goodwife Kemble nervously tapped her foot as if she were feeling wadgetty, too. "Do not tarry, Girl," she blurted, clearly unable to stand the silence a moment longer. "There is work to be done."

Doing the laundry was a backbreaking job. First Philena had to haul piles of firewood to the yard. Then she had to fill a great kettle with water carried in buckets from the spring. She collected the dirty clothes by the armful. Dark woolen jackets and petticoats went from year to year without seeing a kettle of suds. But there were always plenty of shifts and aprons, handkerchiefs and shirts to wash.

Philena set a great fire burning in the yard and laid a kettle over it. Once the water was boiling good and steady, she added the strong lye soap and carefully dropped in the dirty clothes. She stirred them with a beating staff. Smoke blew in her eyes and made her wince and blink. As best she could, she picked up a soggy, steaming bunch of clothing with the long pole, then plopped them into another washtub of fresh rinse water. She bent over and wrung out the clothes with her hands and hung them on the line to dry. She did not feel like singing. *Who would join me at the chorus?*

Once each item was dry, she collected them from the line or the bush where they hung and carried them into the kitchen. Here she pressed the clothing carefully on the table using smoothing irons fitted into a heater, which she filled with coals from the fire. Ironing was the part of the job she hated most: walking back and forth from hearth to table to hearth again to stoke the heaters that kept the heavy irons warm.

Philena leaned against the table. With one chapped hand, she rubbed her eyes. She wondered what her sister might be doing at this very moment. *Not laundry, certainly.*

Suddenly, Philena felt jealous. What was so difficult about riding a horse? Certainly there were dangers, but at least life did not seem so abominably boring as what she was experiencing. Her back and arms ached. Her hands and wrists were sore. Doing the laundry alone was going to take the better part of two days.

Wearily, she sat down on a stool.

"What are you doing, idle creature?" Goodwife Kemble declared. "I thought you were tending the kitchen halyards."

Philena jumped to her feet. "I was, Mistress. Just resting, Mistress."

Goodwife Kemble sat down wearily. "Ah, me. We can look out for squalls all we can, but they still come upon us unawares."

"Mistress?" Philena asked, wondering if the old woman was feeling ill. "You seem a bit peaked."

"I'm bung up and bilge free, same as usual," Goodwife Kemble declared heartily. "It's my daughter I'm worried about."

"Bad news?" Philena asked anxiously. Her worst fears for Hester flashed before her. *Eaten by a bear. Scalped. Drowned.* "Tell me, please. I must know."

Goodwife Kemble placed her tight fist on the table, palm down. She turned over her hand and opened her knobby fingers. And there lay a curious object. It was shaped like a tiny glittering hoof no bigger than a man's finger from the knuckle to the tip. A leather string had been looped and tied at one end. "What is it?" Philena whispered.

"I've seen sailors carry such potent amulets for good luck. It's a guinea deer's foot dipped in real gold."

Philena dared not touch it or get too close. She knew Goodwife Kemble understood and followed all sailor omens and superstitions. This object clearly unnerved the old woman. Philena did not wish to tempt fate by doing the wrong thing. "Where did it come from?"

"West Africa."

"No, I mean how did it come *here*?"

Goodwife Kemble moaned. "When I was cleaning Mr. Trowbridge's room I decided to turn his mattress. And when I did, I discovered this fallen upon the floor. It must have belonged to him." She added in a sorrowful tone, "Don't you see? We cannot simply keep it or heave it overboard. We must return it with the other possessions, for it is certainly valuable and much too powerful for us to keep."

"Too powerful?" Philena gulped.

"We used to bury such things at sea with a sailor when he died," Goodwife Kemble said in a low voice. "But that's not possible, seeing as how Mr. Trowbridge is seven feet underground."

Philena tapped her finger against her nose to help her think. "We could return it with the other belongings to Mr. Trowbridge's family. In that way, *they'd* have to decide what to do with it."

"How? My daughter already has a day's sail ahead of us."

Philena thought hard. "Cato. We could send Cato. He's a good rider."

"If he clipped along," Goodwife Kemble said, nodding. Then she frowned. "The boy won't make it no matter how fast he goes. Some buccaneer will kidnap him. Or he'll sail off and never come back."

Philena nodded. "You're right."

Goodwife Kemble shook her head and rocked back and forth and cried with confusion. "Oh, my daughter will certainly be angry with me, I know it."

"Now, now," Philena said gently. She hated to see Goodwife Kemble so forlorn. "I could go with Cato," she suggested. The more she thought about it, the more appealing the idea became. *I could see my sister again. I could make sure she's all right.*

Goodwife Kemble seemed to brighten. "You'll make sure he doesn't jump ship."

"I'll be your anchor to windward," Philena said, using Goodwife Kemble's favorite phrase to describe a provision against disaster.

"You're a clever one, Girl," Goodwife Kemble said and smiled. "You must leave immediately. There's not a moment to lose."

Philena grinned. No one had ever called the left hand clever.

Goodwife Kemble handed Philena the guinea deer's foot. "Do not lose it. And as soon as you make the delivery, turn around and come back to port. If you do not return in one day, I shall send the authorities out after the both of you."

Philena made a solemn promise and slipped the deer's foot into her pocket. She quickly wrapped a few pieces of bread and a chunk of cheese in a handkerchief and tucked these in a saddlebag while Cato harnessed the horse. He seemed thrilled to escape from his endless chores. Philena tried to feel brave as she climbed up behind him and held tight to him and the saddle.

"Greasy luck to you!" Goodwife Kemble shouted a whaler's favorite farewell. "Point your bow south toward New Haven. You cannot miss them."

Philena and Cato rode south on the Post Road as fast as the horse would gallop. Their first stop was the Good Woman Tavern. Dirty and tired from riding almost without stopping, Philena felt glad to see a place where they could eat and rest before resuming their journey. She felt sore from bumping along on the horse and looked forward to a hot meal. Goodwife Kemble had entrusted her with a small bag of coins to use to pay for their meals on the way. Cato, too, seemed more than happy to rest.

While he led the horse to be fed and watered, Philena opened the inn door. Once her eyes became accustomed to the lack of light, she walked inside and took a seat at an empty table.

Immediately, all eyes were upon her. She felt the same way she did when she walked among strangers too close beside her sister. Only Hester was not here. She had no one to do the talking for her. She gulped as a tall, sallow-faced man in a dirty apron approached her. His eyes shifted about nervously. "What art thou doing back so soon?" he demanded. "And where is John? I told thou not to eat at this table, and yet thou disregards my advice. Art thou not afeared of ghosts?"

She tried clearing her throat. It took every ounce of courage she had to speak. "I beg thou pardon, sir. I don't know what ghosts thou speaks of. Is one called John?"

The man in the apron leaned closer and gave her a dark look. "Has some misfortune befallen him that thou now calls him a haunt?"

Philena felt confused. "I call him that only because *thou* does."

The man snapped the towel and hit a fly squarely. "Thou art a bold one to come in alone. And what happened to the older noisy woman and her pretty daughter? Have thou done away with them, too?"

"You mean my mistress," Philena said eagerly.

"Yes. That is the one I mean. She lured John away from his own wife and fire. Perhaps you were working together. I have heard of such thieves on the road."

Philena stood up. Her hands were shaking. "When was my mistress here? Yesterday?"

"You play the part of the stupid calf very well," the man with the apron replied. "But thou shalt not get away so easily." He lunged forward as if to grab Philena by her arm. But Philena was too quick. She darted out of his grasp and ran for the open door in terror.

"Trouble?" Cato demanded. He stood outside and was nearly knocked over by her.

"No time to explain," Philena said. "Get the horse."

Cato did as he was told. He jumped onto the horse's back and pulled Philena up behind him. An excellent horseman, he seemed delighted to spur the great horse and gallop away at full speed. They hurried off just as the owner of the tavern came outside and shouted to them to stop. They ignored him and rushed on. Philena held on for dear life. When they reached a forest, Cato slowed the horse to a trot and then to a walk.

Philena's breath came more regularly now. She had been so terrified, her hands were nearly cramped from holding on so tight to the back of Cato's saddle. "We are lucky to have escaped," she said. "That man is quite mad. He wanted to capture me and send me to jail."

"Why?"

"He thought I was a murderer."

"You?" Cato laughed derisively. "Who you murder?"

"It doesn't matter," Philena said and pouted. She did not like to be made fun of, especially by Cato.

"I be careful," he said, grinning over his shoulder. She did not speak to him again until they entered a dark forest.

In the distance they saw someone approaching on a slow horse. The stranger waved at them. "Where to?" the stranger demanded. His flushed face was friendly until he saw Philena. Suddenly, all the color seemed to drain away. "These woods must be haunted or I do need another drink," he said, his voice trembling. "Art thou not the girl I just left many miles away? How did thou get all the way back here and not once pass me on the path? Art thou a spirit?"

Philena smiled. "You must mean my sister. Where did thee see her?"

John seemed too terrified to reply. "Goodnight and farewell and do not follow me, spirit!" he cried and kicked his old horse hard so that it leapt around them and galloped away.

"They must be up ahead not too far," Philena told Cato once they entered the swamp. For the first time, self-assured Cato seemed frightened. "Ancestor spirits," he said and motioned with one hand.

Philena glanced nervously about the misty place. "Are you sure this is the way we should go?" Philena asked.

Cato shrugged. "Only way south," he said and pointed to the sun.

Cato's sense of direction did not make sense to Philena. She had seen other trails wandering off from the main one. What if they had picked the wrong way to go? Meanwhile, Cato skillfully managed to guide and cajole the big horse around the muddy places. Philena felt relieved when at last they came upon a house. "We'll stop here," she said. Her stomach growled and she realized she had not eaten anything since they left Moon Street.

As soon as she knocked on the door, she wished

she hadn't. "You!" a frog-eyed woman screeched. "Thief!"

Philena backed quickly away. Without a word, she scrambled back on the horse. Cato kicked the horse hard, and they were soon rushing into the darkening trees.

Chapter

6

Night was coming and they still had not found Madame Knight, Hester, and Polly. Unwilling to take another chance at an inn where they might be chased away or locked up or worse, Philena wondered if they might be better off resting anywhere they could and then setting off at first light.

"What about Goody?" Cato asked. "She think we run off." He was referring to Goodwife Kemble and her threat to send slave catchers with dogs after them.

"What else can we do? We can't go back until we make the delivery." Deep down, she wanted to see her sister again. She wanted to see for her own eyes that Hester was all right.

Geese soared overhead in the darkening sky. The noisy flock moved like one giant V-shaped bird with slender, trailing wings. Their haunting farewell cries filled the evening and made Philena shiver. The geese were journeying far away. She wondered when she, too, would see her sister or their home again.

"Are there bears in these woods?" Philena asked in a small voice.

Cato shrugged.

"Catamounts?"

He shrugged again. "Maybe wolves, too."

This made Philena feel more nervous than ever. She did not like the idea of traveling in the dark when there might be so many vicious hidden creatures waiting to eat them.

"We stay there," Cato said. He pointed to a dilapidated log house half-hidden by trees.

"Do you think anyone's there?" Philena asked. She looked for signs of smoke coming from a chimney or a light at the windows. The place seemed to be deserted. Wind rattled nearby tree branches. Reluctantly, she agreed to go inside the abandoned shack. She and Cato climbed off the horse. After removing the saddle, Cato hobbled the horse so that it could not wander far as it grazed whatever it could find to eat.

"Hello?" she called as bravely as she could.

An owl hooted and startled her.

She pushed open the rotting wooden door. Something scampered past her foot. She stifled a scream.

"Mouse," Cato said.

The one-room house was no bigger than the keeping-room. The walls, made of half-hewn logs, had great gaps and there was a hole in the ceiling. The place smelled damp and moldy, as if it were slowly becoming part of the forest again.

"See? No one here," Cato declared. He began collecting wood to build a fire in the middle of the room. He took from his pocket two small pieces of flint, which he struck together until he made a spark. Carefully, he blew on the little, smoldering pile of pine needles and dried moss. Soon the fire grew and he added bigger chips of bark and small branches. Smoke rose out the hole in the roof.

Once the flames began to roar, Philena felt safer. *No wild beasts will come close now.* She unpacked their bread and cheese and sat inside the circle of light and warmth with her cloak wrapped around her shoulders.

Cato joined her. He stared into the fire and slowly chewed the bread and cheese. Philena had never had a real conversation with Cato. Her sister usually did all the talking. Even though she had ridden with him all day, they had not really exchanged more than a few words. Now she felt awkward. After several moments of silence, she blurted, "You ride a horse very well."

Cato smiled. "My father teach me."

"Do you ever think about your family? Do you think they wonder where you are?" she asked, surprised how easy it was to think of something to say.

"Always." He poked the fire with a stick.

"You can remember them. You are lucky."

Cato smacked a stick against a smoldering log. Sparks flew. He stared into the fire and scowled. "Lucky, hah!"

Philena had never considered that having a few memories, however scanty, might be worse than having none at all. She and her sister could invent their mother. Cato knew his mother existed, but he could neither see nor hear her. He couldn't visit her. He could only remember. "I am sorry to have made you sad and worried," Philena said.

Cato looked up briefly at her and for a split second, his angry mask seemed to fall away. He was no longer the bragging, joking, defiant Cato. He looked vulnerable and afraid. And then, just as quickly, the mask went up again. "You the one should be worried," he said.

"Why?" Philena asked nervously.

"I hear Mistress say she can't keep two of you no more. She say she go sell your sister's time. That why she make trip."

Philena gulped. "She took my sister to work for somebody else? She's separating us for good?"

He nodded wisely. "She keep good secret, but not from Cato."

Philena was stunned. Suddenly, everything made sense. The hurry. The lies. The promises. Madame Knight had not even told her own mother the truth. *Goodwife Kemble never would allow us to be split apart. Never.* Philena felt sick to her stomach. With every passing moment, her sister was moving farther and farther away from her, never to return.

Cato jabbed the stick in the dirt. "Mistress say she get plenty money."

"We have to find them. I have to warn my sister. I have to stop Madame Knight," Philena said. Her voice sounded high-pitched and frantic. "We must go right away. What if we're too late?"

Cato motioned toward the open doorway and the darkness beyond. "Too dangerous now. Go in morning. Get some sleep." He threw a few more branches on the fire and curled up on the ground with his back to the flames.

He doesn't care. She's not his sister. Philena wrapped herself in her cloak. Her mind raced with terrible possibilities. *What if I never see her again? I never told her I loved her. I never said good-bye.* The dirt floor felt prickly against her shoulder. She tried not to sleep. She had to think of a plan. But her eyelids were so heavy, she closed them. Soon she was asleep. That night she dreamed she was searching for her sister in an enormous, echo-filled house. She called her sister's name over and over in the empty rooms. "Hester-Phina! Hester Phina!" Her sister never answered.

Philena awoke the next morning exhausted and disturbed. Her cheek was imbedded with a twig and a small pebble. She sat up shivering and brushed the dirt from her face. *Where am I?* The fire had dwindled to glowing ashes. She could see no sunlight through the cracks in the walls and the hole in the roof. Outside the open door swirled damp, cold mist. Everything was quiet.

Too quiet.

"Cato?" she called in a hoarse voice.

No answer.

She scrambled to her feet. "Cato?"

Frantically, she searched the shack, then hurried outside. The horse had vanished. So had Cato.

In disbelief she called to him again and again. Perhaps this was some kind of joke. He liked to play tricks. Perhaps he was hiding, watching her panic, laughing. "Cato!" she called as loud as she could.

Something large and gray flapped noiselessly overhead. Instinctively, she raised her arms to her face and bent double. For several moments, she wasn't sure how long, she crouched on the ground. Her heart pounded.

Finally, she stood up. The owl was gone. Cato was gone, too. She was completely alone. For the first time in her life, she had no one to tell her what to do, what to think, what to say. No one to make the fire. No one to show her the way. Her sister's words echoed in her ears: *a bigger fool than I thought.*

Shocked and confused, she went back inside the shack and kicked a few dry twigs into the ashes. *Perhaps Cato will come back.* The fire smoldered. Wisps of smoke rose. She sat down and watched the feeble flames. She felt inside her pocket. The guinea deer's foot. *Perhaps he went to find something for us to eat. I'll just wait for him.* She watched the flames sputter, then disappear. She did not know what else to do. She sat there a very long time, her knees bent, her arms wrapped around her legs.

And still he did not return.

The sky began to lighten. She was cold and hungry. More geese passed overhead. This time she felt their cries mocked her. *Cato's never coming back.* He had purposefully left her here to make his escape. She wondered how long it would take him to ride to the Carolinas. Although she felt betrayed, she could not blame him.

At last she stood up. *I must find my sister.* She would have to figure out a plan on her own. Slowly, carefully, she wrapped the cloak around her shoulders and lifted the hood over her head.

She knew then that she could no longer stay where she was. She had to hurry and keep moving south on the Post Road. She had to catch up with Madame Knight, Polly, and her sister.

As soon as she began to walk faster, she felt warmer. Mist lingered in the hollow places. Birds chattered. The fragrant path, thick with pine needles, was soft and springy under her feet. She paused to watch a squirrel dash up a tree. And for the first time she realized she was making all her own decisions. She could walk fast or slow, south or north. She could stop or sleep, and no one was there to tell her what to do or how to feel or what to think. To her complete surprise, she began to laugh.

The squirrel seemed to find her behavior very strange and dashed out of sight.

Suddenly, she heard an odd sound behind her. *A bird?* She paused and listened. No, it was a man singing. The words floated between the trees like an enchantment:

> *"One night when the wind it blew cold*
> *Blew bitter across the wild moor,*
> *Young Mary she came with her child*
> *Wand'ring home to her own father's door."*

She bit her lip and wondered what to do next. Goodwife Kemble warned her to be always on deck, ready for anything. *Do Mohawks sing English songs?* What if the fellow had a scalping knife? Or perhaps he was just another traveler. Should she hide? Should she run? Or should she join him? There might be advantages to having a companion while walking through the woods. To scare away wolves and—

"Hello?"

Too late. Philena turned and could see the man coming closer. He wore a black cloak and rode a tall, dark horse. The man gestured to her with a half-eaten apple. "Where art thou going on such a beautiful morning?" he called in a friendly manner. He did not seem the least startled to see another lone traveler so early.

Speechless, she stood looking up at him. Vapor steamed from the horse's nostrils. Instinctively, she took a step back, fearful of being crushed. The stranger halted his horse, leaned forward, and stared down at her. His black, wide-brimmed hat was pulled down so she could not see his eyes. He had no beard. A deep dimple in his chin danced when he chomped another bite of apple.

"I . . . I am seeking my mistress . . ." She could not think of anything else to say. The horse stomped impatiently. She moved to the edge of the path as if to let him pass. But he did not budge.

"Hast thou never observed a passion for going abroad to attend a guilty conscience?" The stranger's voice was melodic and deep. He used the kind of fancy, confusing words Madame Knight sometimes employed, which made her think he must be a man of distinction and learning. "The jolting of a horse and the company of strangers seem to act as opiates upon it."

"Sir?" she said, not understanding a word of what he was saying. She stared at the apple in his gloved fist and licked her lips.

"Art thou hungry?" he asked kindly. His saddle creaked as he reached back and produced from his saddlebag three bright red apples. His hand was so big, he easily held all three apples at the same time.

She took a step gingerly forward toward the steaming, snorting horse and quickly took the apples from him. "Thank thee kindly, sir," she said and bit into one almost immediately. Until that moment, she had almost forgotten how long it had been since she had had something to eat.

He smiled as he watched her eat. With a gloved finger, he pushed back his hat and she could see his eyes. They were careful green eyes that reminded her of a cat. He seemed old, but not as old as Madame Knight. "Traveled far?"

Apple juice dribbled down her chin. Her mouth was too stuffed to speak. She shrugged. The journey had seemed endless. But she could not say how many miles she had gone. She wiped her mouth with the back of her hand. Patiently, he seemed to wait for her to speak. *Say something.* "I left from Moon Street."

"Boston?"

She nodded.

"A fair and amiable city. I have always had a natural tendency to seek seclusion. But Boston is a wonderful town to ramble in. Once a year or thereabouts I like to take an excursion there. Is Moon Street home?"

"My mistress's home," Philena said and felt a sharp pang of homesickness. For the first time, she felt so far away from everything familiar that she wondered if she would ever see her sister or Goodwife Kemble again. Her existence on Moon Street seemed to have taken on a shadowy, unreal quality. She bit into the second apple to make sure she wasn't simply dreaming.

"Thou art a servant with papers?" he asked, not unkindly.

She paused, uncertain how to answer. *Papers?* She had no papers. Goodwife Kemble had warned her what might happen if she were found on the road traveling alone. An indentured servant who had run away. *Locked up.* That was what she had said. *Has he been sent by the authorities already?* She thought of Goodwife Kemble's warning and shivered.

The stranger did not pursue this line of questioning. He seemed to have made up his mind about her. "Perhaps thou would like to travel along with me for company?"

Philena glanced up at him and felt strangely grateful for his kind suggestion. He seemed like an honorable gentleman. "I am in a hurry on an important errand." She took the guinea deer's foot from her pocket to show him. "I must deliver this to Madame Knight." She explained all the particulars about Mr. Trowbridge and his belongings. But she did not tell him the real reason why she was in such a hurry to find her mistress. She did not mention her sister or Cato for fear he might dissuade her from her mission or alert the authorities about a runaway slave.

"It is a beautiful object," the stranger said. He leaned over and took the guinea deer's foot by the string so that it dangled and glimmered.

"Dost thou suppose the gold is real?" she asked.

The stranger chuckled. "I doubt it. But I shall keep this safe until we find thy mistress. Climb up." He slipped the guinea deer's foot into his pocket and extended a strong hand to Philena. Faster than a cat lapping chained lightning, she was pulled up behind him on to the horse and was soon trotting along at a pace much faster than she could walk. *What good luck!* She gripped his smoky-smelling cloak tightly and felt hopeful that soon she would see Hester safe again.

"Sir, what day is it?" she asked as the wind whipped in her face.

"Sunday."

Sunday! Ordinarily, she would be sitting at the meeting house all day in strict observance of the Sabbath. But instead, here she was riding along on a stranger's horse, pursuing her mistress and her sister. Although she had only been away from

Moon Street for a little over a day, so much had already happened that she felt as if she'd been gone for weeks.

"Hold on," the stranger said. The big horse picked up speed and the trees rushed past in a dizzying blur.

Chapter

7

Sunday—We came upon a place called Devil's Foot rock, a ledge with many marks like that of Great Heels walking. It was a curious site because the footprints seemed to vanish at the edge. I asked my Deer mother what could have made such a thing but neither she nor our feeble guide seemed to know. The Foot Rock was named by Indians, says he. And I should not be surprised to find a skull or wampum here and was glad to continue our journey and who should we hear calling to us from behind shouting but the other madeservant. She galloped behind on a strange gentleman's Horse. We were so surprised we nearly plunged to the ground. The man stopped, not without some reluctance. He demanded to have a *reward to return the wayward girl who slipped from the saddle before he could catch her. "What reward?" my mother demanded. "She's runaway without papers," he says. And both madeservants begin to wail and cry and cling to each other. "Sir," says my mother, "I thank your for your Kindness to Return her to me. You are a Grifter I can see that." She gave him a few coins to make him go away. He was furious but did her bidding and galloped off. And so now we must travel with both girls on one horse, irritating as they are and my mother quite furious for it is too far to send this other one back and we have lost Cato and the horse. "Oh," says Girl, "he took the deer foot." We don't know what she wails about but its Too Late to call back the Wicked stranger. It is a good thing Mama seldom leaves my Grandmother in charge for look what misfortunes and confusions befall us.*

Polly glanced up from her journal at Philena and frowned. They sat at a table at Haven's Tavern, waiting for Madame Knight, who was busy speaking to the innkeeper at his desk near the door. Hester had gone with her.

Miserable Philena tried not to look at Polly. *No one understands. No one listens. Not even Hester-Phina.*

What had begun as a magnificent attempt to save her sister had ended abruptly as her own rescue by Madame Knight.

"You are ruining everything, Girl," Polly grumbled. "You lost my mother's slave, her expensive horse. You cost her money for your own ransom. And because of you, we may not arrive on time."

"Sorry, Mistress," Philena replied. She was glad that Polly did not mention the disappearance of the guinea deer's foot or the stranger's threat. "Thou wilt regret this." She felt cursed enough. How would she ever find a way to keep Madame Knight from separating her from her sister? To make matters worse, her sister was not taking Cato's warning seriously. Her sister's words rang in her ears: *You're too trusting. You believe everyone.*

Meanwhile, at the innkeeper's desk Madame Knight carefully penned a message on pieces of foolscap. It took her several moments to decide upon the reward. When she completed the last line, she gave the piece of paper to the innkeeper to give to the eastward-traveling postrider, who would take the copies with him to post at taverns along the route. "And here's a copy of the notice for the *Boston News Letter* for publication in the next issue," Madame Knight said. She handed the innkeeper another folded piece of paper for the postrider that said:

Five pound Reward. Ran away on Saturday
from his mistress in Boston, a Sirranam
Indian manslave, named Cato, aged about 14
years old, black short hair, markt upon his
breast with the letters SK; has on a black
brooadcloth jacket, under that a frize jacket
and breeches, a crocus apron, gray yarn
stockings and mittens, and speckled neck
cloth: speaks good English. Riding good Bay
mare.

"Hast thou any news for Madame Sarah Knight?" she inquired of the innkeeper.

He gazed at her with gray, squinting eyes. He seemed to have no age—neither very old nor very young. He tucked a large pinch of snuff inside his cheek and then searched through a box at his desk, heaped high with scraps of paper and nubs of goose quills. "Nothing here," he said.

"Art thou sure there's not a message from someone called E.C.?" she demanded in a low voice.

She was unaware that Hester, lingering nearby, was intently listening to every word.

The innkeeper shook his head. "Sorry."

"Something must be amiss," she said and sighed. "We have come so far already. We must simply go on and hope for the best."

The innkeeper scratched his stubbly cheek. "Wilt thou be needing a guide? The postrider going west should be here soon."

"Good. In the meantime, we will have something to eat," Madame Knight said, her old decisiveness returning. She turned and saw Hester watching her closely. "What are you staring at?"

"Nothing, Mistress," Hester said in an innocent voice. "I am only very famished." *Something amiss. What does that mean? And who is E.C.?* She followed Madame Knight through the taproom, filled mostly with drinkers. It was nearly two o'clock in the afternoon and dinner, the largest meal of the day, would not be served until three. In a corner they found Philena sitting with her hands folded at a table, keeping a safe distance from Polly.

As Hester came closer, she inspected her twin critically—the way a stranger coming into the tavern might. For the first time she noticed that

Philena's face was smeared with ashes and dirt. Her sleeves were muddy. "You look hard used," Hester hissed in her sister's ear as she sat down. Hester felt embarrassed to sit in public beside someone so filthy who looked exactly like herself.

"I cannot help my appearance," Philena whispered, startled and hurt by this comment. "I slept upon the ground last night in a filthy hovel. I hurried here to rescue you."

Hester did not seem the least impressed. "Rescue me from what?" she demanded in a low voice.

Philena tilted her head in the direction of Madame Knight.

"From our mistress?" Hester said in disbelief.

Philena coughed once.

"Would you two please stop your incessant back and forth?" Polly said in a critical voice. Then she turned to her mother to complain. "Mama, what took you so long? I am about to faint for want of food."

"Be patient, daughter," Madame Knight said in a tired voice. "I am moving as quickly as I can."

Polly sniffed. "Mama, your maidservant smells quite loathsome. Must I sit beside her?"

Madame Knight did not appear to be listening. She was anxiously counting her coins and gazing up at the sign above the bar that read:

**My liquor's good, my measure just,
but honest sirs I will not trust.**

The innkeeper's wife, a walnut-colored, thin woman in a dirty dress, brought something that looked like a piece of twisted cable to the table. She dropped it with a clunk. "They twins?" she asked, motioning with her head toward Hester and Philena.

Before Madame Knight could respond, Hester replied, "I am. She's not."

When Polly laughed, Hester seemed very pleased. Philena wasn't the least bit happy. She blushed and felt small and awkward and neglected. *The left hand again.* Why had she never noticed before how bossy her sister was?

The woman trudged away, looking confused.

"Can't you take a joke?" Hester growled at her sister.

Philena's eyes narrowed. She had also never noticed before how her sister could be quite cruel when it suited her.

Polly pushed the bread toward Hester and said in a friendly voice, "Give it a pull." She and Hester worked together to claw off one stale end.

Philena took a small piece and ate ravenously. *Why won't my sister listen to me?* She watched the other two girls nibbling and giggling and wished that she were home again where her sister considered *her* her best friend—not Polly.

The walnut-colored woman brought a dish of pork and cabbage. She dropped this unceremoniously on the table with a fistful of dirty spoons.

"What's this? The remains of dinner from last night?" Madame Knight demanded. She scooped a bit and held it up to the light from the dim window.

"The sauce is purple," Polly complained.

Hester and Philena inspected the meat closely and discovered that Polly was right. "Woman?" Madame Knight called in a loud, sending voice. "Hast thou made our meal in your dye kettle?"

The innkeeper's wife shuffled over to the table and scowled at them. "Nothing wrong with that pork and cabbage," she murmured. "Thou will be charged whether thou eats it or not."

Philena's stomach roared with hunger. She did not care what color the cabbage was.

"I'll not eat of this," Polly announced and crossed her arms in front of herself.

Philena, worried that the meal would be taken from them because of Polly's complaints, grabbed a spoon as if ready to take a bite.

Madame Knight sighed. She scooped a bit of purplish vegetable on to her spoon. Amazingly, she managed to get a little down. "What cabbage I swallow will surely serve me for a cud tomorrow," Madame Knight grumbled.

Hester gave her sister a secret sideways glance and winked. Philena smiled. In their private jokes they often referred to Madame Knight as Madame Cow.

"What is so amusing?" Polly demanded.

"Nothing," Hester insisted. She could not look at Philena or she'd start laughing, too.

"You are rude," Polly said. "Both of you."

For the first time since she'd been reunited with Hester, Philena felt as if she and her sister might be comrades again. Twin souls invincible.

When the postrider finally arrived, they began their journey toward New Haven again. He barely stopped to change to a fresh horse and seemed not pleased to have a bossy woman and three girls tagging along behind him to the next stop. "I am in a hurry." He glanced at each of them, his eyes filled with doubt. "If you can keep up, I'll take you. If not, you're on your own and God help you."

Philena did not find his manner or speech very comforting. Clearly, he meant to abandon them if they could not keep pace. Hester turned to her sister behind her in the saddle and demanded, "Weren't you afraid to stay all night in that place you described?"

"I did not know I was alone until I awoke. That's when I was fearful," Philena admitted. She looked behind her down the path through the trees. She wondered what had happened to the dark stranger. What if he were following them? "We must think of a plan," she said softly so that Polly, on the horse ahead of them, could not hear. "Madame Knight means to sell you and separate us."

Hester thought about the conversation she had overheard at the last inn. *Maybe there's some truth in what she says.* "Madame Knight seems in a hurry to meet someone," Hester admitted. "She asks for messages from E.C. Who can that be?"

"Maybe someone she plans to be your new master."

Both girls were silent for several moments. "We could run away," Hester said.

Philena thought of Cato. "How far would we get before we were captured? And you know the punishment."

Our remaining time doubled. "We'd be old women before we're free," Hester said slowly.

The horse picked up speed. They bounced along. With every step, they seemed to be carried closer and closer to the moment of separation. Hester pulled on the reins and the horse slowed to a trot. "We could both pretend to be ill. Who wants a sick servant?"

"Madame Knight is no fool," Philena replied. "She can always tell when we're pretending."

"We could simply refuse to be separated. We could put up a terrible fuss. A howling fit."

Philena shook her head. "We tried that already. And you know what will happen if we make Madame Knight mad enough . . ."

"We'll be sent to Virginia." Hester sighed. Their situation seemed hopeless.

"We'll think of something," Philena insisted,

even though deep down she did not feel the least bit confident.

After several miles, they came upon a wide river. Brown water splashed and gurgled past. The postrider stopped, stared for a moment at the swollen current, then kicked his horse. The beast splashed up to its haunches in the water.

"Sir!" Madame Knight called. "We cannot swim."

The impatient postrider gave her a scornful look. "The horses know what to do." He splashed deeper.

"Sir!" she cried again, louder this time. "We must have a proper boat."

"A boat, your ladyship? Where dost thou expect me to find a boat?"

Madame Knight's face turned red with anger. "I appeal to thee as a gentleman. We must have a boat or we cannot cross."

"What about the horses?" he demanded.

"Ferry us across in a proper craft, then herd the animals across," Madame Knight announced.

Polly's horse pawed the ground nervously. Her face looked even paler than usual. Hester and Philena glanced into the current. *How deep?* Philena wondered.

The postrider spit and cursed. He swung his leg off his saddle and tied his horse to a leafless willow. Without saying a word, he stomped upstream through the underbrush.

"Mama, I am glad you are so forthright," Polly murmured in approval.

Madame Knight seemed pleased with herself. "It is a helpful talent for any woman," she said.

Time passed and still the postrider did not return. Hester slid from the saddle to the ground, then held the reins so that her sister could also climb off the horse. Hester glanced about uneasily.

"Do you suppose there might be Indians here?" Philena whispered, saying aloud her sister's very thoughts.

"Do not speak of such things."

"What if he doesn't come back?" Philena replied. "What will become of us?"

"Be quiet," Hester hissed. "Stop plaguing me with your questions. He left his horse. He has to return."

"What if he's been ambushed?"

Suddenly, their horses whinnied. Branches broke. Footsteps crashed through the bushes. *Indians.* Philena froze. Hester squeezed her eyes shut.

Chapter

8

Through the trees appeared the postrider. He trudged along the river with a paddle over his shoulder. In one hand he tugged a rope attached to an ancient canoe. "Here's a boat," he said angrily to Madame Knight.

Madame Knight came closer to the shore to inspect the craft. Water sloshed in the mossy bottom. She sniffed disapprovingly. "Doesn't look seaworthy."

The postrider spit with great vehemence. "It's this or nothing. Get in."

The boat bobbed. Madame Knight clucked her tongue but did not say another word. She lifted the hem of her skirt, extended her hand to the postrider, and stepped cautiously into the dugout.

The boat tipped and teetered. She shrieked. "Sit down!" the postrider barked.

Madame Knight did as she was told. Water splashed in her lap. She sat rigidly upright and gripped the sides of the dugout with both hands. The boat wobbled as the postrider climbed in with the battered paddle. He sat down quickly. The slightest movement caused the craft to buck and plunge. He shoved away from the shore and headed for the opposite side. For once, Madame Knight was speechless. With awkward, choppy strokes, the postrider splashed and paddled the dugout across the river. He leapt out on the opposite side, wet his boots, and cursed loudly. Madame Knight clumsily rose and stumbled to shore. Her dress was so wet, she wrung it out with her hands.

Philena watched nervously as the postrider returned to their side of the river. "Thou art next," he barked at Polly.

Lighter than her mother, Polly slipped into the boat and took a seat. The postrider crossed her without mishap. When he returned, he shouted to Hester and Philena, "Come on. I'm in a hurry. Climb in."

For a moment Hester and Philena stared at each other in panic. "We go together," Hester said.

"Not separately," Philena added.

"The boat won't hold three," the postrider said.

"Then we won't go," Philena insisted. Hester looked surprised. Ordinarily she was the one who made the decisions and talked to strangers.

The postrider swore a string of oaths that were so awful, Philena pressed her palms against her ears. "All right, then. Get in," he grumbled. "Can't weigh together as much as the old she-beast."

They did as they were told. A wave smacked the boat and splashed their faces. By mid-river, cold water sloshed up to their ankles in the bottom of the boat. Hester's teeth chattered. "Will we capsize?" Philena asked, too terrified to move.

"Bail!" the postrider said between clenched teeth. He paddled faster. "Use anything."

Hester and Philena cupped their hands and lifted water out of the boat. Hester used her soggy shoe to scoop more water out of the boat. Philena did the same. The waterlogged boat managed to arrive safely on the opposite shore. Each of the girls held a damp shoe in one hand and jumped to the muddy shore. The postrider tipped the boat to drain it of water. "It's a good thing we know how to work together," Hester told her sister.

Philena nodded. "Two shoes are better than one."

But when Polly saw them standing shoeless in the mud, she laughed loudly. "Look at your stockings!"

Hester and Philena felt chagrined.

"How far to the next stop?" Madame Knight demanded of the postrider when he returned from swimming the horses across the river.

"Four miles," he replied. He adjusted his saddle, tucked his soggy boot into the stirrup, and swung his leg up into the saddle.

"Pray, dost thou know the condition of the rest of the road till we reach that place?" Madame Knight demanded. It took all three girls' great effort to help her climb up on to her horse again.

The postrider scratched his dirty head. "There's a bad river to ride through."

"Another bad river?" Madame Knight asked in a nervous voice.

"So very fierce a horse can sometimes hardly stem it," he said. "But it's narrow. Thou should soon be over it."

Hester gave her sister a terrified glance. She could hardly imagine anything worse than what they had just crossed. Madame Knight and Polly seemed unusually quiet and nervous as well as they rode along into the darkening trees. "Sometimes I see myself drowning," Hester whispered to her sister. "The blackest idea of my approaching fate."

"Don't say that," Philena said. "It's bad luck. We'll think of something." She wished she still had the guinea deer's foot. They needed every bit of luck they could muster.

The path took them again through the woods. Something scrambled past unseen in the shadows. Tree branches creaked in the wind. In the inky blackness the only light came from the dull glow in the western sky and scattered stars overhead. "Can you see or hear our guide?" Hester demanded.

Philena shook her head. The postrider had galloped too far ahead for them to make out his shape or detect the jangling of his horse harness. *Not that he'd be any protection,* Philena decided. As they rode along, every lifeless trunk, every stump looked like a hiding Mohican or a tall, dark rider.

"Sir!" Madame Knight's loud voice made Philena and Hester jump. "Wait for us."

Their horse picked up a dangerously fast pace that made Hester and Philena grip the saddle with both hands as they bumped along. Trees swallowed them and suddenly they found themselves slipping and faltering down a steep hill. "Hold tight!" Hester shouted as she nearly plunged over the top of the horse's head. The horse righted itself and splashed through up to its haunches. Hester and Philena shrieked as the cold, black river swirled around their legs. Philena shut her eyes, certain of a watery death.

As abruptly as the river had appeared, it seemed to disappear. They were suddenly climbing up another hill, dripping and terrified but still alive. "Narragansett country," the postrider called over his shoulder.

"What's *that* supposed to mean?" Polly demanded.

No one knew—least of all Hester or Philena. And in a few moments, the postrider had galloped out of sight again. The path narrowed. Unseen tree branches clawed at their legs as they rode past. Bushes seemed to jump at them from nowhere, tangling their skirts and tearing at their feet. The darkness was terrible. Worse yet, the guide trotted so far ahead, they could no longer even hear the drumming of his horse's hooves.

Philena sensed that Hester was terrified. So was she. *What should we do?* Their exhausted horse seemed about to collapse. Even Madame Knight's mount—the largest of the group—wheezed badly, as if it might expire at any moment.

At last, with much effort, the horses and their weary riders made it to the top of the hill. Finally, they had traveled out of the woods. The night breeze felt warm. "Look!" Polly called. In the distance they could barely see a faint light. This gave them all hope. The moon appeared from behind the clouds. Inspired, Madame Knight happily recited an original poem:

> *"Fair Cynthia, all the Homage that I may*
> *Unto a Creature, unto thee I pay."*

Madame Knight paused, as if she could not think of anything else. Boldly, Hester chimed in to help her:

"In lonesome woods to meet so kind a guide,
to me's more worth than all the world beside."

Madame Knight laughed. "Look above us, girls. See in the night sky the constellation of Gemini? And there—the twin stars of Castor and Pollux."

"And who are they?" Polly demanded. She sounded as if stars were the last thing she wanted to hear about.

"Identical sons of Jupiter, who disguised himself as a swan. Their mother was human, but they were born in a large egg. And when they grew up, Castor and Pollux were inseparable."

"Who was Jupiter?" Hester asked.

"The pagan ancients believed he was the king of the heavens," Madame Knight replied.

"Perhaps my sister and I were born of royalty, too. Just like Castor and Pollux," Hester said in a hopeful voice.

Polly laughed derisively, then turned toward the twins and announced, "Perhaps you also were born in a bird's egg, which may explain why you are so peculiar."

Hester scowled.

"Pay her no mind," Philena whispered. She

liked the story of Castor and Pollux. It seemed a sign—maybe something that meant they should not lose courage.

In the distance a horn sounded. A faraway horse whinnied. "That must be the postrider. He's reached the inn," Madame Knight announced, "and signals for us to hurry. Come now. We must keep on schedule. I cannot miss the appointed hour for this meeting. It may be my one and only chance."

As Madame Knight galloped ahead, an idea fluttered in Philena's head at almost the same time it appeared in Hester's. Neither girl spoke. Neither needed to. What if they were to make sure that Madame Knight never arrived on time with the delivery of her servant for E.C.?

Hester smiled at their brilliance. *If she's too late, the agreement will be cancelled. We will be saved.*

Their horses did not need any urging. They picked up a rolling speed as they hurried down the path toward the stable.

Monday—*Mama enjoins it upon me to write more details in my journal of the Events that Happen to*

me, of Characters that I converse with, and objects I
see from Day to Day; while I am convinced of the
utility, necessity & importance of this Exercise, yet I
do not have perseverance & patience enough to do it
so Constantly as she does. Will I have the mortifica-
tion a few years hence to read a great deal of my
Childish nonsense? Or shall I have the Pleasure
remarking the many steps I shall have advanced in
taste judgement and knowledge? First I should
describe my travel companions: two Girls who look so
much alike and speak so much alike they are like mirror images were it not for clothes. I have never known
such strange and unnatural girls. One answers for the
other as if she knew words before they came into her
mouth. They laugh at silly things like the Shadow of
Mama upon the wall and they walk arm in arm and
never go out of step with one another. Sometimes they
do not speak but one gives the other a look and then
the receiver smiles as if a message was sent. How can
that be? I know they do not like me yet I try to think
that their Hatefulness is a sure means of Improving
myself. If I were their mother I would have
Abandon'd them too. Here I have only them and
They do not need anyone except each other. On this
journey my journal is my only true friend. The

innkeeper when we arrived saw to our Comfort. She took our damp clothing and offered to make us a meal, tho dinner was long over. But Mama, fearful of upsetting her delicate stomach and giving herself nightmares by eating so late, said that all we needed was chocolate mixed with hot milk. I was hungry and so disappointed, but did not complain tho sorely vexed by the long looks of the other Girls who whispered and made unpleasant remarks I know were about Mama. Their insolence confounds me.

Chapter

9

That evening at the inn near Kingston, Madame Knight received a message from the innkeeper's wife. "A letter delivered by the eastbound post-rider," the woman told her. Madame Knight sat with the three girls at a table in the empty tap-room, finishing their hot milk and chocolate. The girls watched Madame Knight break the waxy seal and unfold the paper. She perched her tiny glasses on the end of her nose, read silently, and smiled.

"What does it say?" Polly demanded.

Hester and Philena exchanged anxious glances.

Her mother refolded the letter and looked up, startled, as if Polly's question took her by surprise. "Nothing," Madame Knight replied.

Polly pursed her lips and let out a great gasp of air. "I saw you reading. Those words were not nothing."

"Nothing for *your* eyes is what I meant," Madame Knight replied and smiled mysteriously. "I'll say this much. We have a change in plans. We must go to New York."

"New York? But Mama, you promised," Polly whined. "You said we'd go to the dressmaker in New Haven. You said you'd buy me new clothes."

"There are dressmakers in New York, too. Now go to bed," Madame Knight said. "We have a long journey ahead of us tomorrow." She twisted the paper, went to the fireplace, and dropped it into the flames.

Hester sighed. *We'll never know what else is written there.* In seconds the letter became ashy, shriveled, and fragile as a dead leaf or a lost dream.

"Mistress, did your letter mention Cato? Was he captured?" Philena asked.

Madame Knight sighed. "No, not yet," she said. "Time for bed, girls."

Reluctantly, the girls did as they were told. They followed the tavern owner to their room—a small area partitioned off from the kitchen by a few rough boards. The bed was hard and narrow, barely big enough to accommodate plump Madame Knight. For once Hester was glad she did not have to share a real bed the way Polly did. At least her sister did not snore and take up all the space.

Hester and Philena curled up on the floor atop a lumpy pallet stuffed with corncobs. Soon Madame Knight began making noises that sounded like wind howling down the chimney.

When she was sure that Polly and Madame Knight were asleep, Philena sat up and nudged Hester. "We must make sure we never arrive on time," Hester said. "We'll plan a mutiny before we reach New York."

"That won't work. We're always outnumbered." Philena held up three fingers. "Madame Knight, her guide, and Polly."

Hester frowned. "A diversion then. We'll raise a false flag. We'll use cannons and surprise the enemy."

Philena sighed loudly. "What makes you think you're Long Ben the pirate? He had a privateer and a crew. What do we have? Nothing." She emptied her pocket on the bed. Out fell a paper of pins, a hank of yarn, a favorite shell, and a few coins that were given to her by Goodwife Kemble. Not enough to get them very far. "What do you have that we can use?"

Hester smiled. She was not going to allow her sister's lack of enthusiasm to annoy her. She emptied her pocket. A pinecone, a half-eaten doughnut, a comb. "And this," she said proudly, and pointed to the silver thimble that was worth more than everything they had together.

"Where did you get that?" Philena said suspiciously.

"Found it."

Philena scowled. "Tell me the truth."

"The woman wasn't using it. Didn't even appreciate such a fine thing. Said it was a mere trifle. She said—"

"*Who* said?"

"Don't be so loud," Hester whispered. "You want to wake everyone? The woman on the road—"

"You *stole* it?" Philena could hardly believe her ears. "Stealing is a sin."

Hester picked up the thimble. She tried it on her finger and admired it. "I was going to give it back. Just as soon as we passed her house again."

Philena groaned. These pirate stories had gone to her sister's head. "Whose house? Where does she live?"

"I don't know her name. She's a horrible woman, really. Lives near a swamp. Bulging eyes. She talks too much. She's got the worst fleas in her house I ever saw. Bit me all night." Hester pouted. "I thought you'd like it. I was going to give it to you as a present."

"I don't want it!" Philena exploded. "Look," she said, lowering her voice, "you can't give away something that doesn't belong to you." For a moment, Philena said nothing. She felt as if she were going to be sick. *How can she take such an awful risk?* Then Philena remembered the woman who came out of the house and called her a thief. That had to be the thimble's owner. "Don't you realize that when you do something like this, I can get accused?"

"We share everything," Hester said and smiled. "Even trouble."

Philena groaned and flopped back on the pallet. Her sister was impossible. Absolutely impossible.

"When Madame Knight finds out, you'll be beaten."

"What are you saying? She doesn't beat us. She—"

The bed creaked. "SHSHSH!" Philena sat up and slapped her hand over her sister's mouth. Madame Knight's breathing stopped. Then her snores began again to steadily yip and yap, yip and yap.

"You've got to give it back," Philena hissed in her ear. "You'll go to Hell. You'll burn in everlasting damnation. At this very moment you're—"

Something crashed on the other side of the thin wall that separated their sleeping chamber from the taproom. Hester tore her sister's hand from her mouth. "What's that noise?" Frantically, she tucked the thimble back in her pocket. A man laughed loudly and there was a steady *thud, thud, thud* upon the floor that rattled Hester's and Philena's teeth.

"What?" Madame Knight sat up, fairly shouting. "You can't come in."

"Mama, who is it?" Polly said fearfully. Now she was awake, too. It sounded as if half of the colony of Rhode Island were carousing in the taproom.

Hester bravely tiptoed across the cold, wooden

floor and put her ear against the wall. "What are they saying?" Philena demanded.

"An argument," Hester said. "About where the name Narragansett came from."

"Drunken scholars," Madame Knight said with disgust. "Now we'll never get a wink of peace and quiet."

"Named by Indians," a loud voice exclaimed, "because of a great, high briar. Narragansett means 'bush.'"

"No it don't. The name's from a spring," another fellow replied. "I know right where it is and how cold the temperature is in summer and hot in winter. Narragansett means 'hot and cold.'"

The noisy men thundered as if they were all hitting their fists on the table at the same time.

"Soon they will begin to debate how to make a triangle into a square," Madame Knight grumbled. She was wide awake and furious.

"A toast to you!"

"And to the King!"

There was a great clanging of tankards, then silence.

"Can you give us a song, Philip? Or perhaps a story?"

"I'll tell you one," a gruff voice said. He seemed so close that Hester wondered if perhaps he was leaning his chair back against the wall closest to the bedstead.

"Did you hear about Hannah Duston, the famous American Amazon who stabbed her would-be Indian killers and then brought back ten scalps so she could collect bounty? Ten scalps."

"Did she do it for the money or the glory?"

"I heard Cotton Mather's famous sermon after the execution."

"The execution of the Indians?"

Someone belched.

"No, the execution of Hannah's sister, Elizabeth Emerson. Do you not know of her fame?"

Madame Knight was clearly becoming agitated. "When will they please shut up so that we can sleep?"

"Now, Mama. Don't go out there," Polly pleaded. "Please, Mama. Don't do it. I can't bear the embarrassment."

Hester and Philena were fascinated. Here was something worth watching—Madame Knight in a fisticuffs with the town drunks. Heedless of the danger they were in, the men rattled on and on about the terrible hanging of Hannah Duston's sister, Elizabeth. They described the size of the crowd and the day and the weather and how she was one of the few women in ten years to have such an awful fate, for killing her own children, so she deserved to die. "Could any two sisters be any more unalike?" Philip said in a low baritone. "One a heroine; the other a criminal."

For a few moments, there were no voices, no sounds. Madame Knight sighed and leaned back on her pillow. Perhaps the party had ended.

But just as suddenly as the noise stopped, it began again. In a fury, Madame Knight sat bolt upright. "This is not talk for ears of impressionable young females." She pushed herself out of bed, lit two candles, and began pulling on her dress. Without bothering to remove her nightcap or fasten her shoes, she stomped from the sleeping chamber carrying one candle.

"Mama!" Polly said weakly. "Don't—"

Her protests made no difference. Madame Knight was on a mission. "Sir, will you be silent?" her voice boiled in the next room. Hester nudged Philena with her elbow. They held their breath.

"Will you, I pray, speak with softness? We are weary travelers trying to sleep."

"And we are weary drinkers trying to stay awake," someone replied in a slurred voice. The men laughed.

"What if they punch her?" Polly whispered. "What will we do?"

"I pity the man who tries to lay a hand on your mother," Hester said in a low, amused voice.

"What?" Polly demanded.

"Nothing," Hester said. "Only I am sure you do not wish to become an orphan."

"Like *you?*" Polly replied in a cold voice. She took a small scrap of paper from her journal and handed it to Philena. "Perhaps you might be interested in this."

Philena bit her lip. The paper seemed to have been torn from a newspaper. Her sister leaned over her shoulder. By flickering candle light they read silently:

Likely servant maid's time for nine years to be disposed of. Works well with needle.

For several moments, neither Hester nor Philena spoke. On the other side of the wall they heard the men arguing about their horses. "And can she run?"

"Yes, she can."

"Where did you find this?" Hester demanded. She tried to keep her voice calm. *A likely servant maid . . . to be disposed of.*

Polly raised one eyebrow. "It does sound like one of you, doesn't it? The notice fell from among my mother's papers. I picked it up."

Nervously, Philena scanned the small, mysterious scribbles. *How do we know she's telling the truth?* She wanted to look into her sister's eyes, but she was afraid her expression would betray them both.

"I suppose New York is as good a place as any to sell unexpired time, don't you think?" Polly carefully refolded the paper. She smiled as if everything about their journey suddenly made perfect sense. "I would be telling a lie if I said I will miss you. Either of you."

Hester gulped. "It doesn't say our names. It doesn't mention Madame Knight."

"Dear, ignorant girl! Newspaper advertisements do not give names. No room." Polly smiled her most charming smile, leaned over, and tucked away the piece of paper just as her mother reappeared in the room.

Madame Knight's nightcap sat askew on her head. Her outfit and her expression gave her the same crazy look as old Widow Bumpus, who roamed Moon Street with her cats trailing behind her. She parted the curtains and placed the candle on the windowsill. "I plan to seek revenge the only way I know how," Madame Knight announced. She opened her saddlebag.

"Now, Mama. There's no need for violence. A pistol never solved anything," Polly said in desperation.

"I have no pistol," Madame Knight replied angrily. "But I have something more powerful." She pulled from the saddlebag a small leather-bound commonplace book, a bottle of ink, and her goose quill. She sat on the bed, dipped her pen in the ink, and began scribbling furiously.

"Read it aloud, will you, Mama?" Polly said.

Madame Knight cleared her throat and read:

"I ask thy aid, o potent rum!
To charm these wrangling topers dumb.
Thou hast their giddy brains possessed—

the man confounded with the Beast—
And I, poor I, can get no rest.
Intoxicate them with thy fumes:
Oh, still their tongues till morning comes."

Hester applauded. She gave her sister a jab in the ribs to do likewise. Philena's applause was halfhearted. "Did you go to the hanging?"

"What hanging?" Madame Knight said, looking surprised.

"Elizabeth Emerson's," Philena replied.

"Such events are meant to chastise the wicked," Madame Knight said. Her voice sounded flustered. "You girls must go to sleep. Tomorrow will be a long ride."

Polly lay down on the bed with the pillow over her head to block the noise. Hester did as she was told as well. But Philena could not go back to sleep. She kept thinking about the newspaper notice. *We will be separated forever.*

She tossed and turned. *One a heroine; the other a criminal.* She thought of the stolen silver thimble. If Hester were a criminal, did that mean she was bad, too? The very idea of the gallows made her cringe. *What if they came to take Hester to jail but took me instead?*

"What's the matter?" Hester whispered.

"Nothing," Philena replied. She turned away from her sister so that she could not see her face.

Hester tried to imagine what Philena was thinking. The harder she focused, the more hazy and impossible the task became. For the first time she could not read her sister's troubled thoughts.

Chapter

10

Tuesday—A great affliction I have met withal by our maid servants; at first reunited on the journey they carried themselfs dutifully as became servants; but since through my mother's forbearance toward them for small faults they have got such a head and gowen so insolent that their carriage toward us especialle myself is insufferable. If I bid them doe a thinge they will bid me to doe it myselfe. If I tell my mother of their behavior towards me, upon examination will deny all they hath done or spoken, so that my dear mother vexed as she is by the speed of our journey knows not how to proceed against them. What trouble and plague to have had two such creatures travelling to contradict and vex me! And oh if my dear Mother would only tell me for what reason we make this dangerous pilgrimage. I am weary of seeing the world and we have not come close to our journey's end.

Madame Knight was so eager to be off on an early start the next day, she hurried everyone out of bed at three-thirty—so early the moon still shone and so cold that they could see their breath. She told the sleepy girls they were on their way to New London, then on to the Connecticut River to Clinton, Madison, Guilford, Branford. They would travel west along the coast into the colony of Connecticut. "Once we arrive at New Haven," Madame Knight said cheerfully, "we have but three days' journey to New York."

"Three days!" Polly said. "I fear cannot live that long at this pace."

"Hurry now," Madame Knight replied.

"I am so very hungry I will collapse," Polly grumbled.

"No time," Madame Knight said. She ushered Polly, Hester, and Philena out the door. Wearily, they mounted their horses. They were accompanied this time by a French doctor. He was a quiet, short man who wore a fashionable wig and rode a handsome dappled mare. "Good morning, *monsieur,*" Madame Knight said in a bright voice.

The doctor lifted one finger to his fine felt hat, but said nothing in reply. As the horses trotted through the darkness, Madame Knight boldly continued her conversation with the doctor. "Did you sleep well?"

"Well enough, *s'il vous plait,*" he replied in a haughty tone.

"And what do you think of these most unfortunate Indian wars that plague our colonies?"

"I do not discuss politics so early in the morning. Especially with women," he said.

Madame Knight made a low "harrumph" and trotted along in silence. Hester and Philena were glad for the quiet. They were almost too sleepy to stay atop the horse.

"Mama?" Polly whined. "When shall we stop for breakfast?"

"To think he would not deign discuss politics!" Madame Knight grumbled to no one in particular. "Such a coward! I should ask him about the French and their guns and their friendliness to certain red-skinned barbarians."

"Mama! Do you listen? I am hungry," Polly

insisted. When her mother still did not reply, she announced, "No one pays any attention to me. I should never have come. Never."

"I shall certainly not disagree with that," Hester said in a low voice. Philena giggled.

"What did you say?" Polly demanded.

"Nothing," Hester replied. "Except that your mother says we must travel nearly twenty-two miles—a long way with no tavern to stop beside the long way."

"Twenty-two miles!" Polly exclaimed. And she began to weep, but her mother still did not pay any attention. This only made Polly sob louder.

"What ails you?" Philena called to her, unable to bear the sounds of her distress any longer.

"Everything. Simply everything!" Polly declared. She stripped a twig from a bush as they passed. She flicked it against her horse to make him gallop faster so that she might escape from the maidservants.

"Look at her fly," Hester said dryly.

"You might try to be a bit more pleasant to her," Philena suggested. "Why try her patience? She intends to make our lives more miserable if she can."

"I'm not afraid of her," Hester said.

"You should fear her mother," Philena replied.

"Aren't you the saucy one, full of advice!" Hester replied. "You never were so full of high spirits and big words on Moon Street. This journey has made you bold."

"You're the bold one," Philena said in a low voice. "Bold enough to land us both in jail."

Hester did not reply.

"Sir?" Madame Knight called to the doctor. "Where shall we stop tonight?"

The doctor turned and said over his shoulder, "The house of a man called Mr. Devel."

"Devel!" Madame Knight exclaimed dramatically. "Should we go to the devil to be helped out of our affliction?"

The doctor did not seem to understand Madame Knight's joke and kept trotting along without comment.

"Like the rest of the deluded souls that post to that infernal den, we make all possible speed to this devil's habitation," Madame Knight declared, louder this time.

Still the doctor paid no attention.

Hester sighed. "She's once again composing one

of her interminable poems," she whispered to her sister. "I wish she would be quiet for once and give us all peace."

After a long, exhausting ride, they finally stopped. Mr. Devel's house was a grim log cabin located in a clearing of toppled pine trees. Wearily, the travelers lowered themselves to the ground as two women came out to greet them.

"Sisters," Philena hissed. And sure enough, when Hester looked, she saw that the two old, ugly women were every bit alike. They wore the same pale blue dresses, the same white caps. They parted their gray hair the same and wore the same shoes.

"Like a mirror," Hester whispered.

It was so unusual to see such complete, aged twins that Philena stared, too. *One day will we seem this way?* For the first time she wished she were not a twin so that she would not always have to look at her own plainness everywhere she went.

"Can you please provide us with lodging?" the doctor demanded.

The two old spinsters went to find their father after much coaxing. He hobbled from the house in an ancient coat that hung about his arms like the wings of a bat. His bald head shone in the sunlight. His eyebrows stood like white hedges. "No guests," he declared vehemently. "Absolutely not."

"A bite of bread, perhaps?" the doctor coaxed.

"Off my property!" the old man shouted until his face was nearly purple. He shuffled into his house again with such purpose, Hester feared he might return with a gun. The doctor, Madame Knight, and the girls quickly remounted their horses and hurried down the road.

"Will we ever eat or sleep again?" Polly wailed.

Hester complained, "If I could I would just stop here —"

"And sleep along the roadside," Philena added.

"And have the Indians take your scalp?" Madame Knight chided.

At these words, the girls spurred their horses on. Early in the afternoon they reached the Paukataug River, which was running very high and wild. There was no bridge, no boat, no other way across except by fording.

"I dare not venture to ride through. My courage at best is small," Madame Knight announced. Hester and Philena were not impressed. They suspected their mistress's complaint was intended to display a soft, helpless side to the doctor.

The French doctor was not impressed either. "Well then, *adieu,*" he said and gave a little wave. And in a very ungentlemanly fashion, he crossed the river and left them stranded.

Madame Knight cursed all French men. Her feminine wiles unsuccessful, she angrily stormed up and down the river. "Now what shall we do?" She sat wearily on a stump and stared at the treacherous river. There seemed to be no houses nearby where they might find help. The dark forest of oak and chestnut, hickory and hemlock stretched in all directions.

Hester and Philena climbed down from their horse. "This is our chance," Hester whispered. She held up two fingers. "Now our odds are evenly matched. Two of them and two of us."

Philena smiled. She patted the horse and watched Madame Knight talking to Polly. "What do you suggest?"

"I'll wander downstream. When I don't come back for quite a while, you say you're going to find me. You wander in the same direction, keeping the river on your left. I'll give you a signal when I spot you. Then we'll both remain hidden."

"All night?" Philena asked nervously. *What about wild animals?*

"Here they come. Now, remember. The river on your left. This may be our only chance."

Philena nodded.

"Madame Knight," Hester said, "I'll go downstream. I think I spied some smoke in that direction. Perhaps I can find someone who will help us cross."

Madame Knight gazed at her own badly swollen feet. "Do not wander too far," she warned. "Do not take any chances."

Hester winked at her sister as she disappeared between the trees. Philena sat on a stump and waited. She listened to the wind blowing in the trees. Dried leaves blew into the water and skittered across the surface. They floated downriver like dizzy boats.

As Hester walked, she realized how confusing the woods appeared once she was deep inside them. She heard the river rolling and babbling. *As long as I keep this nearby I cannot lose my way. I'll simply follow it back.* She walked and walked. The light shifted and fell in patterns. From her pocket she took a dried piece of bread and nibbled on it. She shuffled her feet through the dried leaves. A bird called. She paused and looked up. A great black-winged shape flew overhead and called loudly. Suddenly, she felt afraid. The bird seemed to be following her. She walked faster. *My bread. It wants my bread.*

The leaves crackled and whispered under her feet. While she struggled to make her way through the fallen limbs and brambles, the bird soared. She gripped her bread in her fist and dodged around trees.

"CAW! CAW!" the bird taunted. The flapping of its wings seemed to brush against the air like breath, like promises.

Hester threw the bread as far as she could, hoping to make the bird go away, to convince it to stop tormenting her. The bird swooped down, grabbed the crust, and flapped its giant wings and disappeared.

Her heart beat in her throat. She sat down, out of breath. *The river.* She looked to her left, to her right. Was it her imagination, or were the woods becoming darker? She jumped to her feet and listened. She could hear the wind, the branches moving. She could not hear the water. Desperately, she tried to remember how she had arrived at this place. *To the left. The water to my left.*

She shuffled through a thick patch of pine needles and around a great tree toppled on its side. *This way.* She kept walking, listening intently for the sound of the current. *This way.* She tried a new direction, wishing she had tried to remember what the trees looked like when she came into the woods. Everything looked the same. Nothing but trees, stark and spindly, leafless as bones.

Finally, when she could walk no farther, she found a sheltered spot near a hollowed tree and sat down to rest. She was so hungry, so tired, so worried. *Where am I? How will my sister ever find me?* What she needed, she decided, was just a few moments to sleep. Not very long. Just a short nap. Then she would wake up and feel refreshed. She'd know what to do.

Hester curled up in the hollow place beside a great fallen sycamore. She shut her eyes. In a moment, she was fast asleep.

Far away where the road met the river, Philena waited. She sat and watched the place where Hester had disappeared. The space between the trees reminded her of an enormous mouth. She wondered when she should stand up and go into the woods, too. Slowly, the sun began to shift in a low arc. She stood.

"Where is your sister?" Madame Knight demanded. No one had passed along on the road. She was clearly becoming impatient. "She should have returned by now."

"I'll see if I can find her," Philena volunteered.

Madame Knight scowled. She did not seem to think much of this idea. "And then what if you don't come back, either? No, I am too old to go tramping through the trees looking for two of you. Polly?"

Polly sat up and rubbed her eyes. She had been sleeping on her cloak spread out in a patch of grass. "What? Are we crossing?"

"No," Madame Knight said. "I want you to go into the woods and call for the other Girl. Her sister will go with you."

"What happened?" Polly demanded. "Is she lost?"

"I can go alone," Philena said in a nervous voice. *Polly was never part of the plan.* "She doesn't need to come with me."

"Mama, I don't really want to—"

"Enough!" Madame Knight said in exasperation. "You go with her. Find her and bring her back. In the meantime, I'll wait here and see if perhaps someone will come along who can help us. Do not squander any more time. Go on!"

Chapter

11

Reluctantly, Polly stood and followed Philena into the woods. Philena moved slowly, calling and searching. She hoped that Hester was hiding and watching them. *The river on my left. On my left.* If her sister revealed herself too soon, they'd have to turn around and go back and the delay wouldn't be long enough.

"Can't you move faster?" Polly insisted. "There are too many shadows. I don't like this place."

Philena had to agree. The forest seemed to be growing darker and more menacing by the moment. She tried not to think how frightened she had been traveling with Cato, who seemed to know where he was and what to do. Here she was trying to find her way with Polly, who was of no practical use whatsoever. *Where is she?* "Hello?" Philena called in a loud voice. "Come out, come out wherever you are!"

Polly shuffled along through the dry leaves. "I'm hungry. Let's go back."

"We can't," Philena said, trying to think of some way to stall Polly. "We have to find her, remember? Your mother will just send us in again. I'm sure she's here somewhere. Let's keep walking." She scanned the fallen logs, the trees. Everywhere she looked she thought she saw eyes watching. "Hester-Phina!" she shouted. "Hester-Phina!"

"That's a strange name," Polly said suspiciously. "I never heard you use that before."

"It's special," Philena admitted. "A name we sometimes call each other."

"You call each other the same name? That's odd," Polly said. "Do you like being a twin?"

Philena shrugged. "Sometimes. And what about you? Do you like being an only child?"

Polly broke a branch and stripped away the dead leaves. "Not really. I always wished I could have a sister." She waved the branch as if it were a wand. "Poof! Suddenly, there she'd be."

"I sometimes think I'd like to use a wand like that and make my sister disappear." She blushed and suddenly felt as if she'd betrayed Hester.

Polly giggled. "You're much more amusing without your sister around." She tossed the branch over her shoulder. "What's your other name? Not Hester-Phina. Your real name."

"Philena."

"That has a musical sound to it. Philena. I like it."

Philena felt pleased. No one had ever told her that she was amusing or that her name sounded like a melody. "Hello! Hello!" Philena called. She was surprised that she was enjoying talking to Polly. *Perhaps my sister will stay hidden a little longer.* As soon as she thought this, she felt a little disloyal.

Philena and Polly walked and walked. They found strange marks on the bare trees and patches of long dark hair caught in the bark. Philena pulled a bit of it away, terrified it might belong to her sister, but it was too tough, too black.

"Odd," Polly said. She pointed to a group of pine trees where the bark had been stripped off near the bottom. The exposed wood was light and sticky. "I wonder how that happened."

"Let's keep walking," Philena said nervously. She didn't want to say what she was thinking. *Claw marks.* As they walked, she kept the water on her left. She never let the current leave her sight except when she had to climb over fallen trees or circle boulders. *Where is she?* Suddenly, she began to worry. *What if she's hurt?*

The trees were becoming so filled with shadows it was difficult to see. "Perhaps we should turn back," Polly said.

"We can't. Not yet," Philena insisted. "Hester-Phina!" she shouted, louder this time. "Hester-Phina, where are you?"

In a group of trees to their right they heard the crunch of branches breaking. A large oak creaked. Suddenly, the girls heard an odd drumming sound. *Pock-pock-pock-pock.* Something pelted and bounced against bushes and fallen leaves on the forest floor.

"Sounds like rain," Polly said.

"It's not rain," Philena said, pointing to the ground. "It's acorns."

Branches overhead heaved and shuddered. More acorns tumbled in a great shower of rippling and leaping. And before either girl could move or breathe or blink, a terrifying furry shape clambered down out of the oak tree.

An enormous black bear.

Spellbound, they watched the bear's muscular back move as it climbed surprisingly swiftly to the ground. The black fur rippled. Its enormous pie-pan-size paws moved gracefully down, down. The bark skittered and ripped under the bear's weight and the razor-sharp tugs of its claws. The moment the bear landed on the ground, it noisily crunched and crushed the bed of acorns.

"Run!" Philena squeaked.

Polly took off at a lope. The two girls sped around trees away from the bear. Philena looked over her shoulder. She saw the bear rise up on its haunches and point its tan snout straight up into the air as if it were sniffing the air. And then the bear turned and came down on all fours. In that glimpse, she saw the great black body turn in their direction, its glittering eyes upon them.

Philena did not slow down. Breathlessly, she dodged around fallen limbs, unaware that her skirt was ripped and her sleeve was torn. She did not feel the scratch of a sharp branch against her cheek. She ran without stopping. "Come on!" she shouted to Polly.

One minute Philena looked and saw Polly holding up her long skirt, leaping like a deer. Her terrified face was bright red. Mouth open, she gulped the air and pushed between the brambles, the brown curled ferns, the branches. And then suddenly the next minute she glanced and Polly was nowhere to be seen.

"Help!" she cried. She was several yards back, her skirt and cloak tangled in the brambles.

Philena sped back to her, even though she knew the bear was coming. When she reached Polly, she grabbed the cloak and yanked as hard as she could. The wool ripped. Polly pulled away, cloak in her arms, and kept running. "Come on!"

Finally they could run no more. They staggered slower and slower, out of breath, out of energy. They struggled over the branches, the bushes. They bent over, trying to catch their breath. In that instant they dared to look backward —

And saw that the bear had vanished.

Philena's heart beat so loudly, she could hear nothing else. Her ears drummed with the sound and she felt as if she might be sick. Her throat was raw and her legs began to shake. She listened for the sound of the bear. She watched the trees for its great hulking shape to reappear.

"Where . . . is . . . he?" Polly asked with a croaking voice. She, too, struggled to breathe.

"Maybe scared away," Philena said. She coughed. Her thirst made it nearly impossible to swallow. *Water.* She looked to the left, then to the right and felt a rising sense of panic. "The river!" she said. "We've lost the river."

"How do you lose a river?" Polly demanded. She wiped sweat from her forehead.

"The water led our way back," Philena said. "Now which way do we go?"

They looked in every direction. In the growing murky darkness, there seemed to be no north or south, no east or west. Polly bit her lip and blinked hard. "We're lost."

After much discussion, they decided not to wander any farther. *The bear.* They never mentioned the word, they only thought of it. Lumbering along at several hundred pounds, following them. "We'll just stay here," said Philena, who wished she knew how to build a fire the way Cato had. A fire would be a comfort.

"What if we hear a noise?" Polly asked.

"We'll climb a tree."

Polly nervously cleared her throat. "The bear climbed a tree, too, you know."

"We'll take turns and listen for him," Philena said. "I'm sure he won't come back."

That night neither of them slept. The ground was cold and damp. They wrapped themselves in their cloaks and covered themselves with pine needles, leaves—anything they could find. Polly listened to the terrifying murmurs and shrieks and calls of the woods. Philena strained her ears for the sound of her sister. She prayed that somewhere in the darkness, Hester was still alive.

It was the sound of howling early the next morning before dawn that startled Philena and Polly into sudden wakefulness. As if from nowhere, a pack of dogs bayed. The ground rumbled. Men's voices echoed through the trees. Terrified, Philena jumped to her feet in time to see lights bob and disappear.

"Someone's coming!" Polly said in a hoarse voice.

"Hello!" Philena shouted. "Over here!"

The sound of the dogs grew louder. There

seemed to be hundreds of them yelping and howling and barking. As they came closer, the sound became more and more deafening. The girls heard men shouting and cursing at the animals as if to hold them back. Philena wondered if their rescuers might also be their own undoing. She had an undeniable urge to climb a tree, just to make sure the dogs didn't tear them to pieces.

"Hello! We're here!" Polly called, tears streaming down her face.

The men shouted back. In moments, they arrived. The dogs leapt and jumped and had to be tied up with long pieces of rope. "You the lost ones?" a man asked in a gruff voice.

"Your mother sent us."

Polly babbled furiously as they wrapped a blanket around her shoulders. She told them about the bear. About how they had run. Only Philena was silent. "Have you found another girl in the woods?" she asked.

The man holding the lantern scratched his head. "Sent out a couple of search parties."

"She's about the same size as me. Looks the same, too," Philena said slowly.

"Maybe she's back at the river crossing. Let's go

see. There's others out in the woods looking. Lucky thing nobody mistook you for slaves."

One of the men laughed. "That's our usual job."

"Where's my mother?" Polly demanded.

"Right this way, Miss. She's probably worried sick."

Philena and Polly followed the men through the shadows for what seemed forever. As they walked along, the men joked and laughed and did not seem the least tired. Philena felt as if she might never find her way out of these trees again. With tremendous relief, she saw a clearing ahead filled with faint morning sunshine. She staggered toward the light, anxious yet terrified. *What if she's not there?*

Polly broke through the trees first and ran to her mother. Her mother embraced her and all the men cheered. Philena looked everywhere among the half a dozen or so men and sniffing dogs. They had built a fire and were standing around smoking and spitting and talking. *Where is she?*

"Hester-Phina!" a voice called. Joyfully, Philena turned in time to see the familiar face of her sister. She ran to embrace her—just to make sure she was really there, really standing before her.

"What happened?"

"Fell asleep. Your face!"

"Are you all right?"

"Girl, that's enough lag-last and shiftless!" Madame Knight boomed. Hester and Philena froze. "Thanks to these kind gentlemen, we shall be able to continue on our journey to New York."

Hester and Philena clung to each other with a sense of unspeakable sadness and disappointment. Whatever they had risked was not enough. In the end, they would be separated.

"Come along now. Have something to eat and we will cross this river on a boat brought here especially for our use," Madame Knight said in a voice loud enough for a gentleman standing beside the river to hear. He bowed. Then Madame Knight turned to the twins. She gave each of them a hard, cold stare. "You can see you have caused commotion enough. Until we reach our destination, I shall keep better watch over you."

Chapter

12

Friday—Days pass and I still dream of black bears. When I try to speak to Phelina she seems to avoid me. She has her sister now I suppose. Tomorrow we meet the man that Mama has travelled so fast and so far to meet. We have hurried through New Haven, Stratford, Fairfield and New Rochelle so quickly I have scarce had time to write here. Yester day we met a man and his daughter traveling to New York. They give us company part of the way. I am pleased to hear this becuuse we have heard rumors of a clever, ghost-like bandit who has been robbing taverns along the route. At three-o'clock the man comes with not one but two daughters about 19 years old, each on a sorry lean jade with only a bag under each for a pillow.

The girls have such jaded faces. When they spy our maidservants they notice their Sameness and ask rudely: "Are you twins? Which one of you did your mother love best?" And of course when the Girls reply that they have no mother, the two travelers whose names are Jemima and Deborah, crow with Glee. "Only animals have broods in big numbers." And for the rest of the journey to the ford neither Girl speaks to the other, as if to distance themselves and pretend they are not what they are. The trail is rough and treacherous. Jemima makes sour faces and calls to her father, "Oh lawful heart! This bare mare hurts me. I'm direful sore I vow." But the man doesn't stop or slow or listen. He laughs and says the horse served her mother fine. And the girls says "I don't care how Mother used to do." He gives the horse a Hard Slap and laughs and that makes it jolt her ten times harder.

At the Harlem River crossing the horses bucked and whinnied as they were loaded onto the flatbed boat. Snowflakes stuck to Hester's eyes, and Philena's cape flapped as they climbed aboard the rocking ferry. The ferryman seemed to watch the sudden change in weather with a wary eye.

"Hurry up!" he shouted. "Stay in the middle together and do not move about."

Hester and her sister wondered if they'd make it across. Their confidence was not bolstered when they observed Polly saying a frantic prayer. The half a dozen oarsmen put their backs to the wind and seemed to pull with all their might, but the ferry made little progress.

Hester felt at any moment that she might be sick. The cold, gray water slapped up against the boat and with every movement of the waves, the horses seemed to become more excitable. The thumping of the hooves and the crashing water only made the craft seem that much more fragile. Finally, one of the passengers was clearheaded enough to tie strips of rags around the horses' eyes so that they could not see the great roiling river, and that seemed to calm them. Philena gripped the railing and stood beside her sister, trying to keep her eye on the gray horizon of the opposite shore.

"Few more days and she'll freeze!" the ferry-man called.

Philena's face was so cold, she wondered if her eyelashes would freeze together. The wind lashed against their bodies and tangled their cloaks. There was a terrible lurch. Without meaning to, Philena screamed. She stumbled against her sister. "We're here," Hester shouted in her ear over the wind. "We made it."

The ferryman threw a rope to shore and lowered a plank to lead the horses across. "We won't go over again today," he said to one of the oarsmen. The snow was coming down faster and heavier now. They could barely see the opening in the trees where the Post Road continued. "Which way to the home of Edward Cook?" Madam Knight shouted to the ferryman.

He waved his arm. "That way. Follow the road. You cannot mistake the place. The biggest on the street."

"Girls!" Madame Knight announced in a loud voice. Her face was bright red and she held her cloak around her with some difficulty. "We have not far to go."

Hester's and Philena's teeth were chattering as they once again climbed atop the great horse. Polly was too cold, too frozen to move nimbly and had to be helped into the saddle by another ferry passenger. "Good-bye!" she called to Jemima and

Deborah and their father as they went their separate ways.

"Good-bye!" the two girls called back.

Hester and Philena did not wave or say farewell. Yet they felt glad to see the insulting strangers go. "Don't pay them any mind," Philena shouted in her sister's ear. Even so, their comments had hurt her feelings. She was not an animal. Neither was her sister. *Why did they say such things?*

New York, smaller than Boston, had houses made of brick in many colors. Sleighs whizzed past at great speed down the snowy streets. As Hester and Philena's horse walked along they noticed the language the people spoke seemed unfamiliar. "Dutch," Madame Knight said and sniffed.

The muddy, rutted road was slick and icy and the snow churned the way black and treacherous. The horses slipped and skittered. Philena and Hester were glad to see the great pillared house made of bricks. "That must be the house," Madame Knight said. A groomsman appeared to take their horses once they arrived. Madame Knight shook the snow from her hood, adjusted her purple gloves, and rapped on the great white door. The door opened.

A pale-faced maid appeared in the crack. "Your name?" she inquired.

Madame Knight stood up very straight, very tall. "Madame Sarah Knight. Please tell Mr. Cook I have arrived."

"He is expecting you. Right this way," the maid said. She opened the door wide enough so that they could spy the great fire burning in the parlor. The house smelled of hot cider and fine bayberry candles. But as soon as the maid took one look at the three girls, she paused, as if to prevent them from stepping on the shining, spotless floor. "Your servants?"

"These two," Madame Knight said, pointing to Hester and Philena. "This," she added proudly, "is my daughter, Polly."

"Separate entrance for servants is in back," the maid replied. She pointed. Just as she was about to push the twins outside and shut the door, leaving Hester and Philena shivering on the front steps, Madame Knight stopped her.

"Mr. Cook wants to make sure they don't run off. I think it would be best if you took them around yourself," Madame Knight suggested.

Hester and Philena looked at each other in

desperation and dread. The maid opened an umbrella and waved angrily with her hand. "This way," she said. The maid rounded the corner quickly and pointed to a set of icy steps that led down to a door to the cellar. She knocked as loud as she could. No one answered. She knocked again.

The door swung open. An even more unpleasant-looking woman answered. "What you doing coming in this way?"

"Servants. A special delivery for Mr. Cook," the upstairs maid replied. She gave Hester and Philena a shove inside. She made her way quickly through the kitchen and back upstairs again.

Their entrance and introduction clearly came as a surprise to the other servants. "Come in already," a woman seated at the table replied angrily. "And shut the door!"

Quickly, Hester and Philena entered and shook the snow from their cloaks. They stomped their feet. For several moments, they blinked, trying to adjust their eyes to the lack of light. A fire burned in what appeared a great fireplace of a kitchen. At a table sat four unhappy-looking women and a man eating something from trenchers. When they looked up at Hester and Philena, they neither greeted them nor smiled.

"We're traveling from Boston," Hester said. She had a sinking feeling in her stomach. *Is this where I will spend the next nine years?* "My name is Hester and this is—"

"Bad weather to come so far," one woman interrupted.

"How long does it take to ride here from Boston?" another inquired.

Hester nudged her sister. "Five days, I suspect," Philena said in a small voice.

"On horseback," Hester added.

"Why, really, I was never on a horse so long in my life!" the woman replied. "But then, of course, I'm already here."

The other servants nodded as if what their companion had just said made perfect sense. Hester looked at her sister in confusion. Snow melted around their soggy boots, but no one invited them inside or moved to take their damp cloaks or offered to give them anything to eat. Hester signaled to her sister. They took off their cloaks and hung them on pegs on the wall. Cautiously, they moved toward the fire.

"Don't block the warmth from the rest of us," a man said, slopping soup into his mouth.

Hester moved over a few inches. "And so, how is the work here?" Philena asked.

Two women looked up with blank faces. "All right if you can stand hard labor," one said. The other smiled as if she were very clever.

"Mr. Cook's not so bad," another said in a surprisingly loud voice. "He's got his good days."

"One or two," a woman said and laughed.

Hester and Philena flinched. In Madame Knight's home, they ate with the family and the other boarders. They shared the same food and slept upstairs in the same room with everyone else. Only Cato slept in the barn. This house was different. The servants seemed to have a completely separate existence.

Hester gazed about the kitchen cellar and noticed how cold and damp it was, even with the fire going. The floor was made of bricks and the plastered walls were cracked. She supposed that upstairs must be far grander than this. And suddenly she wondered what Polly and Madame Knight were doing. *Having a fine time.* Her stomach growled.

A small bell rang above the fireplace. "They probably wants tea," the slovenly maid at the table said. "Priscilla, you gets it."

The younger woman beside her shuffled off to fill a tray with a pot and hot water. She dumped a few pieces of gingerbread on a china plate. Philena licked her lips. "Not for the help," the young woman with the tray said and sneered.

Philena lowered herself onto the bench.

"Pray, may we have some soup?" Hester asked when she noticed how faint her sister appeared. "We've been riding all day and just had a bad crossing on the river. Nothing to eat since early daylight."

"Well, aren't you fine! 'Pray may we have some,' " the woman at the table repeated and laughed. "Such fine Boston talk don't impress us."

"Give them something to eat," the man at the table growled. "They'd do the same for you."

"I ain't never been to Boston and I ain't going," the servant at the table complained. But she got up and filled two cracked bowls with pea soup and thumped them on the table. Eagerly, Hester and Philena took their places and ate every last drop.

"You look to be exactly the same," the man said, gazing at them suspiciously. "Anyone ever told you that before?"

"Never," Hester said with a perfectly straight face.

The woman looked confused. While she seemed to ponder Hester's comment, Hester slipped from the table and filled her bowl and her sister's with more soup.

"You hear about the jewel thief along the road from Boston?" the man asked. "Amazing things we've heard."

"Do tell."

Philena finished the last of the soup, which had been decorated with only a few pieces of grizzled ham. She pushed her bowl toward her sister and winked. "See here, my lass, can't you get me some more ham? These here are a day's sail apart." Just saying Goodwife Kemble's favorite phrase made Philena feel homesick for Moon Street.

"This thief changes shape. He runs off and nobody can catch him."

"Might be a woman," his companion interrupted.

"Might be. As I said," he continued in a perturbed voice, "this is a thief that changes shape. Flies down the road and nobody sees him coming or going. Been known to leap a roof and they say he's got a helper. A small dwarf man on a big bay horse."

"Good way to make a bit of money if you don't get hung first," the maid said in a wise voice.

The servants nodded in agreement.

Hester and Philena squirmed.

That evening very late the girls decided they could not stay at Mr. Cook's home. While they heard snoring in the maids' quarters, they crept down the steps through the kitchen. They did not know where they would go or what they would do. They only knew that they could not remain in such an unhappy house.

A small fire burned in the kitchen fireplace. They hurried into their cloaks. An old woman sat in a chair by the door, her sewing in her lap. She was asleep.

Hester and Philena walked on tiptoe. Just as they were about to pass, the woman's eyes fluttered open. "Where do you think you're going?"

"For air," Hester said quickly.

"It's freezing out there."

"Let us pass," Philena whispered. "We can make it worth your while."

"How?"

Philena nudged her sister. From her pocket, Hester produced the thimble. "Take it and let us go. Don't say you saw us or anything else."

The woman snatched the thimble from Hester's hand. Philena opened the door and they both quickly walked up the cellar steps. They hurried around to the front of the house.

Before they made it to the street, a man's voice called to them. "Hester and Philena?"

Stunned, they stopped and turned. *Who knows our names?*

Long windows were lit up from the inside. They saw the silhouette of a man on the porch. He seemed to be emptying his pipe. "Come back in here," he demanded.

Mr. Cook.

For one second they considered bolting away down the snowy street. But they knew there was no escape. He opened the front door and motioned for them to come inside.

Chapter 13

As Hester and Philena trudged closer to the house, they scarcely dared to look up at Mr. Cook. He made a little bow as he held open the door for them. His fashionable, curled white wig did not match his dark, jumping eyebrows. "Thou art the servants of Madame Knight?"

They nodded, surprised by this question. "We are," Hester declared in her bravest voice. "And we won't be separated. If I go, she goes." The girls stepped past Mr. Cook into the grand hallway.

He examined them with some amusement. "This way. Madame Knight and Polly are in the library."

Madame Knight and Polly! These were the last

people Hester or Philena wanted to see. Their
footsteps echoed across shining wooden floors as
they walked past a ticking clock. A great looking
glass stood on one wall. Hester and Philena briefly
glimpsed their double, startled reflections as they
hurried past. Mr. Cook walked quickly. He
opened an enormous door and motioned for them
to come inside. One wall was lined with books,
more books than Hester or Philena had ever seen
before in one place. On a large table Hester recognized the trunk belonging to Mr. Trowbridge.

Madame Knight and Polly, wearing fine
clothes, looked uncomfortable as they sat in
fancy chairs. They seemed surprised to see Hester
and Philena. "Mr. Cook, why, may I ask, are my
servants joining us now?" Madame Knight
demanded.

Mr. Cook smiled in a charming manner. "I have
decided that this is a good time to inform thee of
why I have made this invitation."

Madame Knight seemed to perk up consider-
ably. Polly leaned forward in anticipation. Hester
and Philena kept their eyes on their hands folded
in their laps. They listened to the clock tick. The
steady noise only filled them with more dread.

Mr. Cook sat down and unfolded some papers. "You have come into some money, I am pleased to inform you," he said. As he read, he tapped one long bony finger on the gleaming desk. "As executor of the estate, I am responsible to inform you."

Madame Knight smiled victoriously. "Wonderful news! I have many things I need for my home and for my daughter. You can see she is a fine girl. A girl worthy of the best."

Polly beamed.

Mr. Cook looked up. His brow furrowed so that his expensive wig moved slightly, like a curled white cat shifting on its perch. "I am afraid that I must make clear for whom the money is intended. It is for the twin daughters of David White, recently deceased. These are the twins I spoke of in my letter, do you recall?" He stared at Hester and Philena. "The amount is fifty pounds."

"Fifty pounds!" Madame Knight said, gasping.

Hester and Philena could scarcely believe what he was saying. *Daughters of David White?* They had never heard that name before in all their lives.

"There must be some mistake," Madame Knight insisted. Her face turned bright red. "What of Mr.

Trowbridge? What of our long hours spent caring for him? What of the danger we exposed ourselves to bringing his only earthly possessions to thee." She gestured to the trunk. She paused and shot Hester and Philena an accusing glance. "I expected the family to be grateful—"

Mr. Cook raised his hand as if to stop the torrent of words pouring from Madame Knight's mouth. "Madame, I do not understand what thou speaks of. In my letter I asked thee to bring along the daughters of Mr. White, if they were still in your employ. I told thee to do this in complete secrecy at an appointed time. This thou hast accomplished with admirable punctuality."

"I always follow the letter of the law," Madame Knight announced. Only the quaver in her voice revealed that she was not speaking the complete truth. She had set out on her journey with only one of the twins.

Philena did not pay any attention to Madame Knight's obvious anxiety. She was too busy feeling relieved. *There is no sale of time. No advertisement for either of us.*

Hester glanced quickly at Polly, whose face had turned bright red. Polly wrapped and unwrapped her dress sash around her finger. She refused to look at either Hester or Philena.

Hester wondered what Polly might be thinking. *No great fortune. No dressmakers, no parties, no marvelous wardrobe purchases.* Polly blinked hard as if she might burst into tears. For the first time, Hester felt sorry for her.

Mr. Cook cleared his throat. "My client, Mr. White, was the father of the twins. Their mother, Sally Pierce, was a single woman from Haverhill, Massachusetts."

Our mother. She has a name. Philena did not need to look at Hester. She did not need to say a word. She knew they were thinking the same thing.

"She is dead?" Hester asked and bit her lip.

Mr. Cook nodded solemnly. "Thou were born May the eighth, 1692," Mr. Cook said, glancing at the paper on his desk. "She died a year later. We have no other details about her."

No details. Philena sighed. She wanted to know what Sally Pierce looked like. How old was she? What did her voice sound like? Was she happy?

"All that we know," Mr. Cook continued, "is that after she died, the twins were given briefly into the care of Goodwife Miller of Haverhill, who in turn gave the infants to the city fathers to take care of when she became ill. And that was how Hester and Philena came under the care and protection of Madame Knight as indentured servants."

"I did the hard work," Madame Knight said in a stunned voice. "I raised them. The money should be mine."

Mr. Cook raised his hand as if to silence her. "When the twins were born, Sally Pierce declared Mr. White, a wealthy merchant, the father. Mr. White was already married. My client contested the claim in court, as was the custom. He won. However, before he died last year, he secretly added to his will that he would bequeath some money to the twins' welfare, if they were still alive by their twelfth year. It has taken me this long to find the girls, whom I discovered were in thy employ. You must understand that my job was secret. No one was to know. Mr. White did not wish to offend his family or surviving legitimate children."

Madame Knight seemed too shocked to respond. "I took them in," she said in a confused voice. "They are very much alive. Sometimes a bit *too* alive, if thou asks me."

Bewildered, Hester and Philena, not knowing what else to do, stood and gave a little curtsy. The information overwhelmed them. Not only had they discovered that they had a mother, they had a father, too.

"I was, of course, glad to find thee in Boston. My search took nearly twelve months." Mr. Cook busily tidied up his papers. "Now thou canst see why this information must remain secret."

Madame Knight did not look pleased that their meeting had clearly ended. "Sir, I have come a long way at considerable expense to bring these two unfortunate girls here. I am not a wealthy woman. In the process of this journey, I have spent a great deal of money on our housing and food and fees for guides. I have lost a valuable slave, a fine bay horse, and much time away from my business."

Mr. Cook rubbed his temples with the tips of his pale fingers. "Mr. White also instructed me to provide a small sum for the caregiver. Naturally, he did not know who that would be. It is not much, but perhaps it will assist you on your return home to Boston."

Hester and Philena looked at the leather pouch

of coins he pulled from the drawer of his desk. "But what of our separation, sir?" Hester asked. "What of the sale of our time?"

"My instructions do not mention anything about that," Mr. Cook said. "Since you are only twelve years old, I suppose you will remain in the employ of Madame Knight."

"Sir," Philena asked, her voice trembling, "might we still be split apart and sent to different households?" She glanced at her sister. "We don't always get along, true enough. But we shall always be sisters. A special sort of bond. That will never change."

"We wish to stay together," Hester said. "And Moon Street is the only home we know. What we want to know, sir, can our time as maidservants be sold separately?"

Mr. Cook rubbed his chin. He shuffled his papers, pausing every now and again to read something. "I find nothing here about that subject."

Hester glanced at Madame Knight, who gave a disappointed sigh. *What we want isn't the money.* Hester looked at her sister and arched one eyebrow.

Philena coughed once. Then she smiled.

"What if, sir, we give the fifty pounds to our mistress?" Hester said slowly. "And then she signs a paper saying she won't separate us—not until we're grown. And we can stay at Moon Street. Is that possible? Can thou write that?"

"An unusual request," Mr. Cook said, "though the money belongs to thee to do as thou pleases." He turned to Madame Knight. "Would you sign such an agreement?"

Madame Knight beamed. She nodded. For once, she seemed speechless.

"One moment," Philena said, raising one finger to her lips. "Not quite fifty pounds she'll receive. But almost."

"What do you mean?" Mr. Cook asked. Madame Knight squirmed uncomfortably.

Hester smiled. "We have another debt to repay."

"How much?" Mr. Cook asked, pen poised above his paper.

"The cost of a returned silver thimble," Hester replied.

Madame Knight looked visibly relieved.

"I also almost forgot something," Mr. Cook

admitted. He pulled out a small, smudged piece of paper folded carefully into a square. He looked at Hester and Philena. "These belong to thee. No reason for me to keep them anymore."

When he unfolded the square of paper, two small, faded ribbons fell on to the desk. One ribbon was green, the other yellow. Each were tied in a tiny bow.

"What are they?" Hester whispered.

"From Goodwife Miller. Her husband saved these and gave them to me when I interviewed him during my search for thee. I believe Goodwife Miller did attach one to each of thee to tell thee apart. Perhaps these ribbons came to her from thy mother. I do not know for certain."

From thy mother. Curiously, Hester and Philena inspected the precious, faded ribbons—their only real connection with the mysterious Goodwife Miller or the woman called Sally Pierce.

"May eighth is our birthday," Philena said in a hushed voice.

"Now at last we know," Hester replied, smiling.

"Mr. Cook, please draw up the necessary papers. I will sign whatever needs my signature. If our business is finished, we will be on our way tomorrow," Madame Knight said. "My tender mother awaits our return in Boston."

Mr. Cook cleared his throat. For the first time, he seemed nervous. "I would hope I might persuade thee to stay a day longer. To join me for dinner. I am a widower and would enjoy thy company. And perhaps I might show thee about New York? It is unusual for me to meet a woman with such a fine appreciation for the law."

Madame Knight fluttered her stubby eyelashes. Philena smiled. "She also—"

"Writes poetry, sir," Hester added.

Mr. Cook looked impressed. For the first time in ever so long, blushing Madame Knight gave Hester and Philena appreciative glances.

The twins did not notice. They were too busy admiring their precious green and yellow keepsakes. *Someone loved us.* Hester touched the ribbons. She looked at Philena.

Philena nodded. *Someone loved us very much indeed.*

Polly winked mischievously at the two sisters. "Do you suppose when these ribbons were removed from your baby curls, my dear old grandmother may have mixed you up?"

"What do you mean?" Hester asked.

Philena understood. She grinned. "Perhaps I am really Hester." She turned to her twin. "And you—"

"Are really Philena." Hester smiled. The sound of the three girls' laughter echoed out of the room and down the grand hallway. And for the first time, Mr. Edward Cook's house was filled with the unmistakable sound of surprising, sudden joy.

Bibliography

Botkin, B. A. *New England Folklore*. New York: Bonanza Books, 1965.

Crawford, Mary Caroline. *Social Life in Old New England*. Boston: Little, Brown and Co., 1914.

Cronon, William. *Changes in the Land: Indians, Colonists and the Ecology of New England*. New York: Hill and Wang, 1983.

Daniels, Bruce C. *Puritans at Play: Leisure and Recreation in Colonial New England*. New York: St. Martin's Griffin, 1995.

Deetz, James. *In Small Things Forgotten: The Archeology of Early American Life*. New York: Doubleday, 1977.

Dow, George Francis. *Everyday Life in the Massachusetts Bay Colony*. New York: Dover Publications, 1988.

Earle, Alice Morse. *Child Life in Colonial Days.* New York: Macmillan, 1899.

—————. *Customs and Fashions in Old New England.* New York: Charles Scribner's Sons, 1904.

Freiberg, Malcolm, editor. *The Journal of Madame Knight.* Boston: David R. Godine, 1972.

Hawke, David Freeman. *Everyday Life in Early America.* New York: Harper & Row, 1988.

Holbrook, Stewart H. *The Old Post Road.* New York: McGraw-Hill Book Co., 1962.

Marx, Jenifer. *Pirates and Privateers of the Caribbean.* Malibar, FL: Krieger Publishing Co., 1992.

Mitchell, Edwin V. *It's an Old New England Custom.* New York: Vanguard Press, Inc., 1946.

Ross, Marjorie Drake. *The Book of Boston: The Colonial Period.* New York: Hastings House Publishers, 1960.

Ulrich, Laurel Thatcher. *Good Wives: Image and Reality in the Lives of Women in Northern New England, 1650–1750.* New York: Random House, 1991.

Wolf, Stephanie Grauman. *As Various As Their Land: The Everyday Lives of Eighteenth-Century Americans.* New York: HarperCollins Publishers, 1993.

About the Author

Trained as a journalist, Laurie Lawlor worked for many years as a freelance writer and editor before devoting herself full-time to the creation of children's books. She enjoys many speaking engagements at schools and libraries, and her books have been nominated for many awards. She lives in Evanston, Illinois, with her husband, son, daughter, and two large Labrador retrievers. Her books include the *Addie Across the Prairie* series, the *Heartland* series, *How to Survive Third Grade*, *The Worm Club*, *Gold in the Hills*, and *Little Women* (a movie novelization). Her nonfiction work, *Shadow Catcher: The Life and Work of Edward S. Curtis*, won the Carl Sandburg Award for nonfiction (1995) and the Golden Kite Honor Book Award (1995).

Turn the page for a preview of
the next American Sisters paperback

Exploring the Chicago World's Fair, 1893
by Laurie Lawlor

Available May 2002

"Tell it again."

"Which part?"

"Everything."

Dora sighed. She had already told her three younger sisters the story one thousand times since they left the ranch in Saddlestring, Nebraska. As their eastbound train rumbled toward Chicago, she took a deep breath and leaned forward toward Lillian and Phoebe in the facing seat. "At the fair the buildings are white and splendid and big," Dora said. Expertly, she shifted four-year-old Tess, their sleeping youngest sister, in her lap. "The sidewalk moves by itself, and a giant wheel carries people up into the sky. There's a real, genuine castle you can visit and—"

"What if we fall off?" ten-year-old Phoebe demanded nervously.

"Stop interrupting," Lillian said. She was eight and fearless. The Ferris wheel was her favorite. "Nobody falls because they're inside a car like this with walls and a ceiling."

"Oh," said Phoebe. She looked around at the sixty-five passengers jammed into grubby, hard seats on the rocking, rattling Union Pacific car. The hot, close air smelled of whisky, tobacco, and sweat. The ceiling drummed with the sound of cinders belched against the roof from the steam engine's smokestack. Across the aisle a baby wailed. A woman blew her nose loudly and shouted in a strange language at two wrestling boys. A man in a cowboy hat snored. Phoebe decided she'd skip the Ferris wheel.

"At the fair there are many inventions," Dora continued. "I don't know all the names. Electric machines and gadgets and—"

"You forgot to tell about the cheese," Phoebe said.

Dora rolled her eyes. "At the fair there is an eleven-ton cheese and a fifteen-hundred–pound chocolate statue of a beautiful woman named Venus and a real battleship and trained lions, tigers, and elephants and-"

Lillian smiled dreamily. "I'm going to have a little taste." She smacked her lips. "Just a nibble."

Phoebe scowled. "You mean a crumb of chocolate from her toe? You'll get in trouble."

"Nobody will notice. Venus is huge. She weighs tons," Lillian said indignantly. "Do you know how big that is?"

Phoebe shook her head. "Dora, how much is tons?"

Dora, who always impressed her sisters with her knowledge of nearly everything, wasn't listening. She was staring at the scuffed toes of her worn-out, too-small boots. What if all the other twelve-year-old girls in Chicago wore shiny, new shoes?

"Dora!" Phoebe insisted. "Lillian says she's going to steal chocolate. She's going to be arrested."

"I didn't say I'm going to *steal* Venus's toe. I just said I'm going to taste it," Lillian said angrily.

Dora looked at Lillian and Phoebe as if they were both crazy. "Can't you two get along for five minutes? If your shrieking wakes up Tess, you have to play with her," Dora warned. She looked down at her sleeping sister. Tess's matted hair smelled sour and dusty and had left a damp spot on Dora's skirt. Under one chubby arm Tess clutched beloved Nancy, a rag doll with black bead eyes and one arm missing.

"You forgot the camels and donkeys," Lillian complained.

Phoebe pouted. "You forgot the balloon ride and the volcano and the gold mine."

"I'll tell the rest later," Dora said and yawned. "Now leave me alone." She shut her eyes.

Bored, Phoebe sat up on her knees and pressed her sweaty face against the grimy train window. The mark she made on the glass looked like a ghost staring in at her and her three sisters. "See, Lillian?" she said proudly. She ran her finger along the outline of flattened nose, wide forehead, and shallow chin.

"Not as ugly as you in real life," Lillian replied without glancing up. Dainty Lillian was practicing her autograph with a stubby pencil and a paper scrap. Again and again she wrote the stage name she had invented: "LillianLucilleMariePomeroy" spelled altogether so that it would take up as much room as possible on the marquee.

Phoebe frowned and wiped her greasy face mark from the window with her sleeve. She was dark haired like the other Pomeroy girls, but her lips were thin and her ears were overlarge. Mama called her too plain to go on stage professionally, which was fine with shy Phoebe who did not like to sing or dance. Critically, Phoebe examined her dirty sleeve which had now become even dirtier. Her eyes narrowed with anger. She gave pretty, irritating Lillian a swift, secret jab with her elbow.

"Ouch!" Lillian wailed.

"Sorry." Phoebe made a contrite little smile.

Dora's eyes flew open. "Stop it both of you."

"Better not have given me a bruise," Lillian grumbled.

Phoebe stuck out her tongue.

Dora pretended not to notice. The train car bucked and rattled. She wished she could open the window. She wished there'd be a fresh, cool breeze — not more dust rolling from across the plains or more cinders blown in from the smokestack. Her eyelids lowered. Her head drifted against the sooty window frame.

Carefully, Phoebe removed a battered penny post card from her pocket. "Let me borrow your pencil, Lillian," she whispered.

"What for?" Lillian demanded. She held the pencil tightly in her fist.

"I told Florence I'd write her."

Lillian puckered her mouth. "Next thing you'll be asking for a penny to mail it. Well, don't bother because I'm saving my money for the Ferris wheel."

"Just for a minute," Phoebe pleaded. "Come on, Lillian."

At the sound of Phoebe's familiar, high-pitched whine, Dora opened one eye. "Give her the pencil, Lillian. Stop being so stingy for once."

Lillian made a great puffing noise. "Don't use it all up. And don't go biting the wood. 1 don't like teeth marks on my only pencil." Reluctantly, she handed Phoebe the pencil.

"Thank you," Phoebe replied and made a nasty face. Cleverly, she positioned the post card in her lap with one arm wrapped around it so that Lillian sitting beside her could not see what she was struggling to write:

Deeer Florence:
Never got too say good by to you
Papa said we got to skip out at nite
for the sherriff comes I will trie to send
you a reel souveneer post card from the FAIR
do not ever forget your old frend —Phoebe

"Done?" Lillian demanded with her palm outstretched.

Phoebe handed back the pencil. "That's all the words I can fit." She slid the post card back into her pocket.

Dora stretched her arms over her head. Her leg was cramping under Tess's weight. She felt as if they had been travelling for days.

"How far till Chicago?" Lillian demanded.

"Supposed to be there this evening," Dora said. She stared out the window. Dry, gray-green Iowa blurred past. Dark clouds herded against the horizon that stretched like a taut line of barbed wire.

"I liked the ranch," Phoebe said in a quiet voice to no one in particular. "First place we ever lived three years in a row. Our first real house." She sighed. "We even had curtains."

Lillian drummed her fingers on the worn, red

upholstery. "I'm glad we're going to a big city with lots of bright lights. We're going to see the fair. And don't forget the Wild West Show. We're going to be famous this time, just like Mama said. The ranch was dull. Exactly the same every day."

Dora turned and glanced over her shoulder at their mother dozing in the seat behind them. No one would have guessed that the woman in the yellow taffeta silk skirt and knobby broadcloth cape with most of the pearl buttons missing was once a ranch wife in a faded gingham apron. On her lap she clutched her precious, well-traveled hat box. Her chin had dropped to her chest, and the fake blue bird on her gayest fancy straw hat bobbed and leapt as if trying to free itself as the train lurched along.

Dora remembered a meadowlark she had once found caught by one wing on a fence on her way to school. The bird's beating heart, bones, and feathers felt light as wind when she'd let it go. Did the meadowlark remember her? She turned and stared out the window. "No more school," she said in a soft, mournful voice.

Phoebe nodded sadly. "No more friends."

"You'll make new ones," Lillian replied with impatience. "And what was so wonderful about Miss Elvira Simpson and that schoolhouse with the rattlesnakes under the floor boards and those nasty boys lurking around at recess? I hated school. I'm glad we don't have to go no more."

"Any more," Dora corrected her.

"That's what I said," Lillian replied. Her pretty face flushed bright red. "Sometimes I think you two are the dullest creatures on earth. Dora, you with your stupid spelling bee awards and you, Phoebe with your stupid Wards Catalog."

Phoebe frowned. "Wards Catalog isn't stupid. It's beautiful."

Lillian sensed that she had hit her mark. "You're probably the only ten-year-old girl in all of Nebraska who studied the stupid advertisements and cut out the stupid pictures of stoves and tables and chairs and sewing machines—"

"That's enough," Dora said. She could see that Phoebe was blinking hard and biting both her lips at once. To cry signaled complete defeat—something Lillian would never let Phoebe forget. "Don't fight. We need to stick together. That's what Papa said, remember?"

Lillian folded her arms in front of herself and flounced backward against the hard seat. Phoebe ran her fingers down a pleat of her patched serge skirt. Dora tried not to feel angry about Lillian's comment about Miss Simpson and the spelling bees. Dora was proud how well she could spell hard words like *incinerate* and *parallel*. She liked school. She liked doing something besides taking care of her younger sisters.

School was escape. When she went to school she

could practice writing perfectly shaped vowels with elegant wiggly tails and wash the black board better than anyone and read difficult words no one else could pronounce from the McGuffey's Reader. And best of all, Miss Simpson praised her. Dora was special at school. At home she was just somebody who cooked and swept and did laundry. She had to wipe dirty noses and bandage bloody knees and make up games to keep her sisters from killing each other. School was easy. Everything else in Dora's life was hard. Everything.

"Wanna lemonade," Tess said. She sat up and rubbed her grubby fists in her large blue eyes. She stared hard at the boy across the aisle who was sipping something from a glass bottle beaded with moisture.

"Hush," Dora replied. "We don't have any money."

"Wanna lemonade," Tess repeated, more insistent this time.

"Take her for some water, will you, Lillian?" Dora asked.

"Why me?" Lillian demanded. The doll Nancy tumbled from Tess's arms and landed upside down on the seat. "Come on, Little Kisses," Lillian said, using Tess's nickname. Lillian took her thirsty sister by the hand and dragged her down the aisle toward the water spigot, which dribbled warm, rusty-tasting water into a paper-tasting cone.

As soon as Lillian and Tess disappeared, Phoebe asked quietly, "Dora, do you think Wards Catalog is stupid?"

"No, of course not."

Phoebe examined her ragged fingernails. "You think I'm ugly?"

"No, I do not. You shouldn't pay so much attention to Lillian. You know how she goes on and on sometimes just to hear the sound of her own voice. She doesn't mean half what she says."

Phoebe's thin shoulders seemed to relax. She spread her fingers out on her lap. "Twenty times. We moved twenty times in ten years. I counted. You think we'll stay put in Chicago?"

Dora shrugged. She didn't want to give her worried sister false hope. Papa had what he called a natural disposition to remove to a new country. It was in his blood, he said. His papa and his papa's papa did the same. "Pomeroys never settle down," he liked to brag. Like his ancestors, Papa did not need much reason to move on, to pull up roots and head out for a some distant, better opportunity. Dora's family's life was rooted in rootlessness. Sometimes it seemed to her as if they'd played every little run-down theater and two-bit circus act between New Jersey and California, crisscrossing the country from one small town to the next mining camp and back again. In all those years, Dora had been to school a total of only four years.

"Girls!" Mama gave Dora's shoulder a poke. "Will you look out that window? Before you know it we'll be crossing the Mississippi. Oh, I can tell you I can hardly wait to be in a big city again. Chicago! You never saw anything so beautiful in all your life."

Dora twisted in her seat to catch a glimpse of Mama fanning herself with her slender, gloved hand as she bent over the red-faced man sitting next to her beside the window. "Excuse me, sir, but I just have to keep looking for Illinois," Mama apologized in her sweetest melted butter voice.

Unlike Dora, who had dry, frizzy dark hair, Mama's hair was thick and auburn. Mama's eyes were dark and striking and she had high cheekbones, which she said helped her "light up on stage." Dora always knew there was something slightly exotic about Mama's beauty, yet this afternoon she felt as if she were looking at a stranger. That was when she realized what had changed. Her mother was smiling. She had not seen her mother look so happy in years.

"Going home, ma'am?" the stranger asked and pushed his stained, felt hat back on his meaty forehead.

"You might say we're going to our *real* home. The stage. We've been away awhile. Maybe you've heard of the Magnificent Pomeroy Performers and Their Talking Horse?"

The stranger shook his head. Phoebe blushed. Dora wished her mother would speak in a more quiet voice. What if everyone on the train car was listening?

"Well, if you missed our act, maybe you saw me in *Uncle Tom's Cabin* or maybe *The Count of Monte Cristo*."

The man's silence seemed to indicate he was stumped.

Mama did not give up so easily. "I did *Ten Nights in a Barroom* at the Belmont before it burned. A very popular show."

"I seen that! That was good," he gushed.

Mama smiled and fingered one of the velvet rosettes on her hat brim. "Of course that was ages ago. Before all four girls were born. We're starting a new routine. Calling it Barn Yard Musicians. Chicken imitations, dogs jumping through fiery hoops, that kind of thing. I'm quite a dancer and of course, so are my precious little daughters. I have four daughters, sir. Each one more talented than the next. We had a nice act. Of course, that was before we took up ranching. Hated it. Absolutely hated it. Nothing worse than eleven months of wind and winter in Nebraska. After the bank foreclosed we decided to head to Chicago. Like everybody else, I guess," she said. Her nervous laughter sounded musical.

The stranger smiled. One of his front teeth was missing.

"I'm sure you've heard of the Wild West Show and Buffalo Bill?"

The stranger nodded eagerly.

"My husband," Mama said with a dramatic pause, "has been hired by Buffalo Bill himself to be one of the horse handlers. He was a trick rider before he hurt his back. A real professional daredevil."

Dora and her sister shrank lower and lower into their seats as if somehow to become invisible.

"Well Buffalo Bill, Bill as we like to call him," Mama continued, "he heard about my husband and he hired him on the spot. Of course I'm going to audition. Maybe get my babies on stage, too. Ever been to Chicago?"

"Sure. Sure—"

"We're going to be right across the street from the World's Columbian Exposition. We're going to be performing for thousands of folks every day."

"The fair! Now there's something," the stranger managed to interrupt Mama. "Unbelievable. The chance of a lifetime. Why I've heard—"

Before he could get another word in edgewise, Mama burst into a long monologue about their costumes and their songs and their unfortunate contract in San Francisco and how the trick horse died half way across Nevada, which was one reason they ended up in Nebraska and she was certainly glad to be getting back to civilization again. She bet he was glad, too, wasn't he?

"Yes, ma'am," the stranger said with some confusion. He seemed grateful when the train pulled into a water stop for the engine. He stood up and tipped his hat and took a long walk out to the platform.

Dora twisted in her seat. "Do you have to talk so loud to strangers, Mama?" she hissed.

Mama patted her face with a handkerchief and checked her hair using a small mirror from her cheap square pocket book made of embossed leather worn white around the ball catch. "Dora," she said, looking with disdain over the top of the mirror. "Never, never underestimate the effect of a little advance publicity." She dropped the mirror in the purse and snapped it shut. "Where's your father?"

"Haven't seen him since Omaha," replied Phoebe, who, like the rest of her sisters, knew very well where Papa had gone. Phoebe didn't want to tell Mama for fear of a scene. Besides, she was enjoying Mama's rare, good mood.

Mama arranged her cape and glanced cheerfully up and down the car, which was emptying of the crowd of ragged families, limping cowboys and down-on-their-luck salesmen traveling on the cheapest fares possible. "Do you think all these people are out of work?"

Dora shrugged. It was unusual for Mama to think about other people's circumstances. How many times had she reminded Dora and her sisters that other people's troubles were just too depressing? She had enough problems of her own, she liked to say, to worry about anybody else.

Mama peered happily out the window and sang in a soft voice:

"Then come sit by my side if you love me;
Do not hasten to bid me adieu.
But remember the Red River Valley
and the cowboy that loved you so true..."

The familiar tune made Dora smile at Phoebe. Neither girl had heard their mother sing "Red River Valley" in a long, long time. "Remember?" Phoebe whispered to her sister.

"Haven't heard it since before the El Grande Theater in Leadville," Dora replied. She smiled. Maybe everything was going to work out fine after all. Maybe Chicago and the Wild West Show would be their lucky break.

The train whistle wailed. "All aboard!" the conductor shouted.

Dora glanced at Nancy sprawled in the seat across from them. She jumped to her feet. "What's wrong?" Phoebe demanded.

"Tess and Lillian! Where are they?" Dora said. Desperately, she pushed her way up the aisle through the crowd of passengers piling back on the train again. What if her sisters wandered off the train on to the platform?

"Tess and Lillian!" she called in desperation.

"Last call! All aboard!" the conductor called. A bell rang.

Dora looked out on to the empty platform. What if they'd been kidnapped?

Look for the next American Sisters title

Exploring the Chicago World's Fair, 1893
by Laurie Lawlor

Available from Aladdin Paperbacks

The
Submissive
Wife

A N D

Other
Legends

The
Submissive
Wife

A N D

Other
Legends

MARSHA DRAKE

BETHANY HOUSE PUBLISHERS
MINNEAPOLIS, MINNESOTA 55438
A Division of Bethany Fellowship, Inc.

Published by Bethany House Publishers
A Division of Bethany Fellowship, Inc.
6820 Auto Club Road, Minneapolis, Minnesota 55438

Printed in the United States of America

Library of Congress Cataloging-in-Publication Data

Drake, Marsha.
    The submissive wife and other legends.

    Bibliography: p.
    I. Title.
PS3554.R233S8   1987   813'.54   87-682
ISBN 0-87123-926-4 (pbk.)

Dedicated to:

The Reverend L. H. Shonfelt

Table of Contents

1 / Sunrise

"So why do you call me 'Lord' when you won't obey me?"[1]

I woke with a start. A feeling of foreboding washed over me. I listened for house sounds, familiar or disastrous. No crackle of fire creeping along the hall carpet. No rumblings of hurricane or roar of earth's vibrations signaling an earthquake.

Quickly I tuned into John, sleeping next to me. "Zzzz, cough, whistle. Zzzz, pause, whistle."

"So far so good," I whispered, hopping out of bed.

Hurrying down the hall, I peeked in on each of my three children. John Jr. and Joe shared a room. The fighting stopped only when they slept. "J.J. snores louder than his father," I whispered to myself, pulling his covers up over his broadening sixteen-year-old shoulders.

"Joe," I sighed, "you're going to give yourself brain cancer all huddled under your blankets like this." I struggled against my middle son's strength to untangle his head.

"Stop it!" Joe yelled in his sleep, grabbing his covers and disappearing into the center of his bed.

"I hate age fourteen," I muttered. Turning my back on him, I headed toward baby George's room.

"Ah, my baby." I stood at the doorway and watched my eleven-year-old son sleep in splendor. Light brown hair framed his freckled face. His breathing pattern revealed the glint of braces now and then. "I know he will be handsome with straight

9

teeth," I said softly as I pulled his curtain closed against the early morning light. "Maybe we can get him contact lenses too. I know how much he hates his glasses."

Realizing all was well, I padded softly in my housecoat and slippers into the living room to have a look at the Chief. The Chief, my favorite mountain, and I had been friends for a long time. The gigantic feldspar quartz cliff towered over the small town where we lived.

Opening the drapes wide, I beheld the Chief silhouetted against a powder blue sky. Rose-colored clouds hovered above his head.

"How are you today, Big Fella?" I queried.

Mentally I traced the outline of an Indian chief lying on his back gazing with stone eyes forever into the heavens. Dawn had not yet touched the tip of his nose. "What do you see up there?"

As usual he did not reply.

I never tired of discovering the many facets of his face. "Even for one day I'd like to know all you've seen, lying there for centuries," I stated to the silent mountainous monolith, the Chief.

Shoving my thoughts aside, I directed my attention to the present. "Daylight changes things. As soon as the sun comes up, warmth enters all creation and exposes nonexistent creatures of the night."

Standing in front of our large picture window, I expected happiness to sweep over me. Instead, an uncomfortable sense of impending doom chilled my bones. "I must have been dreaming again," I commented uneasily.

Grabbing my Bible, I headed for the sofa. "It happens sometimes," I comforted myself. "Last week the pastor preached about that. He said he sometimes awakens and feels low for no apparent reason."

"But *he* has never had *dream attacks!*" My mind hissed.

I shoved the thought away. It had been a long time since those dream attacks and my struggle with identity.

Leafing through the pages, I turned to Proverbs 31, beginning at verse ten. I reread the description of the virtuous wife whose reality had plagued me for more than a year. The more I had tried to become like Her—that woman liberated beyond belief—the deeper I had sunk into un-Christlikeness.

Dream attacks had caused me to wake up nearly screaming. Perspiration formed along my hairline, and John and the children grew leery of my wide-eyed stare and effervescent enthusiasm.

"But I'm over that now. I've realized that the secret of being like Her is obedience to every Word of God—just like the Book says." I settled myself more comfortably on the couch and wrinkled my brow. "Then why am I uneasy?"

A subtle finger of fear touched my heart, leaving its mark.

"Probably nothing," I told myself roaming through my Bible. "I wonder what the Lord has for me today." Lazily, I let my eyes drift across the pages.

Then it happened. One little word sprang off the page at me. The word *obeyed*. "Thus Sarah obeyed Abraham, calling him lord, and you have become her children . . ."[2]

That verse struck a gong in my subconscious. Immediately, terror took over.

"Cute, however quaint." I spoke with courage, but my soul *knew* beyond the shadow of the Chief that I would never again be the same.

Jumping off the sofa, I began to prowl around the living room. "Imagine! The idea of me calling John *lord*! *Me?* Bowing and scraping? No one would expect such a silly thing like that today!"

Peering out my picture window at the Chief, I delighted in the pure glory of watching the dawn. Pink clouds retreated before the approaching sun. "The power of our Creator God is awesome," I exulted.

Scurrying to the kitchen, I prepared a pot of coffee. The warm steam and friendly aroma soothed me.

Sitting at the kitchen table by myself, I sipped the piping hot, black brew and pondered the word *obey*. "Probably the Bible means to obey God and *get along* with John. That makes sense." I shuddered to think of what my life would be like if I actually gave way to John.

Like a moth drawn to the incinerating flame, I swooped over

to my Bible concordance to locate the word *obey*. "I'm going to be sorry I'm doing this," I admonished myself.

Running my finger down the *o* section, I spied the term *obeisance*. "What's this?" My curious nature demanded a dictionary.

No dictionary in sight.

"John Jr. probably has it under his bed again," I decided, tiptoeing to his room.

J.J. lay on his back, snoring. Specimen, John's gigantic, black labrador-mutt mixture, had managed to sneak up the basement stairs and snuggle his way deep into the clean comforter on top of the bed. His huge paws lay across J.J.'s chest. Upon seeing me, he wagged his tail—slap, slap—against the wall.

"Specimen!" I exclaimed under my breath.

He pulled himself along the bed toward me.

"Specimen, get down!"

Rolling his sorrowful brown eyes in my direction, he lumbered off the bed and stretched his massive frame out on the carpet beside the bedstead.

I got down on my hands and knees to peer under J.J.'s bed. "Specimen, you're supposed to be downstairs or outside. When are you going to learn that?"

He slurped me right in the eye.

"Think you're pretty smart, don't you?"

He rolled over on his side and closed his eyes.

"Nobody pays any attention to what I say—even you!" Giving him a shove, I crawled past him and squeezed myself under the bedframe.

With a practiced eye I picked out the dictionary—just to the left of an old sandwich.

"Why didn't you eat this, Specimen?" I fumed furiously as I struggled to reach the book and the sandwich. "Just a little more . . . got it!"

Bumping my head on the box springs, I slithered out Green-Beret-style on my elbows, balancing the book and sandwich on the back of my right hand. "So far so good," I puffed.

Disgruntled, but victorious, I made my way to the living room with the dictionary. The sandwich, which I placed in the garbage disposal, irritated me. "I won't think about it. Not now."

The digital clock on the stereo displayed one half hour before John would waken.

"Anyway, it's Sunday," I mused while thumbing through the dog-eared dictionary for the word *obeisance.*

"I've always loved Sundays with John," I spoke to myself softly. Closing my eyes, I envisioned John across the kitchen table from me, sharing coffee and conversation before the children woke for Sunday school.

Sometimes we held hands—even after all the years together.

Love for my husband swept over me just as I found the term *obeisance.* Pronounced o-bay-sense, it meant a bow, curtsy, genuflection in token of respect, submission, or reverence; also, deference, homage.

Until I reached *homage* I felt comfortable—even sleepy.

"Homage?" My eyes widened. "How did I get into this?"

"You found it in the *o* section of the concordance on the way to *obey,*" replied my mind.

"Why," I whispered, "was I looking up *obey?*"

"You wanted to see if it was in the Bible," my gray matter reminded me.

"That's ridiculous!" I said in a normal tone. "Of course the word obey is in—"

"Of course," mocked my cerebrum.

I took a moment to remember. "Yes, I recall it now. I was reading my Bible, and I came across the word *obey,* and that led me to this *obeisance* nuisance in the concordance and I wanted to find out what it means."

"It means *homage,*" interjected my brain.

Goose bumps raised on my kneecaps.

Ignoring *obeisance,* I moved on to *obey* and discovered it meant to be obedient to; execute the commands of; also, to execute, as an order—to be ruled or controlled by; to follow guidance, operation of, as to obey, to yield obedience.

The dictionary had delivered my death warrant. "Thus Sarah was *controlled* by Abraham!" My heart pounded at the thought.

I slapped the dictionary shut.

Does God expect that? Would He allow John to rule me? Control me? I shivered.

"I need a plan. Didn't Alexander Pope say in 1688 that everything is a maze without a plan?"

"Lord—" I dropped to my knees by the sofa in the living room with the drapes drawn open so even the Chief could see that I meant it—"You know I love you and want to obey you, but I can't do *that*! Please." I whimpered a little for effect.

"Thus John *controlled* Martha," my brain drawled.

Rising from my knees, I swayed a little. "I need another cup of boiling coffee to stop these shivers." In my mind I heard the cup rattling on the saucer, beckoning me.

My feet landed like lead with each step I took toward the kitchen. Waves of uneasiness washed through me like ill tides of a fateful wind as I put the coffeepot on the burner and flipped on the heat. "Terrible," I told the stove, "to learn how to become virtuous and discover the reward is to be ruled like a robot."

Peace vanished as misery set up housekeeping in my soul.

"Mom?"

"A-a-a-h!" I nearly jumped out of my skin at the sound of my youngest son's voice. "Yes, George." I tried to sound calm.

"I'm hungry, Mom," George responded, his blue eyes glued to the chocolate double-fudge cake on the counter. The super-moist delicacy was covered in his favorite chocolate-candy-velvet-smooth frosting.

My knees sagged. Prepared for disaster and finding none, my body almost collapsed in exhaustion. "There's cake on the counter, George," I replied in a monotone.

"Are you okay, Mom?" George eyed me suspiciously.

"Have a piece of cake, George." I sat down.

"At dawn?"

"Yes."

"Yes?"

"Fine."

George came closer and pushed his face into mine. "Mom." He cleared his throat. "Have you been *dreaming*?" he asked, stuffing a big bite of cake into his mouth.

"I'm not well, George." I smoothed my hair into place.

"How 'bout milk?"

"What?"

"Can I have milk, too?"

"Sure. Fine."

"Would you like some, too?" He smiled brightly.

For the first time that morning, I looked at my offspring. His sandy hair stood up all over his head, and he had chocolate frosting smeared all around his mouth. "My stomach doesn't feel good, George. I don't want pastry right now."

"Do you want me to get Dad?" He pulled up a chair beside me.

Coming out of my near comatose state, I recovered quickly. "George, *what* is your problem? I told you that I don't want anything now, and that is final!"

"But, Mom," whimpered George, "pastry is pie."

"What?" I glowered in his direction.

"Pie, Mom. You made cake, not pie." For a moment he stopped inhaling chocolate.

"Look, George, just take your food and go to bed. I have to check on Joe. I hear noises." Totally frustrated at the meaningless conversation, I put my head in my hands.

My baby, my own, patted me on the back before he left the kitchen.

Meanwhile, I, unaware of my son's real problem—me—tripped off toward middle son's room.

"If Joe's sleeping," I muttered to myself, "then what was the noise I heard?"

Suddenly it came to me, a hazy notion too vague to understand and too frightening to contemplate. "Maybe I *have* been dreaming again!"

Shock propelled me toward the living room as I tried to remember.

"Mom?" George was back.

"What, George?" I stood with my back to him, staring out the picture window at nothing.

"I'm going to put my plate in the sink."

"Good."

"Are you still mad because we never washed the kitchen

walls yet from making pancakes?"

I stood mute, fumbling for words.

George picked up the ball of communication and tossed it my direction. "I love you, Mom."

"I love you, too, George," I replied from the depths of my heart. "Mothers aren't perfect."

"I know." He came and stood beside me, exhibiting a serious glance out the window. "Are you going to talk to the Chief today?"

I put my arm around my eleven-year-old. "Honey, please don't worry. Everything will be fine."

Smiling into my face, he gave me a bear hug and ran back toward his room.

Standing there, staring out the glass, I felt warm prickles of pride in my son. "But he had to bring up the pancakes. Yes. That was nearly a year ago."

I guess it had all started when John suggested that we let the kids cook dinner while we went to the town council dinner. "They'll be fine, Martha," he assured me.

"I'm not so sure."

"You worry too much. John Jr. can handle it."

When we arrived home from the banquet, the police, the fire department, and an ambulance greeted my horrified eyes. "I was just *french frying* the flapjacks, Mom!" John Jr. defended.

I had resented the whole thing so much that I'd said little. The griddle cake batter still decorated the kitchen walls like little globules of beige cement.

The kids never did clean the walls the way they promised, my mind clamored.

Resentment flowed afresh. "I think it's time I clean these walls. Maybe John will help me." Purpose quickened my step as I charged for our bedroom.

"John!" I shook my husband by the shoulder. "Wake up, John."

"What is it?" John bolted upright. "What's wrong?" His red-rimmed eyes tried to focus on my bright hazel orbs.

"Let's wallpaper the kitchen today." I sat down on the bed

beside him and bounced up and down a bit to jar his consciousness.

"Martha," he groaned and lay back down. "Today is Sunday." I thought I detected a note of disgust in his voice.

"Oh," I pouted.

"And," continued my spouse, "I think I feel sick."

My temper flared. "You'd say anything to get out of papering the kitchen. Those cement blobs are still up there from last year." Whirling on my heel, I vanished from the bedroom.

Stomping my way back to the kitchen, I mumbled, "Why did John have to get the flu on Sunday?"

"Sunday!" I put my hands on my hips. A glaze covered my eyes. "That means I teach Sunday school. Then I fix dinner, complete with dessert. Then I . . ."

Self-pity jumped on my soul and hung on.

Impulse prompted me to open the refrigerator door. "Terrific," I said to the door. "Somebody has broken an egg and left it for me to clean up." I followed the trail of cream-colored goo from the top shelf to its drizzled destination—a mustard jar.

Temper suddenly erupted. "I hate Sunday!" Shocked at my own outburst, I clasped my hand over my mouth as guilt joined the fray. Confusion reigned.

It's not your fault! hissed my brain.

"I know. I'm not to blame for this mess. Look at these walls! What am I to this family, anyway?" My throat constricted.

A maid, my mind answered.

The telephone rang.

"Hi, sweetie! How ya doin'?" My friend Jean's warm greeting hadn't changed in fifteen years.

"I'm leaving John," I responded.

"Oh, is that all?" She chuckled.

"This isn't funny, Jean. Do you realize *obey* means obedient, obeisance means curtsy, it all means submit, and everything means *control*?" Like a geyser, I blew.

"Maybe you should start at the beginning," she suggested.

"Submissive means a letting down, a lowering, and I can't do it."

"Of course you can't." She paused. "Do what?"

"Be a vassal, subservient," I answered honestly.

"Hold on."

"Where are you going?"

"To get a cup of coffee. This sounds good!"

For an hour—John's and my coffee hour—I tried to explain the unexplainable.

"Martha!" John called out from the bedroom.

"Uh, Jean, my friend, I have to go. I think it's starting already."

"How are you feeling, John?" As I hovered sympathetically at his bedside, my congenial attitude surprised him.

John's usual tranquility carried him through all the inherent disasters of living with me. Today, however, he scowled as I pulled the pillows out from under his head, fluffed them vigorously, and stuffed them back again. "Head hurt?" I smiled sweetly.

"Aaaaah-choo!" he replied.

"Hmm," I responded lightly, quickly assessing his condition. "Not so good."

"I feel terrible!" He blew his nose mightily. "Why didn't you wake me up?"

"I did—about an hour ago."

"No, I mean I can't teach Sunday school this morning."

"Oh," I commented.

Laying his head back and closing his eyes he said, "You will have to call Wesley Ward and tell him to arrange for somebody else to do it."

"I can't do that." I shifted my weight from one foot to the other uneasily.

"Why not?"

"I'm busy," I said.

"Doing what?" His query raised my hackles.

"Doing what? How can you be so callous?"

"Callous?" John's ill eyes clouded with anger. "Not now, Martha."

"Not now what?" I topped his irritation with an icy reply.

"Martha," John sighed. "I am sick. Really ill." He raised a finger and pointed it in my direction. "Now I want you to get the kids up, and call Mr. Ward, the Sunday school superintendent, to inform him that I cannot teach my class today."

Orders! My minds screamed. *He wants you to obey orders!*

"John—" I crossed my arms in front of me. "I won't be controlled."

"Martha, have you had one of your *dreams* again?" His voice sounded impatient, accusing, cold—like that of a master to his slave.

I stared at him in disbelief. *Obedience is like submission; submission is like subjection; subjection is lowering; and lowering is to bite the dust with one's face!*

I opened my mouth to speak, but I stood silent.

"Just call him, Martha. It's a simple request." His tone cut me in two.

"As you say," I said distantly, responding as I would to a stranger.

Isolation.

2 / Twilight

"Thus Sarah obeyed Abraham, calling him lord, and you have become her children if you do what is right without being frightened by any fear."[3]

Fearing the worst, I stood in the kitchen by the telephone. "It's silly to be afraid of Mr. Ward," I comforted myself. "He will understand that John cannot make it to teach Sunday school today, and neither can I."

Feeling better, I dialed his number and waited for him to answer. Somehow our Sunday school superintendent reminded me of my hard-nosed elementary school principal from childhood. I remembered the terror I experienced when Mr. Nix whirled his key chain round and round as he paced up and down the rows of desks. If a pencil fell, his keys rapped the knuckles of the offending hand which had allowed the "unnecessary noise."

"Hello?" Wesley Ward's voice struck insecurity into my soul.

"Uh, good morning, Mr. Ward." I groped for the right words. "John, or rather, John and I, most probably I, but certainly John—"

"What is it you're trying to say, Mrs. Christian?" he rudely interrupted.

"Just that John can't teach his Sunday school class today. He is sick—I mean, indisposed," I apologized.

"Indisposed?" His response thundered with accusation.

"I, uh, well . . . He says he won't be able to . . ." I grasped for confidence and missed.

"*John* says he can't? Well then, obviously he won't be able to teach his class this morning," he announced cheerfully.

"That's right," I agreed like a small child with rapped knuckles.

I heard Mr. Ward rattling something. Then he pronounced in dictatorial tones, "You can put his class in with *yours*." He waited for my reply.

"I can't do that!" My voice squeaked with indignation at the thought of combining fifteen seventh graders with thirty preschoolers.

"That will be fine then," he decided, ignoring my objection.

"Mr. Ward," I lowered my voice to sound authoritative, "do you realize that twelve-year-olds do not mesh with toddlers?" I let my statement stand with a dramatic pause for effect.

I heard him clear his throat. He said nothing.

"Perhaps I could handle that," I continued. "But I don't see how."

"Certainly, Mrs. Christian. Don't be late," he admonished, terminating the conversation.

Irritation rose as I put my mind into reverse and floored it. "Of all the nerve!" I began straightening things on the kitchen counter, lining up the flour and sugar containers and folding the dishcloth into a neat square. "If it isn't bad enough that John is giving me orders, now I'm going to have a riot in my classroom in twenty minutes. Twenty minutes? Oh, no!"

I raced down the hall to George's room. "George!" I shrieked. "Get up! Right now!" Yanking back his covers, I clapped my hands for emphasis. Ben, the guinea pig, began squealing at the top of his lungs. "That's right, Ben," I cheered. "*You* get him up!"

Running back down the hall, I pounded on J.J. and Joe's door. "Guys!" I yelled through reddish-brown wood. "Get up! Immediately!"

Knowing Joe would never respond to any call, no matter how earsplitting, I roared right past the DO NOT ENTER sign on the door and flipped his pillow out from under his head. Pulling at his blankets, I shook him by the shoulders and shouted into his left ear, "Joe! Get up! We have to be at church in fifteen minutes!"

Joe wrenched his comforter from my grasp, threw it over his head and mumbled something about "forty more winks and painting the world."

I responded by firmly gripping the immovable bedcovering and pulling with all my might. "Joe!" I yelled, bouncing the bed and shaking him all around.

"What, Mom?" My middle son pulled himself to a sitting position, hanging on to his quilt for dear life.

"Joe, we have to get to church!" I screamed. "Dad is sick, and I want you to get up *right now!*"

"Okay," he replied, lying down again.

"Joe!" Dragging him out of bed, I rolled him onto the carpet. "If you don't get up, we can't leave. Do you understand that?"

"Stand up?" He smiled from the Land of Nod.

"Okay, Joe!" I screeched, stomping out of the room, "I'm going to get a glass of water and I will dump it on your head if you are not up by the time I come back."

As I darted into the bathroom to make good my threat, I spied Specimen skulking down the hallway. "John Jr.!" I shouted. "Get this dog and escort him out of the house before I—"

"I'll get him!" George raced by, hollering.

Meanwhile, John Jr. ambled out of his room, rubbing his eyes.

"Shhh, Mom, you're screaming." John Jr., my oldest, spoke to me as though I were out of control. "Have you had one of your dreams again?" He put an arm around my shoulder boy-scout-style and smiled at me ingratiatingly.

"John—" My voice cracked as tears threatened my eyes. "You have to help me! I must teach Dad's class and mine, and then sing my solo, and there's still pancake batter on the kitchen wall, and—"

"No problem," he replied evenly. "We can handle it." He sounded just like his father.

And I believed him.

We arrived very late to Sunday school. Tears alone could not express the pain in my heart over what happened in my classroom.

The twelve-year-olds decided they wanted to play games with the toddlers, resulting in bedlam. Huge pre-pubescent heads popped in and out of the small playhouse intended for little ones, while cries of "Gimmee another ride, horsy!" rang out at fifty thousand decibels. Mock fights broke out between horsies and their riders, while real altercations took place over blocks, trucks, and patchwork puppets.

Finally it was over.

After Sunday school came church, accompanied by the choir robe ordeal.

Mine was nowhere in sight. The only one left sported a blue ink stain on the collar and smelled of moth balls. Bent pins replaced the broken zipper.

"This must have been meant for a six-footer," I sighed, struggling to pin it shut.

My five-foot frame, although round, couldn't begin to fill the allotted space. I stood in a pool of blue satin.

Stumbling into line, I gathered some fabric in each hand, clasped the hymn book, and opened my eyes wide to project a picture of serenity.

Hallelujah! I quavered, tripping my way to the choir loft.

As soon as we had sung the opening hymn, "Submit and Surrender," I settled myself among the folds of blue, took a deep breath, and wondered where my kids were and what they were up to.

Glancing at the congregation, I spotted John Jr. He sat in rapt attention, eyeballing the new girl in church. To his left, and three rows back, Joe and George were giggling uncontrollably.

They refused to acknowledge my raised eyebrows or my hand signals. "I'll wait until after the next prayer to try again," I promised myself. Anxiety crept up my spine.

"George!" I heard Mr. Wesley Ward's voice ring out in harsh correction.

My youngest's face turned crimson then white when he looked in my direction. My countenance registered, *Kill!* My insides collapsed in abject humiliation. Joe, however, smirked.

"I'll get him, and when I do . . ."

I was late for my solo. My preoccupation with the children mesmerized me, causing me to miss the organist's opening chord.

"Martha!" the choir director whispered.

Scarlet ribbons of embarrassment traced their way from my neck to my hairline. Smiling all the while, to portray self-possession, I lurched my way forward to sing.

"Take it to the Lord in prayer," I trilled—without instrumental accompaniment. *Guess I grabbed the wrong song.* I hung my head in shame. The organist managed to follow me as I warbled.

Then I tripped on the way back to my seat, and I hoped I would die before noon. Such was not the case. Punishment comes in droves, as I was soon to learn.

The sermon title should have warned me—"Surrender to Win!" Shock left me limp as I heard the pastor announce, "Our text for today is from the book of Ephesians, 'Wives, submit yourselves unto your own husbands, as unto the Lord.' "[4]

Cold sweat broke out on my forehead while nausea twisted my mouth into a horrible grimace.

Immediately my mind began, *Submit! Submit means to subject, and to subject is to lower . . .*

It might have been the heat that caused the room to swim before my eyes. It could have been the oversized robe and the smell of moth balls that made my stomach retch and my mouth quiver as I struggled to gain control over my body.

Whatever it was that triggered my response of denial, the stage was set for the inevitable result—submission would be repressed, sublimated, and obliterated from my consciousness. Insurrection and I began wandering the path to hopelessness.

The rest of the service was automatic—that is, *I* wasn't there. I did not hear the service, I did not respond to gentle suggestions offered by the pastor (most carefully so as not to offend), and I did not pass "Go" or collect my spiritual "two hundred dollars" to lay up with the rest of my treasure in heaven.

My *body* stood up and sang, sat down and pretended to listen, and emerged from the enveloping folds of blue, looking like me.

But it was an *alien* Martha who retrieved one son from a cozy conversation with the new blond, blue-eyed bombshell, yanked her youngest from the middle of a newly formed mud puddle, and grabbed Joe by the ear, vowing, "You'll get yours when we get home!"

Strangely silent, I drove home. After fixing John some chicken noodle soup for lunch, I fed the kids peanut butter sandwiches. My lunch consisted of two cookies and a glass of milk.

Once the boys were off to their own pursuits, I stood staring at the spotted kitchen walls.

"How will I ever get these walls clean again?" I moaned in horror as I chipped away at the cement-like structure of each pancake batter globule scattered up and down the peach walls.

The urge to cry overwhelmed me. Instead, I hurried to the basement, located the putty knife, and began scraping in earnest. Soon the kitchen looked like the remains of a bomb site. For some reason the paint adhered to the plaster, which fell out in large chunks.

"Martha!" John's voice broke through the sounds of scraping.

"What?" I yelled back.

Silence from our bedroom.

"What, John?" I screeched a little louder while continuing to dig at the wall above the kitchen sink.

Still no word from darling husband.

"Maybe he's had a heart attack!" Suddenly I was anxiously alert. Dropping my scraper and jumping over the piles of accumulating plaster, I hurried to our bedroom.

"John!" Breathlessly, I flew through the door. "Are you—?"

John, propped up in bed reading the newspaper, grinned. "Oh, hi, honey. I was wondering if you'd made any of your special Sunday morning coffee cake. I'm feeling hungry." He laid the paper down and gazed expectantly in my direction.

Putting my hands on my hips, I glared silently at John. Fearing what I might say, I clamped my mouth shut. Once I'd gained control over my outrage at being asked to wait on him after the morning's misery, I spoke to him in dulcet tones. "No, dear," I said, spreading my lips over my teeth to resemble a grin.

"What are you doing?" He seemed curious.

"Reconstructing the kitchen," I replied simply.

"Well," his brows scrunched together, "how long should that take?"

"Considering the fact that I'm going to have to hire someone to replaster the walls, and then you will need to repaint the entire kitchen, it could take me a couple more hours."

Suddenly his face went dark. He no longer looked like my beloved John. He reminded me of a mad thing from one of my childhood nightmares. "Martha," he spoke slowly and distinctly, "what have *you* done?"

The *you* finished me. "What have *I* done?" Tears sprang to my eyes and blurred my vision of my now ugly knight in shining armor. Furious blinking, accompanied by rubbing my dusty fingers in my eyes, I cleared my sight enough to see that his hair (what was left of it now that he was beginning to bald) was standing straight up, and he needed a shave. I took a deep breath. "*You* did it John! You are the one who wanted to leave mere babes to cook for themselves!"

Storming from the room, I ran to the kitchen to put on a pot of coffee. John did not follow after me as I hoped he would.

"Well, I'm just not going to say anything else about this," I pouted. "That is the godly way—*silence.*" I bent my efforts to the task at hand and finished destroying the walls in just over an hour. I could not see me as John saw me. Self-pity, spawned from fear, controlled my mind.

Finally, curiosity took over, and I tiptoed back to see snoozing John. "Oh, I do love him so," I whispered softly from the doorway of our bedroom. In sleep his face resembled that of an angel (Michael, the archangel, I think). His snoring comforted me.

Feeling sorry about everything I'd said, I hurried to the kitchen and started peeling apples for his favorite coffee cake. My spirits lifted at the thought of his joy when I surprised him with this tender, tasty treat.

I was just dumping cinnamon into the mixing bowl when the telephone rang. "Mrs. Christian?"

"Yes?" I slurped out as I licked the tasty batter-coated spoon.

"We need your services at the hospital." The male voice was so deep and authoritative, it sounded like God calling.

"My services?" Instantly, I perked up at the thought of being needed.

"Yes," the well-modulated, articulate voice continued. "We require another Smock Lady, and your name was given to us as a potential volunteer."

"Oh, my!" I patted my hair into place. "I'm honored!" Beaming, I poured the cake batter into the floured pan. "When do we begin?" Needles of excitement prickled the skin on my forearms.

"Would tomorrow be too soon?" The deep baritone words were music to my soul.

Balancing the telephone receiver between my left ear and shoulder, I managed to pop the cake into the oven without frying the phone. "Tomorrow would be wonderful! What time?"

I didn't hear his reply. Much to my chagrin, the receiver flew off my shoulder and into the bubbly dishwater in the sink. I stared in dismay momentarily before my lightning-quick mind shouted, *He's drowning!* Diving into the hot suds, I said to the foaming mouthpiece, "Hello?"

Without a break of timing, he responded, "Hello! Yes, I'm just wondering if eight o'clock tomorrow morning would be suitable for you to come in? I know you must have a busy schedule." His voice, full of courtesy and respect, comforted me.

Without a thought of John, I enthusiastically promised to meet the alluring-sounding hospital administrator, Drundel Jenkins, at our small community medical facility the next morning. "I'll see you at eight on the dot in the coffee shop!"

Having finished in the kitchen, I took my cold cup of coffee and headed for the living room. "I think I'll look up that Bible passage the pastor was talking about this morning." I settled myself comfortably on the sofa. "Ah, here it is! Ephesians, chapter six." I read in silence for a moment. "He must have said this wrong!" I exclaimed. "Why, this says *children* are supposed to obey their parents and honor their fathers and mothers."[5]

I sat with my finger poised on the side of my nose. "No, he wouldn't have made that mistake. Probably I heard it wrong."

Then panic pelted me. "Oh, no," I whispered. "Maybe I am having *dreams* again after all."

Slowly I rose from the couch, put away the Bible and wandered out to the kitchen. "I need something to do. I won't give in to vague imaginings."

By the time I sniffed the aroma of John's freshly baked coffee cake, I knew that Drundel Jenkins was a gift from God. "A Smock Lady. Imagine me working in a hospital." I grinned. "Exactly what I need."

Softly padding my way back to our bedroom, my spouse's snores informed me of his success at napping. I relaxed. "As long as he can sleep like that, he is mending." Gently I closed the door as I left the room. "Everything will be just fine," I whispered.

Suddenly I remembered the children. "Better call them in from wherever they are," I reminded myself as I hunted for John's physical education class whistle.

My search led me to the basement. "Here it is. Conveniently located next to the screwdriver!" My sarcasm pleased me since I had succeeded in forgetting how much I loved my dearest one in all the world—my husband.

Standing out in the backyard, I blew on the silver instrument with all my might. The sound reverberated off the face of the Chief. "That should get them wherever they are." I spoke to myself with satisfaction.

No response.

"Where are those kids?" Irritation began to rise as I scanned the horizon and saw nothing except seagulls.

"Looking for somebody?" My new neighbor lady poked her head above her fence and peered in my direction.

"Just for my boys," I answered honestly. Guilt for never calling upon her with cookies swept over me. "How's everything?" I inquired, but I didn't really care.

Her head disappeared before she could answer. "Maybe she doesn't want to be friendly, either," I mused.

Waiting no longer, I blew three sharp blasts. The shrill notes set the neighborhood dogs to barking, and I thought I heard a fire siren from downtown.

Still no boys. "That's it!" I announced to myself, stuffing the whistle into my pocket. "I'm going to locate those children and teach them about obedience just like the pastor said!"

An hour later I had corralled John Jr., Joe, and George from their various points of interest (girls, lizards, and dirt) and sat them down on the living room floor in front of me. Trying to soften the upcoming blow, I offered ice cream and cookies first. "So, guys," I trilled, "since the Bible says you are to obey your mothers and fathers—"

"Mother and father, singular," corrected Joe.

"Joe, hush up!" I shouted.

"You're shouting, Mom," John Jr. chimed in.

Glaring at my oldest, I continued. "I feel it is my duty to instill in you this bit of knowledge so that this family can live in peace and harmony." I concluded my opening statement with a broad grin.

"Why isn't Daddy here?" George whined, looking upset.

"Daddy is taking a much-deserved nap because he is ill," I responded, smoothing his ruffled hair.

"So what does sick Dad think of this new deal?" Joe's smart-aleck attitude infuriated me.

"Listen, Joe!" I screamed, "I thought I told you to—"

"Uh-uh!" John Jr. shook a warning pointer finger in my direction.

"Joe"—I lowered my scream to a shout—"the Bible says to obey your *parents*, and since I am also a *parent*, you will obey me right now!" I stomped over to the rocking chair and sat rocking back and forth at a furious rate.

John Jr., wiser than the rest, having dealt with me over a period of sixteen years, stared at the floor, looking worried.

"Besides," I said, softening my voice to pure charm, "I have to begin working tomorrow—at the hospital. I will need your cooperation." I stopped rocking and gazed expectantly at my sons, hoping for approval.

"Working? *You*? Honest?" George's blue eyes reflected real respect.

"Yes, George dear." I showered a smile upon him. "I am going to be a Smock Lady!" I knew he would come through in a pinch.

"Our Lady of the Smock!" Joe roared with laughter and

tipped over backwards, rolling around on the carpet like a chimpanzee.

I glared at him like he was one of those slithery things he loved to play with that sunned themselves upon rocks.

"John, speak to your brother, please." I directed my eyebrows in Joe's direction.

J.J. reached over and grabbed Joe by the arm. "Hey, Joe! Do you want to hear my new record?" he began patting his younger brother on the back.

"What new record?" Joe eyed J.J. suspiciously.

"Come and see for yourself!" Looking distraught, he maneuvered Joe out of the room.

"Well, George," I smiled charmingly at my youngest, "what do you think?"

"You'll be terrific, Mom!" His eyes glowed with excitement.

"You will obey quickly and quietly, won't you, George?" I handed him a large double-fudge cookie loaded with frosting.

"Sure, Mom!" He responded with glee and grabbed three more cookies from the plate on the coffee table.

"That's a good boy. Now, I'm going to wake Daddy and see how he's feeling. Would you like to watch television awhile?" My dulcet tones charmed me most of all.

"Wow, Mom! Sure! How come you're letting me watch TV on Sunday? Usually you yell—"

"Nonsense, George," I corrected. "You must have been having one of your dreams again!" I chucked him playfully under the chin.

As I headed down the hall toward our bedroom to wake John, I heard him singing in the bathroom. "Feeling better, dear?" I placed my nose against the door and shouted above the noise of the shower.

"Terrific!" he yelled back happily. "How are *you* feeling?"

Instantly I knew what he meant—my little attack of temper earlier. "Fine now," I replied, opening the door a crack. "Sorry I got upset." I started to poke my head inside.

"Shut the door. It's cold in here!" It seemed to me a selfish remark, totally uncaring.

I slammed it shut. Standing back, I roared, "By the way, I'm going to work tomorrow!"

"Tell me later," he hollered back. "I can't hear you over the shower!"

I left him to finish his shower—undisturbed.

3 / Hospital

"As they observe your chaste and respectful behavior."[6]

My new Purple Cross nurse's shoes squeaked as I raced down the hospital corridor. The smell of alcohol and disinfectant assured me that this was the right place to achieve my mission of mercy.

"Where is the supply room?" Tension tightened my already worried expression to one of panic.

"Lose somethin'?" The lazy drawl of an orderly startled me. I whirled around. "Where did *you* come from?"

His pale blue eyes, framed by red lids, twinkled. "I'll bet yer lookin' for the supply room," he continued.

"Well, er, yes, I am." Quickly I regained my composure as I straightened myself as tall as possible. "Would you happen to know where it is?"

A sardonic grin revealed one missing front tooth. "Yer standin' next to it!" Guffawing, he departed down the hall.

"Where did *he* come from?" I asked myself as I pushed my way through the door into the pitch black of the supply room. Irritation jabbed at me.

You couldn't even find the supply room, my ever-busy mind accused.

Standing there in the dark, I reviewed my morning's activities. . . .

"You'll be a terrific asset to our little staff." The voice of Drun-

33

del Jenkins, the hospital administrator, sent chills of being necessary down my spine.

I stirred my black coffee vigorously. "Are you always so courteous at eight o'clock in the morning?"

"You've spilled your coffee," he noted. "Here. Let me help."

Awestruck, I sat transfixed in my chair as Mr. Jenkins patted the amber pool of liquid dry and then carefully placed a clean, white napkin between the coffee cup and the saucer.

"Why, thank you, Mr. Jenkins," I said sincerely.

"Call me Drundel," he responded evenly, patting my hand.

Momentarily I allowed myself to stare into the face of the handsome executive. His heavenly-blue eyes bored into my being. "Would you please pass me the sugar?" Shyly I dropped my gaze.

"You're too sweet to need sugar," he suggested boldly.

"Oh, my," I replied, spilling sugar into the now cold beverage.

He took command of the situation. "As soon as you've finished, I'll show you around."

"Oh, yes, by all means. Show me the hospital!" Excitement grabbed my heart.

First he introduced me to Mrs. Lill, the head nurse.

"This is our new Smock Lady, Lill. Give her your best attention—for *me*." He winked, then vanished into his office.

After showing me around at warp speed, Mrs. Lill gave me my first assignment. "Would you please get a flower vase for room 202?"

"Oh! Yes!" I ran down the hall in search of the supply room. . . .

"Now where would they hide a light switch?" Blinded by the blackness, I groped around the walls. "Terrific!" Nervousness threatened to overpower me, but valiantly I fought it. As I stood feeling the outline of something cold, the door behind me whipped open, flooding the small room with light from the hallway.

"Hi!" Simultaneously I saw the light flick on and heard the high-pitched voice of a young woman.

"Oh!" I screamed.

"Are you looking for a bedpan?" The white uniform housed a tiny girl, certainly not old enough to be employed.

"A bedpan?" My surprise heightened my guilt about not being able to find the supply room.

"You're holding one." She smiled patiently. "I thought you wanted a bedpan because you're holding one." She looked puzzled.

"Oh, yes!" I lied. "For one of the patients." I set my face to appear competent.

"Good!" She grinned from ear to ear. "Most Smock Ladies won't even *touch* a bedpan. You must be something special!" Her admiration at my pretense stabbed my soul.

"Are you a nurse?" Suddenly I felt sick.

"No"—she leaned back against the wall and relaxed—"just a nurse's aid. Usually *I* have to take care of the bedpan."

"Sherry!" Suddenly Mrs. Lill's voice sounded just outside the door.

"Coming!" The little one I was leading astray bolted from the room.

"Mrs. Christian?" The head nurse peered through the open doorway.

Penitent, I jolted to attention ,waiting for Mrs. Lill to discover my lie. "Yes!"

"The vases are in the far corner to your left, dear." She seemed unconcerned. "I'll meet you in room 202." Her tone was more tender than when she spoke to Sherry. I wondered why.

"Yes, of course," I replied, scurrying to find a flower container.

Self-reproach burned within me as I examined the plastic vases. "What size?" I wondered. Sweat beaded along my hairline as I struggled to decide. Finally I settled for three sizes and ran out of the room.

Once in the hall, I discovered the room numbers began at *ten*. "Oh, no," I moaned. "There is only one floor of this little hospital, and I'm certain Mrs. Lill mentioned less than fifteen rooms. Now where can the two hundred series be?"

Weariness descended, weighing my shoulders down in defeat. "It's not even lunchtime yet, and I'm exhausted." I stood alone in the hall, holding three flower vases and feeling stupid. "How can I be so dull-witted?" I asked myself. I recalled feeling like that as a child—the time I was lost in a huge department store. I had wandered around, crying until someone found me and restored me to my frantic mother . . .

"Mrs. Christian?" A strong arm encircled my waist. I caught the scent of an expensive aftershave or cologne.

"Oh! Mr. Jenkins!" I cried out in surprise. "Does everyone around here sneak up on everyone else?" In my anxiety I spoke rapidly, giving little thought to what I was saying.

"Has someone frightened you?" The resonant voice comforted while two arms wrapped around me.

"Mr. Jenkins!" I squeaked and wriggled away.

Smiling, he replied, "Call me Drundel."

"I think I need to call home," I responded. "John Jr. is sick. I should check on him." I heard myself lying for the second time in less than an hour. *At this rate I should have a dream attack any day*, I thought, chagrined.

You've forgotten everything you ever learned. My disgusting brain always came through in my hour of need.

"Of course, Martha!" Suddenly Drundel's voice boomed into my consciousness. "You can use my office!"

I looked blankly in his direction. "What?"

"To call your son." Mr. Congeniality waited expectantly for my answer.

"Yes. Thank you," I mumbled, rearranging the vases in my arms and dropping one on the floor. "I will call him later and check on him." Regaining my composure, I continued, "I promised Mrs. Lill I'd get these vases to her right away. So I should find room 202 now, if you can just tell me where it is." I smoothed my voice to condition-calm.

Drundel bent over and gallantly replaced the flower container in my arms. "Martha," the sympathetic tone threw me. "May I call you Martha?"

"Yes, of course, Durndel, I mean Drundel." I flushed in embarrassment.

"Martha"—the voice oiled away my inner pain—"everyone finds it rough the first day. Don't give up!"

I stood pinned to the spot—the embodiment of guilt, failure, remorse, and curiosity.

"Now," he continued, assuming a businesslike air, "room 202 is at the end of the hall." He put a hand on each of my shoulders and pointed me in the right direction.

"Thanks," I responded numbly, heading toward the elusive room.

"See you at lunch, Martha," he boomed as he clicked his heels and departed.

My spirit whirlpooled downward as I raced toward room 202. "How could that have happened?" I asked myself. "I love John. I'm happily married. Am I giving the wrong impression?"

Then I heard a voice at the back of my brain whispering almost audibly, *Has God said you cannot feel good? What's wrong with a little happiness?*[7]

If I had recognized the voice of temptation, I wouldn't have answered, "No. God never said I can't feel happy, but I think there's a verse in the Bible that says something about having only one person to love as my husband and care for."

Where is that? I heard a faint hissing sound.

"What?" I stood looking at the white starched form of Mrs. Lill.

"I said that I've been waiting for you!" The head nurse's full-bodied voice blasted my brain. "Did you find a vase?"

"Oh, yes!" I held up my three flower containers for her approval.

For the first time that day she seemed disappointed in my performance.

"I wanted you to have a choice," I explained clumsily. (Lie number three—an unholy trinity.)

Just after I'd arranged some flowers and emptied a few bedpans for Sherry, I sat down on a patient's bed to rest.

"Mrs. Christian, there's a telephone call for you." Sherry beamed. "And thanks again for all your help."

"Think nothing of it," I responded wearily, following her.

Putting the cold receiver to my ear, I heard, "Martha?"

"John!" I exclaimed in horror. "What are you doing phoning me at work?"

John probably interpreted the tenseness in my voice as caustic rudeness.

"Excuse *me*, Martha." His response stung.

"John—" I groped for words to explain the pressure I felt. "I . . ."

His silence chilled my soul.

"Oh, there you are, Martha!" Like the roar of a friendly lion, Drundel's approaching presence filled me with dread. "Let's go for lunch!" His resonant baritone voice bounced off the walls, soared into the telephone receiver, and landed in John's left ear.

"I'll let you go, Martha," John replied in snappy staccato.

"Fine," I lied, gritting my teeth in rebellion. "Are you ready for lunch, *Drundel?*" I smiled as I spoke.

"Yes, indeed!" He grinned happily and held his arm out to me. "My privilege!"

I took hold of his arm without showing a trace of the sinfulness I felt.

Lunch was a lie. Outwardly charming, I churned inside over my unhappy conversation with John. Then I ate a calorie-laden dessert.

"My, young lady, what an appetite you have for such a little person!" His eyes glowed. "I like to see a pretty woman eat what she likes. I'm glad to see you don't diet like so many females I meet." He reached across the table and tried to pat my hand as it carried a spoonful of whipped cream to my mouth.

I said nothing. The sweet taste turned sour on my tongue. Shamed, I remembered the chicken pot pie loaded with gravy, the heavily buttered dinner rolls, and the potato pancakes I'd just stuffed in.

The hospital administrator seemed oblivious to my turmoil. Gallant in every way, he swooped down to pick up my check and guided me toward the door.

"You really mustn't, Drundel," I objected lamely.

"Nonsense, Martha, my dear! It's my pleasure." He paid the bill and escorted me from the coffee shop.

The rest of the afternoon I ran from room to room emptying bedpans, delivering flowers, watering plants, fluffing pillows, dusting dirty windowsills, carrying books and magazines to various patients, and I even began teaching an elderly lady to knit. She had arthritis in both hands.

"Whew!" I mopped my perspiring brow. "I'm beginning to think being a Smock Lady is a little like being the low person on a totem pole." I groaned as I sat down in a corner in the supply room.

Racing ahead of John by accepting the position at the hospital—without a thought for his opinion—seemed to be plunging me into hot water.

"I'm leaving now, Drundel." I spoke wearily as I stood in the doorway of his office.

"Good! Fine! See you Wednesday then!" He flashed me a gregarious grin, and I was dismissed.

From the hospital parking lot, I ran to the car and squeezed grocery shopping, banking, and a trip to the post office into the time I usually spent combing my hair.

Arriving home disheveled and worn, I heard George call out, "Mom?"

Instantly alert, I dropped the groceries in the kitchen and raced to his room.

"Hi, Mom," George said shakily. He lay flat in his bed looking whiter than the most sun-bleached sheets in town.

"George! What's wrong? Are you all right?" I flew to the side of his bed and sat down next to him. Placing my right wrist against his forehead, I could tell he was burning up with fever.

"I don't feel so good, Mom," he softly replied. "I've been losing my breakfast all day."

"Oh, sweetheart!" Remorse at not being there when he needed me ripped my heart. "I'll go make you some tea right now. Or would you rather have gingerale?"

His wan face lit up a little. "Can I have cookies too?"

Tenderly I kissed his crimson cheek. "How about some crackers instead, just until your tummy settles down."

He nodded affirmatively. "I feel hot!"

"Well," I smiled knowingly, "a Popsicle should help that!"

"Yeah!" Then he gazed at me with a seriousness that belied his age. "Mom?"

"Yes?"

"Does *working* mean you won't be here when I'm sick anymore?"

Deeply struck in my soul, I covered with a light remark. "Nonsense, my dear. This is just an unfortunate incident!"

By the time John returned home from teaching school around 5:00 p.m., we had encountered another problem.

"He's gone! Oh, Mom, he's lost!" Joe watered the floor with his tears.

"Who is gone, Joe?" Wrapping my arms around him, I hugged him tightly.

He pulled back quickly, glared at me, and retorted, "Hampst the Second, my hamster! That's who."

Feeling his pain, I replied softly, "Honey, I'm so sorry."

"If you'd been here, he wouldn't be missing!" His fury almost toppled me.

"Let's look for him right now, okay?" I remembered to be gentle.[8]

I found John in the kitchen. "John, can you help us look for Joe's hamster?"

Flashing me a look of irritation, he answered, "Martha, I am busy rebuilding the kitchen as a result of your cleaning project. Can't you find one small rodent?"

By dinnertime frustration enveloped me. As I tried to cook food in the midst of paint fumes, sobbing and sick children, and one unsupportive husband, rebellion rose within.

Slamming pots and pans, I muttered, "All I am to anybody is a *slave!*" Simultaneously, I prepared three dinners—chicken broth and jello, steak and french fries, and tea and toast for me. "At least at the hospital somebody appreciates what I do with my time!"

I failed to speak to God at all that day.

By bedtime I wasn't talking to John either.

Tuesday was another day of sadness. Hampst II did not appear. Visions of him stuck in a heat duct or lying cold somewhere in the dark recesses of the basement left me miserable.

Joe trudged off to school too quiet, and when I kissed him goodbye, I felt wetness against my cheek.

Meanwhile, George recovered rapidly. He bounced from

room to room, talking incessantly.

Once I'd corralled him, I sat beside his bed on a straight chair and picked up my knitting. "So, George! How did it happen?"

"How did what happen, Mom?" His blue eyes twinkled.

Gazing at my son who was surrounded by cookies, comic books, and cracker crumbs, I smiled. "Your stomach, remember?" I busied myself with the clickety-clack of the knitting needles.

"Oh, that!" He grinned enthusiastically. "All of a sudden (his eyes grew wider with each word) I lost my breakfast at school! Then I called Daddy at *his* school because I didn't know where you were. Then Daddy fixed it so somebody came and got me and drove me home. Daddy said to go home and go to bed. So I did!" He chomped a cracker with a mighty crunch.

"Did anybody *see* your breakfast?" I tried to ask in an offhand manner.

"Don't be silly, Mom!" George settled himself more comfortably against his pillows. "Who would want to see my a-b-c breakfast?"

"A-b-c?" I put my knitting in my lap and waited for an explanation.

"Already-been-chewed!" His laughter salved my guilty conscience a little.

"Okay, champ." I leaned over and ruffled his hair. "I think you're well enough to go back to school tomorrow."

"Aw, Mom, I was just starting to enjoy being sick."

At supper George pigged out on chicken.

"You're looking better, son," remarked John, helping himself to more potatoes and gravy.

"I feel better, too!" George spoke around the drumstick he'd stuffed into his mouth.

Meanwhile, Joe said nothing.

"Any word from your hamster?" John tried to cheer Joe by kidding him.

"Can I go to my room, Mom?" Joe choked out the words, shoved back his chair, and fled to the safety of loneliness.

Not knowing what else to say, I addressed John Jr. "How's school?" I queried brightly.

Turning his sea blue eyes in my direction, he replied, "What's ever good about disgusting school?"

"Oh." I responded.

The rest of dinner was silent.

Wednesday morning I returned to my job at the hospital.

"Martha!" Drundel's welcome soothed my sore spirit as he clasped both my hands in his. "Good morning!" He led me toward his office.

Tears filled my eyes and my feet glued themselves to the floor. "I'm not feeling well, Drundel," I lied. "I think it must be what George had."

"George? You mean *John*, of course." He wrapped an arm around my shoulders. "Say, that's too bad, Martha."

Red tinged my face as he corrected my slip about George and John. *On Monday you told him John Jr. was sick, and he wasn't!* My brain mocked.

Guiding me back toward the main hall, he suggested, "You just take it easy today. That is, if you think you're strong enough to last the day." He paused to give me time to think about it. "Are you?"

Caught off guard, I responded numbly, "I can make it." I dragged myself toward the locker room to locate my smock.

My first duty was to be sandwich lady. It gave me a chance to put my life into perspective. Lining up the entire loaf of bread on the counter, piece by piece, cleansed my thinking processes. Then I piled luscious fillings on each piece. "I can make thirty sandwiches in one shot," I thought gleefully.

"What am I doing here?" I asked myself. "And what am I doing with my life? Maybe I should stay at home." I chopped lettuce into fine shreds and decorated each half-made sandwich.

My thinking wandered about, concluding nothing while I wrapped each filled and topped sandwich half.

"Do they really miss me at home? What's wrong with wanting to find out who *I* am?"

Then I discovered I'd made two-toned creations—white bread on the bottom, whole wheat on the top. I didn't care. "No one appreciates me anyway," I sulked, piling the finished product on trays and stuffing them into the giant refrigerator.

I did, however, realize that a union of self-assertion and self-pity gives birth to trouble. I would have to speak to Drundel about quitting my job at the hospital until I had time to work it out. "I need a vacation. That's what I need!"

I sped out of the kitchen and searched for Mr. Jenkins.

Does the enemy of our souls ever aid us in doing right?

I couldn't find Mr. Jenkins.

"He's downstairs checking some laundry equipment, Martha," Mrs. Lill informed me. "By the way, could you take this blanket down there with you?" She was polite but abrupt and commanding.

Taking the hospital bedcovering from her, I bit my lip. *How many Smock Ladies do they go through in a month around here?* I wondered.

"Certainly, Mrs. Lill," I responded with sickening courtesy.

"Don't get lost now, the way you usually do!" She smirked. "And, bring a clean cover for room eighteen—not eighty-one!" Laughing loudly at her own humor, she tripped off to the nurse's station.

Gathering the bulky blanket in my arms, I headed straight for the exit sign. I can't explain how it happened. I only recall my terror as I tumbled down the stairs, screaming all the way.

"Martha!" Instantly Drundel Jenkins stood beside me. "What happened?"

"I fell," I replied simply.

"Are you hurt?" He began hauling me to my feet.

"Ow!" I screeched.

"Here, let me help you!" Drundel tried to pick me up, but fell sideways.

"No!" I yelled. "It's my ankle! I must have broken my leg!"

"Be calm, Martha. Hysterics never help." He grabbed my right arm, threw it over his shoulders and stood up.

Pain shot through my entire right side. "Let me go!"

He did.

From my vantage point on the basement floor I spoke softly. "Would you give me your arm?"

He held out both hands. "I heard the noise—"

Interrupting him, I shot back, "You heard the sounds of bone and flesh colliding with cement."

As Drundel dragged me up the stairs, he remarked, "What can be better than to fracture a leg right near X-ray!"

Clenching my teeth in agony, I endured.

John rushed to the hospital in response to a nurse's call.

Meanwhile, I waited in a wheelchair at the front entrance. "What did the doctor tell you?" I inquired as my husband helped me out of the chair.

"You have some bone chips floating free, and a break in the ankle. You'll be using crutches along with the current cast until you're ready for a walking cast." His matter-of-fact assessment complemented his comfortable care. John opened the car door, lifted me into the passenger side, and shoved my crutches into the back seat.

"How long?" Fear gnawed at my nerves.

"As long as it takes, I guess. He didn't say." My lifetime friend started the car and steered out of the parking lot.

As long as it takes! My brain repeated. *You're in for it now.*

"Thank you for coming to pick me up," I said quietly.

"Anytime." John reached over and squeezed my hand.

Watching him at the wheel, I admired his skill in handling the car. I respected him. "I love you, John."

"I love you, too."

I knew he meant it, and I resolved to be a better wife.

Peace?

4 / Buddy

"Because He is your Lord, bow down to Him."[9]

"Crutches and housework don't mix!" I leaned on the kitchen counter and let frustration reign. For four days I'd hobbled around the house, hauling my right leg, which I could no longer see since it disappeared into its white prison.

Tossing the dishcloth into the sink, I hippity-hopped toward the living room sofa. "I can't do what I did before. Nobody seems to realize that."

My self-pity felt good. "I'd like to cry, but it would probably give me a headache," I muttered as I pulled myself painfully along on my crutches.

Placing my ill-fated crutch tip on an uneven place on the floor, I slipped sideways. "Oh, the pain," I moaned, recovering my balance. Then I noticed a pile of double-fudge cookie remains before me. "Even the crumbs are waiting to get me," I grumbled suspiciously. "I must speak to George about carrying food all over the house."

Finally I flopped on the couch. A throbbing pain tortured my right armpit. I hadn't been able to master the art of using my crutches properly. Instead of putting the weight on my hands, I leaned heavily on the tops. "At this rate my shoulders will be even with the top of my head." Lifting my cast-covered leg with my hands, I plopped it atop the coffee table, leaned my head back, and closed my eyes.

I recalled my early morning conversation with John. "John! Look at this!" I pointed to the purple bruise under my right shoulder.

John, who was busy shaving, barely blinked an eyelid. "Look at what?" Skillfully he cut a swath through the white foam on his face, exposing rose-hued skin.

"This!" I leaned myself against the bathroom sink and showed him my shoulder.

"Nice!" He spoke admiringly.

"I'm talking about the *contusion* from my crutches." My impatience with his insensitivity showed.

"What's a contusion?" John riveted his eyes to the mirror and resumed scraping away at his neck.

"It's hospital talk. It means a black-and-blue mark." I adjusted my crutches for better balance.

"Martha! Ow!" He jumped and dropped his razor in the sink. "What are you trying to do, destroy me?"

When I saw blood oozing from his neck, I stood dumbstruck. *You made him slice his neck,* my helpful brain accused.

"Martha," John remonstrated, taking a deep breath and enunciating each word carefully, "your left crutch is stationed on my foot!"

"You're bleeding, John!" Quickly I grabbed a facial tissue and began daubing at the red river running down his neck.

"Please don't help." He grabbed the tissue and pressed it hard against the nick in his neck.

"You just don't care what happens to me, John." I stood firmly on my familiar tripod of one foot and two crutches. Sensing an argument in the making, I leaned heavily on my wooden supports for balance.

"Martha, you're still on my foot. Can't you feel it when you're off-balance?" His voice seemed a trifle louder than usual.

"I'm sorry," I replied simply. "These crutches don't have much feeling, you know."

Suddenly his countenance changed. "Martha, how long are you going to carry this on?" He washed his hands and tossed the disposable razor in the trash.

"You look ridiculous, John," I pointed to the tissue stuck to his neck. "Why don't you just use a little piece instead of a whole sheet?" I laughed a bit to demonstrate my amiability.

John, however, saw no humor in the matter. "*What* are we having for breakfast?" he retorted. "And *when* do you think it will be ready?" The remark hurt, but the look in his eyes and the tone of his voice devastated me.

Whirling around on my crutches, I hobbled as fast as I could toward the kitchen and started pulling boxes of cereal off the shelves.

He just wants to use you. My mind was right on schedule with its ill-advised comment.

"That's right," I agreed while propping myself against the kitchen counter to pour milk into the pitcher. "If he did care about me, he wouldn't get mad over a little thing like accidentally standing on his foot."

He didn't even want to see the abrasion on your armpit, my ever-busy brain continued.

"Yeah, I'd like to see how fast *he* could go to work on crutches!" I chimed right in, unaware of the subtle influence of my thought life.

He's abusing you, concluded my cranial matter.

"Abuse?" Pondering that, I decided that an insult was abuse.

Breakfast, a silent affair, mercifully ended. The family troops stormed from the house, and I was left alone. Almost alone. Self-pity, martyrdom, and selfishness crouched close by, waiting for a chance to catch me and my mind in the snare of my old nature—*self.*

"Now I'm sitting on the sofa, and they've all gone to school, and nobody cares about me." I'd raised my head from the sofa back, opened my eyes, and spied my imprisoned leg afresh.

I paused and allowed the quiet of the house to overtake me. "My skin won't be able to breathe in there," I mentioned to the silent room.

Remembering the doctor telling me to prop my leg up, I groaned, "I think it should be higher than my heart." Carefully I hoisted the dreadful burden up and over until it rested upon the arm of the couch. This forced me into a reclining position.

The clock ticked.

The furnace came on.

"I'm a vegetable," I complained.

I noticed the ceiling had a hand print on it. "Looks like Joe's," I observed.

Finally I could stand it no longer. Struggling with the heavy cast which had gobbled up my leg, I managed to position the hateful thing on the coffee table. By the time I'd shoved a pillow underneath my heel, sweat poured down my back from the exertion.

Then the cushion slipped. The cast slid off and sent new shocks of pain to the lame leg housed within. "Terrific!" I exclaimed sarcastically, "the table is scratched." Shoving the soft support back underneath my leg, I tried to relax.

The silence of the house swept over me. It should have meant peace—that state of freedom from war, but to me the quiet meant misery.

In my mind's eye I could see John and the children walking, jumping, running! I saw me withering away with atrophied muscles.

"This is terrible," I complained. The statement flowed out of my ungrateful heart, rolled from my tongue, and wafted through the house until every room picked up the negative atmosphere.

It didn't occur to me to be thankful for my life as it was, "for this is God's will for you who belong to Christ Jesus."[10] Furthermore, it didn't dawn upon me that perhaps I'd had anything to do with my predicament.

I sat on the sofa, sulking about the hardship of my existence. A distant clock tick-tocked. The refrigerator whirred. Otherwise, silence.

"You could read your Bible," a tiny voice somewhere inside suggested.

"Forget it!" I articulated aloud. "I've seen enough since I saw the part about Sarah bowing and scraping to Abraham."

Quiet. Tick tock. Whir.

Boredom set in. My leg felt like knives were stabbing at me, my toes throbbed, and my insides churned.

I began to tap my fingernails upon the padded armrest of the couch. "It seems to me that Socrates said, 'The life which is unexamined is not worth living.' "

Silence. Whir whir. Tock tick.

After I examined my existence briefly, I decided that I needed comfort, someone to lighten my burden. "The Bible is big on sharing burdens.[11] I'll phone Jean!"

My spirits lifted at the thought of feeling better. I had a goal—solace, and a target—the telephone.

"Careful! Careful now," I admonished myself. Painfully, I edged forward on the sofa and seized my wooden support system.

Hope lightened my burden as I swung myself into "moving" position. "Jean knows me better than anyone else I know. She'll understand. A friend is an important asset."

"Swing-drag! Swing-drag!" I cheered myself along as I pulled myself toward the telephone in the kitchen. By the time I'd arrived, exhaustion set in.

Propping myself against the kitchen counter, I dialed Jean's number.

"Busy!" I shrieked. "Why, why, *why* can't I have a long telephone cord like other women?" Seething inside, I recalled John's answer to me when I'd requested a twenty-five-footer.

"No."

"How about a cordless telephone so I can go anywhere in the house, even outside in the garden?"

Veto.

"Hmm," I grumbled. "If I were to let John have his way around here, I'd probably be sending smoke signals to my friends and chewing his shoes into softness!"

Dialing again, I gave up when the irritating noise blasted my eardrum.

"Jean doesn't care either," I pronounced, slamming down the receiver. "If she did, she would have called me to find out how I'm doing."

Self-inflicted misery knows no bounds. "I'll just lurch my way to the kitchen sink and do the breakfast dishes alone. *Somebody* has to do them." Stuffing my hands into hot, sudsy water, I remarked, "I have noticed that Jean doesn't care about me lately. She's getting very selfish." By the time I'd finished scrubbing the soft-boiled egg pot, I couldn't stand my own company. That didn't dissuade my negativity either.

My self-pity was surpassed only by my martyr complex. I decided to clean the oven.

While squirting the foul-smelling chemicals, I thought about old Hampst the Second. "I did love the little fella. Joe had no reason to get mad at *me* over his pet's disappearance."

I crawled along the floor to reach a rag for wiping the oven clean. "On the other hand," I observed, "losing Hampst must have been a great shock to him. He needs another pet to love."

I decided cleaning the stove would be impossible in my condition. "Maybe I can talk John Jr. into finishing it for me."

Creeping along the kitchen floor to the dining room rug, I pulled the telephone cord until the receiver dropped into my lap.

"Information, please," I said politely.

"You can dial it yourself, ma'am," replied a rude voice.

I dialed information. "Hello. I would like the name of a pet store—"

"Don't you have a telephone directory, madam?" The operator interrupted.

"What?"

"I'll have to charge you if you require a number for a local call. If, however, you would like to contact the long distance operator—"

I cut the connection.

A few minutes later I sat in a kitchen chair with my leg propped on a stool, a cup of steaming coffee at my elbow, and the telephone directory in my hands. I flipped the pages ferociously.

"Hmm," I said to myself. "Here's a good one—the Mice Is Nice Nook." Quickly I twirled the telephone dial.

"Hi!" I gave a friendly greeting to inform the storeperson of my sincerity. "What have you got to replace a hamster for a fourteen-year-old?" Ignoring the pain of my lame leg, I spoke brightly.

"We don't carry fourteen-year-old hamsters," replied a decrepit male voice. "Most of them die by age two."

"What?" I inquired, nervously twiddling the telephone cord.

"What?" echoed the ancient, croaking voice.

"Let's begin from the beginning," I suggested. "You see, I'm looking for a fourteen-year-old boy, and *he* wants a cinnamon-bear hamster. Preferably a baby." Perspiration popped out along my hairline.

"Cinnamon-what?"

"Hamster."

"Listen, lady, if this is a joke, I can just call the phone company and—"

"Look!" I raised my voice for emphasis. "Is this the Mice Is Nice Nook or not?"

"Oh!" He gasped for air and wheezed. "You want the Mice Is Nice Nook?"

I waited for him to gather enough energy to continue.

"There isn't one that I know of." He coughed. "What town are you calling from?" Suddenly he seemed sympathetic.

"I am calling from the same city!" Provoked, I decided to display patience. "You see, your telephone number is in my phone book, and that's how I got the idea to telephone you. I'm looking for a hamster to *replace the one that died* not too long ago." I took a breath and held it.

"Died?" He choked and coughed mightily. "Say, that's too bad! How did it die?"

Fearing for his life, I asked, "Have you seen a doctor lately?"

"Bet you fed the little fella popcorn, didn't you? That'll do it every time!" He inhaled noisily.

"Popcorn?" Tingles of guilt attacked my throat.

"I can usually tell," he barked. "Some folks read minds. I recognize popcorn people."

I heard the sound of a match being struck, then the click of plastic against ivory. "Are you lighting a pipe?" I could almost smell the acrid odor and see the smoke obscuring his face.

He gagged and hacked. "Say, that's pretty clever! What did you say your name was?"

"Martha. My name is Martha. I'm trying to get a hamster for my son Joe. To replace the one that is lost, maybe dead." Tears filled my eyes and I couldn't speak for a moment.

"Hello?" His gravelly voice came through.

"I didn't give Hampst popcorn," I confessed in a whisper.

"I know you didn't, lady. Don't take it so hard. Maybe you should blow your nose or something." His concern caused me to snivel some more.

"Can I buy a hamster from you?" I sobbed quietly, sniffing steadily.

"No, lady. We only sell mice. I'm really sorry, though." He gasped. "Why don't you start at the beginning?"

An hour later, after I'd told him of my accident, he filled me in on the details concerning his car wreck. "Finally, after the gangrene set in, they had to cut off my foot!"

Suddenly the pain in my leg seemed minor. "What did you say your name was?" Patiently I waited.

"I didn't." He hacked again. "But I enjoyed talking to you!" He hung up.

Stunned at the strangeness of the conversation, I spoke to myself. "What a caring man! I wonder who he is." Still musing, I began my search for a telephone number once again. "This looks good. The Pet Store." I dialed the number.

"The Pet Store!" intoned a musical female voice.

"Hello," I began, "I'm looking . . . or inquiring about looking for . . ." Sadness swept over me. "Do you sell hamsters?"

"Sorry," she lilted callously. "Would you like anything else?"

"What else do you have?"

"Birds," she replied easily. "We only carry birds."

"Birds?" I questioned.

"Just birds." She warbled in agreement.

"Why is this called the *Pet* Store?" I tried to sound casual.

"Birds are pets," she responded patiently as though speaking to a turtle. "Quite good pets. Ever had a bird in your house for a pet?"

"No, but I've fed a few outside," I answered honestly.

By the time the boys arrived home from school, I'd ordered a blue parakeet for Joe.

"You'll love it, Joe!" Enthusiastically, I encouraged my middle son to love his new feathered friend. "You and Dad can get it as soon as he comes home."

"I hate birds!" Joe yelled.

"Stop shouting!" I screamed back. Once he'd hung his head in gratitude, I began explaining the wonders of the bird world.

"And, so, Joe," I concluded, "a bird in need is a friend indeed!"

Worn out, and missing Hampst, he inquired, "Why can't we get another hamster?"

"Because there aren't any in town." I made the statement and waited for him to see the light.

"Oh." He stared at the floor.

"Joe," I suggested gently, "why not try one? Baby budgies are cute."

"Just out of the egg?" His face brightened.

"I think so," I replied, trying to inspire some interest.

"Do they have big feet?" Curiosity sparkled in his eyes.

"Why not go today with your father and look at them?" I began to arrange myself in an easy chair.

"Here, Mom, allow me to assist you!" Joe, with unaccustomed chivalry, shoved a footstool over and propped my leg on a pillow.

"Thank you, Joe!" I beamed.

"Think nothing of it, Mom," he charmed back. "When do you think dear old Dad will be home?"

"Did I hear my name being called?" John's deep voice floated up the stairs from the front door.

"Dad!" Joe whooped, bounding away toward the front hall. "Yippee! Hey, Dad!" My middle son raced toward his father "Can we go get me a baby parakeet? Right now?"

I heard John's hushed tone and a couple of whispers.

"No, Dad. She won't care!" My son's fourteen-year-old vocal cords couldn't keep pace with his excitement, and high-pitched squeaks intermingled with his emerging baritone. "It's *her* idea!"

While my darling husband hauled his two youngest children off to the pet store, my dear oldest son, John Jr., brought me a cup of tea. We had a nice conversation together, and the last thought in my consciousness before drifting off to sleep was, *I'm going to treat them all better. I have a very special family.*

"Mom! Look at this!" I opened my eyes and stared into a pile of heavenly-blue fluff. It was the tummy of a parakeet.

"Hold him, Mom!" Joe commanded, pushing the bird into my face.

Shifting my gaze from the delicate blue bird to the soft brown eyes of Joe, I marveled at the awesome power of God to create different beings. "It's lovely, Joe."

"See his yellow beak, Mom? And the stripes on his wings?" He danced around in excitement. "We got the best one in the place, didn't we, Dad?"

"Better put him back into the cage," warned John. "You don't want him to fly before he knows the way around the house, do you?" He patted Joe's shoulder affectionately.

"Right, Dad!" Tenderly our child placed the white-faced, royal-blue-tailed parakeet into the new cage.

"Peep," said the baby.

"He talked, Dad!" screamed Joe.

"Not yet he hasn't, but he will," John predicted. "Especially if you spend some time with him each day and teach him."

Sitting there in the easy chair, listening to the two of them communicate, it amazed me how one word from John could carry the weight of thousands of my sentences. Joe never listened to me. John Jr. would when it suited his plans, and sometimes George did, but never Joe. Not to me. Too often I responded to Joe's stubbornness with anger, and it never worked.

"Mom?" Joe's voice broke into my reverie. "Are you in there?"

Smiling, I ignored his question. "What are you going to name him? I think Burgess would be nice," I offered, showing my support.

"I'm going to call him . . ." He paused dramatically. "I think I'll name him Buddy. Because he's gonna be my best friend!"

Lowering my eyes to hide my disappointment at Joe's refusal to consider my suggestion, I busied myself with arranging my cast-encased foot to a more comfortable position. "Buddy," I repeated.

"Buddy it is then," agreed John.

Why does Joe hate me, God? I felt the tears sting my eyes.

John must have realized my pain because he came around to the side of my chair and kissed me on the forehead. "Your face feels hot. How are you doing?" His concern unnerved me.

"I'm okay," I lied.

"It's all going to work out. You'll see," he comforted.

"I know," I fibbed.

"Well, Joe," John addressed his enthusiastic offspring, "where shall we put your best friend?"

"In my room!" Joe yelled excitedly. Grabbing the bird cage, he raced down the hall.

"Wait for me!" George hollered, running after his brother.

"What's going on?" John Jr. shouted from the basement.

"Are you going to be all right?" John asked casually.

"I'm fine," I prevaricated.

"Good." He squeezed my shoulder softly like a person testing bread for freshness in the supermarket. "I'll go help the boys."

Staring after his disappearing back, I thought, *Lord, why do I feel so alone?* Tears filled my eyes, then spilled down my cheeks. The conflict in my soul tore at the center of my being. "I'm going to call Drundel and quit. I can't take this anymore. I feel like an outsider in my own home." Struggling against crying, my throat closed, and I felt fifty pounds of weight on my breathing spaces.

"Where did they go, Mom?" My oldest son's voice rang out from the kitchen.

"To Joe's room," I lifted my voice to sound normal.

"Great!" he yelled back. "See ya!"

Sitting there in my living room, I didn't understand the struggle my soul faced. Neither did I realize that the forces of darkness had trained their best weapons upon me—a searching wife and mother—in order to create chaos in our family. Without knowing it, I could be the razor that cut my family to ribbons. All Satan had to do was *suggest*. I would do the damage. Sowing the wind of my own selfish discontent, I would reap the whirlwind of devastating results.

War.

5 / Drundel

"Then Sarai said to Abram, 'It's all your fault. For now this servant girl of mine despises me, though I myself gave her the privilege of being your wife. May the Lord judge you for doing this to me!' "[10]

Cuddled in my favorite easy chair, I cooed in satisfaction as I admired my brand-new white plaster foot-prison. "This walking cast is shorter and fatter than the other one. *Walking!* No longer struggling with crutches. Now I can get anywhere *independently!*" I turned the cast from side to side. "And, I especially like the blue heel." The bulb-like fixture attached to the bottom for walking attracted my attention.

Remembering my struggle with immobility—tripping over chairs, people, and slippery crumbs—the pain of frustration stabbed me one more time.

"But now it will be a different story!" I gloated as I envisioned my driving the car to town—a little too fast, perhaps—to do the shopping.

"Independence. Freedom from care. That's what I need." My eyebrows drew together as I concentrated. "Doing what I want to do when I want to do it. Yes. That is true freedom."

Somewhere in the depths of my soul a still, quiet voice whispered, "John advised against driving, didn't he?"

Don't be stupid! My mind screamed. *John just wants you to be dependent.*

"However, I can see that John would like my dependency.

Didn't I read something the other day about the male ego?" I reached over and ruffled through a stack of magazines. "Yes, here it is, 'The male ego needs to dominate an unsuspecting wife in order to achieve masculine supremacy in the home. Men cannot stand competition.' "

I listened again for the gentle whisper.

It had faded into nothingness.

"Hmm." I pulled myself up out of the easy chair onto my good foot and my white plaster-foot, "I wonder *why* John said not to drive? Drundel says he's anxious for me to resume my duties at the hospital."

Chills tingled in my arms as I recalled Drundel's words. "Martha, you are sensitive, compassionate, and lovely to look at. You are a wonder of mercy!"

"Oh, anyone could have done it, Drundel," I'd responded.

"You should have been named Florence, not Martha," he insisted.

I began to pace around on my plaster. "That's what I need to do. I'll call Drundel right away and see how soon I can come back to work."

On the way to the telephone a soft suggestion blew my way, "Wouldn't it be wise to ask John first?"

Hurry, hurry! shrieked my brain. *Someone else may get the job before you can call!*

Frantically, I dialed the number.

"Martha? How good to hear your voice again!" Immediately Drundel recognized me. Warmth exuded through the telephone wires right into my disobedient heart.

"Hello, Drundel."

"How are you, 'Florence'?"

"I'm fine. Getting around almost like normal," I replied.

"Wonderful," he responded.

Like a cat watching a grasshopper, my mind waited for his next question.

"When are you coming back to work, Martha?" the perfect gentleman inquired.

"When would you suggest?" Scarlet-the-sinful purred.

"As soon as possible. We've missed you."

Overwhelmed, and without a thought for John's approval or opinion, I agreed to return to work. "I'll be in right at eleven, Drundel."

"Get a little extra sleep, Martha," Drundel suggested. "Then you won't be too tired."

"Of course, Drundel," I agreed. "See you tomorrow."

I flew the rest of the day—preparing pizza for the kids, steak and french fries for John, and a pan of fudge for me. "I'll need some extra energy."

At the supper table I was energetic and excited as I passed around the family's favorite foods.

"Wow, Mom!" Joe exclaimed, wolfing down a large piece of pepperoni pizza laden with melted mozzerella cheese. "Now you're cooking like other mothers!"

"What does that mean, Joe, dear?" I serenely inquired.

Gulping down a horrendous mouthful of cola, he stated simply, "Usually we have to eat what's *good* for us instead of what we want." He grabbed another pizza wedge.

"Oh," I replied, repressing guilt pangs.

"J.J., I want to thank you for your help in finishing the oven." I handed him a piece of devil's food cake, thick with marshmallow icing.

"Think nothing of it, Mom!" He grinned broadly. "That was a long time ago."

"Can I have more cake, Mom?" George licked his fork and held out his plate.

"Certainly, George, darling." I cut a large hunk and hefted it onto his dish.

"What's the catch?" John's voice penetrated my soul like a rapier.

"Whatever do you mean?" I forced a look of innocence.

"Let's discuss it after supper," he announced to an audience of one—me. He said nothing else throughout the entire meal.

The remainder of the evening strained itself into a thin line of courtesy between my husband and me. The children didn't notice, however, because Buddy, the bird, entertained by hopping along after Ben, the guinea pig, all over the living room carpet.

"Go get him, Buddy!" Joe yelled and cheered, emitting shrieks of delight.

"No! Buddy!" George screamed, grabbing his pig. "You're not gonna get Ben, you mean bird!" He stuffed Ben under his shirt.

"Aw, don't be such a crybaby, George," grumbled Joe. "Buddy won't hurt your dumb pig."

"He's not dumb!" Tears leaked from George's eyes. "*You're* dumb!"

"Yeah? Well you're a jerk!" Joe shoved his chin out and took a step toward his younger brother.

George darted from the room.

"Mom, aren't you going to say anything?" John Jr.'s tone tunneled into my consciousness.

"What?" I looked up from my knitting.

"George is crying, Mom." J.J. sounded concerned. "Usually you yell at Joe."

"I'm not raising my voice anymore," I recited confidently. "All of you children are old enough to look after yourselves. I read that in the newspaper the other day."

John appeared in the archway into our living room. "Martha, what's wrong with George?"

"He's all right," I commented, resuming my needle-clacking.

"He is crying, Martha." John's concern momentarily arrested my attention.

"Then you solve it, John. I can't be everybody's slave all the time." Knitting consumed my concentration.

John stared at me in disbelief, then announced, "John Jr., time for bed." He walked over and rubbed J.J.'s shoulder gently. "See that your brothers brush their teeth, will you?"

"Sure, Dad," mumbled John Jr. "Come on, Joe, help me pick up George's soldiers."

For once Joe had no retort, and the boys disappeared into their room.

John pulled up a straight chair close to where I was knitting. "Martha, let's talk."

"Okay," I vocalized, still knitting.

"Could you stop what you're doing?" His articulation sounded rather aggressive.

"About what, John?" I responded lightly.

"About the fact that you're planning to go back to work at the hospital again tomorrow," he pronounced. "Isn't it bad enough that George had to tell me where you were the last time he was sick at school?"

Guilt grabbed hard. "How did you know—about tomorrow?"

That's why he called you at the hospital that time. He was checking up on you! concluded my cranium.

Riveted to my chair, I saw the hurt in John's eyes.

"Mr. Jenkins telephoned while you were in the shower." His commanding blue eyes bored into my defensive hazel ones. "He called to see if 10:30 in the morning would be possible rather than the previously agreed time of eleven."

"Oh," I said in a small voice. Taking a deep breath for courage, I rejoined, "I figured I would have everything arranged by this evening, and, since you've been taking the kids to school anyway, I thought that perhaps Drundel—"

"Drundel?" His eyes narrowed. "You call your boss Drundel? When did that start?"

"Don't be silly, John." I laughed nervously. Powerless to stop whatever raged inside me, I picked up my knitting needles and began concentrating on counting stitches.

With a touch as gentle as spring rain, John covered my hands with his. "Please don't do this, Martha."

"Do what, John?" Feeling his concern, but certain I was right, I made light of his request.

He let go of my hands and replaced the chair in the corner of the room. "I'm tired. Guess I'll see you tomorrow."

For the first time that I could remember, except when I was in the hospital having our children, John didn't kiss me good night.

"Call after him," suggested a quiet voice.

Well, what do you think of that! My mind went for the jugular. *You married a chauvinist. You showed him!*

"Oh, be quiet, brain." I ached with uncertainty.

Later I crept into bed.

"Wake him and apologize," the Quiet One prompted.

I lay there staring at the ceiling, full of misery. John didn't snore, and I wondered if he was sleeping.

The silence of darkness stabbed my spirit. Though tears filled my eyes and inexpressible grief at my wrongdoing tore through my heart, I could not or would not reach over and waken my husband.

Finally, unable to sleep, I stepped softly out to the living room to read my Bible. Flicking on a dim light, I sat on the sofa.

"I don't understand myself at all, for I really want to do what is right, but I can't. I do what I don't want to—what I hate. I know perfectly well that what I am doing is wrong, and my bad conscience proves that I agree. . . . But I can't help myself, because I'm no longer doing it. It is sin inside me that is stronger than I am that makes me do these evil things. . . . It seems to be a fact of life that when I want to do what is right, I inevitably do what is wrong. I love to do God's will so far as my new nature is concerned, but there is something else deep within me . . . that is at war. . . . Oh, what a terrible predicament I'm in!"[13]

I should have read on, but I didn't. Instead, I listened as rain fell softly on the roof. Later, when I woke on the couch with my Bible in my hands, I hurried off to bed.

By that time John was sleeping soundly.

I must have drifted off, too, because the next time I opened my eyes it was nine o'clock in the morning. John and the children had gone to school.

Now you've blown it, chided my cranium.

Ignoring the thought, I rambled through the house.

"Everyone's gone," I commented sadly as I put the kettle on to make coffee.

I paced back and forth in the kitchen, watching the kettle for signs of steam. "But what is so terrible about wanting to fulfill myself as a person?"

A watched pot never boils, advised my mind.

"I'm beginning to think that *you* don't know much either," I said out loud to my brain. I didn't stop to think about what kind of person talks to herself. I didn't care. Anger replaced my anxiety, and I felt a burst of adrenaline.

I thumped my plaster foot and me to the bathroom to wash my face. "Cold water feels great." I tried in vain to encourage myself. Then I looked in the mirror. "I've aged overnight!"

What do you expect, house-slave? The word slave hissed at me.

Still looking at myself in the mirror, I waited for that small voice to speak.

Silence.

Often I'd felt it must have been God speaking to me in a quiet way, but I wasn't quite certain. That serene sound somewhere inside urged me to follow after the better part of myself. "I wonder if other women hear voices," I inquired of the person in the mirror.

Don't be stupid! squealed my scraggy brain.

Weariness settled around my shoulders as I sipped my coffee. "I know what I have to do."

Dragging my heavy foot with my healthy foot, I stood beside the telephone. "I'll have to quit. It's the only way."

Unwilling fingers stuffed themselves into the dial. My ears listened to the buzz of numbers lining themselves up in a distant computer. A moment of silence. Then the ringing.

"Mr. Jenkins, please." I sounded as pleasant as I could.

"Mrs. Christian?" The voice replied. "Great to hear from you! How is your ankle?"

"What?" Confusion crept around me. "Do I know you?"

"Of course not," answered the friendly female at the other end of the telephone line, "but we all know you!"

"Oh," I said numbly.

"You will want to speak to Mr. Jenkins, of course," she continued. "One moment, please." The musical quality of her speech seemed to indicate happiness in her job.

"Martha!" The resonant baritone boomed. "You're not going to be late, are you?" His voice mesmerized me.

"Well, actually, Mr. Jenk—"

"*Drundel,*" he corrected me as a schoolteacher reprimands an erring reader.

"Yes," I responded dutifully. "I wasn't going to come in today because I—"

"Are you in pain, Martha?" His sympathetic approach crumbled my resolve to resign.

"Just a little," I lied.

"Well, we can't have our favorite Smock Lady hurting!" His energy gave life to my rebellious tendencies. "Tell you what"—he lowered his tone to confidential comfort—"you come in late today. I'm off for lunch around noon, so I'll swing around, pick you up, and you can try it for an hour."

I hesitated. "Just for an hour?"

One hour can't hurt anybody! You-know-who screeched.

"What do you say?" His voice—so smooth, so pleasant, so soothing—created chaos in my being.

"Well, I . . ."

"You do know how much we need you, don't you?" He wheedled.

"Yes, but . . ."

"And we're *counting* on you." He chuckled. "Why, just the other day Mrs. Hillvalley asked about you!"

"Me? She did?"

"She wondered where that Wonder Of Mercy disappeared to, but I assured her that you would be back today to start her on that new sweater you promised to help her knit." He paused to let the information sink in. "Remember?"

I remembered.

You can do it! My cranial cheering section roared.

"I don't think I can . . ." Faltering, I struggled to hear the Quiet One.

Nothing.

Do it! Do it! Do it! My bossy brain seemed to jump up and down, demanding to be obeyed. *You can tell him while you're there at the hospital that this will be your last day,* it continued, crooning compromise.

Within the depths of my being it seemed I recalled a verse from my Bible, something about compromise being like a polluted spring.[14]

"Martha? Are you there?" The commanding sound startled me.

"Yes." Unable to stand the pressure, I stood in my house and allowed myself to be swayed. The "I'll be ready" didn't come from me. It couldn't have.

"Wonderful, Martha! See you at noon." He hung up.

My spirit sank lower than the sole of my good foot as I shakily dressed and combed my hair. Inside I felt like a tomb.

Just as I donned my coat, however, the unexplainable happened. (Later I discovered that people feel this way just before suicide.) Lightheartedness seemed to create an atmosphere of euphoria in my head.

On the way past Buddy, the bird, I said, "Hey, my blue-feathered friend, this isn't going to be so bad after all." I had no clear evidence. I didn't need any. Self-assertion carried the day.

Quickly I thumped down the stairs to the back door and waited.

"That's unusual," I said, checking my watch. "Drundel, who is always early, is late." I gasped for air. "This cast weighs a ton!" I pounded my way over to a chair and flopped in it.

While waiting for Drundel, I puzzled over my sudden happy-go-lucky attitude. "Wonder what it means?" I asked myself. "Sometimes I feel like two people live inside me. Martha and Martha."

Pacing over to a window, I peered outside. "Other women work at jobs away from home. Why can't I? What is wrong with self-expression?"

Drundel was nowhere in sight. "After all," I reasoned to myself, "that verse about Sarah obeying Abraham was written for women who lived thousands of years ago. Any modern woman knows that slavery went out with bound feet and suffocating veils."

The Quiet One spoke, "What about the thoughts of My heart?"[15]

The soundless tug at my spirit dispersed cloud nine immediately.

By the time Drundel arrived, I knew I needed to talk to someone. "I can't unravel this mess by myself."

As I stepped onto the plush carpet of Drundel's yacht-sized car, I made another decision. "It won't be John I discuss this with."

That evening John discovered I'd gone to work—without his consent, against his expressed wishes. "Hiroshima" best describes our evening.

"You did what, Martha?" Devastation.

"Just for one hour, John!" Annihilation. "You can't tell me what to do. I am not a child. I am not a slave."

It was at that point that I got confused, but the result was my sitting in the living room on the sofa hours after everyone else lay sleeping. John sawed logs loudly as if nothing had happened.

I uncovered Buddy. "You know, little bird, I've read that men who bomb cities don't feel very good later."

Buddy opened one eye then closed it. I covered the cage.

Reaching for my Bible, I thumbed the well-worn pages. "Hmm. I don't remember seeing this, 'This wise woman builds her house, but the foolish tears it down with her own hands.' "[16]

I heard the Quiet One. "Do you realize what you are doing, Martha?"

As tears moistened the page, a gentle peace wrapped around my spirit. Truly sorry for causing John pain, I no longer cared about being right.

"I've hurt him, Lord, and I'm sorry."

Relief.

Joy flooded my soul as I raced to our bedroom to tell John the great news. I rehearsed it as I thumped my foot down the hallway. "I'm going to quit my job because this was all *Drundel's* doing, John . . ."

John, however, didn't respond the way I'd hoped.

Acting like a child, I reaped an adult lesson. Damaging another person causes one to feel very much *alone.*

6 / Valerie

"An excellent wife is the crown of her husband, but she who shames him is as rottenness in his bones."[17]

". . . and, so, Drundel, John would prefer it if I didn't work right now—with the children so young and all. . . ."

Taking a deep breath, I tried to calm the jitters which shook the telephone receiver in my hand. Waiting, I hoped the hospital administrator would accept my resignation graciously.

Silence.

"Are you there?"

"Certainly, Martha." The cold, crisp tone threw me. "Whatever you wish."

Panic gripped my stomach. "It's not what *I* want at all, Drundel." I pleaded for his understanding.

I was greeted with a soundless chasm of misunderstanding. The pain of isolation engulfed me.

"As you say, Martha. It cannot be helped."

The click of the phone severed my attempts at reconciling my two lives. I quietly replaced the receiver. The separation was complete.

Fighting back tears, I heard the thump of my walking cast as I made my way to the living room. Standing before the large picture window, I watched the sky.

"Why is it, Chief, that the sun still shines outside when it's raining in my heart?"

No answer.

Futility crept along my shoulders and weighed them down in defeat.

Before I could prevent it, heart-wrenching sobs shook my whole body.

Giving up my position as Smock Lady shouldn't have been so traumatic. But to me, a woman searching for myself, it seemed the end of the line.

"Well, I know one thing, God," I cried out as I dragged my heavy foot over to the box of facial tissues. "I must accept this because it is for my good."[18]

Resigning myself to what was "good," I felt better. I remembered reading somewhere that accepting things brought peace, and I determined to try it.

Yet hidden underneath it all, anger at John still lurked, waiting to pounce.

Almost immediately the telephone rang.

"Maybe it's John calling to tell me he's changed his mind about my working at the hospital!"

Happily I picked up the receiver. "Hello?" I intoned expectantly.

"Cough. Gasp. Martha?" The ancient, rasping voice sounded vaguely familiar.

"Yes?" I tried to recall who it might be.

"Did'ja ever get yerself yer hamster?"

"What?" My trauma left me in no mood for funny phone calls.

"Don'tcha remember me, Martha?" A mighty bark, hack. "I'm from the Mice Is Nice Nook."

"Oh! But yes, of course, Mr. . . . ."

"Just thought I'd give ya a call and see how yer doin' with that hamster you were trying to get, cuz I can get you one if you want it." He tried to inhale and choked.

"Thank you very much," I replied. "It's considerate of you to remember, but we wound up with a bird instead."

"They're good too," he uttered over a wheeze.

"How are you, anyway?" I inquired, trying to get to the bottom of his cough.

"Fine," he responded just before another great hacking session. "How is your leg?"

During the hour that followed, I found myself telling him all about my job at the hospital and how sad I felt to be quitting.

"What yer lookin' for is you, ma'am." Another cough. "Yeah." He whooped. "It's hard for people nowadays to know what they are—what with women's *libation* and all."

"Do you have family?" I inquired, hoping he would tell me his name.

"Nope. I'm all that's left." Sounds of him lighting his pipe rattled over the wire. "Oops! Got a customer. Gotta go. Nice to talk to ya again."

And I was alone.

Even my brain would have been some company, but it remained silent. The Quiet One also had nothing to say.

For the next few weeks my life existed in nothingness. Day after day I trudged through my housework—cooking meals, scrubbing floors, picking up after John and the kids.

Week after week I felt that my mind stagnated as I mechanically reminded the children to brush their teeth, brought coffee to John in the evenings, and watched the sun come up early in the morning when I couldn't sleep.

John seemed indifferent to my turmoil.

He's making you pay for what you did, going to work without his permission! my brain accused.

"Yes," I agreed, eagerly talking with myself to break the cycle of loneliness. "John should be over being mad by now. What's wrong with him, anyway?"

I bumped around the living room, watering house plants. "After all, *I'm* the one who has no goals for my life. Day after dreary day I do the same things. I never get out of the house. Sometimes I don't think God cares either." I slopped water all over the giant philodendron.

What you need is a diversion, my cranium suggested.

Wandering over to the sofa, I flopped down on it and grabbed a magazine. The feature article entitled "Shopping Beats Stress" intrigued me.

My eyes glued themselves to page fifty-three where I read,

"You, too, can beat the household blues by spending money. Do it today!"

"How long has it been since I bought *me* anything?" I stared off into space.

Too long! you-know-who yelled.

Before ten minutes had passed, I'd telephoned Jean and asked her to pick me up. Then I grabbed the checkbook and a couple of John's plastic cards.

"Martha . . ." The Quiet One barely had time to whisper my name before I was modeling a new outfit in front of Jean at Chic Boutique.

"What do you think of this one, Jean?" I swished past her in an alabaster-white silk pantsuit trimmed in red braid.

The corners of her mouth turned down. "I don't think John will like it."

"I didn't ask you what *John* would like," I replied saucily. "What do *you* think of it?" I paraded around the store.

"Well—" She hesitated as she zipped and unzipped her purse nervously. "I know that John prefers you to wear skirts—especially to school and town meetings." She lifted her eyes to meet mine. "Where would you wear that?"

"Jean!" I put my hands on my hips. "*Everyone* wears pants *everywhere* these days. Women don't have bound feet anymore." Throwing her a look of disdain, I grabbed a bright scarlet scarf and wrapped it around my neck.

While admiring myself in the store mirror, I spied the saleslady behind me. Turning toward her, I asked, "What's that in your hand?"

"These are simply *gorgeous!*" she responded as she clipped huge, fire-engine-red ear bobs on my ears.

Jean said, "Where is the ladies' room? I don't feel well."

By the end of my shopping spree, I was dressed in red from head to toe.

My lips were creamy crimson, my fingernails glowed with ruby, red-hot bracelets jangled on my wrists, and my good foot squeezed into half a pair of low scarlet pumps. I shoved the other half into my shopping bag to save for post-cast days.

Quietly, Jean drove me to my house.

"Well, Jean!" Grinning, I opened the car door and hopped out on my good foot, dragging my purchases with me. I poked my head back inside the car window. "Thanks!" I offered.

"Sure, Martha," she answered without turning her head in my direction. She backed out of the driveway without waving.

"I don't know what's wrong with Jean," I muttered as I hefted my spoils up the stairs and dumped them on the dining room table.

About a half-hour later I realized that shopping hadn't beat the household doldrums the way the article promised. Putting the packages away without John knowing, I resolved to take everything back first thing in the morning.

After breakfast I approached John as he drank his second cup of coffee. "Would it be all right with you if I take the car today?"

His face lit up like it hadn't for a long time. "Sure, honey," he replied, "just bring it home in one piece, okay?"

Back in the store I faced the saleslady. "Somehow I don't think this outfit will work for me."

"Certainly, madam," she retorted icily.

I hadn't learned my lesson, however.

By the time a person could say, "Wives should obey their husbands," I'd discovered the brand-new supermarket in town.

Grand opening! Prizes! I couldn't turn down the chance to win something—anything.

"Wow!" I stared at the bright lights, the wide aisles, and the efficient store personnel. That was aisle number *one*.

By aisle fifteen, section B, I'd had it. My good foot ached. "These concrete floors are something!" My plaster foot itched, and my eyes burned. "How can anyone read the prices when they're in fine print, hidden along the edges of the shelves, and covered with LOOK HERE! signs?"

Along with apples, oranges, meat, eggs, milk, and other delicious edibles, my grocery cart overflowed with frustration.

"All of this just to get my money!" I groused as I wandered down the primrose path to poverty.

They're all out to get you, crooned my cranium.

As I approached the checkout line, a bleeping sound interrupted my tirade.

"What's that noise?" I inquired of a portly gentleman standing in line in front of me.

He chuckled at my question. "Just the computer. It's reading the packages." He pulled out a pipe and chewed on the end. "Yes, sir! What a world we live in now. The grocery checker doesn't even have to know what things cost anymore."

I wondered if he could be the Mice-Is-Nice-Nook man. "Do you sell hamsters?"

"What?" He sized me up as though he'd encountered a deranged mind.

"Do you work at the Mice Is Nice Nook? I didn't get your name," I responded cheerily.

"Uh, no," he mumbled, turning his back.

Flushing in embarrassment, I began digging in my purse for money to pay for the groceries.

Then it was my turn at the till. Fascinated, I watched as the lady in blue slowly pulled an item across futuristic red lights which glowed from a square window housed in the counter. A guard of black plastic fingers covered the glass. When one of my purchases crossed the red glow, a bleep blipped, and the price flashed on the cash register screen.

"Amazing!" I exclaimed to the young woman processing my order.

"Yes," she responded, weighing oranges. She tapped some keys on a board in front of her, and *Oranges—99¢*, flashed on the cash register.

"How does it know?" I inquired.

"Know what?" She answered without looking up from her work.

"Know how much everything is?" I responded brightly.

Lifting her gaze to meet mine, she engaged my hazel eyes. Then she resumed her work.

"Oh," I whispered. "Guess you're pretty busy." Suddenly I felt out of place, antiquated, obsolete.

You blew that one! my gray matter chattered.

Finally the grocery checker looked up and said, "That'll be fifty-two dollars."

Like the child of old with rapped knuckles, I paid the price and left.

Arriving home disgruntled, I decided to talk to Joe's bird. "I know what is wrong with me, Buddy." I made a few clicks with my tongue. "I need to become *creative* with my housework."

Buddy chirped happily in his cage.

"No sense moaning about nothing." I continued talking to myself while I put away the groceries. "I think I'll bake John his favorite apple pie!"

By the time John and the boys arrived home, I'd produced a tender, flaky piecrust stuffed full of juicy sliced apples, spiced with cinnamon, and topped with real butter.

"Hi, John!" I ran to meet him and threw my arms around his neck.

"What's the catch?" he asked suspiciously.

"No catch," I answered, giving him a quick kiss. "See what I made for you!" Grabbing him by the arm, I hauled him out to the kitchen and displayed the pie.

"Nice," he responded absentmindedly just before heading for his study to grade papers.

Realizing he was busy with report-card time approaching, I didn't mind—much.

When the kids, however, complained about the lovely dinner of roast beef, mashed potatoes and gravy, rolls and butter, candied carrots, and pie a la mode, I began a slow burn.

Nobody in this family cares what you do. My gray matter gave notice of my situation.

A hot steam of anger began somewhere in my midsection and seeped slowly through my system.

"Why should I try at all?" I slapped the dishes in the sink. "Nobody even noticed my hard work today." Self-pity ate like a cancer into my spirit as I finished the supper cleanup by myself.

"All the kids care about is cars, lizards, and bikes!" I hung the towel carefully on the rack to dry.

The kitchen sparkled.

"Now it is time for me to clean up a few other matters!" I set my face as I whipped my apron off and threw it at a chair.

With a confident stride I covered the distance to John's study, where he labored at grading papers. With a grip born of raw courage I turned the doorknob and entered his sanctuary. With the voice of a loudmouth I delivered my earsplitting ultimatum.

"John!" I paced about the room vigorously. "The Declaration of Feminism drawn up in Minneapolis in 1972 stated, 'Marriage has existed for the benefit of *men!*' Therefore, 'the end of the institution of marriage is necessary . . .' "

I paused, staring at the hunched-over figure working at his desk. "John, you're not listening to me!" I screamed.

John slowly straightened his shoulders. Carefully he laid his red pencil on a piece of paper already covered with scarlet comments. In one movement he spun his swiveling desk chair to face me.

Immediately I realized I'd bitten a wormy apple.

"I have a lot of papers to get through. Surely you can see that." His icy tone cut me to the quick, but his complete disinterest in my pronouncement disintegrated me.

Trying to recover my damaged assertiveness, I cracked. "Well, then, I guess it's the end."

Pivoting his chair, he picked up his pencil and resumed grading tests.

Stunned, I stood facing his back. Pain, fury, anxiety, and terror enveloped me as I slowly turned away. Softly I closed the door. I ran to the bathroom and sobbed, unable to see the forces of the satanic world working on my husband and me to divide us. I failed to realize that the truth of God's Word for wives would set me free.[19]

Instead of consulting the Bible, I counseled myself. I was unable to pray because of my anger, so I reacted. "John is wrong! Dead wrong."

After another sleepless night, I realized by morning that I would have to find my own fulfillment in life if I was to survive.

My brain and I joined forces to achieve and ensure my happiness.

Our first move, sneakiness, went off like clockwork.

Breakfast—eggs on a raft, surrounded by crisp bacon slices and accompanied by hot apple muffins—soothed what I now considered a savage beast, John.

Next, as soon as the children and he departed for school, I consulted the classified section of the daily newspaper. Sporting a large black felt marker, I prepared my attack on the work forces of our area.

Just then the telephone rang. "Martha?"

"Hello! Jean, dear!" I trilled.

"Uh oh," she replied.

"Not at all," I lilted.

"How are things?" Jean inquired in a worried tone.

"Never better!" I enunciated clearly. "I'm job hunting."

"Triple uh oh," she whispered.

"Jean, I've decided that John and the boys are now able to look after themselves. It's time I find *myself*." I paused to let it soak in.

"Have you spoken to John about this?" she queried gently.

"Not exactly this, but we've been discussing my life lately."

Don't tell her anything! my ally in sneakiness advised.

"What's new at your house?" I asked abruptly.

"Martha, I thought you liked staying home." She sounded like George when he wouldn't give up asking for chocolate cake.

"Correction, Jean, my friend. I *did*. But now I am no longer needed the way I was. Life changes." Firmly I stated my case.

"Oh," she commented.

"Surely you can see that we must remain flexible if we are to survive this vale of tears." I shamed her into agreement.

"Martha," she replied, "I think somebody's ringing my doorbell, and I'm meeting Hub for lunch."

After hanging up the telephone receiver, I hurried back to my newspaper and opportunity.

One hour later, I'd accumulated a list of numbers and a heart full of hope—for me.

"A working person drinks a lot of coffee," I mentioned to myself as I put the coffeepot on to perk. "And," I patted my hair into place, "I'll need to go to the hairdresser for a new coiffure."

With no job in sight by the end of the day, I tossed the black marker onto the table. "I'm going to have to really apply myself if I'm going to succeed in cracking the job market," I announced. "In the meantime, positive thinking should carry me. I'm certain it was Francois Duc de La Rochefoucauld in 1653 who said, 'To succeed in the world, we do everything we can to appear successful.' "

Fatigue drove me to shelve the project till morning.

Bright and early the next morning, after John and the children left for school, I sat at the kitchen table with my coffee and list of telephone numbers. "Let's see," I mumbled to myself, "I could be a Nanny/Housekeeper."

Don't be ridiculous, advised my ally with a superior air. *That's what you are already!*

"Right," I agreed, pushing onward down the classified ads.

After ten minutes, I decided I needed a break and phoned Jean. "Hello, Jean?"

"Hi, sweetie," she responded amiably.

"Are you going anywhere today?" Her friendship comforted me, but I hesitated to say it.

"Not today," she replied warmly. "Anything you need?"

"Don't you think that's boring?" I asked honestly.

"What's boring?" she inquired without irritation.

"Staying home all day." I explained my position patiently. "Don't you realize nothing different will happen to you today?"

Uproarious laughter floated through the telephone lines. "Are you kidding?" More giggling. "You should *see* what Hub has planned for the day!" She broke up again. "I'll be lucky to survive"— Another snigger. "But it won't be dull!"

"Oh," I mumbled, feeling totally cut off from my best friend.

"Martha," she said, suddenly serious. "Are you all right? You're not . . ." She paused. "Have you had one of your *dreams?*"

"Jean," I snapped, "why is it that when I want to find myself, fulfill my life, that everybody thinks I'm losing my mind? I'm getting really tired of it!"

The silence at the other end of the telephone cut me to the core.

"I'm sorry, Jean," I instantly covered. "Maybe I am dreaming, or troubled somewhere in my subconscious, and don't know it."

"Martha—" Her voice gentled my spirit. "Have you tried

reading your Bible lately? Maybe that would help." She cleared her throat nervously as though another outbreak from me would sever our relationship.

Tears filled my eyes.

"Martha?"

"I have read it, and I can't do it. That's the trouble." Speaking over a lump in my throat forced the words out in little blasts.

"Would you like to talk about it?" Her concern came through.

"No," I said simply, cutting our communication. I realized Jean wanted to reach out and help. "It's not something I can explain right now," I said. "If I had the answer, then I could share it, but I don't."

Jean's type of love didn't push, but I felt I'd caused a misunderstanding between us.

Later I had a little conversation with our resident parakeet. "You see, Buddy, the problem with Jean is that she can't understand me. She always does what Hub wants to do. It's easy for her to submit to him, but I honestly don't see why she's not a vegetable."

Swinging happily in his cage, Buddy replied, "Peep."

"Moreover," I continued my discourse, "Jean lucked out when she married Hub. I bet he never gets moody or inconsiderate like John."

Putting my forefinger through the bars of Buddy's cage, I tickled his chin.

"Chirp!" he responded cheerily.

I delivered my conclusion. "This time Jean and I will have to go our separate ways."

"Peep. Tweet," Buddy commented.

Thus assured, I returned to the table, my cold coffee, and my lists.

Later that afternoon, I mopped my perspiring brow. "Becoming a member of the work force isn't as easy as I figured!"

Dinner—homemade spaghetti and chocolate cake—passed quietly.

By the next morning, undaunted, I attacked the telephone with full vigor.

"What can you do?" a female voice drawled.

"Well, I . . ." I reached for an answer and came up empty-handed.

"Can you type?" The threatening questioning continued.

"I took typing in high school," I offered.

"How many words per minute?" She sounded bored.

"Oh, let's see." I tried to remember. "How does twenty-five hit you?"

"Like a bomb," she replied just before she hung up.

The employment office gave me no hope.

The local career center suggested I start my life over again.

The college nearby said I could enter as a "mature student."

Completely frustrated by midafternoon, I called the man with no name at the Mice-Nice store. "Hello?"

Busy with customers, he offered to hypnotize me sometime, "so's you can be free to be yourself."

Finally I reached the end of my rope and decided to try God. But not directly.

"Pastor Jim?"

He answered his phone on the first ring.

"I wonder if I could get in to see you this afternoon. . . ."

Whipping my coat on, I procured a ride from a neighbor, and I arrived at the pastor's office within fifteen minutes.

Nervously, I sat in a soft chair across from his desk.

"Martha!" His broad smile and twinkling eyes welcomed me instantly. "How are you today?"

"Fine," I lied.

The visit produced nothing in terms of my relationship to God. Unable to unmask my real feelings of futility for fear of what Pastor Jim might think of my spirituality, I spoke of favorite hymns and the upcoming choir party. And I promised regular attendance at Bible studies.

He responded with, "Let's pray."

He asked God to bless me and my family, praying long and hard for *John*.

It wasn't Pastor Jim's fault.

A week later I knew that no one in the world wanted me to work for them, and that I had no skills worth hiring.

Finally John noticed me withdrawing from life.

"Martha." He approached me gently. "What can I do to help?" Gone from his eyes was irritation or anger.

"Oh, John." I dropped my head and stared at my feet. "I need something to do!"

He scratched his head and cleared his throat. His countenance conveyed calm. "It seems to me, Martha, that you complain of being too busy."

Looking into his eyes, I searched for a trace of his love.

He doesn't understand either, my mind-mentor yapped.

"You don't understand," I repeated the suggestion.

His pure blue eyes turned to azure-ice. Pacing the room, he addressed me, his audience of one. "Martha."

I waited.

"Just tell me what you want so we can get on with living, will you?" He stood across the room.

I didn't know what I wanted. I only knew I hurt inside, and I wanted him to touch the ache and share it. Probably fear prompted my response. "John, I want a *computer!*"

"A computer!" Incredulous at my request, he asked, "Do you have any idea what a computer costs?"

"I don't need one as big as they have at the supermarket, John. I'll find a cheap one." A computer seemed a good answer the more I thought about it.

"What are you going to do with it?" He folded his arms across his chest.

"Be a home secretary!" I replied confidently.

"For whom?" he questioned.

"For whomever!" I shot back enthusiastically.

Stuffing his hands in his pockets, he shrugged his shoulders and surrendered.

Recognizing his defeat, I smiled in anticipation.

"Maybe it will help, Martha. I can't take much more of your moping around the house. Possibly it'll help you pass the time while you're waiting for the cast to come off your leg."

Victory tasted sweet. "Thank you, John." I gave him a big grin.

"I didn't have any choice." Vanquished, John vanished from the room.

In less than a week's time I sat before my new computer. It didn't cost much. The warehouse needed to rid themselves of a discontinued line of home computers. We bought it at cost.

Locating an old desk, I stashed the entire computer, including the printer, on the top and sat in my old sewing chair.

"Perfect!" I ran my hands over the keyboard. "I'm certain John won't mind it being in the living room, even if it does take some extra space. After all," I congratulated myself on my ingenuity, "now he won't have to buy a *monitor*."

I recalled John's scowl when he heard the cost of a viewing screen and the salesman's fast reply, "You can hook it up to your own television set!"

Then I remembered Joe's reaction when we brought the versatile machine home. "Great! Now we can play computer games!"

"No," I'd firmly pronounced. "*You* will not touch it! This is for Mom's work."

Storming out of the room, he informed George and J.J., "Mom's ugly computer is a piece of junk, and we're not supposed to touch it!"

"I won't even mind Joe's horrible temper, which he obviously inherited from John," I soothed myself. "Soon they'll appreciate me when I'm earning a few dollars myself."

"John will love it in time," I mused while removing tags and stickers from the sides and top of the printer. "Even smells new. And look at this! Five books to read to learn how to operate it! Why, I'll be a computer whiz by the time I've finished these. It won't matter at all how fast I can type, either. The salesman said so!"

The days following, while John and the boys were at school, I wiled away the hours, pushing buttons and discovering it was going to be a bit tougher than I expected. Robert Lewis Stevenson stated it well in the eighteenth century, however, when he wrote, "Give us grace and strength to forbear and to persevere. Give us courage."

Sitting before my machine, an idea hit me. "This computer needs a name!"

How about Val? suggested the cranium.

"Val." I tumbled the name off my tongue. "Yes. I like it. Has a nice ring to it—rather like the famous space computer Joe's always talking about."

Covering Val in plastic to keep out the dust, I remembered hearing something about a Valerie in Norse mythology.

That's Valkyrie, corrected the cerebrum.

"Yes, Valkyrie. Those were the maids who conducted the heroes to their heaven, Valhalla, I think." I stared at the wall, trying to remember. "Yes, I know. Then they all had a feast with the main god, Odin."

"Yes," I repeated, thumping my plaster foot out to the kitchen to prepare dinner. "Val, the *maid,* will serve us well!"

I should have recalled, however, the Valkyrie, Odin's awful, beautiful maidens, hovered over the field of battle, choosing those who would be *slain.*

7 / *Clouds*

"Obey the king as you have vowed to do."[20]

"Hey, Mom, who is *Meppbitis*?" Chomping a crunchy chunk out of his ripe, juicy apple, George gazed expectantly at me.

"Not now, George. I'm cleaning strawberries." Hearing nothing but munching, I glanced at my youngest and spied a royal pout in progress. "Don't you have some homework to do?"

"No." He threw his apple core at the waste basket and missed.

I stabbed myself with the paring knife. "Ow!" I yelled. Blood flowed from my left thumb while torment assaulted my entire nervous system.

"That's okay," my offspring commented. "It's the same color as the jam you're making." He yawned.

Clenching my teeth, I held my thumb against my forefinger to stop the bleeding while uttering in a monotone, "Would you please get me a bandage from the bathroom? I feel sick."

"Sure, Mom, anything you say." Shoving his hands in his jeans pockets, he ambled to the top of the basement stairs and screeched, "Hey, Joe! Mom cut her thumb! Wanna get her a Bluestar bandage?"

Closing my eyes, I leaned against the kitchen counter for mental and physical strength. I remembered the time I'd fallen in the strawberry patch while going for a walk with the kids. By the time I'd extricated myself from the low wire fence, they'd disappeared.

You could die while waiting. On cue, my cranium clarified the circumstances.

Like a robot, unable to alter the situation, I stood by.

"What?" Joe's adolescent croak drifted up the basement stairs.

"Never mind!" George wandered back into the kitchen. *"I'll* do it!" he shrieked.

"I asked *you* to get it in the first place!" My temper pounced on my son.

"Well," he drawled, "somebody has to guard you."

"Get the bandage, please," I whispered through pursed lips.

"Would you like a red one with satellites?" he inquired.

"Just don't bother, George." I glared. "I'm feeling stronger now. The strawberries will have to wait. I'll get it myself. Thank you anyway."

"You're bleeding, Mom!" Suddenly my solicitous son noticed the blood oozing through my fingers, heading toward my wrist.

"Yes," I agreed. Thumping my cast-encased leg past my eleven-year-old protector, I hurried to the bathroom.

While rummaging around the medicine chest for a bandage of any color, a recent scene with George and me and bandages flashed before my eyes. . . .

"Hey, Mom, what are you doing in the rocking chair?" my inquisitive one had asked.

"Knitting, George." Preoccupied, I'd hoped he'd go away.

"I'm bored." He began rocking the chair from behind.

"I know," I'd responded, guardedly, bracing myself for the next question.

"What can I do?" His thin tone seared my sympathetic nervous system.

"Find something, George." Planting my feet firmly on the floor, I managed to stabilize the rocker. "You'll think of something."

"Can't *you* think of something?" Wheedle, cajole. "It's raining." The whine crept up from behind as George circled to face me.

Cornered, I'd concentrated on the difficult sweater pattern I'd tried to master. "All right, George. What do you want?"

If I'd looked up from my clicking needles, I would have seen his exuberant smile of victory. "Can I make something out of adhesive tape?"

"No," I'd said flatly.

"Why not?" he whined, pacing around my chair.

"Because I said so." Holding on to my sanity, I waited for his familiar retort.

"That's no reason!" He gave my chair a mighty yank.

"George!" I roared. "You are not a baby anymore! Now occupy yourself just until I get this pattern worked *one time*! Can't you?"

"How about bandages?" The bargaining began.

"What?" I stalled for time.

"Instead of adhesive tape. We've got lots of bandages." Gaining momentum, he danced around my chair.

"Fine," I surrendered, dropping a stitch. "But just *one*."

Faster than I could finish the word *one*, he had disappeared. . . .

"And now so have all the bandages!" Still trying to hold my thumb and forefinger together, I decided not to scream at anyone. "Boys will be children," I comforted myself while searching the house for a suitable bandage.

Finding nothing, I headed for the basement. "Maybe there's some tape in the tool box," I suggested to myself. Meanwhile, the scarlet riverlet crept toward my elbow.

"Wow, Mom, look at your hand!" Joe breathed down my neck as I plowed through John's tools and workbench. "What are you doing?"

"Looking for tape," I answered defensively.

"Why?" His eyes gleamed with excitement.

"No reason," I replied lightly. Grabbing the almost nonexistent roll of black electrical tape, I thumped my heavy foot back toward the stairs.

"Going to do some wiring?" He followed me so closely my composure continued to disintegrate.

"No." Without a backward glance, I climbed the stairs.

"You sure are a crab."

"Joe! Enough!" I screamed.

Storming back down the stairs, two at a time, Joe wisely retreated.

Entering the bathroom, I tried to turn my full-boil anger down to slow simmer as I stopped the bleeding with bathroom tissue and electrical tape.

Heading toward the couch in the living room, I beheld George glued to the television set.

I decided to reconnoiter. "George, dear," I trilled, "how are things at school?"

"What?" He stared at the idiot box.

Charging to the set, I terminated the program with one finger. "I said I would like to see your lessons for the day."

Wrinkling his face in torment, he pleaded for mercy. "I don't have any."

"Find some," I ordered.

Like a shot he disappeared into his room.

While waiting for his return, I took up a post on the sofa and propped my right leg up on the coffee table while elevating my left thumb above my head.

George arrived a few minutes later, smoothing some sheets of crumpled paper on his chest. "See?" He handed me the top piece. "I got an *A* on this one."

"This is art," I responded dryly.

"Yeah, I know. Isn't it good?" He flashed me a gregarious grin.

"What's that other piece of paper you're holding?" I pointed to what looked like an arithmetic assignment.

Dutifully he handed it over.

"It's not finished, George." I handed it back. "See you later—after it's finished."

"Aw . . ."

Settling myself on the sofa, I picked up my knitting and remembered Joe calling me a crab. "I'm going to tell John he simply must do something about Joe's mouth." Furiously my needles clacked. "I'm tired of tangling with him." I adjusted my sore thumb to avoid the yarn. "Joe never listens to *me*."

After working one entire pattern in peaceful tranquility, I decided to check on George and his studying.

Bumping the floor as quietly as possible with my cast, I made my way to the den of my youngest.

"George?" I peeked in. "How are you doing?"

He sat crosslegged on the floor in intense concentration—both fists on his head, earphones on his ears, and guinea pig in his lap.

The pig heard my arrival and squealed a greeting.

George, however continued to gaze at the paper in front of him.

I tapped him on the shoulder. "George?"

"Yipe!" He jumped as he grabbed his fuzzy study-buddy. "I'm stuck on this one problem," he explained good-naturedly.

Curling up on the rug beside him, I joined the scholarly group.

After a half hour I had to admit, "This is too hard for me, George."

"Me, too!" he smiled ally-to-ally.

"I better get back to the strawberries," I said wearily hauling myself to a standing position. "Do you want to help?"

He narrowed his eyes behind aviator glasses. "Do I get to eat some?" the ever-ready bargainer asked.

I pondered the prospect. A few berries (a pittance) against good public relations with my son (a prize). "You're on." I steadied myself on his right shoulder. "But," I squeezed my eyelids together cowboy-style, "the pig stays here!"

"You've got a *deal!*" He whooped and raced ahead of me to the kitchen.

By the time I arrived, he was elbow deep in berries, popping the fleshy fruit into his mouth as fast as his fingers could fly. "How about some sugar, too, Mom?"

Removing the strawberries from his grasping paws, I queried. "What were you asking about Mepp—somebody-or-other?"

"Oh, *Meppbitis!*" He shoved a few more bits of cardinal-colored fruit into his mouth and swallowed them in one gulp, "Meppbitis was this guy in the Bible, and I think his mother dropped him on his head or something because . . ." He threw back another strawberry. "Well, I'm not sure why she let him fall, but anyway, I think he got hurt or something." He grabbed a handful of freshly cleaned berries from the bowl I'd filled.

"Cleaning is difficult enough with nine fingers," I interjected. "Slow down, George."

". . . and, anyway, Meppbitis got to eat at the king's table, and everybody else had to wait on him and take care of him." Taking a deep breath, he eyed the berries as I dumped them from the shiny metal bowl into a large kettle on the stove and pulped them with the potato masher.

"Want to measure the sugar?"

"Sure!" He dived for the sugar cannister.

"Better get the new sack," I advised, hiding my smile as he raced to the supply closet.

George dashed back carrying the bag of granulated goodness.

"You may have ten berries dipped in sugar—for your trouble." I flipped the stove burner on high and stirred the fruit.

"How about twenty?" he negotiated.

"Fifteen," I bargained back.

Silently, I watched the bubbling berries. "Smells good," I commented. "What was the point of the story?"

George looked puzzled.

"*Meppbitis.* What was the point?"

Vacant stare.

"Did you *learn* anything?"

"Oh!" He clued in. "No. The teacher, Miss Dwyer, got called to the telephone, and she bumped her head on the door because one of the kids had locked it."

"It's okay, George. I'll find it myself in the Bible concordance and let you know what happened."

By the time George and Joe were flying kites outside, and the jam was cooling in the jars, I realized why I'd never heard of Meppbitis. "Because there isn't one, that's why," I muttered as I made my way through the big concordance.

Later that evening, after the supper dishes were put away, I approached John. "Who's Meppbitis?"

"Who is who?" he asked, settling himself comfortably on the sofa with the evening paper.

"You know, *Meppbitis*." I raised my voice for emphasis.

John picked up the newspaper and began to read. "Will you look at that! They won!" The sports section began to vibrate slightly.

"Don't you care what happens to George?" I sat down beside him and stared at the side of his head.

"Of course I do, dear," he absentmindedly passed the time of day. "George who?"

I snatched the news from his relaxed grip. "John!"

"Just kidding! Just kidding!" he laughed, wrapping his arms around me.

I sat like a stone. "I'm serious, John."

"Of course you are," he kidded. "How about a kiss for a hard-working husband?"

I kissed him. "Now who is the Meppbitis-person in the Bible?" I snuggled in the crook of his arm.

"Hmm," he communicated thoughtfully. "The only person who even sounds like that is Mephibosheth, Jonathan's son. Why not try that?"

Early the next morning, as soon as the boys and John had departed for their schools, I researched Mephibosheth. Our concordance referred me to second Samuel, chapter nine, verse six, "And Mephibosheth, son of Jonathan, son of Saul, came to David and fell on his face and did obeisance."

My eyes widened in surprise. "There is that word *obeisance* again!" My mouth twisted into an unnatural shape.

There is that word again, drawled my brain.

"You're behind this time, oh, cranial counselor," I murmured. "I already saw it."

Continuing my search for two hours, I discovered *two* Mephibosheths had lived, and one had died by hanging. Chills swept over me as I hypothesized, "Hanging must hurt terribly. Obeisance seems to offer a slightly better alternative than a noose."

That afternoon after school, I tried to tell the tale to George. "And, so, George, Mephibosheth—"

"Mef—who?" Totally absorbed in his project sprawled about

him on the living room rug, his disinterest reminded me of his father's.

"What are you doing, George?" I eyed the shoe box loaded with his live guinea pig, and a neat pile of wooden sticks stacked nearby.

"Do we have any electrical tape?" He didn't look up from his concentrated effort to keep Ben in the box.

"Why?"

"We're all out of the other tapes," he responded easily.

"Oh. I used it for my thumb." I cleared my throat to gain his attention. "Now about *Mephibosheth*. You'll be the star of your Sunday school class with this information!"

Ignoring me, he bent his back to his work.

"What's that?" I couldn't help asking the question.

"A ramp." He sighed, shoving his glasses up on his nose with his forefinger. Then he leaned back on his heels and announced in satisfaction, "Now Ben can walk into the elevator by himself!"

"Oh." I didn't bother to ask why Ben would want to take an elevator—or to where.

Rubbing my eyes to improve my concentration, I came out with, "Now Meppbitis . . . I mean Mephibosheth . . . didn't fall on his head. No, his nurse dropped him on his legs. He spent the rest of his life crippled."

"Excuse me, Mom. I'll be right back." George left the room, then returned with hammer and nails. He began pounding nails into sticks.

"Certainly." I continued, "Jonathan and King Saul were killed when Mephibosheth was five years old—where are you going?"

"Be right back, Mom." George departed and returned with a ball of string.

Could be a noose, my brain jumped in.

"However, King David, Jonathan's blood brother—"

"Like Cochise?" George didn't bat an eye as he wound string on cardboard.

"What?" I tried to assimilate my son's statement and failed. "But the king . . ." Like a machine gone berserk, I could no longer compute the information flooding my system.

"Did ya get lost?" solicitous son inquired.

"I have dusting to do," I replied uneasily.

"That's okay, Mom!" He called after me as I fled from the room. "I didn't get the point in Sunday school either!"

Grabbing a dust cloth, I worked my way through the house. "I had a point," I muttered. "I know I had a point." My brows converged in the center of my forehead.

You are losing your grip, nagged my mind.

Furiously, I dusted the back of an overstuffed chair. "It's this obeisance business that's causing a crazed mind to flourish. I need diversion." Leaving the cloth on the back of the chair, I headed for Val and a new lease on life.

Turning the switches on, I found the hum of my friendly computer comforting.

By the time George had his elevator working, I'd read two computer operation manuals.

The evening passed uneventfully.

John did reprimand his mouthy son. "Your mother is not a crab, Joe."

Ben survived the elevator ordeal, John Jr. managed to connect with the tennis ball enough to win a short match with John, and I absorbed another computer instruction book.

Early the next morning, I sat before Val. "Val, you are a great convenience. Together we'll address envelopes, write letters, do shopping lists, create better budgets, and plan next year's activities. Perhaps we can assist John by organizing his school class lists and grading system!" Sighing in satisfaction, I flipped the switches to *on* and proceeded to computerize the upcoming choir party.

As soon as John Jr. arrived home after school, however, I met him at the door. "J.J., you have to help me!"

"What's the matter, Mom?" Instantly alert, his eyes bored into mine.

"It's Val!" I wailed. "It—she knows more than I do, and whatever I do is *wrong*!" I wrung my hands.

My sixteen-year-old son flashed me a reassuring smile. "It's a *machine*, Mom." He put his comforting arm around my shoulders. "Show me."

I did. For two hours of his study time. "You see, J.J., she does not print the words on the printer. She makes exclamation points whenever she likes, and the words vanish from the screen. I'm having an anxiety attack. The stress is killing me."

"Computers are stupid, Mom." Patiently he probed Val's memory bank. "You have to tell it what to do." Quickly he tapped out a message on the keyboard, and the screen obediently flashed responses.

"Impressive!" My eyes danced with excitement. "Can I do it?"

John Jr.'s encouragement turned the tide.

The following week I bragged to everyone at the choir party. "It's as easy as one, two, three!"

"This is a terrific choir-party-picnic," I announced to a blade of grass while munching a muffin.

"Were you talking to me?" A pleasant young lady passed by.

"Oh, hello! Do you have a computer?" In a couple of minutes she introduced herself as Sara Dwyer, George's Sunday-school teacher.

"George tells me you're interested in Mephibosheth." She stood smiling before me.

"Yes! As a matter-of-fact I am!" Beaming, I explained. "I read from second Samuel, chapter four, all the way to chapter twenty-one, and wound up completely confused. Why did they hang him?"

She laughed, then seated herself beside me on the live green carpet. "There are two Mephibosheths. The Mephibosheth we studied establishes a biblical principle for us today. Probably you realize he was Jonathan's son, and the grandson of King Saul."

I nodded enthusiastically. "They hanged the other one."

"When Mephibosheth was five years old, King Saul and Jonathan were killed. And, as if that wasn't bad enough, the nurse dropped Mephibosheth, causing him to be lame."

"I knew about that part," I offered.

"When David was king, he wanted to show mercy and kindness to the offspring of Jonathan because of his love for him—"

"They were blood brothers," I interrupted.

"Yes," she agreed. "Because of David's previous oath to Jonathan, he gave Mephibosheth all the land of his grandfather Saul along with Saul's servants who were expected to farm it for Mephibosheth. Then the lame young man was granted the right to live at the palace in Jerusalem and to eat at King David's table for the rest of his life."

Toying with a blade of grass, I posed my next question carefully. "What about—obeisance?"

"Pardon me?" She looked puzzled.

"Obeisance." I stared casually at the ground.

"Do you mean Mephibosheth *bowing* before the king?"

"Yes," I replied nonchalantly. "How important was *that*?"

Arranging her skirt around her, she answered, "To me, the bowing simply opened the way for the king to bestow his favor. If Mephibosheth had refused to come to the king in obedience, he would have missed the blessing of being taken care of for the rest of his life. King David protected him."

I sat transfixed to the spot.

"I believe," she continued, "that as we bow before the Lord in obedience and submission, we open the way for God to bless us today. After all—" she seemed to look far away into another time, another place—"we will eat at our King's table in heaven forever, won't we?"

I bobbed my head up and down in wholehearted agreement.

"And we'll be taken care of for all eternity." She seemed to drift away from the present altogether.

Carefully I considered her angelic face, framed by dark brown curls cascading around her shoulders, and her quiet manner. She reminded me of what I thought Sarah, Abraham's wife, would have looked like as a young matron. "Are you by any chance married?"

She blushed. "Why do you ask?"

"Oh, no reason," I blandly replied. "Just wondering."

Her celestial countenance blessed me. "Maybe someday—when the right man comes along. I'll want to obey him, you know. I want to wait for God's best for me." Her voice seemed to ring heavenly chimes as she spoke.

"Are you from around here?"

The question rolled off my lips just as my rowdy son Joe ran in front of me showering me with grass and dirt.

"Mom! Mom!" he screeched. "Dad says you have to help haul sand! Hurry up!" Grabbing me by the arms, he dragged me to my feet.

"Thanks!" I managed to holler back to the saintly Sunday-school teacher. Joe pushed and prodded me along.

"Slow down, Joe!" I yelled.

"Mom, Dad says the men are going to play horseshoes, and the women have to haul the sand!" Irritation flashed in his eyes.

Miss Dwyer's angelic attitude faded. My devilish dander took over. "Oh, he did, did he?" I plopped down on the nearest lawn chair. "Well, I'm not going, and that's final!"

Joe swung his head back and forth slowly. "Dad's not going to like this."

Later that evening, after the kids were asleep, John asked, "How come you missed the horseshoe game?"

I told him why, concluding with, ". . . and I'm not going to be anybody's slave!"

The atmosphere chilled our breakfast cereal the following morning.

The chasm between John and me widened. It should have concerned me. Instead, I turned to my own pursuits—and Val.

"I know what I'll do, Val. I'll become employed—at *home!* Then I'll have the best of both worlds."

My reasoning kept pace with my typing as I furiously pounded the keyboard, computing everything from brooms to the household budget.

Sitting there, I envisioned me as a secretary. "A home secretary!" As though tapping fresh eggs, I touched the keys and watched the screen. *MARTHA—THE HOME EXECUTIVE SECRETARY!* Then I changed it to *MARTHA'S HOME EXEC-SEC-RETARIAL SERVICE!*

I pushed the *print* button and waited for Val to do her stuff.

"Meanwhile, I'll watch television!" Switching the switch on the back of the TV from *computer* to *TV*, I rolled my steno chair in front of the screen.

"You can be healed today!" Excitedly the speaker waved his hands while roaring his message.

"What's this?" Immediately curious, I concentrated my attention on the television picture.

Your ankle should be cured, whispered my busybody brain.

Eyes glued to the set, I rolled my chair over to Val and shut everything down. "This is too good to miss!" I exclaimed, positioning myself for better viewing. I looked down at my walking cast, then addressed the orator in the box. "My cast is due to come off tomorrow, but the doctor said it won't be completely healed. What about that?"

"God doesn't want you to hurt!" he boomed back.

"I wonder if he heard me."

By the time the program was over, the speechmaker had convinced me.

"I am healed! I can't wait to see the doctor's face tomorrow. He's in for a major surprise!"

The next afternoon, while the serious physician concentrated on cutting off my cast, I giggled and grinned.

My levity vanished, however, when he pronounced, "Just as I thought, Mrs. Christian. You will need a cane as well as physical therapy."

"What?" I couldn't believe my ears.

"You remember. I informed you that this would probably be the case. A few weeks more . . ." He patted my shoulder.

"Why does my leg look shriveled?" In shock I stared at my withered, white limb.

Driving home, I muttered, "Maybe God is punishing me."

My ankle folded repeatedly as I struggled up the basement stairs to the kitchen. "This cane is worse than crutches!" A tear dribbled down my right cheek.

While trying to pace back and forth in the kitchen, I realized what I had to do. "Prayer changes things," I admonished myself.

Off to the living room—hippity-hop—down on my knees before the rocking chair, I droned out, "God, I'll tell you what. I'll make you a deal. You fix my leg, and I'll obey John. You know I can't stand much more of this hobbling around the house."

I lay down on the floor to rest while I waited to get healed.

Certain I'd made God a deal He wouldn't want to refuse (after all I was dealing in His Word), I relaxed.

"I can't miss with this one," I cooed. Stretched out on the carpet in the middle of the living room, in front of the big picture window which framed the sleeping monolith called Chief, I drifted off to sleep.

In my dream, clouds covered the Chief. Storm shrouds obscured my vision and curled confusion around the house where I lay on a mat. Feeling pain in my legs, I noticed I could not move them. "Help me!" I cried out in terror.

Two young men appeared beside me and carried me to a low table. After settling me on a pillow, they brought me fruit and cheese. "The King wishes to see you now," advised one.

"I'm not moving from this spot," I retorted, sick with self-pity. "I hate being lame!"

"As you wish," said the other.

Instantly the gigantic black clouds moved right into the room with me, and formed a figure larger than life which boomed threateningly, "You will remain a cripple for the rest of your days for your lack of obedience!"

"Mom?" Gently George's voice drifted into my nightmare.

"George? Is it really you?" Opening my eyes, I welcomed the sight of my freckle-faced son.

"What are you doing on the floor, Mom?" He took a large bite from his ever-present apple.

"Oh, nothing," I replied. "Just resting."

"Hey, you got your cast off," he grinned. "Think I'll give Ben another ride in his new elevator." He skipped happily toward his room.

Pulling myself to a standing position, leaning on my cane, I recalled my promise to God, "I *will* obey John."

Uneasiness crept along the back of my skull.

You've done it this time! My brain screamed in pain. *You've gone and grabbed a tiger by the tail!*

"Yeah," I agreed shakily. "And I know the big cat's name."

Obeisance.

8 / *Grounded*

"One who doesn't give the gift he promised is like a cloud blowing over a desert without dropping any rain."[21]

By late May I walked without a cane.

Guilt gripped me, however, because I still did *not* obey John. Unfaithful to my promise to God, I expected misery and disaster from above, but the sky continued to dawn blue above the Chief.

Then the rigor mortis of disobedience set in, stiffening my backbone against every suggestion of John's. Try as I might I could not truckle to my husband.

One sunny spring day as I watched Buddy the bird run and hop around the living room carpet, I spied a raven swooping past our picture window.

Viewing Buddy from my vantage point in my rocking chair, I realized Joe's little bird had a problem. "You don't *fly*, Buddy. You walk!"

"Cheep! Peep!" He tore across the rug and snapped up a cookie crumb in his beak.

I rocked back and forth, observing his behavior.

Maybe he doesn't know how to fly, offered my mind.

"I'll bet you don't know how to get off the ground, Buddy."

(I should have known better than to touch Joe's parakeet without informing him, but people sometimes devise other projects when not wishing to tackle their own, and I hated ironing.)

"Chirp! Chirp!" My feathered friend seemed willing to learn.

Slithering out of the rocking chair, I slowly slid myself next to him. Beak to nose we stayed for a while as I spoke softly to him to get his attention. "How's it goin', fella?" I clicked my tongue against the roof of my mouth to make bird sounds.

Tilting his head to one side, he blinked, opened his beak wide, and made a burping noise.

"Wouldn't you like to wing your way through the house?" I inquired gently.

He fluffed his feathers and stretched his wings.

Excitement stirred me to greater effort as I carefully crept my hand over next to him.

He jumped backwards.

"Now, now, Buddy, this won't hurt a bit!" I stretched my right arm forward and laid it like a log on the floor beside him.

He stood stationary and stared at me with one eye.

Ever so slowly, I inched my fingers toward his feet, clucking and chirping as I went.

The heavenly-blue fluff of feathers watched me.

Tingles of exhilaration overcame the cramp in my arm as I laid my forefinger right on top of both his feet.

Warily, he watched for my next move.

"Hop on my hand, Buddy," I coaxed.

Cautiously, he pulled a yellow foot from underneath my finger and placed it on top.

Holding my breath, I hoped he would follow with the other one.

He pulled his foot back again.

My nose itched, but I didn't move a muscle. Time seemed suspended as mother and warm-blooded vertebrate with feathers and wings encountered each other.

Then lighter than a feather's touch, he hopped on the human perch.

Victory! my brain squealed.

"Nice bird," I crooned softly, pulling myself to a sitting position to ease my aching back.

"Peep." He shifted back and forth on my finger.

That completed lesson number one.

"You're going to be great!" Proud of my future feathered flier,

I hummed happily while transporting him on my hand across the living room to the large picture window. "See? You, Buddy, my boy, will soar like the eagles!" I chirped a little more in the interest of good communications. "Won't Joe be surprised?"

Just as I managed to get him back into his cage, a bell rang in the kitchen. "Ah," I said in satisfaction, "the oven is responding nicely to my new meal-planning system devised by Val and me." Staring off into the distance, I could see the entire house run by robots—and me moving into more productive pursuits.

Ambling over to the rocking chair, I plopped down and swung my previously injured right leg up over the arm. "How silly!" I exclaimed. "I don't have to prop my leg anymore." Leaning my head back, I rocked to and fro for a moment, just before guilt swept through my nervous system again with great discomfort. My healed leg reminded me of my unkept promise to God to obey John.

Leaping up from the chair as though I'd sat on a tack, I headed for Val. "The computer noise will do me good," I mused. "All those blips and beeps comfort a frayed nervous system." I positioned myself in my steno chair. "I think I'll surprise John! Won't he love it when he finds his class records systematized by Val!"

I flipped the computer switches to *on*, and the telephone rang.

I raced to answer it. "Hello?"

"Hi, sweetie. What's wrong with your voice?" Jean chuckled.

"I'm practicing a professional sound. Like it?" Without waiting to hear her answer or her giggle, I dashed to my computer work-area and switched everything off. Then I tore back to the telephone.

"Busy?" Jean inquired good-naturedly as I picked up the receiver.

"No. Be back in a minute." Bustling to the kitchen, I poured myself a cup of cold, black coffee, pulled a chair close to the phone, and prepared to chat. "I'm glad you called. There's something I want to ask you."

"What?"

"Something has been bothering me for a while now—you

probably haven't noticed—and I want to know what you think."
I took a sip of cold blackness to brace myself.

"What's the problem?"

"Not really a problem," I defended. "Do you remember my ankle?"

She roared with laughter.

"What's so funny?" Slightly miffed, I waited for her to control herself.

"You mean the one you hurt?" She sounded serious again.

"Yes. Well, I asked God to heal it." I paused to get my thoughts in order for a good presentation of my case.

"Great! Now it's healed. What's the problem?" She muffled laughter.

"This isn't funny!" I snapped.

Don't tell her anything. What does she know? My brain leaped into action.

"There are 'friends' who pretend to be friends, but there is a friend who sticks closer than a brother."²² The Quiet One brought me a scripture verse I'd read and placed it softly in my thinking.

Holding the receiver thoughtfully near my ear, I pondered the meaning.

"Martha? Sorry I teased you," Jean's voice interrupted. "Are you still there?"

My eyes half closed as I decided to tell Jean *some* of the truth. "Yes. It's okay. But how do I know God healed my ankle?"

"What?"

"How do I know it wasn't a coincidence?"

"A coincidence?" She sounded puzzled.

"It could have healed anyway, whether I asked God or not, couldn't it?" Carefully, I explained my case.

"Martha, why do I have the feeling there is more to this than you're telling me?"

"Jean, what I'm trying to say is this—if God healed my leg, He would have done it overnight, or at least fast, wouldn't He?" Holding my breath while she weighed her answer, I waited for the statement which would set me free from my vow to God to obey John.

"That's a difficult question." She cleared her throat. "I'll ask Hub what he thinks when he comes home tonight. We'll pray about it, and I'll let you know."

You're not going to take that, are you? You're not going to let her husband tell you what to think, are you? My gray matter was giving me an instant headache.

"What's Hub got to do with it?" Guardedly, I grilled my dearest friend.

"Let a woman quietly receive instruction with entire submissiveness,"[23] Jean responded softly.

"What?"

"That's a Bible verse, Martha. First Timothy 2:11."

Struck to the core of my being, I closed my mouth. Then I chuckled artificially, "Can't argue with that!"

"*You* might try," she replied seriously.

I terminated the conversation and stomped back to Val. "What does she know?" I muttered. "We have *never* agreed on this issue, and we never will! She has her way, and I have mine, and our ways will never be the same." I flopped down on my secretarial chair. "I realize she believes that submitting to Hub is the only way, but I can't see the point. John and I get along just fine the way we are!" I fumed, crossing my arms in front of me.

"Why don't you ask John what he thinks?" the Quiet One breathed gently.

Jumping up from my chair, I stormed out to the kitchen. "At least one thing is certain. I don't have to keep my promise to obey John because even Jean said it could have been a coincidence."

I looked down at my healthy leg. Quickly I forgot the pain of immobility, the discomfort of the cast, and the dependence I'd felt upon others to help me.

By the time I returned to Val, after taking an hour to cool off, I'd managed to rationalize the entire issue.

"Certainly God will understand *my* point of view," I argued, pacing around the living room. "I would have tried to jump through the hoops for John if I'd really been healed, but my ankle got better normally. Therefore God had nothing to do with it.

He won't hold me to something like bondage. After all, this is the twentieth century!"

By late evening, while John and the kids lay sleeping, I completed my thought processes concerning my promise to God. Knitting needles clacking, I muttered to the sweater heating up in my sweating palms. "I know who got me into this!" I dropped a couple of stitches. "It was that man on television. I'm sure there's a Bible verse about people like him!"

Throwing my knitting into my work basket, I hurried to the Bible and flailed through the pages. "Ah, here is one!"

"They are like clouds blowing over dry land without giving rain, promising much, but producing nothing."[24]

Somewhere in celestial realms angels wept over my hasty interpretation, and my application to someone other than myself.

Having sold my soul to foolishness, the next day I moved ahead.

"I will help John with his schoolwork! He's going to love this," I predicted, snitching his class records from the files in his study.

On the way to Val I passed Buddy. "I'm going to teach you to fly later, Buddy!" I announced. "Won't that be fun?"

Busily I tapped Val's keyboards, storing John's grade records in her memory banks.

My mind worked as fast as my fingers flew. "John will have this information already typed on his report cards. That way, when he pulls them out of his files to make them out, half the work will be done before he begins!" I paused to straighten my aching back. "Val, you are going to promote a class of children to the next grade. What do you think of that?"

"Blip. Blip. Bleep. Blip," Val responded.

Once finished, I decided I deserved a treat.

In no time at all I stood before an appliance store admiring a dishwasher. "Everyone has one nowadays," I rationalized, walking inside.

The pleasant salesperson concluded my purchasing deal with, "We'll deliver it by the end of the week, Mrs. Christian."

On my way out of the store I discovered the world of *timers*.

"John will really appreciate the modern world of machinery with a few of these!"

Not long afterward, I waltzed around the house looking for places to install timing devices. "We'll save on electricity and conserve our own energy too. Jean may submit to Hub, but our entire house will serve John!" Gloating over my discovery, I hooked John's favorite reading lamp to one. "He will love it coming on automatically."

I peppered the house with square timing boxes. "The toaster will be terrific. The coffeepot too!"

Finally I attached John's electric blanket to one. "He keeps it too hot anyway, and he will be crazy about the savings."

Walking through the rooms, admiring my work, I amazed myself with my accomplishments. "And in such a short time!"

At the end of the week, however, John shocked me into complete chagrin. "Martha! What is this dishwasher doing in my kitchen?" he roared most unbecomingly.

Striking my best battle stance, I declared, "It's my kitchen, too. Furthermore, I am the one who works out here!"

Facing a hysterical female usually threw John off balance, but not this time. "Take it back," he ordered.

"Back?" My eyes pleaded with him to be understanding.

"Return it to the store," he commanded.

"What don't you like about it?" My desperation rose.

"We can't afford it."

"Oh," I replied, thinking of the things he could afford for himself.

Bright and early the next morning, however, I telephoned the appliance store. "Will you please come and get the dishwasher delivered to the Christian residence yesterday afternoon?"

"Sorry, lady," a strident male voice replied.

"I'm sorry too, but we can't seem to fit this appliance into the scheme of our budget right now." I waited.

"We don't do pickups on Saturday, lady. Call Monday morning and talk to somebody then." Abruptly he hung up.

Staring at the dead receiver in my hand, I toyed with the idea of phoning back but thought better of it.

"Maybe we can keep it after all," I mumbled to myself, hunting through the house for John.

I found him down in the basement, sanding a table. "Looks nice," I began.

"Uh huh, and we're not keeping the machine, Martha," he replied without looking up from his work.

I decided to eat humble pie. "I'm sorry." Yet underneath my peace initiative lay deep indignation at John's apparent lack of interest in providing me with proper working conditions. (I'd been watching a lot of television while waiting for Val to do printouts.)

"They can't pick it up until Monday," I announced.

"Just as long as they get it." John continued to apply muscle to sandpaper on the old folding table.

"Where did you get that?" I marveled at the oak appearing from under a coat of white paint.

"School. Thought you might like it for the house."

"Oh." Shame began to melt my hardened heart. "Thank you."

"Why not tell him how you really feel?" the Quiet One softly suggested.

For a moment I wavered.

You can't tell John you feel unappreciated, my cranium countered. *He'll think you're crazy!*

So the communication gap between me and my husband widened over the weekend. While John sanded and varnished the folding table for the front hall, I discovered a myriad of household chores to attract my attention.

When Monday morning rolled around, I couldn't wait to get John and the boys off to school. Now I could clear up the dishwasher dilemma.

"What do you *mean* you won't take it back?" I couldn't believe the message transmitted to me through the telephone. "Where is the person I bought it from?"

"If you would like a replacement, or repair," the voice continued dryly, "we can handle that." His insensitivity appalled me.

"Never mind. I'll call back." The staggering blow caught me

off guard. "What am I going to do?" I twiddled the telephone cord.

You're not prepared to deal with this, my traitorous cerebrum stated the obvious.

My body trembled with agonizing anxiety. Sitting down at the kitchen table, I manicured my nails, allowing time for the circumstances to clear themselves.

"Oh, no. Oh, no," I muttered to myself as I furiously filed my fingers down to stubs. "There's no point in asking Jean for help. She would have told me to ask John's permission in the first place."

An hour later, I paced the living room rug and wrung my hands behind my back.

When John arrived home from school that afternoon, I rushed out to the car to meet him. Adopting a posture of abject misery, I complained, "John, they won't take it back. They'll only replace or repair the dishwasher. And I don't know who sold it to me." Tears filled my eyes.

Stepping out of the car, his blue eyes appraised the situation. "What happened?"

"Nothing happened, John. That's the trouble. They absolutely refuse to take back the dishwasher!"

John opened the door to the house and held it for me to enter. "I'll handle it," he said in a clipped tone.

And he did. Within one hour the kitchen no longer housed a machine for washing dishes.

"I'll be forever grateful," I announced to the soap bubbles after supper while scrubbing pots and pans. "It is, however, a *man's* world. They wouldn't listen to me at all."

After that I intended to consult John more often about things, but human nature took over. Spiritual discipline needed to take root before it could grow. My promise made to God in desperation withered faster than a sapling on a scorching summer day. Until my heart condition changed, my home life would remain dry, lifeless.

Filled with my own miseries, I didn't see John retreating into himself. Neither of us realized the pressure conditions developing in our home.

The first pitfall lay dead ahead.

Three days later, when I answered the door in the middle of the day, I faced the blue uniform of the law. Sniveling next to the officer stood Joe. Fourteen years of training down the tube. "May we come in, Mrs. Christian?" The authoritative voice requested.

Numbly I nodded assent and stepped back. Terror tore through me.

"He was caught shoplifting." The law officer explained before I could ask.

Blood rushed to my head, and my ears pounded. Unable to speak, I motioned for Joe to go upstairs.

Somehow we arrived at the kitchen table, seated ourselves, and I listened to the detailed account of my son's crime.

"The store proprietor phoned us. Your son and a few other punks tried to help themselves to hunting knives."

I couldn't believe my son had earned the label *punk*. My laser-like eyes pierced the gaze of my guilty offspring. "Joe, is this true?"

"I guess so," he mumbled, hanging his head.

"Don't you know?" my voice squeaked.

Joe stared down at the table.

"May I see you for a moment privately?" The officer broke the heavy silence.

"Certainly." In humiliation I led the way to John's study.

"It's a first offense, Mrs. Christian."

Trying to decipher his feelings toward me and my son, I stared mute at his black moustache.

"He gave us no trouble in apprehending him. However, he bears watching. A court appearance won't be necessary. No charges—as long as he makes proper restitution. And," he adjusted his gun belt, "the owner wants to meet the parents of each offender."

"Yes, of course," I agreed in the agony of degradation.

After the law left, I sat down at the kitchen table with Joe. "Joe, why?" I tried to keep my voice low.

"I dunno!" he snapped.

"Don't you have anything to say?" My temper sparked.

"No."

An impasse. Stone wall against cement building blocks.

"Then go to your room." My last resort.

He went.

Crushed, I sat alone at the table. Putting my face in my hands, I wept.

Finally I remembered to fix supper. Since John had a dinner meeting, and John Jr. had gone to a barbecue, I hunted around the kitchen for something to feed Joe and George. "Hot dogs will have to do. I feel sick," I said, hauling weiners out of the freezer.

"Suppertime!" I hollered to the house.

George arrived at the table, hungry and talkative. "Great hot dogs, Mom! You really outdid yourself this time! Where did you get these weiners?" My youngest loaded the bun with catsup, then gingerly placed the meat in the middle.

"Don't squeeze it, George, or you'll have it all down your arms." He took a large bite, and the contents exploded.

Ignoring the "I-told-you-so" opportunity, I asked, "Would you like some potato chips?"

"Yeah!" His eyes widened with delight as he helped himself to huge handfuls and loaded them onto the catsup pool on his plate.

I watched him inhale the food.

"Aren't you hungry, Mom?" He stopped chomping long enough to inquire.

"Not very." I got up from the table. "Would you like some ice cream for dessert?"

"Where's Joe?" He hefted a spoonful of chocolate swirled in vanilla and stuffed it in his face.

"In his room. He's not hungry either."

"Oh," he responded, licking his bowl.

Once finished, George raced out to play with his friends. I breathed a sigh of relief and cleared the table.

By the time I sat down in the living room to put my feet up, I heard George running up the stairs two at a time.

"Mom," he whimpered, "I can't find Specimen."

"Why is your brother's dog loose?" Slowly I pieced the information together and realized what had happened before George explained the situation to me.

"I took him with me to Johnny's house." Fresh tears streaked his cheeks.

"Oh, George, no." Discouragement settled in my soul. "We better get going and find him before J.J. comes home."

Eleven-year-old George's head drooped. "I'm sorry, Mom."

"I know you are. Let's go." Grabbing a light jacket. I raced out the door with my sorry one. Up and down the streets we called for an hour. No Specimen.

Wearily, we walked home together. "Bedtime, George."

"Okay, Mom," he replied sadly, heading for his room.

Approaching Joe and John Jr.'s room, I tapped lightly on the closed door.

No answer.

Peeking in, I discovered Joe sound asleep in his clothes. I decided not to wake him.

Turning my back, I tiptoed toward the living room. "Lord, please help me," I whispered. "Why is this happening?" Ruefully, I remembered my promise to obey John. "I won't make another vow I won't keep, Lord, but Specimen is what John Jr. loves most in the world."

Hearing the back door slam, I hurried down the stairs.

"Hi, Mom." J.J. tossed the words over his shoulder while parking his bike.

"Specimen is lost," I ventured. "Could you—"

Hopping back on his bike, John Jr. rode through the door and out the driveway.

Rushing after him, I watched as he disappeared from sight, hollering for his dog. When his voice faded, I walked slowly back upstairs to wait.

An hour later John Jr. returned without his canine companion.

"When Dad gets home, we'll use the car to look for Specimen," I promised.

"Wake me if you find out anything, will you?" Bravely he faced the unknown.

I hugged his man-sized frame. "God knows where Specimen

is, J.J.," I comforted softly. "God knows."

He straightened his shoulders and cleared his throat. "Where's Joe?"

"Asleep." The memory of the day stabbed my heart. Realizing J.J. wanted comfort from his younger brother, I couldn't tell him about Joe's transgression of the law.

"Good night, Mom."

I kissed him on the cheek and patted his shoulder.

Walking outside in the evening air, I hoped to see Specimen's gigantic jaws carrying a bone home. I called softly, I hunted, and I prayed to find him.

Trudging home by myself, I climbed the stairs. Twilight descended.

As I sat alone in the living room, the timer turned on John's reading lamp, chasing away the shadows.

"What am I going to tell John?" I listened for his key in the lock and heard it.

John.

9 / Checkout

"A dry crust eaten in peace is better than steak every day along with argument and strife."[25]

"Well, kids, how does it feel?" Placing a platter of steaming scrambled eggs and crisp bacon on the table, I scanned my sons' faces.

George grinned mischievously. Joe quietly grabbed the serving spoon.

John Jr. swooped down with his own spoon and helped himself first to the eggs. "You mean the last day of school?" he asked.

"Exactly that," I commented, snatching the plate and handing it to George.

"Where's your father?" I asked, popping bread into the toaster.

"He's coming, I think," responded George while piling jam onto his plate.

"I'll go and see. Watch the toast, will you J.J.?" Wiping my hands on my apron, I walked toward the back of the house.

"John?" I found him hard at work in his study. "Aren't you coming out for breakfast?"

When he turned around in his chair and faced me, his frown could have leveled a skyscraper.

"What's wrong, John?" I inquired innocently.

Removing his reading glasses, he said coldly, "Martha, your computer failed every child in class. You promised you would check your work." Whipping his chair back around, he resumed writing.

Horrified, I stared at his back. "Does that mean you're not coming to breakfast?"

"At least that, Martha."

"Can I help?" My voice sounded small.

"You already did." John refused to look at me.

Retreating from the room in silence, this fresh wound opened a wider gulf between me and my husband.

You ruined his report cards, chided my cranium. *Why don't you quit getting in his way?*

Returning to the breakfast table, I managed to continue casual conversation with the children.

The boys chattered happily, delighted to be nearly free of educational bombardment.

"No more homework, Joe! Isn't that great?" John Jr. slapped his brother on the back.

"Yeah," he mumbled, stuffing toast into his mouth.

"I passed, Mom! I know I did!" George's eyes beamed with victorious achievement.

"Dad's not very hungry this morning," I introduced out of context.

Suddenly John appeared at the table, making a liar out of me. "Any eggs left? I'm starved!" He winked at George.

My eyebrows arched. "Is everything all right?"

"It will be, Martha." He grinned at J.J. and playfully cuffed Joe on the chin. "Hand me the plate, will you, Joe?" He motioned toward the half-empty serving platter.

Not long afterward, the empty house and dirty dishes reminded me that my family had begun their day. Hurrying to my computer desk, I flipped Val on.

"What happened?" I asked myself while waiting for the screen to display what Val had printed on the report cards.

YOUR CHILD HAS FAILED THE CURRENT GRADE LEVEL PASSED.

"Oh, no!" I breathed in dismay.

Leaning back in my chair, I tried to reconstruct the moment of Val's programming. I remembered. When I tried the *move copy* feature, I never moved *passed* next to *failed*! Disgusted with my imperfect performance, I started to reprogram the sequence.

YOUR CHILD HAS PASSED FAILED THE CURRENT GRADE LEVEL. John was supposed to circle *passed,* or *failed.*

So much for your help, goaded my mind.

"That does it. I'm not cut out for this. If I'm going to work, I'll get a job outside the house!" Shutting down Val, I covered the computer in plastic, realizing I'd never use it again.

The telephone rang.

"Hi, Jean," I answered.

"How did you know it would be me?" she inquired brightly.

"Who else calls every day at this hour?" I quipped without humor.

"Right," she responded warmly. "What's wrong?"

"I ruined John's report cards," I confessed without my usual preamble.

"How did it happen?" My dear friend's patience in my time of need comforted my soul.

After I explained my mistake, I said, "Jean, things aren't going well these days."

"Do you want to talk about it?" Her tone was gentle.

"I think I need to try this submission situation differently. Oh, Jean," my voice broke, "last week the police brought Joe home for shoplifting." The tension inside me erupted into tears.

"Martha, I am sorry." Warmth wrapped around me. She cared.

"John will go with Joe to make restitution. I can't." Tears ran off the end of my nose.

"Anything I can do to help?" Love flowed through the wires. Jean didn't crack jokes when I needed her.[26]

"Thanks, Jean. You're a true friend, just like the Bible says."[27] Taking a deep breath, I wiped my eyes and continued. "At least we found Specimen."

"I didn't know you lost the dog, too!"

"George took him to Johnny's house without permission, and Johnny shut him down in their basement for some unknown reason without telling his mother. The upshot of the story is that Specimen spent a lonely night, John Jr. didn't sleep a wink, and

John's electric blanket timer malfunctioned."

"Malfunctioned?"

"Didn't I tell you? I've put timers all over the house for convenience. Things happen all by themselves!" I gathered momentum. "It would be glorious if the house could be completely automated!" I paused. "Anyway, the electric blanket shut off unexpectedly in the middle of the night, leaving John in the cold."

"What does John think of the new system?"

"I dunno. He didn't say."

"Have you ever read the Book of Esther?"

"Certainly. She's the one who saved her people. Why?" I wrinkled my brows in confusion, surprised at the sudden change in conversation.

"I wonder if you'd be willing to read Esther eight, verses one through eight. Maybe it will help."

Hurting too much too argue, I promised to read it.

Back in the living room, I read the Esther portion but understood nothing.

"Read all of Esther with an open heart," suggested the Quiet One.

Sore of spirit and weary of work, I turned to chapter one and discovered Queen Vashti. The apple of her husband's eye, she refused to attend his celebration party and shamed him before his guests.

"What a horrible thing to do!" I stated vehemently, reading on.

King Ahasuerus, the embarrassed emperor of one hundred twenty-seven provinces, which stretched from India to Ethiopia, consulted his lawyers before venting his fury upon his wife.

"We suggest that, subject to your agreement, you issue a royal edict, a law of the Medes and Persians that can never be changed, that Queen Vashti be forever banished from your presence and that you choose another queen more worthy than she."[28]

"Banished! Wow!" My eyes widened at the queen's sentence. "At least we can't be exiled today."

But then the king began to brood because he missed Queen Vashti.

That's where Mordecai came in. He had adopted and raised as his daughter, his lovely young cousin Hadassah (Esther) who was then taken to the king's palace and added to his harem.

"Harem!" I almost shouted. Slapping my Bible shut, I put it aside.

"Read all of the book," counseled the Quiet One.

I read on.

The point of the story seemed to be that Esther followed everyone's advice: Hegai, the harem keeper, told her how to dress, while Mordecai advised against admitting her Jewish ancestry.

As a result, King Ahasuerus crowned her *Queen* Esther.

"At least *obeisance* wasn't in this story," I commented, dialing Jean's number.

"What's the point?" I queried as soon as I'd said hello.

"You mean Esther?"

"Yes."

"Did you read it?"

"Yes. The whole thing—all about how she saved her people." Impatiently I drummed my fingers on the kitchen counter.

"Did you happen to notice a difference between Queen Vashti and Esther?"

"Yes. The king banished Vashti, but he loved Esther." I twirled the telephone cord.

"Do you have your Bible handy?" Patiently she probed my mood.

"Right here. Just *tell* me, Jean. You always do this to me."

"Would you please read chapter eight, verse eight out loud to me?" Her calm dissipated my irritability.

I read, "Now go ahead and send a message to the Jews, telling them whatever you want to in the king's name, and seal it with the king's ring, so that it can never be reversed."[29]

"Hmm, that's not bad," I commented. "I thought you'd have me reading the part about her falling down at his feet!"

"Be serious, Martha," she gently admonished.

"Sorry." I needed Jean's help and I knew it.

"Now please read Esther chapter nine, verse thirty-two," she urged.

Turning the page, I began. "So the commandment of Esther confirmed these dates and it was recorded as law."[30]

"Hmm, not bad," I pronounced, raising my eyebrows in approval. "I still don't understand."

"Martha—" Jean's patience was inexhaustible. "Esther's submission gave her the rights of the king."

I felt a stirring deep within my soul, a glimmer of light in the dark tunnel closing in on me.

Pondering the information, I terminated our conversation, then spent some time in prayer. Looking at the Book of Esther again, I noticed that she seemed willing to be led.

"Is that what it means to be submissive, Lord? Willing?"

Walking over to our picture window, I watched the clouds skim the sky. "That seems too easy," I remarked to the quiet world outside.

"For My yoke is easy, and My load is light."[31]

"Cheep! Peep! Chirp!" Buddy the bird called from his prison.

"Want to go for a walk, do you, little fella?" Still thinking about Esther, I strolled over to his cage and stuck my hand in. He hopped on the human perch. "At least you remembered that much from our last lesson," I joked. Carefully I placed him on the rug and sat down in the rocking chair to watch him hop.

I rocked to and fro for a few moments, then I decided suddenly, "Today is the day to sell Val. No sense wasting time."

Feeling a sense of urgency, I penned an advertisement, "Computer for sale—*cheap!*"

Then I telephoned the local paper and made arrangements for payment. "Soon I will be rid of that headache forever," I sighed in satisfaction.

When I returned to the living room, I noticed Buddy's cage door open. "Oh, no," I whispered. "I forgot. Buddy is loose!"

Frantically, I crawled around the living room rug, searching for our blue bird. "Not another pet gone," I moaned, knowing Joe's anger would follow as surely as thunder after storm clouds.

Finding nothing, I sat up and listened for a peep. "I wonder if he would come if I call him?"

He can't even fly! He won't know his name, sneered my gray matter.

Standing up slowly, I ignored my cranial adviser and counseled myself. "He can't have hopped far."

Worry grabbed the pit of my stomach and dug in for the duration.

"Oh, Lord," I prayed, "don't let Buddy be permanently lost. Joe and I already don't get along. He will blame me. I know it."

No Buddy.

Visions of an injured bird tormented my thinking as I searched the house in vain. "This must be how George felt when Specimen disappeared. I will be more understanding next time," I promised myself.

"He could be flying," a soft thought soothed.

I began to call. "Buddy! Buddy, where are you? Come on, little fella, it's me."

I heard a faint cheeping noise. My heart leaped as I followed the sound.

"Buddy?"

"Peep! Chirrup!" The sound floated from our bedroom.

Hurrying to the door, I called out, "Chirp! Cluck-cluck!" Peeking into our room, I searched in earnest and listened.

"Chirp! Chirrup!"

"Buddy!" My eyes riveted to the top of the bedroom draperies. "Buddy, you *flew!*"

The yellow-beaked ball of blue fluff puffed out his chest and preened his feathers.

Joy, relief, and frustration characterized the hour it took me to capture Joe's parakeet and return him safely to his cage.

Buddy, on the other hand, loved every minute of it. Recaged, he sat happily on his swing and blinked his eyes contentedly.

"You did it all by yourself, Buddy! I didn't even have to teach you."

I wondered if Jean felt the same satisfaction as I moved through the house, straightening, dusting, and picking up the children's litter—gum wrappers, marbles, and socks. Jean seemed to fly in relation to her husband and family, while I hopped along the ground. "I'm certain there's a lesson in it somewhere," I muttered. "But I'm not ready to leap into thin air."

By the time I stood scouring the sink, I prayed, "Why am I different, Lord? It seems easy for Jean. She doesn't have the huge upheavals with her children either."

Keep on with that lily-livered-mollycoddle-attitude, and you'll be bowing and scraping before you know it, my sly mind warned.

Shouts from the back door informed me that motherhood would be my full-time job until fall.

"Hey, Mom! We're home! H'ray!" chorused George.

"Get out of my way!" middle son grumbled.

"Then *you* move over!" oldest son argued.

Taking a deep breath, I prepared for the onslaught.

Thundering feet stampeded up the stairs to the kitchen where I stood waiting.

"Whoopee!" shouted George. "It's over!"

"What have you got to eat around here?" inquired John Jr., owner of two hollow legs.

"Joe," I tried to be heard above the din, "Buddy flew today. Isn't that wonderful?" The good news fortified me against the reality of school's end.

"Did you take him out?" Joe frowned and curled his lip as he flung his accusation my way. "You could have lost him, you know."

Anger straightened my backbone. "Joe—" I shook my finger in his direction. "I've had just about enough of your backtalk."

"Yeah, well, I've had enough of you!" Slamming the remains of his cleaned-out locker on the floor, he stormed out of the kitchen.

Shock cemented my feet to the floor.

"What's wrong with him?" asked George innocently.

Mad as a *toro* in a bullring, I held my tongue and clenched my fists.

"Never mind, Mom," John Jr. comforted. "He's disgusted with the world today."

My anger was suddenly transformed into investigative research. Mother love made inquiry. "Why?" I asked J.J.

J.J. responded like a funeral parlor attendant—partly sympathy, mostly business. "He flunked three subjects," he informed me.

"*Failed?*" I couldn't accept the unacceptable word. It was foreign to our standards for a bright boy who needed an education in order to survive.

"Yup." J.J. opened the refrigerator door and eyed the contents.

"It's not time for supper," I said mechanically, closing the door.

"Aw, Mom." Now George tried to pull it open.

"Out!" I screamed.

They cleared the decks.

Failure flowed through my veins. The stress of family life held no rewards for me. "John will blame me for this. I know it." I spoke to an empty kitchen. "That's it! Staying home doesn't work."

I imagined me—hair neatly coiffured, high heels clicking—walking into a place of business I could call my own. "I am getting a job!" I slammed a cupboard door to show I meant business. "Only this time I'll get one, and nobody will stop me."

Hands on my hips, I yelled, "Hey, you kids, get in here!"

"You just told us to leave!" brave George hollered from his room.

"I changed my mind!" I screeched back.

They appeared.

"Let me see your report cards." I stuck out my right hand.

Dutifully, George plopped his into my waiting palm.

J.J., with nothing to fear, announced, "You're going to like this!"

I glared at Joe. "Yours first, Joe."

Red-faced, he handed over his report card and waited for the maternal volcano to erupt.

Ripping open the envelope, I slowly surveyed the sheet. "Go to your room, Joe," I stated in clipped tones. "I'll speak to your father when he gets home. *Now move it!*"

Mercy might have restrained me from shaming him in front of his brothers.

"The anger of man does not achieve the righteousness of

God," breathed the Quiet Spirit.[32]

Complimenting John Jr. on his high grade average, and commenting on George's improvement in the area of citizenship, I tried to cover the pain Joe brought to my heart.

When John arrived home, weary with year-end work, I met him at the door with, "Joe failed *three* subjects, John. You have to talk to him."

Worry lines etched his face as sadness dulled his deep blue eyes. "All right, Martha," he replied, heading for Joe's room.

The following day John and Joe kept their appointment with the store proprietor in regard to the hunting knife episode.

Anxiously, I waited at home for the results.

"If Joe and the others will spend the next four weekends picking up garbage around the parking lot, the owner won't press charges." John aged ten years as he reported the results to me.

"I guess we can be thankful it won't appear in the newspaper," I offered.

"I'm going to take a nap," John wearily responded.

As the week went by, John's spirits continued to dip lower.

Worried at his pale appearance one day, I felt his forehead with the back of my hand. "Do you feel all right, John?"

"I'm fine." Dejection tinged his voice.

Our family activities dissolved into nothingness as Joe spent more time away from home with his friends, John Jr. found a girl who stole his senses, and George rode all over town on his bike.

When I eventually sold Val for a little less than the purchase price, I thought John would be pleased.

"Fine, Martha," he said without feeling.

When Buddy molted for the first time, nobody but me noticed.

Finally John told me what he thought of my timing devices planted around the house.

"Martha, the doorbell refuses to ring, the hot water is cold, my electric shaver doesn't realize summer means different hours, the toaster only works at 7:30 a.m., the lamp turns *off* when I read the newspaper, the stereo blares while I sleep, and my side of the electric blanket runs day and night. Remove them—all of them!"

"Oh," I pouted. In my opinion he stated his case coldly.

Hurt that he didn't appreciate my ingenuity, I ripped the timing devices from the wallsockets and stored them in the attic.

John's cordiality ceased completely when he discovered that my constant use of Val had obliterated the television picture tube.

"Martha! The baseball game vanished in the final inning!"

He was still shouting something about bases being loaded as I telephoned the TV repairperson to come right away and fix it.

I also suspected that John blamed me for Joe's recent misbehavior. I, on the other hand, felt John should have spent more time with his son, or at least put a stop to Joe's constant sassing.

While John retreated, I escaped into "holiness."

"Look at this!" I exclaimed, excited by my find in the Good Book.

Carefully I copied, "But women shall be preserved through the bearing of children if they continue in faith and love and sanctity with self-restraint."[33]

Suddenly my trials had purpose. "I will continue in the faith," I said, crossing the threshold of a nearby Christian bookstore.

Returning home with pamphlets, books, wall plaques, posters, and gummed labels sporting the slogan, SMILE! YOU'RE GOD'S CAMERA ANGLE!, I instituted my own holy crusade.

John didn't seem to notice me stuffing my head full of sanctified information.

He did, however, register surprise when I met him at the door bowing very low with my right palm plastered against my forehead.

"Got a headache, Martha?"

"This is a *salaam!*"

"Is it related to salami, or bologna?" He chuckled, walking past me.

Not long after that I tried reading books on how to interest my husband in his wife.

Finally, disheartened about life in general and motivated by severe inner tension, I decided to approach John about my finding full-time employment. Instigating an early evening stroll, I began our conversation with, "Nothing like an old-fashioned walk to clear the sinuses!"

"Usually you say summer pollens give you a headache," he commented.

"Oh," I responded.

Hit him where it hurts! the wizard of trouble advised.

We walked silently around the familiar neighborhood block. Finally I asked, "John, what's wrong with us?"

He didn't break his stride. "Everything will be fine, Martha. Don't worry about it."

Tension bore a hole in the pit of my stomach. "I need something to do."

"You have too much to do now, don't you?" He gazed steadily ahead.

"Nobody in the family appreciates what I do now."

Silently we matched our steps as I took his arm.

"John, I would like to get a job." Anxiously, I watched his face.

He blinked once, set his jaw, and said nothing.

"Maybe if I go out to work," I continued, "I could find myself."

John bent over to tie his shoe.

"Would it be all right with you?" I stood next to him, listening to my heart pound.

"If that's what you want, Martha." He spoke quietly. "It's getting late," he said, glancing at the darkening sky.

"Tell him you love him," suggested the Quiet One.

My self-assertive rebellion sealed my mouth.

Just then George raced by on his bike. "Hey, Mom!" he squealed happily. "Hey, Dad! I can ride no-handed!"

"Great, George!" my husband called after his speeding son.

By the time we reached home I'd buried my feelings in the growing pile of confusion within.

Early the next morning I again began combing the classified section of the newspaper.

Deep down I knew that John hadn't given his enthusiastic

approval, but I figured he could mind the boys during the summer months while I adjusted to a new job. "He won't mind once he gets used to it. The extra money should help, too."

Close examination of the short column of employment opportunities revealed what I'd discovered during my previous job search.

"Nobody wants what I have to offer." Disappointment settled around me like a dark cloud.

Life is passing you by, agreed the whiz of dissension.

"I'll make a list," I uttered with firm resolve. "I must have *some* marketable skills! I've had enough of volunteering."

Grabbing pen and paper, I drew a line down the middle of the page, and another one across the top. On the left side I wrote, *Current Skills,* and on the other I penned, *Past Experience.*

CURRENT SKILLS	PAST EXPERIENCE
housecleaning	Smock Lady—volunteer
laundry	
nursemaid	
free taxi service	
message-taker	
cook	
dishwasher	
mother	
wife	

Discouragement hit like a freight train. "Who wants any of that?" I questioned.

Housefraus are history, sneered the skull. *Nobody pays good money for unskilled labor.*

Uncertainty gripped me. I paced around the house, thinking.

Spotting the big Bible on the coffee table in the living room, I picked it up, closed my eyes, and opened it at random.

"These older women must train the younger women to live quietly, to love their husbands and their children, and to be sensible and clean minded, spending their time in their own homes, being kind and obedient to their husbands, so that the Christian faith can't be spoken against by those who know them."[34]

The telephone is ringing, interjected my brain.

I leaped to answer it. "Hello?"

"Hack. Cough."

"Is that *you*?" Instantly I recognized the man from the Mice Is Nice Nook.

"Heh, heh. How'd ya know it was me?"

"Just lucky, I guess," I chuckled. "But I'm glad to hear from you because maybe you can tell me where I can find a job." Hoping he might hire me to sell mice or run the cash register while he sold them, I held my breath.

"Well, that's why I called, Martha." He clicked his pipe against the telephone and hacked out a mighty cough. "Must be ESP, or somethin'." Inhaling enough air to squeak and wheeze, he continued, "One of my customers bought a nice white mouse last week. Yes, sir, a plump little rodent with pink eyes." Choking, he cleared his throat. "Come to think of it, maybe the little rascal just had one pink eye. . . ."

"What about the job?" I interrupted.

"The job?"

"You mentioned you might know of something from one of your other patrons who bought a mouse last week." I tried to refresh his memory.

"Don't push me, Martha. I have to tell it my way." Another wheeze whistled through the wires.

"Certainly," I responded impatiently.

"Oh, yeah, now I remember!" I heard the sound of a match being struck. "Say, Martha! Do you know anything about computers?"

"Computers?" Shivers of recognition ran along my spine.

PAY DIRT! My pesky brain howled with delight.

"Hush up! I can handle this myself," I muttered in a loud whisper.

"Are you talkin' to somebody, Martha?" The ancient ears had heard.

"No. Nobody," I replied, firmly, then changed the subject. "Now about computers?"

By the end of the following week, I stood at the checkout of a small supermarket not far from home. Dressed in a resplendent cardinal-colored uniform, I nervously fingered the keys of the gleaming computerized cash register in front of me.

"I've finally made it," I told myself proudly. "I am *employed*!"

10 / Oxymoron

"God wants to know why you are disobeying his commandments. For when you do, everything you try fails. You have forsaken the Lord, and now he has forsaken you."[35]

Incredulously, I stared at my oldest son across the checkout counter. Beside him stood a slip of a girl barely old enough to be allowed out of her backyard.

"Hello," I replied, glaring at John Jr. "Why are you *here*?"

"Babs wanted to see where you work," explained my offspring casually, throwing a starry-eyed glance at his sandy-blond-haired companion.

"Hi, Mrs. Christian," chirped the sweet young thing. "My, what a lovely supermarket!" Her washed-blue eyes engaged the scene.

"Yes," I responded with suspicion.

"Excuse me," interrupted a young mother pushing a cart loaded with babies and groceries, "May I check out now?"

Embarrassed, I quickly waved J.J. aside and began processing the young mother's purchases.

"See you later, Mom," J.J. cheerily waved back at me as he opened the door for his petite female friend.

"Bye, bye," she trilled. Tossing her head in my direction, she wrapped an arm around my son's waist!

I concentrated on the price of lettuce and continued pulling items across blinking red scanning lights until I'd reached the end of the young woman's order. "Will that be all?" I plastered a smile on my face for customer courtesy.

"It's too much already," she answered, eyeing the amount.

"That will be one hundred twenty-seven dollars and seventy-six cents," I droned mechanically while putting things in bags.

"I can't do it," she announced softly.

I continued stuffing groceries into sacks oblivious to her plea.

"Stop. Please." Touching my arm, she spoke louder.

"What?" Busy thinking about J.J. and *Babs*, I jumped.

"I can't pay for it," she declared, hanging her head.

By this time her two-year-old toddler had escaped out the front door. Her year-old twins screeched when she set them down on the floor on either side of her.

Meanwhile, a line of people formed behind her. Heads bobbed up and down with curious irritation.

Nervous perspiration beaded along my hairline. "How much can you pay?" I inquired gently.

"I left my checkbook at home," she whispered in shame.

What a pain, my sassy brain sneered.

Gritting my teeth, I sized up the situation. The poor bedraggled woman needed food and understanding more than my condemnation.

"It's all right," I said magnanimously. "Bring it to me whenever you can. I'll be here till five o'clock this afternoon."

Awestruck at my apparent sainthood, she gathered her groceries and her children and disappeared.

The rest of the afternoon was a torrent of busyness as I checked groceries, stocked empty shelves, and cleaned windows.

When five o'clock rolled around, my feet hurt and my head throbbed with fatigue.

"You can go now, Martha," announced Mr. Kleaver, the store manager.

"Thank you," I responded wearily, stepping over beside the door.

My employer changed my cash drawer, installed a new checker, and headed for the stockroom.

I, on the other hand, shifted from one aching foot to the other, anxiously searching the faces of passersby. "Where can she be?" I sighed.

Mr. Kleaver came out front again. "Are you waiting for a ride, Martha?" he asked.

"No." Tension tightened my already fixed smile. "I'm waiting for someone." Adjusting my stance to look comfortable, I said casually, "She should be here any minute now."

Smoothing his heavy black moustache with his thumb and forefinger, he admonished, "We close at six."

"I realize that," I said uncomfortably. "I'll give her another five minutes." I spread a convincing smirk across my face.

"See you tomorrow then, Mrs. Christian," he replied, sticking his black marking pen over his left ear.

"Telephone. Mr. Kleaver, telephone." The public address system accented a woman's nasal twang.

At five-thirty p.m., my heart sank beneath the soles of my shoes. "She isn't coming back." Crushed with disappointment, I shuffled through the huge glass doors.

You did it this time! accused my mind. *One hundred twenty-eight smackers!* My head ached. *Wait until John hears this one! Wow! Are you in for it!*

Trudging toward home, I tried to restrain the flood of fear coursing through my veins.

Tiptoing up the front walk to our house, I couldn't believe my eyes. John Jr. and Babs lay sunbathing arm in arm on our front lawn. I stood above them and blocked the sun's rays. "Where is your father?"

"Hi, Mom!" my son said cheerily. "You're making a shadow."

"Hello, Mrs. Christian," whispered his companion, taking his hand.

Terror-born fury rose to my throat; I spoke through a set mouth. "John Jr., I think it is time for Babs to go home *now*."

His blue eyes flashed. "Supper isn't ready," he argued.

My right eye began to twitch. The lump of gall acidifying in my stomach rose to my chest. "You heard me!" I snapped. Turning on my heel, I stormed toward the house.

Whipping open the door, I yelled, "John! John? John! Where

are you, John?" I ran upstairs toward his study.

"Who are ya lookin' for Mom?" George shouted from in front of the television set.

Rushing toward the sound of a human voice, I screeched to a stop. There sat my youngest, surrounded with candy and gum wrappers. "George!"

"What's the matter?" he whined.

Clenching my teeth, I waited for a moment before I roared, "*Where* is your father?"

"I dunno," he responded with a complete lack of concern. He popped a chocolate drop into his mouth. "I know where Joe is, though. Will that help?" He flashed a gregarious grin.

The smile unnerved me. "George," my voice softened, "what about your braces?" I gestured toward the litter surrounding him.

"Oh, that." He sniggered. "It's *sugarless!*"

I decided to let that one pass. "Where is Joe?"

"I knew you would want to know, Mom, so I found out the three guys' names he went with," he said, gathering the candy papers.

"Don't end a sentence with a preposition, George." Perplexed, I scratched my head and wrinkled my brows. "I'm certain I gave him some chores to do around the house today."

"He went with Rat, Duke, and Punk." My youngest blithely offered his information, then stuck out his hand.

"What's that for?" I stared at his chocolate-stained palm.

"Stool pigeons always get paid!" He stood up and stuck out both hands.

"Don't be ridiculous, George," I answered, gripping my purse tightly under my arm. "Where are you hearing such things? I thought we had a rule about what you watch on television." I stopped and eyed him carefully. "Come to think of it, why are you sitting in front of the TV? Where is your father?"

"I already told you. I don't know!" He crossed his arms in front of his chest and stuck out his chin.

"Never mind." Sighing heavily, I dragged my feet toward the bedroom to change my clothes. "We can talk about it later."

By the time I arrived at my next workpost, the kitchen, the

rest of the family had landed in various parts of the house.

John Jr. and Joe yelled and screamed their way to their room, where they wrestled around the beds knocking over lamps and shaking pictures off the walls. George played with his guinea pig, Ben, in the middle of the living room rug. John stretched out on the sofa for a nap before supper.

During dinner I spoke up, trying to instigate order. "Where were you today, John?"

"I had some business to attend to," he responded mysteriously.

"Is *to* a *proposition*, Dad?" George jumped into the conversation.

John gazed steadily at his youngest. "Why?" he asked slowly.

"Mom said people aren't supposed to end a sentence with a *proposition*. Can I have some jam?" He poised himself on the edge of his chair, ready to race to the refrigerator.

"*May* I," John corrected. "Oh. No you may not." He suddenly realized what George wanted.

Silenced, George sat back, looking confused.

Joe and I remained quiet while the rest of the family indulged in table talk.

When are you going to tell John about the hundred twenty-eight big ones? my gray matter tormented.

"Pass the salt please," I addressed John Jr.

Who are the guys called Rat, Duke, and Punk? The cranium reminded me of unfinished business.

"Please pass the pepper, George." My mouth spoke automatically.

John is up to something, nagged my noggin.

"What *business*, John?" I inquired pointedly.

"Just a job offer, Martha. Nothing, really." He continued his eating.

"Oh." I responded sarcastically. "Is that all? I'm glad you let me know."

His retort, a brief angry glance, fried my brains to a crisp.

"If you have all finished, I'll get dessert," my weary voice announced to everyone, changing the subject.

"Yum! Dessert! What are we having?" George asked.

"A light, nutritious bowl of fruit, fresh from my store."

Suddenly no one seemed hungry anymore.

By the time I cleaned up the kitchen, washed my hair for the following work day, pressed my uniform, and picked up some of the clutter around the house, everyone else in the family lay sleeping.

An uneasy knot formed in the pit of my stomach and refused to budge. "It's the money," I moaned to myself, lying in bed with my eyes wide open. "Here I've just begun the job, I haven't received my first paycheck, and I'm already over a hundred dollars in the hole."

"But seek first His kingdom and His righteousness; and all these things shall be added to you,"[36] whispered the Quiet One.

In the still of the night the familiar scripture soothed my soul, and I slept.

"Ah, Mrs. Christian!" My boss waited for me just inside the huge glass doors. "I wonder if you would step into my office for a brief moment?" Mr. Kleaver's smile seemed strained.

"Certainly, sir." I answered from the pit of guilt. Dutifully I followed him to the back of the supermarket—the manager's cubicle, where thorny problems were smoothed.

Once seated, my middle-aged, balding boss looked me straight in the eye and wasted no words. "An envelope containing one hundred twenty-seven dollars and seventy-six cents came through our night letter deposit slot last night. It was addressed to you."

Uh, oh, mocked my mind. It's adieu for you!

"Do you know anything about it?" He leaned back in his two-arm desk chair and waited for my response.

My heart forgot to beat.

The Quiet One spoke. "O Lord, who may abide in Thy tent? Who may dwell on Thy holy hill? He who walks with integrity, and works righteousness, and speaks truth in his heart. He does not slander with his tongue, nor does evil to his neighbor, nor takes up a reproach against his friend . . . He who does these things . . ."[37]

"Mrs. Christian? Did you hear me?" Mr. Kleaver's voice

broke through the scripture flooding my spirit.

"Oh, yes. I'm sorry, Mr. Kleaver." Taking a deep breath, I plunged right in. "The truth is, a young woman came in here yesterday with crying children and couldn't afford, or rather forgot her checkbook." I twisted my hands in my lap.

Adios, amigos, sneered my smart-aleck cerebrum.

"I gave her the food, and she promised to come back yesterday afternoon and pay me, but she didn't, and I should have told you then, but I didn't." The words rushed out, propelled by the terror of losing my job.

"Are you religious, Mrs. Christian?" My employer leaned forward in his chair.

"Religious?" Flustered, I floundered. "No."

A look of disappointment crossed his face. "I thought maybe you might be." Leaning back, he balanced a pencil between his two forefingers and studied it.

"Am I fired?" I blurted.

"Of course not, Mrs. Christian. It's your first offense. Thank you for telling me the truth. Some people would have tried to lie their way out. You didn't. I find that interesting."

"Really?" I squeaked.

"However, you won't do that again, will you?" He frowned and smiled at the same time, a strange expression.

Relief swept over me as I hurried back to my post at the cash register.

"Heh, heh, gimme some of that pipe tobacco, Martha." A gnarled old man choked and coughed across the checkout counter from me.

"Mr. Mice Is Nice!" I exclaimed.

"Yup, Martha," he chuckled and hacked. "Thought I'd stop in and see how yer doin'."

"Fine! Just fine. But I am worried about my son, Joe. Do you happen to know three boys named Rat, Duke, and Punk?" I packaged the tobacco and handed it to him.

He inhaled noisily. His darkened face scared me.

"Are you all right?" I asked, trying to remember the symptons of a heart attack. "Can you breathe?"

Scowling, he looked steadily into my eyes with the wisdom

of the ages. "Where did he hook up with those thugs? They're not boys, they're—"

"Mrs. Christian?" Mr. Kleaver's voice shot through me like lightning.

"Yes, sir!" Busily stocking my checkout lane with neat stacks of sacks, he whispered, "You have other customers." He motioned for me to hurry Mr. Mice along.

"Certainly, Mr. Kleaver." I looked up at my gravel-voiced friend. "See you again, Mr.?"

"You better watch out, Martha," he replied sourly. Then he disappeared through the huge glass doors.

The day dragged on for me with worry dogging every step. While stacking some cans, I decided to tackle my home problems one at a time. "I'll begin with John Jr."

That evening at home I called my oldest out to the kitchen table for a chitchat—just after I'd finished doing the dishes.

"J.J., I've discovered that a good way to deal with situations is to talk about what bothers people. It's a tool I'm learning to use at work." I folded my hands and waited for his interchange.

John Jr. grabbed an apple from the fruit bowl and took a large bite.

"Yes," I continued, "it's good to discuss things. Just because you are a teenager and I am a grown-up doesn't mean—"

"Are you putting me down, Mom?" Instantly alert, he leaned forward in his chair.

"Of course not, J.J."

"That's good," he replied, "because a lot of parents do that, and I wouldn't want to have to leave home. Babs said—"

"Babs is just the subject I'd like to discuss with you," I interrupted, trying to sound casual.

"What's this? The inquisition?" He chomped another bite out of the apple.

Stunned, I stared at my sixteen-year-old son, who now shaved at least twice a week, sometimes three, if he wanted razor burn. "How can you say that?"

"A lot of parents get pretty nosy when they're your age," he said knowingly.

Suddenly I felt isolated from my oldest. "Wait a moment. I'll be right back," I promised. "I need to get something."

"Okay." He leaned back and put his feet up on the table.

I returned in a flash with my Bible. " 'Children,' " I read aloud, " 'be obedient to your parents in all things, for this is well-pleasing to the Lord.'[38] Now get your feet off the table, J.J."

"Let me see that!" Grabbing the Bible from my hands, he carefully scrutinized the scriptures.

Watching his face, I waited contentedly for him to see my point of view.

He raised his eyes to meet my gaze, then articulated in his best debating tone, "*Two* points, Mother of mine: first, the Bible also says, a verse or so away from the one you found, 'Wives, be subject to your husbands, as is fitting in the Lord.' "[39]

Laying the Bible down on the table in front of him, he clutched the sides preacher-style and continued his oratory. "Now I am not going to impose anything upon *you* that I don't do myself. I ask you clearly, how would you feel if you had to *obey* Dad? Do you really think this type of philosophy can survive in today's world?" He closed the Bible and laid it aside.

The telephone rang. "It's for you J.J.!" George yelled from ten feet away. "It's Babs!"

While my "adult" child spoke to his lively lassie, I explored my memory bank. "It seems to me Antoine de Saint-Exupery said in 1943, 'Grown-ups never understand anything for themselves, and it is tiresome for children to be always and forever explaining things to them.' "

The conflict deep within my soul raged as I sat at the table with my chin propped up on my fists. "What was J.J.'s *second* point?"

"So, hey, Mom, how about Babs coming over for supper tomorrow night?" He reappeared, full of creative ideas.

"Who will cook it?" I asked sarcastically.

"Babs!" His eyes gleamed with excitement.

An hour later as I tidied the house before bedtime, I mumbled, "Dealing with John Jr. is like being tied to railroad tracks, waiting for the next train to blot me from the face of the earth."

By morning I decided to elicit John's aid. Handing him his morning coffee, I inquired, "What do you know about Babs?"

"Nice little girl," he commented, yawning.

"She's not a little girl, John. Girls her age get married," I replied firmly.

"You worry too much," he remarked, sipping his coffee. "Where's the morning paper?"

"On the table beside you," I answered, frustrated at his lack of interest in our son's upcoming marriage. "I'm going to be late for work," I announced, changing the subject. "Do you need the car?" I shoved the newspaper closer to his hand.

"As a matter-of-fact, I do today. I need to see a few people on business." His top-secret attitude bothered me.

"Where'd you say the other teaching position is?" I asked, affecting disinterest while collecting my things.

"I didn't," he said, opening the morning edition and settling down to read. Obviously he refused to share—whatever his reasons.

"Babs will be here for dinner tonight. I've put a roast in the oven. Would you please turn it on at three o'clock?" I watched his eyes zipping across the page.

"Rather hot for a roast, don't you think?" My husband took off his reading glasses and rubbed his eyes.

"You decide," I responded, putting on my running shoes.

"You don't mind walking?" John got himself another cup of coffee.

"It's good for my waistline," I joked. "Anyway, it's only a few blocks." Blowing him a kiss, I raced for the door.

At the end of my day at work I felt exhausted. Furthermore, several errors appeared on the cash register tape, and my cash count came up short.

"It often happens in the beginning, Mrs. Christian," comforted my patient employer. "You'll get better. We won't begin docking your paycheck for mistakes until next week."

"Thank you, Mr. Kleaver," I said gratefully.

While tramping home, apprehension hurried me along. "Who is this Babs person?" I asked myself. "Only two weeks have passed since I began this job, and already I feel like I don't live in my own home anymore."

Walking up the driveway, I smelled the delicious aroma of charcoal-broiled steak.

"Hi, Mom!" George raced out to meet me. "Babs is cooking steaks, and we're having corn on the cob and hot-fudge sundaes with real homemade ice cream!" He danced around the drive in front of me.

"Oh," I replied. "That's nice. Where's your dad? Why aren't we cooking the roast?"

"He hasn't come home yet," George recited, "but he said to tell you he'll be on time for dinner. He doesn't want to miss the steak."

Tension began at my toes and rocketed to my neck where it erupted in an instant headache.

They don't need you at all, chimed my cranium.

Dinner passed. My impression of Babs was that of a boy-crazy, rambunctious, woman-child who talked too much.

"Isn't she terrific, Mom?" John Jr. glowed after he had taken her home. "She made all that dinner by herself, and she's short—just like you!"

I could see the handwriting on the wall which meant a *coup d'état* for Miss Babs and my dethronement as queen of my home if I didn't act quickly.

If you can't beat 'em, join 'em, advised the wizard of ego.

"Yes, J.J. She did a beautiful job," I agreed with a sly smile. "Maybe she would like to help you again tomorrow."

"She would love it, Mom!" John Jr.'s face shone like a beacon. "Babs knows how to cook, clean, and bake. She wants to be a nurse or an actress someday, and she's terrific at arranging flowers!"

"What's her family like?"

"I've never met her mom or dad, but she has a little brother, Johnny. She takes care of him all the time." He began getting dishes from the kitchen and putting them on the table. "Have you ever heard of the word *oxymoron*?"

Chuckling at his enthusiasm and good humor, I replied, "I think it's a cross between an ox and a moron—meaning a stupid, bullheaded person."

"No, Mom," he corrected me in a serious tone. "It's the way

you put words together—for epigrammatic effect. We learned about it in English class last year in the poetry section." He reached in his shirt pocket and pulled out a crumpled piece of paper.

Suddenly I felt old.

"I've written something," he announced, carefully unfolding the well-creased page. "With cruel kindness she took my heart." He paused.

"Is that *it*?" I inquired cautiously.

"That's it!" Puffing out his chest, he put the paper back in his shirt pocket and resumed setting the table.

I watched him suspiciously. "Why are we doing this?" I posed the question gingerly.

"We are doing this so that you don't have to do it tomorrow morning before you go to work. Babs said to me, 'Sweetie, you should help your mother more. She must get awfully tired helping to earn enough money for your family.' "

"Thoughtful child," I replied with dry wit.

"I told you she's terrific," he agreed, not noticing my remark.

"J.J., I'll finish this. It's been a long day. Thanks for your effort, though."

"Sure, Mom." He slapped me on the back. "I'll call Babs and tell her to come over tomorrow morning!"

"Tomorrow *afternoon*," I corrected quickly, "when your father is here to keep an eye . . . on *George*."

"Anything you say, Mom!" He tore to the telephone.

Later that evening while shampooing my hair, I reviewed the recent events in our family life.

"John and I live on separate planets, communicatively speaking. John Jr.'s romance could cost him his grades next year unless he settles down. Joe is running around with criminals, probably breaking and entering by now. George, my baby, is rapidly becoming an orphan from lack of company."

The comfortable, warm water soothed my scalp, and my hair squeaked with cleanliness. "Oh, Lord," I prayed, "I'd like to be that clean on the inside, in my spirit."

A hush surrounded me, and I felt the Living Water touch my soul with purity.

That night while I slept, a deep quiet descended upon my spirit. "For what is a man profited, if he shall gain the whole world, and lose his own soul?"[40]

My eyes flipped open. I sensed the presence of my Savior, Jesus Christ.

"Are you here, Lord?" I whispered to the dark room.

I listened intently but heard nothing.

John, however, moved restlessly in his sleep.

Lying as still as a stone, I confessed softly, "We are not well, Lord. The wall between John and me gets higher every day."

"If you cling to your life, you will lose it; but if you give it up for me, you will save it."[41] The voice of the Master spoke.

Deep within my soul I saw my lack of obedience to John as rebellion in my life against God's Word.

The warfare inside raged until, in the darkest past of the night, I faced the sin of wanting my own way and vanquished it. "Lord, I don't know how I can let somebody else control my life, but if You will take charge, I will trust You. I promise I'll obey John no matter what he says, and I will leave the results in Your hands."

Dawn.

11 / Sunset

"And you will seek Me and find Me, when you search for Me with all your heart."[42]

"What do you think, John?" Patting my newly bleached, freshly coiffured hair, I twirled around in front of my husband and waited for his approval.

Folding his afternoon edition of the newspaper, John eyed my head. "What's wrong with *brown* hair?"

"Don't you like it?" I pivoted slowly on one foot for full effect.

"I liked it before," John answered carefully, as though approaching an electric eel.

Anger rumbled inside me, gathering force like a small tornado. I readied my retort beginning with, "Well, if *you*—"

"Remember your promise," interjected The Quiet One.

Leaning back on my heels, I quelled the storm. "You mean you prefer it dull, drab, mousy, disgusting brown?"

"Martha, if you don't want my opinion, don't bother to ask." John picked up his newspaper and stuck his head inside.

"I thought blond would look nice with my red uniform." I heard myself beginning to argue, but I couldn't help it.

Engrossed in the sports section, my spouse remained silent.

Plastering a smile across my face to cover my disappointment in his reaction, I asked, "Okay if I take the car?"

"Go ahead," came the reply from behind the newsprint shield.

By the time I'd found a parking space in town three blocks from the drugstore, I'd already shed a few tears. "I knew it would be tough, Lord, but did we have to start right at the top?"

"If you keep my commandments, you will abide in My love; just as I have kept My Father's commandments, and abide in His love. These things I have spoken to you that My joy may be in you, and that your joy may be made full."[43]

"Yes, Lord," I responded, grateful for the support. With firm resolve I locked the car and trooped my way down the block toward the pharmacy.

"Martha? Can it be my little Martha?" The familiar baritone made me wish for an "invisible" potion.

"Mr. Jenkins!" I wriggled away from his encircling arm.

"My, my, the blond hair brings out the hazel in your eyes!" Admiringly he stepped back and pretended to whistle.

I flushed in embarrassment.

"You look ten, no, *fifteen* years younger!" His white shirt collar dazzled me.

"Do you really think so?" I relaxed under his effusive praise.

"I see your leg looks good, too." His gaze shifted to my right limb. "Would you consider coming back to the hospital?"

Standing a little taller, I replied confidently, "I would love to, Mr. Jenkins, but I can't. I'm working full time now at a supermarket near our house."

"Full time?" he queried purposefully. "I thought you barely had time to work a little as a volunteer. What happened?" He bent knowingly toward me and used a confidential tone. "Financial trouble? You can tell me. We go way back, don't we?"

Guilt feelings propelled my feet forward toward my destination—the drugstore. Waving over my shoulder, I hollered, "See you sometime, Mr. Jenkins! Thanks for everything!"

Mopping my perspiring brow with the back of my hand, I hurried to the hair-color section of the store.

"Martha?" Jean's voice spoke from right behind me.

Unable to locate a hole in the floor where I could disappear, I decided to answer. "Hi, Jean," I whispered, feeling a choking sensation in my throat.

She smiled warmly. "Do you have the day off?"

Expecting a blast about the bleach job on my hair, I replied in a daze, "What?"

"Aren't you working at the supermarket today?" Patiently, she rephrased her question.

"Oh, that!" I gasped. "I thought you meant *this!*" I pointed to my golden-haired head.

"Why did you do that?" She studied my eyes.

"It seemed like a good idea at the time," I replied, twisting my fingers. "And," I dropped my gaze to the floor, "I thought maybe John would notice me. He's pretty withdrawn lately." I began picking up hair coloring products at random.

"Want to go for coffee?" Warmth radiated from her.

Fingering a bottle of dark brown, I hesitated. "I was going to go right home and dye my hair dark again."

"Can you do it later?" Jean never forced, just asked.

"All right. Meet you at the Tea Shop in ten minutes."

As soon as she'd vanished from view, I began reading the fine print on every box. "I can't afford to go back to Fifi at the Sans Salon and tell her to dye my hair dark," I muttered to myself. "In fact, I'll never be able to go there again!" Perspiration beaded on my forehead as I traversed the complicated world of hair color.

"May I help you?" A young girl the age of Babs appeared at my elbow.

"Yes," I gratefully replied. "I want to dye my hair brown, and I don't know what to buy."

"Hmm," she studied my flaxen locks with a critical, inexperienced eye. "Brown is blah," she finally announced.

"My husband doesn't like it lightened," I confessed, wondering how I ever let Fifi talk me into it. Remembering her convincing conversation, I had allowed her to subtly suggest changing my appearance without first asking John what he thought.

"*C'est magnifique* to colourrr yourrr trresses!" Fifi had swooped her arms outward and swirled enticingly around me while I waited nervously in her chair.

"Does that mean it will look good?" Anxiously, I fingered my cheeks and stared in her mirror, trying to envision my face framed by light yellow.

"Certainemént, madame! *Très* terrrific!" She had begun to mix chemicals while continuing her sales pitch. "We 'ave la special price this week only!" She wrapped a plastic drape around my shoulders and fastened it tightly around my neck.

Tension quivered in my covered arms, jiggling the vinyl cape slightly.

"Ooo-la-la, madame! Your neck muscles tighten!" She rubbed the back of my neck vigorously. "You will love it!" She kissed the ends of her fingers and swept out of the room. "Un moment, s'il vous plaît."

Before I knew it I'd been bleached, fried, and combed. Gingerly I felt my scalp. "Will it continue to hurt like this?"

"Mais non!" Patting my back while pushing me toward the cash register, Fifi had ignored my complaint.

"What do you think of 'Bomber Brown'?" The store clerk touched me on the elbow.

I evaluated her. "How old are you?" I abruptly asked.

"Sixteen," she answered, looking confused. "Why?"

"Do you know Babs?" I took the box marked "Bomber Brown," trying to imagine my face surrounded by it.

"Babs? Babs who?"

"I guess you don't," I replied handing the package back to her. "Do you have anything like my previous hair color?"

"What color was that?" With the intensity only the young can muster, she furrowed her brows in concentration.

"Brown. Just brown." I hoped she could interpret that into one of the potions lying around.

"Blah brown?" Trying to he helpful, she began rummaging through color charts.

"More like mousy brown," I offered.

"Hmm," she replied thoughtfully. "Aren't most mice gray?"

"I could ask the Mice Is Nice man," I mumbled to myself.

"Do you know Mr. Mice?" she queried excitedly.

"Is that his name? I've been trying to find it out for months!" My enthusiasm matched hers.

"Oh," she giggled. "I don't know his name. I just call him Mr. Mice. I never thought of him having a name."

"I'm not surprised," I muttered to the shelf. Turning toward her I asked, "How about 'Disgusting Brown'?" I snickered inside.

"Perfect!" she exclaimed, digging around through a basket of bottles. "I know we have that one!"

Shocked, I stood still and waited.

"Here it is!" She stuck her hand into a dusty bin and pulled out an antiquated-looking container.

"It looks pretty old to me," I pronounced, turning it over in my hands. "How long have you had it lying around the store?"

"Not very long." She answered the way George would if I caught him with his hands in a full cookie jar.

"Not very long?" I repeated suspiciously, checking the label for an expiration date. There wasn't one.

"Would you like to take that one then?" The youthful clerk fidgited, straightening boxes on the shelf.

Checking my watch, I realized that fifteen minutes had passed since promising to meet Jean in ten minutes at the Tea Shop. Impulse prompted me to take anything just to get the blond on my head back to brown.

While crossing the clerk's dainty palm with greenbacks and silver, I asked, "What color is that on your hair?"

"Oh," she giggled. "It's my own. My mother won't let me dye mine."

"Oh," I replied and left.

A few minutes later, sitting across the table from Jean, I sipped steaming tea sweetened with honey. "Good," I remarked congenially.

"Would you like something to eat? My treat." She smiled and opened the menu.

"Great!" I agreed wholeheartedly. "It's my day off from the supermarket—and my diet."

As soon as we munched carrot muffins loaded with coconut and raisins and spices, I found to my dismay that we had nothing to talk about. "How's the garden?" I inquired politely.

"Really good," Jean responded cheerfully. "I'm managing to can, freeze, and make jam as well this year."

"Oh," I remarked. Twirling my teaspoon in my cup, I said,

"Joe is running around with some kids named Rat, Duke, and Punk."

"Oh?" Her face darkened.

"Do you know them?" I questioned my best friend, dreading her reply.

"I know of them," she answered, pouring herself more tea. "They're bad news I'm afraid, Martha."

"In what way?" I dumped two spoons of honey into my half-filled cup of tea.

"Oh, look at the time!" Jean suddenly began gathering her things. "I must go."

"Jean, in what way?" I reached out and touched her arm to restrain her. "Please."

Perching on the edge of her chair, she picked her words carefully. "Each one has been to jail at least once, and Duke has spent most of his life in a juvenile home for boys."

"Where did you hear that?" Fear gripped the pit of my stomach.

She studied my face. "Believe me, Martha. I know it's true." She stood to leave. "Ready to go?"

Worry transported me home in a flash. Roaring into the driveway, I glanced around for signs of Joe. No bike parked by the back door.

I rushed into the house and called up the stairs. "Joe? Joe! Where are you?"

The ominous silence of our abode unnerved me. Slowly, I climbed the stairs. Goosebumps rose along my forearms. "Something is wrong," I announced to myself. "This place is never quiet."

Hurrying to the kitchen table where we often left notes, I read, "Martha, I am at the police station. Call me there. John."

I watched the paper tremble in my hands. Pain unlike anything I'd ever known—even worse than childbirth—swept through my system as I hunted through the telephone book for the number of the police station.

Fighting back tears, I dialed the first number I saw.

"Is this an emergency?" a male voice boomed.

"What?" I replied numbly.

"Is this an emergency?" the law enforcer repeated.

"Yes." I paused to reflect. "No."

"No?"

"Yes," I agreed.

"Which is it?" he snapped.

"Don't you yell at me!" I shot back, tears falling freely onto the receiver.

"Why are you calling?" His tone softened slightly.

"My husband told me to call him at the police station," I defended.

"Ma'am, this is emergency dispatch. Just a moment. I'll give you the correct exchange."

By the time John's voice came on the line, I sobbed in earnest. "What happened?" I sniveled. "Is Joe in jail?"

"Calm down, Martha." John's comforting expression he used in all cases of crisis soothed me. "I just didn't want you to worry. We'll be home in a while and I'll explain then."

My heart slowed down to a dull thudding. I returned to the table to look for a note from J.J., who was also missing.

"Dear Mom, Babs and I have taken George swimming. See you for supper. Love, J.J."

Too upset to sit down, I decided to dye my hair back to brown while waiting for everyone to come home. Then it hit me. "George can't swim!"

Panic-stricken, I poured the bottle of dark goo on my head and paced the floor.

The front doorbell chimed.

"Oh, no!" Hoping nobody would think I was home, I stood still, barely breathing.

A loud pounding commenced at the back door. "Maybe it's George!" Visions of my drowning son raced before my eyes as I rushed down the stairs and ran toward the rackety knocking.

Whipping open the door, I faced our paper boy. Chubby, about ten years old, his brown eyes seemed squeezed between his cheeks and his forehead.

"Collecting." Wrinkling his freckled nose, his expression never changed, but the whites of his eyes grew larger as he stared at the top of my head.

"Not today," I announced, shutting the door.

The knocking resumed steadily like boulders falling off a mountain onto a wooden roof.

Gritting my teeth, I decided I'd have to answer it. "Yes?" I glared.

"The lady here yesterday told me to come today," he groused, folding and unfolding his receipt pad.

"How old are you?" The nonsequitur question surprised him.

"Eleven," he mumbled. His wide eyes never left my foamy head. "I think she said her name was Babs."

"Just a minute," I replied, slamming the door and hurrying back up the stairs to find some cash.

"Somebody has raided my coffee-can-change." Exasperated, I left the empty container on the kitchen counter and headed for J.J.'s room.

"He always has money! Even John borrows from him," I muttered, plowing through his dresser drawers.

Finally I raided George's piggy bank.

"Here it is!" Opening the back door, I spied our local newspaper carrier sitting down on the cement. Specimen licked his face.

"Nice dog," he said, jumping up. Our mutt sat beside him.

I stood on one foot and then the other as he rummaged around in his pockets for a pencil. "It's all right," I countered. "I don't need a receipt."

Locating a pencil stub, he carefully printed his name and telephone number on a tiny slip of paper. Handing it to me, he held out a grimy palm for money.

Dropping the cash into his hand, I tried to shut the door.

"Wait a minute!" He stuck a toe across the threshold. "I have to *count* it." Pocketing the bills, he put the coins in a pouch.

"You have a hole in your running shoe," I commented casually.

"That foam on your head is turning green," he disclosed in return. Hopping on his bike, he waved.

Horrified, I flew up the stairs past the ringing telephone.

"Hurry, hurry, hurry," I said to myself as I turned on the hot water and stuck my head under the tap.

Grabbing a towel and blotting my head, I raced to the bathroom mirror.

"My hair is green!" My shoulders sagged as I heard cries of "Hey, Mom! We're home!"

Sticking my head out of the bathroom, I yelled, "Is George all right?"

Silence.

Throwing the towel over my head, I ran to the top of the stairs and screeched, "Is *George* with you?"

"He's better now, Mom." John Jr. spoke from the bottom of the stairs. "He swallowed a bit of water, though."

"I'm really sorry, Mrs. Christian." Babs appeared at J.J.'s side. "I didn't know he couldn't swim." She began to cry.

Standing at the top of the stairs with a towel over my head and my heart in my mouth, I was overwhelmed with compassion for the young lady standing next to my son. "Don't worry, Babs," I comforted. "These things happen."

George arrived next to the other two. "Hi, Mom!"

"Why didn't you tell Babs you can't swim?" I queried.

"I thought she knew!" His face suddenly flushed bright red, and *he* began to cry.

"The telephone is ringing, Mom," advised John Jr.

"I heard it a little while ago, too," I responded, heading toward the jingling that was jangling my nervous system.

"Martha?" John's irritated tone threw me. "Why aren't you answering the phone?"

"If I'd known it was you," I snapped, "I would have stood here and waited for it to ring!"

He ignored my biting comment. "I'm taking Joe out for dinner. I just wanted to let you know," he said.

"Oh," I replied. "Why aren't you coming home?"

"I'll explain later," he said and hung up.

"Who's on the phone, Mom?" John Jr. appeared at my left elbow.

"Just your father," I answered.

"Why?" George inquired as usual.

"He's taking Joe out for supper," I reported, "and I don't know why."

"Why doesn't Babs stay for supper here?" My oldest son tossed the remark casually as though Babs wasn't standing two feet away from us.

Cornered, I agreed. "We can have take-out chicken. At least it's fast."

"Hooray!" George shouted, hopping around the kitchen.

"John Jr., please go to the store and get some paper plates and cups, will you? You can get the chicken at the same time."

"What do I use for money?"

"Don't you have any?"

"Aw, Mom, that'll wipe me out," he objected.

"I'll pay you back later," I promised.

By the time J.J. and Babs returned from gathering dinner from the chicken place and the corner grocery store, I'd tried washing and scouring my hair to no avail.

The kids knew better than to laugh at my sea-green locks.

"My scalp is so tender I don't think I can touch it," I complained in between bites of a juicy, fried drumstick.

"It will be all right, Mrs. Christian. I'm sure it will," comforted the fourteen-year-old female whose name, according to our dog-eared dictionary, meant *foreign; strange.*

"Thank you, Babs," I replied sincerely.

After we finished eating, while Babs was helping me clear the table, she dropped George's half-filled cup of milk. Instantly, she burst into tears. "Oh! I'm so sorry!" she cried, running from the room.

"J.J.," I called, "come here."

Hurrying from the living room, he saw me soaking milk from the rug. "Need some help, Mom?"

"What's wrong with Babs?" I phrased my question carefully. "Babs?"

I peered into his innocent eyes. "Babs. Yes. She is the girl you sat next to at dinner tonight."

"Oh, Babs!" Suddenly he clued in. "What's wrong?"

"That's what I'm asking you, J.J. All she did was spill a little milk and she broke up crying and ran out of the room. Is she sick?" I rinsed the rag out under the kitchen tap and sat down at the table.

"Oh, I guess I know what's wrong." My eldest sat across the table from me. "Her parents are separating. She just found out this morning."

"I am sorry, J.J.," I said. "Anything I can do?"

"Naw, her mother works all the time anyway, so they'll be all right. I guess her dad's moving out of town the end of this week, and he wants to take her little brother, Johnny, with him."

I leaned my head on my hand. "Ow!"

"What's the matter, Mom?" J.J. looked concerned.

"I don't know, but my skin feels sore." I gently touched the back of my head.

"Let me see," J.J. pronounced, digging around in my greenish curls. "Oh." He tsk-tsked. "This looks bad. It's bleeding!"

"Mom, my stomach hurts!" George shouted from in front of the television set.

"You probably ate too much chicken, George," I hollered back. "Why don't you rest awhile?"

"Okay, Mom, but I'm not kidding this time," he moaned.

Babs sniffled as she pulled up a chair and sat down next to John Jr.

"How much water do you think George swallowed?" I spoke under my breath to J.J. and friend.

"It's hard to say, Mom," my twenty-five-year-old teenaged son replied seriously.

"I'm sorry to hear about your parents, Babs," I said quietly.

"Oh, it's okay, Mrs. Christian." Her face crumpled into tears again. "But I'm gonna miss my little brother!"

Grabbing a couple of facial tissues, I handed them to her while wrapping my arm around her trembling shoulders. "It will be all right, Babs. I'm sure it will."

"He, my father, doesn't like it when she's working all the time." She blew her nose and sniffed heartily. "She said she's not—"

"You don't have to tell me, Babs, if you don't want to," I interrupted.

"That's okay, Mrs. Christian." She took a couple big breaths and continued. "She, my mom, said she's not going to have a ring in her nose, or an hourglass waist, or a hundred-pound jug on her head, or bound feet either!" She sighed deeply and sat back in her chair with her arms crossed.

"I guess nobody would want all that," I replied. Handing her another tissue I sat down.

Babs looked at me seriously. "I wish my mom were like you!"

"Me? Are you kidding? I've got green hair!"

"No," she replied honestly. "You're sort of . . . sweet, and you don't tell your husband what to do all the time, either."

"Mom!" George's scream cut through me.

"What, George?" Leaving John Jr. and Babs, I ambled into the living room expecting to see George lying on the floor wearing a smirk on his face with his eyes glued to the television tube.

"Mom," my youngest whimpered and grabbed my hand. "It hurts!" Pulling his knees up, he groaned and twisted his face in pain.

"Honey, what is it?" I plopped down beside him and cradled his face in my hands.

"My stomach." He rolled back and forth in agony. "It hurts so bad!"

"J.J.! Go get a blanket, will you?" I shouted.

"What's wrong, Mom?" John Jr. answered casually from the other room.

"John Jr.!" My nerves, already strained, exploded into a command that seemed to come from somewhere else. "Now!"

"Sure, Mom, anything you say." He raced toward George's room.

Checking George over, I noticed his face turning gray. "Do you feel hot, sweetheart?"

His upper lip trembled. "I dunno."

"Here's the blanket, Mom." J.J. covered his brother.

"Get me the thermometer, please, J.J." Tenderly, I stroked George's forehead and removed his glasses. "Can you show me where it hurts?"

"Here." He pointed to his abdomen.

"Here's the thermometer, Mom." My oldest son gazed at his

brother with real concern. "It's probably the water he swallowed."

"It's all my fault," sobbed Babs, now next to J.J.

My head reeled with the discomfort of my scalp and all the worried tension.

"Babs, stop crying. It's all right." I turned my gaze to my eldest son's concerned eyes. "Look, why don't you two go to the drugstore and find some black dye for my hair?"

"Black?" His face crumpled in disdain. "Black is bleak."

"J.J., for once in your life would you do as you're told?" I glared at him.

"What do I do for money *this* time?" he quipped sarcastically.

Babs took his arm quickly. "I have some money. Come on, let's go."

Without another word, J.J. escorted his life-saving girlfriend out to the car.

My insides seethed as I sat with George, rubbing his forehead. Clinging to hope, I waited for improvement. "Any better now?"

"It might be," he answered.

By the time J.J. and Babs returned with the bottle of black, George lay sleeping on the floor.

"Shhh!" I hissed as they bounded up the stairs. "Your brother is sleeping!"

"I knew he'd be okay," J.J. sounded off. "He's too tough for a little water!"

"I'll help you with your hair, Mrs. Christian," offered Babs. Her worried expression tore at my heart.

"Fine," I answered without enthusiasm. "J.J., you stay with your brother, will you? He has a slight fever."

"Anything you say."

"J.J.—" I paused, searching for words. "I'm sorry about raising my voice to you. It's been a long day."

His eyes searched mine. Finding no malicious intent, he responded, "It's all right, Mom. Parents are people too."

"Thanks, J.J." I headed for the bathroom and the black-repair-kit.

Gently, Babs daubed the smelly goo on my hair. "It won't

hurt as long as I keep it off your scalp," she comforted as she worked. "My dad wants my mother to move to where he's going, but she won't." Like a fountain, Babs poured out her family's problems. "What do you think Mom should do?"

"Therefore, wait for Me, declares the Lord."[44] The verse whispered peace through me.

"Babs—" I spoke candidly. "I'll tell you a secret nobody else knows." I flashed a confidential smile. "Are you good at keeping secrets?"

"Oh, yes!" She sat down on the edge of the bathtub, giving me her full attention.

"I have recently come to believe that it works best for a wife if she tries to please her husband. How about fetching my Bible for me? We have a few minutes before rinsing my hair, don't we?"

Instantly she disappeared, returning seconds later.

"That was fast," I said, taking the book from her outstretched hands.

She sat down and waited.

Thumbing the familiar pages, I read, "Let the wife see to it that she respect her husband."[45]

"Wow!" Babs exclaimed with stars in her eyes. "Maybe I should show that to my mom."

"Might not hurt," I answered, identifying with her mother's struggle. "It's not easy to make a marriage work, Babs, but I believe God shows us the way. After all, He brought Eve to Adam, didn't He?"

She turned her attention to my hair just as the phone rang in the other room.

"Mom," J.J. called, "it's Mr. Kleaver!"

"Shhh!" I hissed. "Babs, will you ask J.J. to tell Mr. Kleaver I'll call him back?"

"Okay," she answered lightly.

An hour later while George still slept, I, the raven-haired mother of three, spoke softly into the phone. "Yes, Mr. Kleaver, I'll be glad to come in early tomorrow morning."

"Fine, Mrs. Christian," my employer intoned heartily, "I'll explain everything then."

"Mom." John Jr. touched my elbow. "Something is wrong with George."

One look at my oldest son's expression brought panic. "I'll see you tomorrow then, Mr. Kleaver." Quickly, I hung up the receiver.

Hurrying to the living room, I saw George doubled over, crying with pain.

I touched his forehead. His fever was rising rapidly. "Where does it hurt, George?"

"Here," he whimpered, touching his right side.

Remembering my first aid training as a young girl, I ran to call the doctor. One word crowded my brain.

Appendicitis.

12 / *Liberty*

"The Spirit of the Lord is upon me, because he hath anointed me to preach the gospel to the poor; he hath sent me to heal the brokenhearted, to preach deliverance to the captives, and recovering of sight to the blind, to set at liberty them that are bruised."[46]

"Martha, I'm taking Joe with me on a short vacation." John made his announcement as we stood waiting for George to come out of surgery. "And a job interview."

"What?" I squeaked. "You have to be kidding, John. George is now on the operating table, and I'm due for work in a few hours after having no sleep." Spying his stony glance, tension tore me in two. "What job interview? Where? When? Teaching? John, how can you be so insensitive?" My mouth motored right along while my desperate eyes searched his face for compassion.

"Martha, this is neither the time nor the place to . . ."

"Mr. and Mrs. Christian?" The surgeon's voice behind us interrupted our strained conversation. "Your son is in recovery."

"Is he all right?" I felt my face blanch.

"He's fine," the surgeon answered reassuringly. "He'll be brought to his room later."

"Thank you," I said, feeling my legs go limp.

"Don't worry, Mrs. Christian." He laid a steadying hand on my shoulder. "By the way, who is Ben?"

"Ben is George's guinea pig," John replied for both of us.

"Oh," he chuckled, adjusting his half-spectacles. Then a

frown crossed his face. "But I wonder why he wanted him on an elevator."

"Ben has his own elevator at home," I explained. "George built it for him."

"Thank you for everything, Doctor," John interjected, shaking the physician's hand.

Feeling numb, I stood still—the way Ben does when he feels frightened. "John, will you wait a minute for me, please?"

Nodding affirmatively, he found a chair and sat down.

Racing to the supply room of the hospital where I'd spent many miserable hours as a Smock Lady, I hurried inside without turning on the lights. The silence of the room seemed heavier than the darkness. A feeling of isolation pushed me toward hysteria.

"Oh, Lord—" I shook inside. "John is going to leave me. I know it! Just like Babs' father. First he will take Joe away for a holiday, and then . . ." Holding my ice-cold hands to my eyes to will back tears, I whispered, "Lord, what will I do?"

"Offer the sacrifices of righteousness, and trust in the Lord."[47]

The dark room seemed less lonely.

Pacing back and forth, I almost laughed when I remembered the scene at home as we had waited anxiously for the doctor to return my telephone call.

"I don't know which shocked John more when he and Joe walked into the living room—my black hair or my white face."

Still pacing, I remembered John's calm under fire as he took charge of the situation.

It wasn't so bad—following his orders. Actually, he did quite well. Pride in my husband welled up inside me as I thought back to the turmoil. In no time at all he had sent John Jr. and Joe to bed, taken Babs home, and driven George and me to the hospital emergency room.

"Mrs. Christian?" Instantly I recognized Mrs. Lill's commanding tone. "Are you in here? Your husband is asking for you."

Feeling like a small child hiding in the closet to avoid drying dishes, I reluctantly responded. "Yes, I'm here." Taking a deep breath, I walked toward the door and expected the worst.

"Quiet in here, isn't it?" Mrs. Lill inquired without turning on the lights. Suddenly, a tiny sunbeam slipped through the window, breaking into the darkness and giving warmth to the room.

"Sorry," I said quickly. "I shouldn't have come in here since I no longer work at the hospital." Tears filled my eyes.

Mrs. Lill wrapped a comforting arm around my shoulder. "Martha, I've spent many hours right where you've been standing—crying, thinking and praying."

"Wow, Lord!" I whispered excitedly as I walked away from the supply room. "I didn't know she believed in you!" My load lightened by one who cared,[48] I straightened my shoulders and hurried toward John.

"Trust in the Lord with all your heart, and do not lean on your own understanding. In all your ways acknowledge Him and He will make your paths straight. Do not be wise in your own eyes; fear the Lord and turn away from evil. It will be healing to your body, and refreshment to your bones."[49] The Quiet One comforted me all the way back to where my husband sat waiting.

"Hi, honey," I said, managing a grin.

"Ready?" My soul-mate hardly looked at me.

"Sorry I took so long," I apologized as meekly as possible.

"You'll be late for work," he replied.

I am trusting in you, Lord, I thought on the way home, *and it's a good thing, too, because otherwise I might just tell John what I think about how cold and unfeeling he is just when I need him the most.*

"We're home, Martha." John turned off the car motor, opened his door and unlocked the door of the house almost before I could say, "Sorry, Lord. I *am* trusting in you."

Once in the house, I thought I'd try that sweet, quiet spirit Jean always talked about.[50] "Would you like a cup of coffee, John?"

"Fine," he replied, heading toward the living room with the newspaper.

Resentment against that useless, attention-demanding paper

threatened my heart. I took a deep breath and put the kettle on to boil.

"Lord," I prayed inside myself, "you know I can't take too much of this without blowing my top!" Angry tears erupted, then vanished as I set my face like a flint to do God's will.[51]

A few minutes later I sat beside my husband on the sofa watching him sip his steaming coffee. Joy crept into my spirit. "Would you like me to see if we have some coffee cake in the deep freeze?"

John looked at me out of the corner of his eye, opened his mouth to speak, then quietly set his cup down on the table beside the couch.

"Martha, when I telephoned to say I was taking Joe out to dinner . . ."

My heart pounded in my ears.

". . . I told you I would explain."

"Yes." I said through frozen lips. "Where's Joe?"

"J.J. and Babs are spending the day with him. They'll be back this afternoon before you're home from work. I've given them some chores to do around the house."

"What chores?"

"Yard work, Martha." He leaned back on the sofa and turned to face me. "When I was called to the police station, I discovered that Joe had been seen breaking and entering along with Rat, Duke, and Punk."

"Oh, no," I uttered softly. My stomach sank.

"Oh, yes," John quipped without humor.

"The officer said he *might* be able to get the charges against Joe dropped," he continued, "but for his cohorts it will be a different story."

My stomach churned with relief and fear.

"Joe, however, refuses to discuss anything with anybody because he doesn't want to fink on his friends." John's face sagged.

"Oh, John, I am sorry." I blinked back the tears and tried to steady my voice.

"I just finished reading a report on working mothers." John leaned back and sipped his coffee. "Would you be interested in the results?"

"It seems that this recent study demonstrates that children of mothers who work outside the home have more trouble with the law, with drugs, alcohol, and . . ."

I raced out of the room to get more coffee and to calm myself. "Lord!" I whispered furiously. "He's going to blame *me* for this! And what about *him*, Lord? Doesn't *he* work outside the home?" Instead of slamming a cupboard door to relieve the tension, I stood next to the kitchen counter, gripping it tightly, waiting for the head of steam to evaporate. I couldn't explode now.

"Coming back, Martha?" John called from the living room.

"Yes," I called, "but I have to leave soon, so I thought I'd clean up the kitchen a little."

He appeared at the doorway and continued. "I think I need to take Joe away for a while—a holiday. Maybe a move away from here would be beneficial for Joe." The air between us hung heavy. "Maybe I need a change too." He sighed, shrugging his shoulders in defeat.

"When?" I turned my back to him so he couldn't see the anguish in my eyes. Somewhere I'd lost touch with my life-mate.

"Actually, Martha," he continued, setting his cup on the counter, "I had been planning it anyway. Joe tells me he seems to fight with you much of the time, and I thought it would be a good idea for me to spend some quality time with him alone."

"You also have two other children, John." I tried to keep my voice low.

He didn't answer.

"Excuse me a moment, John." I walked quickly to the living room, grabbed my Bible, and closeted myself in the bathroom. While I ran the water and cried, I flipped through God's Word looking for help. I found it.

"But thanks be to God that though you were slaves of sin, you became obedient from the heart to that form of teaching to which you were committed, and having been freed from sin, you became slaves of righteousness."[52]

By the time I reappeared in the living room, my tears were dried, and my spirit at rest.

John sat dejected on the couch, his paper lying on the cushion next to him.

"Sorry I ran away like that," I said as lightly as possible. "I'm due at work in a few minutes. Mr. Kleaver telephoned last night, asking me to come in early, but I'll call in and cancel if you think I should."

"That's not necessary, Martha," John replied.

Foregoing my chance to retaliate against his working-mother comments, I inquired, "When will you and Joe be leaving?"

"This afternoon." John stared straight ahead.

"Oh." I fought the impending terror attack. "When do you expect to be back?"

Heaving a huge sigh, John picked up his paper, folded it, and laid it down again. "Labor Day." The finality of his tone hit my heart heavily. "I'll decide about the other teaching opportunity by then too. It doesn't start till January anyway."

My throat constricted. "Will you need any help packing?" I couldn't ask where he would be teaching in January. Fear froze my mouth shut. What if he said Australia or Alaska?

"No thanks, Martha."

"Well, then, I'd better get to work." Leaning over, I kissed my husband's tense forehead and quietly left the room.

Moments later I arrived at the supermarket without noticing how I got there.

"Ah, Martha!" My boss beckoned me to follow him to his office. "I've been waiting for you!"

"Good morning, Mr. Kleaver," I intoned like a robot. "You wanted to see me?" I waited for his dark moustache to move.

Walking slowly around his desk, my balding employer sat down, tipped back in his chair, and carefully lined up the fingers of his pudgy hands.

I shifted uneasily on my feet and waited.

Lifting his eyes from his fingers to my face, my stout superior's gaze penetrated mine. "Sit down, Martha." He gestured toward a straight-backed, slightly peeling kitchen chair—obviously a reject.

"Thank you." I slid onto the seat, anxiously awaiting his next move.

"Are you happy here, Martha?" Mr. Kleaver straightened a few hairs struggling to grow at the front of his scalp.

"Yes, sir!" My right hand had the urge to spring forward in a military salute.

"Good. Good." He smoothed his moustache. "I've decided to promote you to assistant manager."

"Oh." I sagged on the seat.

"What's wrong, Martha?" His eyes narrowed suspiciously. "Don't you like the idea?"

"Oh!" Nervousness crept up my spine, leaving a trail of goosebumps.

"Well?"

"Oh."

"I take it you mean that to be an affirmative reply." Standing up, he leaned forward on his desk, pointed to the door with his left hand, and announced, "I will give you your duty sheet later."

I shot to a standing position and instructed my feet to move toward the door.

"By the way, Martha," Mr. Kleaver's voice stopped me en route, "this means a raise in salary as well." He shuffled some papers on his desk.

"Raise?" My eyes lit up with excitement.

"Yes. Fifty dollars bimonthly plus a grocery discount."

"Discount?" I parroted.

"On day-old bread and discontinued merchandise."

"Oh." Stumbling through the door, I made my way back to my computerized cash register. Ten people waited impatiently for me to process them through the checkout lane.

"Good morning," I mumbled, picking up a can of peas and pulling it across the red sensor lights. Nothing happened. "Hmm," I said, dragging the peas across one more time. Nothing.

"Why don't you get one that works?" groused the elderly gentleman fidgeting before me.

Ignoring his comment, I tapped out the price of the peas on the computer keys and sent him on his way.

The next customer stood patiently as I pulled, dragged, and slowly drew and redrew each and every item of her huge order across nonblinking scarlet scanners.

By the time I finished bagging her groceries, nervous exhaustion had set in. "Thank you." I plastered a grin on my face. "Come again."

"I doubt it," responded the tired lady.

"Excuse me, sir," I chirped brightly to a gentleman holding two boxes of instant rice. Reaching over to the right, I picked up the in-store telephone. "Mr. Kleaver." Crossing my arms in front of me, I waited for him to reply from his office.

"Maarth-a . . ."

"Mr. Kleaver?" Anxiously I listened.

"Help," came a hoarse whisper. Anxiety hit.

As calmly as possible I closed my checkout lane and sped on tiptoe to Mr. Kleaver's office. When I found him on the floor, I telephoned for an ambulance, organized other employees to pinch-hit, and resumed my station at my cash register while calming people along the way.

"Lord, this is not going according to plan," I groaned inside. "Home is a disaster area, and now this!" I continued smiling and checking groceries as I prayed.

"The one who obeys me is the one who loves me; and because he loves me, my Father will love him; and I will too, and I will reveal myself to him."[53] The scriptures soothed my soul as I allowed the Quiet One His way in my thinking.

During my lunch hour I handled a myriad of Mr. Kleaver's duties and read my Bible as well.

"I wonder what the rest of that verse was?" I pondered excitedly while stuffing a sandwich in my mouth with one hand and flipping pages with the other. "Ah, here it is!" I settled down to read.

"Judas (not Judas Iscariot, but his other disciple with that name) said to him, 'Sir, why are you going to reveal yourself only to us disciples and not to the world at large?' Jesus replied, 'Because I will only reveal myself to those who love me and obey me. The Father will love them too, and we will come to them and live with them. Anyone who doesn't obey me doesn't love me. And remember, I am not making up this answer to your question! It is the answer given by the Father who sent me. I am telling you these things now while I am still with you. But when the Father sends the Comforter instead of me—and by the Comforter I mean the Holy Spirit—he will teach you much, as well as remind you of everything I myself have told you.' "[54]

"Wow!" Sparks of spiritual stimulation ignited a flame of love for God in my heart, and I read on.

" 'I am leaving you with a gift—peace of mind and heart! And the peace I give isn't fragile like the peace the world gives. So don't be troubled or afraid.' "[55]

Sitting alone in Mr. Kleaver's office, I sat at the feet of the Master as He spoke to me through God's Word. I could see in my mind's eye Jesus Christ, Savior of the world, hanging on a cruel cross for me. Tears filled my eyes. "Lord, I recognize it now. It isn't my husband who is the issue. It's You! You want me to trust you enough to die to myself so that I can live for *You*." Cleansing teardrops formed shining trails down my cheeks while an overflow of peace rushed through me.

That same peace of mind and heart given to me personally by the Comforter himself—the Quiet One—sustained me throughout the rest of the day. Calling a brief staff meeting, I announced, "Mr. Kleaver made me assistant manager this morning."

"What happened to him?" Our teenage stock boy blurted out the question they all had on their minds.

"I'm happy to say he will mend. He's had a mild myocardial infarction." I stared at blank expressions. "A heart attack," I explained. "He's in a stable condition and will be returning to work as soon as he is able to do so."

"Will you be taking over?" A slightly antagonistic expression darkened the face of one of the other checkers who had worked at her job far longer than I.

"I will need all the help I can get from *all* of you." I smiled at her scowling countenance while praying for strength. "I'm certain we want to work as a team, don't we?"

By the time I trudged home, I realized for the first time that everyone at work depended on me to keep things going. "And now that John is away, it will be tough to handle J.J. and visit George in the hospital as well," I said to myself as I walked up the driveway and into our comfortable habitat.

"John Jr.?" I listened for sounds in the house. "I'm home!"

"Hi, Mom!" The familiar screech of my eldest son's voice sounded a symphony in my heart.

"Home is where the heart is," I muttered, heading up the stairs to the kitchen. "Yard looks great, J.J.," I hollered. "Did Babs help you?" Hearing nothing, I searched the house calling, "John Jr.?"

When I walked into the living room, J.J. and Babs jumped up from behind the couch.

"Surprise, Mom!" they yelled.

"What?" Suddenly my sinuses seized upon a floral odor and almost swelled shut.

"Look!" Babs' feverish face and bright eyes beamed above the bouquet of freshly cut blossoms she held in her hands.

"She's decorated the entire place with flowers, Mom!" Proudly, J.J. wrapped an arm around her shoulders.

"Oh." The pain in my face increased in intensity. "That's nice, J.J." I looked at their glowing faces and decided against admitting to my discomfort. "You've been busy I see. The yard will please your father."

"When are he and Joe coming back?" My blue-eyed, sixteen-year-old son faced issues squarely.

"Labor Day," I answered simply.

Excitedly Babs pulled John by the arm. "Let's show her the rest of the house!" In one magic moment they disappeared from behind the sofa and appeared again in front of me. The tour began with Buddy.

"See, Mom?" J.J. bobbed up and down in front of Buddy the bird who sat eyeing him from his cage swing.

"See what?" I inquired gently, seeing nothing but a bird in his cage sitting on a swing.

"Watch this!" John Jr. bobbed up and down in front of Buddy again.

"Hmm," I replied, waiting.

Then Buddy began to bow up and down again and again.

"Very good!" I pronounced in honest appreciation.

Babs hauled me toward the large picture window and pointed

my face to the outside. "See?" said the three-year-old housed in a teenaged body.

Peeking out, I spied Specimen sitting in some sort of enclosure with his tongue lolling out of one side of his mouth.

"What's that?" I questioned carefully.

"The pig pen!" J.J. announced proudly. Sweeping the drapes to one side, permanently pleating them, he pointed to a small object next to our gigantic dog. It moved.

"Ben?" I queried in astonishment.

"Ben!" Babs and J.J. chorused in unison. "Now he won't be lonesome while George is in the hospital, and Specimen can't run away anymore!"

"Excellent idea," I commented approvingly. "Who ever said teenagers can't do a marvelous job!"

The air freshener Babs implanted in the bathroom wall scented the entire house.

"I'm doin' just like you said, Mrs. Christian," Babs explained. "I'm being a helper to John Jr. I found that verse in the Bible you were talking to me about while I fixed your green hair!"[56]

"Oh," I answered, not sure I wanted her applying wife-type verses to herself yet. "That's good."

"I told my mom she ought to do what my dad wants, too, so she's thinking about it right now. Isn't that great?" She scurried from the room before I could answer.

"Where is she going?" Stunned, I phrased my question cautiously.

"To make you a cup of coffee!" J.J. beamed like a lighthouse. "Want to see the deep freeze?"

"The deep freeze?" My heart took up a strange rhythm in my chest.

"Remember all those chickens you ordered from the butcher because you said they were such a great price?" He bounded down the basement stairs ahead of me.

"Yes," I answered, puffing along behind. "Is this the end of the tour?"

"You bet! Well, those fine plump birds are now housed in *your* deep freeze getting a taste of arctic air!" John Jr. lifted the deep freeze lid with the gallantry matched only by the sixteenth century's Sir Walter Raleigh when he laid his cape before Queen Elizabeth so she wouldn't dirty her slippers in a mud puddle.

I peered inside. "Where are they? All I see is bread and beef roasts." A queasy feeling rolled around in my stomach.

Bowing deeply, he projected his right hand in a courtly gesture. "On the bottom!" he announced. "You always say to *rotate* things for freshness!"

"Oh," I articulated while my horror rose. "Were they . . ." I paused to think of a nonoffensive word, ". . . soft?"

"Soft?" He grinned broadly. "Of course! They weren't *frozen* yet!"

"I wonder if I could see one," I commented casually while visions of pancake chickens floated in my head.

"But of course!" With a flourish he rummaged around the contents of the freezer until he produced a compacted chicken. His face fell. "What happened to it?" He held up what looked like a flying saucer frozen in flight.

After appointing J.J. to "prepare dinner," I left to visit George in the hospital.

While backing the car out of the drive, I muttered to myself, "I wonder how we will ever extricate the chicken meat from the bones?"

But greater worries plagued me all the way to the hospital. "Is John leaving for good? What is all this private business he's been doing all summer? Maybe he's moving!" Horror blasted my eyes open. "I'll have to keep my job if he's taken another teaching position somewhere."

"Mom!" George's voice broke through my thoughts as I entered his room.

"Sweetheart! You're sitting up! How are you feeling?" I eyed my youngest from a critical-mother standpoint.

His blue eyes filled with crocodile tears. "It *hurts*."

"I know," I responded sympathetically. Pulling a chair alongside his bed I whispered, "Got a surprise for you!"

"What, Mom?" Instantly he brightened.

Hurrying out into the hall, I grabbed a paper bag of goodies and toys. "Now every time you get lonesome," I warned in mock seriousness, "you dig into this sack and pull out *one* thing."

"Gimme!" He stuck out both arms.

"And you must do exactly as the nurses say."

"You bet!" Closing his eyes, he stuck one hand in the bag and pulled out a puzzle. "One more?" His eyes twinkled with mischief.

"George—" I changed the subject abruptly. "Would you like to move away from where we live now?"

"No way!" My youngest ripped and tore into the puzzle package. "Why?"

"No reason," I replied offhandedly.

"Where's Dad?" He concentrated on the puzzle before him.

"Didn't I tell you? He's taken Joe for a little vacation."

"So that's what it is!" My youngest pounced like a lion in pursuit. "You're afraid Dad is going to leave you like Babs' dad left her mother." His freckled face grew serious, then broke into a sly smile. "Don't worry, Mom. Dad wouldn't do it."

"How do you know all that?" My mouth remained opened in shock-position.

"Oh, I know what goes on around our house. I make it my *business!*" He settled back in triumph, concentrating on puzzle pieces.

Speechless, I sat with my son until he felt sleepy.

"Time to go, Mrs. Christian." A young nurse gently touched my elbow.

Embarrassed to be caught napping in a straight chair, I replied, "I was just telling my son good night."

"Oh," she responded, smiling. "You did a good job. He's been asleep for about fifteen minutes."

By the time I arrived home I knew what I had to do. "I'm going to write to John and tell him how sorry I am about everything, and that I will quit my job, and that I am going to obey him because . . ."

"A wife is responsible to her husband, her husband is responsible to Christ, and Christ is responsible to God,"[57] prompted the Comforter.

"I want to obey as Christ obeyed," I finished my remarks as I entered the house.

Wearily, I made my way up the stairs to the kitchen. "That's funny," I said, wrinkling my nose. "I don't smell dinner cooking."

Panic-generated adrenalin surged through my system, giving new life to my feet. "John Jr.! Where are you?"

By the time I discovered his note on the kitchen table, I was ready for anything. Picking up the crumpled piece of paper, I read: "Dear Mom, Babs got sick and I had to get her home right away. Please call me at her house. Love, J.J."

My trembling fingers managed to dial the right number. "J.J.?"

"Oh, yeah. Hi, Mom," answered my son blithely.

"Is Babs all right?"

"Oh, yeah, she's fine, Mom."

"Well, what happened?" I could see Babs stretched out somewhere.

"She's moving tomorrow." J.J. seemed to be chewing something.

"Moving?" My eyebrows narrowed in consternation. "I thought your note said she was sick."

"Oh, yeah, Mom. She got heatstroke out in the kitchen. She was going to clean the oven for you, but her mother called, and the family is getting together again. So Babs and her mother are moving, and I'm helping them," J.J. explained succintly.

"Oh." I sagged against the wall. "When are you coming home?"

"As soon as we're finished," my practical son replied.

"Thanks for letting me know," I responded weakly. "I'll—"

"By the way, Mom," J.J. interrupted, "Dad called and said he's dropping in this evening."

"Do you know why?" My heart rose to my throat.

"Nope," he answered easily. "Jean called too. Said it was important. Got to go now." He hung up.

Just as I replaced the receiver, the phone rang. "Martha?"

Recognizing my dearest friend's voice instantly, I hollered, "Jean, what is going on?" Unable to stand the pressure any longer, I burst into tears.

"Hold it, Martha," she said as soon as I quit my blubbering. "Joe just wants to know if he can stay overnight here."

"Certainly, but how did Joe get to your house?" Gripping the phone with my white-knuckled right hand, I heard footsteps on the stairs. "Jean," I whispered hoarsely, "somebody is in the house!"

"Martha?" A male voice sounded from the top of the stairs.

"A-a-a-h!" I screamed, dropping the telephone.

"Martha, it's me, your husband—John!" Larger than life my spouse appeared in our kitchen.

Falling into his arms, I cried, "John, I am sorry. I've been horrible. I . . ."

Tenderly, he held me close. "Please let me speak first. I left Joe at Jean's house so we could have some time together—just us. I am not taking another job. I am not leaving again. I'm sorry I've blamed you for Joe's disobedience. Home is where the heart is, they say. And that's *you*." He kissed the tip of my nose.

"A heart needs a *head* or it has no direction . . ." I burst into tears and hugged him, hiding my face against his shoulder.

Gently, John stroked my hair, "While at the lake I read something in the Bible, 'Husbands, love your wives, and do not be embittered against them.' "[58]

I felt his fingers tremble slightly as he traced the tear lines on my face.

"Martha—" He paused to clear his throat. "I've been blind."

"And I've been disobedient!" Joining right in, I covered his face with kisses until we broke into laughter.

Later in the quiet of the evening, we sat together on the sofa sipping steaming mugs of coffee.

"George is getting better," I said.

"Joe is coming along, too," John offered.

"And J.J. will be all right," I stated thoughtfully. "Maybe Babs can come back to visit?"

"Fine with me," he agreed amiably.

"What about my job? Do you think I should quit since Mr. Kleaver has promoted me?" I snuggled into the crook of his arm.

"My dear wife," my sniggering spouse stated with a flair, "please listen to this." Reaching over to the end table, he opened our well-worn Bible and read, " 'Nevertheless let each individual among you also love his own wife even as himself.' "[59]

Holding my breath, I waited for his decision.

"You choose, Martha. I trust your judgment." Kissing my forehead lightly, he leaned back comfortably against the couch.

The Comforter spoke softly to my soul as I nestled in my husband's arms. "He has sent me to bind up the brokenhearted, to proclaim liberty . . ."[60]

Liberty.

Notes

CHAPTER 1

1. Luke 6:46, TLB
2. 1 Peter 3:6, NASB

CHAPTER 2

3. 1 Peter 3:6, NASB
4. Ephesians 5:22, KJV
5. Ephesians 6:1–2, KJV

CHAPTER 3

6. 1 Peter 3:2, NASB
7. Genesis 3:1, (Author's paraphrase)
8. Proverbs 15:1, NASB

CHAPTER 4

9. Psalm 45:11, NASB
10. 1 Thessalonians 5:18, TLB
11. Galatians 6:2, NASB

CHAPTER 5

12. Genesis 16:5, TLB
13. Romans 7:15–24, TLB
14. Proverbs 25:26, AMP
15. Psalm 33:11, KJV
16. Proverbs 14:1, NASB

CHAPTER 6

17. Proverbs 12:4, NASB
18. Romans 8:28, KJV
19. John 8:36, TLB

CHAPTER 7

20. Ecclesiastes 8:2, TLB

CHAPTER 8

21. Proverbs 25:14, TLB
22. Proverbs 18:24, TLB
23. 1 Timothy 2:11, NASB
24. Jude 12, TLB

CHAPTER 9

25. Proverbs 17:1, TLB
26. Proverbs 25:20, TLB
27. Proverbs 17:17, TLB
28. Esther 1:19, TLB
29. Esther 8:8, TLB
30. Esther 9:32, TLB
31. Matthew 11:30, NASB
32. James 1:20, NASB
33. 1 Timothy 2:15, NASB
34. Titus 2:4–5, TLB

CHAPTER 10

35. 2 Chronicles 24:20, TLB
36. Matthew 6:33, NASB
37. Psalm 15:1–5, NASB
38. Colossians 3:20, NASB
39. Colossians 3:18, NASB
40. Matthew 16:26, KJV
41. Matthew 10:39, TLB

CHAPTER 11

42. Jeremiah 29:13, NASB
43. John 15:10–11, NASB
44. Zephaniah 3:8, NASB
45. Ephesians 5:33, NASB

CHAPTER 12

46. Luke 4:18, KJV
47. Psalm 4:5, NASB
48. Galatians 6:2, TLB
49. Proverbs 3:5–8, NASB
50. Ephesians 4:29–32; 1 Peter 3:4, NASB
51. Isaiah 50:7, TLB
52. Romans 6:17–18, NASB
53. John 14:21, TLB
54. John 14:22–26, TLB
55. John 14:27–31, TLB
56. Genesis 2:18, NASB
57. 1 Corinthians 11:3, TLB
58. Colossians 3:19, NASB
59. Ephesians 5:33, NASB
60. Isaiah 61:1, NASB